The hatch opened out onto a ledge of a heavily wooded slope, thick with birches and alders. Many of the trees had gone fiery with the change of seasons. To one side, a creek tumbled over mossy green rocks. Low mountains stretched off into the distance, dotted by tiny alpine lakes that shone like droplets of silver.

They had climbed out of hell into paradise.

But hell wasn't done with them yet.

From the tunnel behind them, a strange yowling cry echoed out to them. Monk remembered hearing the same howl coming from the walled complex that neighbored the hospital.

The Menagerie.

A second and third cry answered the first.

He didn't need Konstantin's urging to keep moving.

Monk recognized what he was hearing – not from memory, but from that buried part of his brain where instinct of predator and prey were still written.

Another howl echoed.

Louder and closer.

They were being hunted.

James Rollins is the author of nine previous hit novels. An amateur spelunker and scuba enthusiast, he holds a doctorate in veterinary medicine from the University of Missouri. He currently lives and writes in Sacramento, California. Visit his website at www.jamesrollins.com.

By James Rollins

Subterranean
Excavation
Deep Fathom
Amazonia
Ice Hunt
Sandstorm
Map of Bones
Black Order
The Judas Strain
The Last Oracle

THE LAST ORACLE

A Σ Sigma Force novel

JAMES ROLLINS

An Orion paperback

First published in Great Britain in 2008
by Orion
This paperback edition published in 2009
by Orion Books Ltd,
Orion House, 5 Upper St Martin's Lane,
London WC2H 9EA

An Hachette UK company

1 3 5 7 9 10 8 6 4 2

A CIP catalogue record for this book is available
from the British Library.

ISBN 978-1-4091-0220-5

Printed in Great Britain by Clays Ltd, St Ives plc

The Orion Publishing Group's policy is to use papers that
are natural, renewable and recyclable products and
made from wood grown in sustainable forests. The logging
and manufacturing processes are expected to conform to
the environmental regulations of the country of origin.

www.orionbooks.co.uk

To Shay and Bryce,
because you both rock

ACKNOWLEDGMENTS

While it may be inspiration that starts a novel, it's the dedication of the folks that surround an author that turn such inspiration into a finished product. In my last novel, I acknowledged the fantastic dream team at HarperCollins, upon whose guidance and expertise I can place no greater value. In this note, I'd like to spend a few words to especially recognize the writers of my critique group. I've been with this group since the beginning of my career (when I was writing horrible short stories that are now safely buried in my backyard), and it was through their counsel and criticisms that I have become a better writer. I'd first like to acknowledge Penny Hill, Steve and Judy Prey, and Dave Murray, whom I lean on too heavily at times for last-minute input. Then there is the core group, who has been with me through the trenches from the beginning: Caroline Williams, Chris Crowe, Lee Garrett, Jane O'Riva, Michael Gallowglas, and Denny Grayson. And the new blood to the group, who always brings refreshing input: Leonard Little, Kathy L'Ecluse, and Scott Smith. Last, there is one gentleman who has since moved across the country but deserves special acknowledgment here as friend, mentor, and colleague: Dave Meek. Beyond the group, Carolyn McCray and David Sylvian stand on either side of me and keep pushing me to loftier heights. I also want to thank J. A. Konrath, author of the wonderful Jack Daniels series, for being there when I needed him during a moment of crisis; Jotu J. Kamlani, for his help in bladed weaponry; and Anthony Ossa-Richardson, for his personal help with the history of Delphi. As to the core of this novel, I would like to especially acknowledge Temple Grandin (author of *Animals in Translation*) for both the inspiration behind this book and for allowing me to quote her. And finally, a special thanks to the four people instrumental at all levels of production: my editor, Lyssa Keusch, and her colleague May Chen, and my agents, Russ Galen and Danny Baror. And as always, I must stress any and all errors of fact or detail in this book fall squarely on my own shoulders.

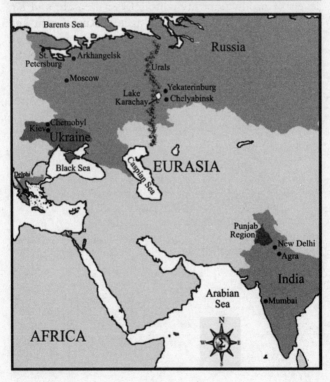

FROM THE HISTORICAL RECORD

The greatest blessings granted to mankind come
by way of madness, which is a divine gift.

– SOCRATES, ON THE
ORACLE OF DELPHI

Ancient Greeks, with their pantheon of gods, held an
abiding belief in the powers of prophecy. They revered
those who could read the portents in the entrails of goats,
who saw the future in the rising smoke of a sacrificial
fire, who predicted events based on the auguries of tossed
bones. But one individual was held in the highest esteem:
the mystical Oracle of Delphi.

For almost two thousand years, a succession of closely
guarded women resided within the temple to Apollo on
the slopes of Mount Parnassus. Each generation, a single
woman ascended to the seat of prophecy and took the
name Pythia. While under a vapor-induced trance, she
answered questions about the future – from the mundane
to the profound.

Her admirers included leading figures of Greek and
Roman history: Plato, Sophocles, Aristotle, Plutarch,

Ovid. Even early Christians revered her. Michelangelo painted her prominently on the ceiling of the Sistine Chapel, foretelling the coming of Christ.

But was she a charlatan, duping the masses with cryptic answers? No matter the truth, one fact is beyond dispute. Revered by kings and conquerors across the ancient world, Pythia's prophecies changed the course of human history.

And while much about her remains shrouded in mystery and mythology, one truth has emerged. In 2001, archaeologists and geologists discovered a strange alignment of tectonic plates under Mount Parnassus that has been shown to vent hydrocarbon gases, including ethylene, which is capable of inducing a trancelike euphoria and hallucinations, the very vapors described in the historical record.

So while science has discovered one of Pythia's secrets, the ultimate truth remains unknown:

Did the Oracle truly foresee the future? Or was it divine madness?

Man, know thyself, and thou wilt know the universe and the gods.

– INSCRIPTION AT THE
TEMPLE OF DELPHI

They had come to slay her.

The woman stood at the temple's portico. She shivered in her thin garment, a simple shift of white linen belted at the waist, but it was not the cold of predawn that iced her bones.

Below, a torchlight procession flowed up the slopes of Mount Parnassus like a river of fire. It followed the stone-paved road of the Sacred Way, climbing in switchbacks up toward the temple of Apollo. The beat of sword on shield accompanied their progress, a full cohort of the Roman legion, five hundred strong. The road wound through broken monuments and long-ransacked treasuries. Whatever could burn had been set to torch.

As the firelight danced over the ruins, the flames cast a shimmering illusion of better times, a fiery restoration of former glory: treasuries overflowing with gold and jewels, legions of statues carved by the finest artisans, milling crowds gathered to hear the prophetic words of the Oracle.

But no more.

Over the past century, Delphi had been brought low by invading Gauls, by plundering Thracians, but most of all,

3

by neglect. Few now came to seek the words of the Oracle: a goat herder questioning a wife's fidelity, or a sailor seeking good omens for a voyage across the Gulf of Corinth.

It was the end of times, the end of the Oracle of Delphi. After prophesying for thirty years, she would be the last to bear the name Pythia.

The last Oracle of Delphi.

But with this burden came one final challenge.

Pythia turned toward the east, where the sky had begun to lighten.

Oh, that rosy Eos, goddess of dawn, would hurry Apollo to tether his four horses to his Sun chariot.

One of Pythia's sisters, a young acolyte, stepped out of the temple behind her. 'Mistress, come away with us,' the younger woman begged. 'It is not too late. We can still escape with the others to the high caves.'

Pythia placed a reassuring hand on the woman's shoulder. Over the past night, the other women had fled to the rugged heights where the caves of Dionysus would keep them safe. But Pythia had a final duty here.

'Mistress, surely there is no time to perform this last prophecy.'

'I must.'

'Then do it now. Before it is too late.'

Pythia turned away. 'We must wait for dawn of the seventh day. That is our way.'

As the sun had set last night, Pythia had begun her preparations. She had bathed in Castilia's silver spring, drank from the Kassotis spring, and burned bay leaves on an altar of black marble outside the temple. She had followed the ritual precisely, the same as the first Pythia thousands of years ago.

Only this time, the Oracle had not been alone in her purifications.

At her side had been a girl, barely past her twelfth summer.

4

Such a small creature and of such strange manner.

The child had simply stood naked in the spring waters while the older woman had washed and anointed her. She'd said not a word, merely stood with an arm out, opening and closing her fingers, as if grasping for something only she could see. What god so suffered the child, yet blessed her just the same? Surely not even Apollo. Yet the child's words thirty days ago could come only from the gods. Words that had plainly spread and stoked the fires that now climbed toward Delphi.

Oh, that the child had never been brought here.

Pythia had been content to allow Delphi to fade into obscurity. She remembered the words spoken by one of her predecessors, long dead for centuries, an ominous portent.

Emperor Augustus had asked of her dead sister, 'Why has the Oracle grown so silent?'

Her sister had responded, 'A Hebrew boy, a god who rules among the blessed, bids me leave this house . . .'

Those words proved to be a true prophecy. The cult of Christ rose to consume the empire and destroyed any hope for a return to the old ways.

Then a moon ago, the strange girl had been brought to her steps.

Pythia glanced away from the flames and toward the adytum, the inner sanctum of Apollo's temple. The girl waited inside.

She was an orphan from the distant township of Chios. Over the ages, many had hauled such children here, seeking to abandon such burdens upon the sisterhood. Most were turned away. Only the most ideal girls were allowed to stay: straight of limb, clear of eye, and unspoiled. Apollo would never accept a vessel of lesser quality for his prophetic spirit.

So when this willow branch of a girl had been presented naked to the steps of Apollo's temple, Pythia had given her hardly a glance. The child was unkempt, her dark hair knotted and tangled, her skin marked with pox scars. But deeper, Pythia had sensed something *wrong* with the child. The way she rocked back and forth. Even her eyes stared without truly seeing.

Her patrons had claimed the child was touched by the gods. That she could tell the number of olives in a tree with merely a glance, that she could declare when a sheep would lamb with but a touch of her hand.

Upon hearing such stories, Pythia's interest had stirred. She called the girl to join her at the entrance to the temple. The child obeyed, but she moved as if disconnected, as if the winds themselves propelled her upward. Pythia had to draw her by hand to sit on the top step.

'Can you tell me your name?' she asked the thin child.

'Her name is Anthea,' one of her patrons declared from below.

Pythia kept her gaze focused on the child. 'Anthea, do you know why you've been brought here?'

'Your house is empty,' the child finally mumbled to the floor.

So at least she can speak. Pythia glanced to the temple's interior. The hearth fire burned in the center of the main hall. It was indeed empty at the moment, but the child's words seemed to whisper at something more.

Maybe it was her manner. So strange, so *distant*, as if she stood with one leg in this world and the other beyond this realm.

The child glanced up with those clear blue eyes, so full of innocence, so in contrast with what spilled next from her lips.

'You are old. You will die soon.'

From below, her patron attempted to scold her, but Pythia kept her words soft. 'We all die eventually, Anthea. It is the order of the world.'

She shook her head. 'Not the Hebrew boy.'

Those strange eyes bored into her. The hairs along Pythia's arms shivered. Plainly the girl had been taught the catechism of the cult of Christ and his bloody cross. But her words again. Such strange cadence.

The Hebrew boy . . .

It reminded her of her ancestor's prophecy of doom.

'But another will come,' the girl continued. 'Another boy.'

'Another boy?' Pythia leaned closer. 'Who? From where?'

'From my dreams.' The girl rubbed the heel of one hand at her ear.

Sensing there were depths to the girl that remained untapped, Pythia plumbed them. 'This boy?' she asked. 'Who is he?'

What the child said next drew a gasp from the gathered crowd – even they recognized blasphemy when they heard it.

'He is the brother of the Hebrew boy.' The child then clasped tight to the hem of Pythia's skirt. 'He burns in my dreams . . . and he will burn everything. Nothing will last. Not even Rome.'

For the past month, Pythia had attempted to learn more of this doom, even taking the girl into the sisterhood's fold. But the child had seemed only to retreat into herself, going mute. Still, there was one way to learn more.

If the girl were truly blessed, the power of Apollo's breath – his prophetic vapors – might burn free what was locked within the girl's strangeness.

But was there enough time?

A touch to her elbow interrupted her reverie and drew her back to the present. 'Mistress, the sun . . . ,' her younger sister urged.

Pythia focused to the east. The eastern skies blazed, heralding the coming sunrise. Below, shouts rose from the

Roman legion. Word of the girl had spread. Prophecies of doom had traveled far . . . even to the ears of the emperor. An Imperial courier had demanded the child be delivered to Rome, declaring her demon-plagued.

Pythia had refused. The gods had sent this child to her threshold, to Apollo's temple. Pythia would not relinquish the girl without first testing her, putting her to the question.

To the east, the first rays of the sun etched the morning skies.

The seventh day of the seventh month dawned.

They had waited long enough.

Pythia turned her back on the fiery legion. 'Come. We must hurry.'

She swept into the temple's interior. Flames greeted her here, too, but they were the welcoming warmth from the temple's sacred hearth. Two of her elder sisters still tended the flames, too old to make the harsh climb up to the caves.

She nodded her gratitude to each in turn, then hurried past the hearth.

At the back of the temple, stairs led down toward the private sanctum. Only those who served the Oracle were allowed to enter the subterranean adytum. As she descended, marble turned to raw limestone. The stairs emptied into a small cavern. The cave had been discovered ages ago by a goat herder, who upon nearing the cavern opening, fell under the sway of Apollo's sweet-smelling vapors and succumbed to strange visions.

Would that such gifts last one more sunrise.

Pythia found the child waiting inside the cave. The girl was dressed in an alb too large for her and sat cross-legged beside the bronze tripod that supported the sacred omphalos, a waist-high domed rock that represented the navel of the world, the center of the universe.

The only other decoration in the cave was a single raised seat, resting on three legs. It stood over a natural crack in the floor. Pythia, long accustomed to Apollo's vapor, was still struck by the scent rising from below, smelling of almond blossoms.

The god's pneuma, his prophetic exhalation.

'It is time,' she said to the younger sister, who had followed her down. 'Bring the child to me.'

Pythia crossed to the tripod and mounted the seat. Positioned over the crack in the floor, the rising vapors bathed her in Apollo's breath. 'Hurry.'

The younger sister gathered up the child and placed the girl into her lap. Pythia cradled her gently, like a mother with a babe, but the child did not respond to such affection.

Pythia already felt the effect of the pneuma rising from the earth below her. A familiar tingle ran along her limbs. Her throat burned warmly as Apollo entered her. Her vision began to close.

But the child was smaller, more susceptible to the pneuma.

The girl's head rolled back; her eyelids drooped. Surely she would not survive Apollo's penetration for long. Still, if there was to be any hope, the girl had to be put to the question.

'Child,' Pythia rang out, 'tell us more of this boy and the doom he whispered to you. Where will he rise?'

The small lips moved in a whisper. 'From me. From my dreams.'

Small fingers found Pythia's hand and squeezed.

Words continued to spill from the girl's lips. 'Your house is empty . . . your springs have dried up. But a new spring of prophecy will flow.'

Pythia's arms tightened on the girl. For too long, ruin had lingered over the temple. 'A new spring.' Hope rang in her voice. 'Here at Delphi?'

'No . . .'

Pythia's breath grew more rapid. 'Then from where will it spring?'

The girl's lips moved, but no words came out.

She shook the girl. 'Where?'

The girl lifted a boneless arm and placed a hand on her own belly.

With that touch, a vision swelled through Pythia, of silver waters gushing from the girl's navel, from out of her womb. A new spring. But was it a vision from Apollo? Or was it born from her own hope?

A scream pierced her daze. Hard voices echoed down. From the stairs, a figure stumbled into view. It was one of the elders who had tended the fire. She clutched a hand to her shoulder. A crimson bloom spread from under her palm. The black head of an arrow protruded between her fingers.

'Too late,' the old woman cried out and collapsed to her knees. 'The Romans . . .'

Pythia heard the woman's words but remained lost in the vapors. Behind her eyes, she pictured the spring flowing from the girl, a new font of prophetic power. But Pythia also smelled the smoke from the Roman torches. Blood and smoke leaked into her vision. The silver spring now ran with a thin stream of black crimson and swept into the future.

The child suddenly sagged in her arms, completely lost to the pneuma's vapors. Still, as Pythia studied the vision, she watched the dark stream form a black figure . . . the shadow of a boy. Flames rose behind him.

The child's words from a moon ago echoed to her.

The brother of the Hebrew boy . . . he who would set fire to the world.

Pythia held the limp girl. The child's prophecy hinted at both doom and salvation. Perhaps it would be best to leave her to the Imperial legion, to end such an uncertain future here. From overhead, hard voices echoed down. There was already no escape. Except in death.

Still, the vision swelled in her.

Apollo had sent the child. To Pythia.

A new spring will flow.

She took a deep breath, drawing Apollo fully into her.

What must I do?

The Roman centurion crossed the hall. He had his orders. To slay the girl who spoke of the empire's doom. Last night, they had captured one of the temple's servants, a maid. Under the lash – and before he gave her to his men – she let it be known that the child still remained at the temple.

'Bring the torches!' he yelled. 'Search every corner!'

Movement near the back of the hall drew his eye – and his sword.

A woman appeared from the shadows of a lower stair. She stumbled forward, weaving two steps into view, unsteady, dazed. Dressed all in white, she bore a crown of laurel branches.

He knew who stood before him.

The Oracle of Delphi.

The centurion fought back a tremble of fear. Like many of the legion, he still secretly practiced the old ways. Even slaughtered bulls to Mithra and bathed in their blood.

Still, a new sun was on the rise.

There was no stopping it.

'Who dares violate Apollo's temple?' she called out to them.

With the stony weight of his men's eyes upon him, the centurion marched to face the woman. 'Bring forth the girl!' he demanded.

'She is gone. Beyond even your reach.'

The centurion knew that was impossible. The temple was surrounded.

Still, worry pushed him forward.

The Oracle stepped to block him from the stairs. She

held a palm against his breastplate. 'The adytum below is forbidden to all men.'

'But not to the emperor. And I am under his edict.'

She refused to move. 'You will not pass.'

The centurion had his orders under the seal of Emperor Theodosius, handed to him personally by the emperor's son Arcadius. The old gods were to be silenced, their old temples torn down. All across the empire, including Delphi. The centurion had been given one additional command.

He would obey.

He thrust his sword deep into the Oracle's belly and drove it full to the hilt. A gasp escaped her. She fell against his shoulder, as in a lover's embrace. He shouldered her away from him roughly.

Blood splashed across his armor, across the floor.

The Oracle slumped to the marble, then to her side. A trembling arm reached to the pool of her own blood. Her palm settled into it. 'A new spring . . . ,' she whispered, as if it were a promise.

Then her body went slack with death.

The centurion stepped over her form and let his sword lead him down the stairs to a small blind cave. An old woman's corpse, arrow-bit, lay in a black pool of blood. A three-legged chair lay toppled beside a riven crack in the floor. He searched the rest of the room and turned a full circle.

Impossible.

The chamber was empty.

March 1959
Carpathian Mountains
Romania

Major Yuri Raev climbed out of the Russian ZiS-151 truck and dropped to the rutted dirt road. His legs trembled under him. To steady himself, he leaned a hand on the green steel door of the battered vehicle, both cursing it and thanking it. The rattle of the week-long trek up into the mountains still made his spine ache. Even his molars seemed loose in his skull. Still, it took such a rugged vehicle to climb the stony switchbacks and river-flooded roads to reach this isolated winter camp.

He glanced over his shoulder as the rear door to the truck's bed crashed down. Soldiers in black-and-white uniforms hopped out. Their winter garb blended with the snow and granite of the densely wooded highlands. Morning fog still hung in hollows like sullen ghosts.

The men swore and stamped their boots. Small flickers of fire sparked as cigarettes were dropped or ground out. With a clatter, the soldiers readied their Kalashnikov assault rifles. But they were only the rear guard, meant to keep all away.

Yuri faced forward as the second in command of this mission, Lieutenant Dobritsky, marched over. He was a blocky Ukrainian with a pocked face and broken nose, outfitted in winter camouflage. Red rings from his snow goggles still circled his eyes.

'Major, sir, the camp is secure.'

'Is it them? Who we seek?'

Dobritsky shrugged, leaving it for Yuri to decide. They'd already had one false alarm, raiding a winter camp of half-starved peasants, who'd been eking out a living by quarrying stone.

Yuri scowled. These mountains were from another era, Stone-Aged, backward, rife with superstition and poverty. Yet the craggy, forested highlands were also a perfect refuge for those who wished to remain hidden.

Yuri stepped to the side and studied the curve of the rutted track that served as a road. Mud and snow had been churned up by the lead vehicles. Through the trees, Yuri spotted a score of IMZ-Ural motorcycles, each bearing an armed soldier in a sidecar. The heavy bikes had swept up in advance and secured the site, cutting off all means of escape.

Rumor and tortured testimony had led to this remote place. And still it had required scouring the highlands and burning a few homesteads to warm the occasional frozen tongues. Few were willing to speak of the Carpathian Romani. Especially with the stories spoken about this isolated clan in particular, whispers of *strigoi* and *moroi*. Evil spirits and witches.

But had he found them at long last?

Lieutenant Dobritsky shifted his boots. 'What now, Major?'

Yuri noted the sour turn to the Ukrainian's lips. Though Yuri was a major in the Soviet army, he was no soldier. He stood a head shorter than Dobritsky, with a slight paunch to his belly and a doughy face. Recruited from Leningrad State University, he had risen to his position through the ranks of the military's scientific branches. At the age of twenty-eight, he was already chief of the biophysics laboratory at the State Control Institute of Medical and Biological Research.

'Where is Captain Martov?' Yuri asked. The representative of Soviet Military Intelligence seldom left Dobritsky's side and kept an officious eye on all matters.

'Waiting for us at the camp's entrance.'

Dobritsky slogged a straight path up the road's center. Yuri sidestepped to the edge, where the ground was still frozen and the walking easier. Reaching the last switchback, the lieutenant pointed toward a camp sheltered in a cover of steep crags and surrounded by black woods.

'Gypsies,' Dobritsky grunted. 'As you ordered, *da*?'

But is this the right Romani clan?

Ahead, the Gypsy wagons were painted in faded hues of green and black, with wheels as tall as Yuri. Some

14

paint had peeled and flaked to reveal bolder colors hidden beneath, peeks at happier times. The tall wooden wagons were piled with snow and fringed by icicles along the sides. Windows were etched with frost. Blackened pits marked old bonfires. Two fires were still lit deeper in the winter camp, casting flames as high as the tallest wagon. Another wagon stood shattered and burned to a husk.

To one side, a few swaybacked draft horses hung their heads dully from beneath a lean-to of salvaged wood planks and piled stones. Goats and a few sheep ambled through the camp.

The soldiers had the site surrounded. A few dead bodies in ragged clothes and furred jackets lay sprawled here and there. The living looked little better. The camp's residents had been hauled from their wagons and heavy tents.

Shouts rose from deeper in the camp as the last of the Gypsies were rounded up. A spatter of automatic gunfire sounded. Kalashnikovs. Yuri observed the grim-eyed crowd. Some of the women were on their knees, sobbing. The dark men were steely in their black regard of the intruders. Most were bloody, wounded, broken-limbed.

'Where are all the children?' Yuri asked.

The answer came from his other side, bright and brittle as the ice frosting these highlands. 'Barricaded in the church.'

Yuri turned to face the speaker, Captain Savina Martov, the mission's intelligence officer. She was buried in a black overcoat with a fur-lined hood. Her black hair was a match to the hood's fringe of Russian wolf.

She lifted a slender arm toward a steeple rising beyond the wagons and tents. It appeared to be the only permanent structure here. Built all of local stone, the church blended into the surrounding crags.

'The children were already assembled in the structure before our forces arrived,' Savina recounted.

Dobritsky nodded. 'Must have heard the motor-cycles' engines.'

Savina met Yuri's eyes. Morning light danced in her green eyes. The intelligence officer had her own thoughts. It had been Savina who had delivered a cache of research papers to Yuri's institute, notebooks and reams of data from Auschwitz-Birkenau, specifically the work of Dr. Josef Mengele, the concentration camp's 'Angel of Death.'

Yuri had many sweat-soaked nightmares after reading through the material. It was well known that Dr. Mengele had performed all manner of horrible experiments on the prisoners, but the monster bore a special fascination for Gypsies, especially their children. He would ply them with treats and chocolates. They came to call him 'Uncle Pepe.' This was all done just to get the children to better cooperate. Eventually he had them all slaughtered – but not before he discovered an especially unique pair of Gypsy twins.

Two identical girls. Sasha and Meena.

Yuri had read those notes with a mixture of fascination and horror.

Mengele had kept meticulous notes on the remarkable twins: age, family history, lineage. He tortured the twins' family and relatives to uncover more details, verified by testing with the girls. Mengele accelerated his experiments. But as the war drew to a close, he was forced to prematurely terminate his tests. He killed the twins with injections of phenol into their hearts.

Mengele had scrawled his frustration near the end.

Wenn ich nur mehr Zeit gehabt hätte . . .

If only I'd had more time . . .

'Are you ready?' Savina asked Yuri.

He nodded.

Accompanied by Dobritsky and another soldier, the pair headed into the camp. He stepped around a corpse sprawled facedown in a pool of frozen blood.

The church appeared ahead. It was all stacked stones,

no windows. A single door stood closed, constructed of hewn beams of stout wood, banded and studded in copper. The building looked more like a fortress than a church.

Two soldiers flanked the doors with a steel battering ram.

Dobritsky glanced to Yuri.

He nodded.

'Break it down!' the lieutenant ordered sharply.

The men swung the ram and smashed the door. Wood splintered. It held for two more swings. Finally the door burst open with a crack of thunder.

Yuri shadowed Savina and stepped forward.

Small oil lamps lit the dark interior. Rows of pews lined either side, leading to a raised altar. Children of all ages cowered among the benches, strangely silent.

As Yuri continued toward the altar, he studied the children. Many bore disturbing deformities: pinheaded microcephaly, cleft lips, dwarfism. One child had no arms at all, only a torso. *Inbreeding.* Yuri's skin pebbled with unease. No wonder the rural folk around here feared this Romani clan, told tales of spirits and monsters.

'How will you know if these are the *right* children?' Savina asked with clear disgust in her voice.

Yuri quoted from one of the tortured interviews recorded by Mengele. 'The lair of the *chovihanis*.' The place was where the twins had been born, a secret kept by the Gypsies going back to the founding of the clans.

'Are these the ones?' Savina pressed.

Yuri shook his head. 'I don't know.'

He continued toward a girl seated before the altar. She clutched a rag doll to her chest, though her own garb was little better than her doll's. As Yuri neared, he noted the child seemed perfect, spared of any of the deformities. In the dim light, the pure crystal blue of her eyes shone brightly.

So rare among the Romani.

Like the twins, Sasha and Meena.

Yuri knelt in front of her. She seemed not to notice

17

him. Her gaze passed straight through him. He sensed there *was* something wrong with this child, possibly worse than any of the other deformities.

Though her eyes never seemed to focus any sharper, she lifted a hand toward him. '*Unchi Pepe,*' she lisped in a thin Romani voice.

A wash of fear swept through Yuri. *Uncle Pepe.* The pet name for Josef Mengele. It had been used by all the Gypsy children. But these children were too young to have ever seen the insides of a concentration camp.

Yuri stared into those vacant eyes. Did the child know what Yuri and his research team intended? How could she? Mengele's words haunted him:

If only I'd had more time . . .

That would not be Yuri's problem. His team would be granted all the time it needed. The facility was already under construction. Far from prying eyes.

Savina stepped closer. She needed an answer.

Yuri knew the truth; he'd known it the moment he stared into this girl's face. Still he hesitated.

Savina placed a hand on his elbow. 'Major?'

There could be no turning back, so Yuri nodded, acknowledging the horror to come. '*Da*. These are the *chovihanis.*'

'Are you certain?'

Yuri nodded again, but he kept his gaze fixed on the child's blue eyes. He barely heard Savina order Dobritsky: 'Collect all the children into the trucks. Eliminate everyone else.'

Yuri did not countermand those orders. He knew why they were here.

The child still held out her hand. '*Unchi Pepe,*' she repeated.

He took the tiny fingers into his own. There was no denying it, no turning back.

Yes, I am.

FIRST

1

It wasn't every day a man dropped dead in your arms.

Commander Gray Pierce had been crossing the national Mall when the homeless man accosted him. Gray was already in a bad mood, having finished one fight and was headed toward another. The midday heat only stoked his irritability. The day steamed with the usual D.C. swelter, baking off the sidewalk. Dressed in a navy blue blazer over an untucked cotton jersey and jeans, he estimated his internal temperature had risen from medium to well done.

From half a block away, Gray spotted a gaunt figure weaving toward him. The homeless man was dressed in baggy jeans rolled at the ankle, revealing scuffed army boots, only half laced. He hunched within a rumpled suit jacket. As the man neared, Gray noted his scrabbled beard was shot with gray, his eyes bleary and red as he searched around.

Such panhandlers were not a rare sight around the national Mall, especially as the Labor Day celebrations had just ended this past weekend. The tourists had retreated back to their ordinary lives, the riot police had retired to the local bars, and the street cleaners had finished erasing the evidence. The last to leave were those who still sought some bit of loose change that might have fallen through the cracks, searching trash bins for bottles or cans, like crabs scavenging the last bit of meat from old bones.

Gray did not sidestep the vagrant as he headed down Jefferson Drive toward the Smithsonian Castle, his destination. He even made eye contact, both to judge any threat level and to acknowledge the man's existence. While there were certainly some panhandling cons perpetrated by a few who were less than needy, most of the men and women on the streets were there through misfortune, addiction, or various forms of mental illness. And a good number of them were veterans of the armed services. Gray refused to look away – and maybe that was what brightened the other man's eyes.

Gray read a mix of relief and hope through the grime and wrinkles. Upon spotting Gray, the homeless man's shuffling gait became more determined. Perhaps he feared his quarry might escape into the Castle before he could reach him. The man's limbs shook. He was plainly inebriated or possibly suffering from drunken tremors.

A hand reached toward him, palm up.

It was a universal gesture – from the slums of Brazil to the alleys of Bangkok.

Help me. Please.

Gray reached inside his blazer for his wallet. Many thought he was a sucker for succumbing to such panhandling. *They'll just use it to buy booze or crack.* He didn't care. It was not his place to judge. This was another human being in need. He pulled out his wallet. If asked, he would give. That was his motto. And maybe at a more honest level, such charity served Gray, too, a balm of human kindness to soothe a guilt buried deeper than he cared to face.

22

And all it cost was a buck or two.

Not a bad deal.

He glanced into his wallet. All twenties. He had just cashed up at an ATM at the Metro station. He shrugged and tugged out a bill with Andrew Jackson's face.

Okay, sometimes it cost more than a buck or two.

He lifted his head just as the two met. Gray reached out with the twenty-dollar bill but found the man's hand wasn't empty. Resting in the middle of his palm lay a tarnished coin, about the size of a fifty-cent piece.

Gray frowned.

It was the first time a homeless man had tried to pay *him*.

Before he could comprehend the situation, the man tripped toward him, as if suddenly shoved from behind. His mouth opened in an O of surprise. He fell into Gray, who reflexively caught the elderly man.

He was lighter than Gray had expected. Under his jacket, the man's body seemed all bone, a skeleton in a suit. A hand grazed Gray's cheek. It burned feverishly hot. A flicker of fear – of disease, of AIDS – passed through Gray, but he did not let go as the man slumped in his arms.

Carrying the man's weight, Gray shifted his left arm. His hand settled upon a hot welling wetness on the man's lower back. It streamed over his fingers.

Blood.

Gray pivoted on instinct. He hip-rolled to the side and dove off the sidewalk, with the man still clutched in his arms. The thick grass cushioned their fall.

Gray didn't hear the next shots – but two ricocheting flashes sparked off the concrete sidewalk where he'd been standing. Without stopping, he continued to roll until he reached a metal-and-concrete sign planted in the lawn of the Smithsonian Castle. It stood only waist high. He huddled behind it with the old man. The sign read: SMITHSONIAN INFORMATION CENTER IN THE CASTLE.

Gray certainly needed information.

Like who was shooting at him.

The solid sign stood between him and the Mall. It offered temporary shelter. Only ten yards away, the arched doors of a side entrance of the Smithsonian Castle beckoned. The building itself rose in turrets and towers of red sandstone, all quarried from Seneca Creek, Maryland, a true Norman castle, a literal fortress. The protection it offered lay only a few steps away, but to cross that open distance would leave them exposed to the sniper.

Instead, Gray yanked a pistol – a compact Sig Sauer P229 – from the holster at his back. Not that he had a target. Still, he readied his weapon in case there was any direct assault.

At Gray's side, the homeless man groaned. Blood soaked his entire back. Gray frowned at the man's continuing misfortune in life. The poor sack had come seeking a bit of charity and got a bullet in the back instead, collateral damage in an assassination attempt against Gray.

But who was trying to kill him? And why?

The homeless man lifted a palsied arm, failing with each ragged breath. From the entry point and amount of blood, the shot had struck a kidney, a fatal wound for one so debilitated. The man reached to Gray's thigh. His fingers opened to drop the tarnished coin he had been holding. He had somehow kept his grip on it. The coin bounced off Gray's leg and rolled to the grass.

A final gift.

A bit of charity returned.

With the deed done, the homeless man's limbs went slack. His head fell to Gray's shoulder. Gray swore under his breath.

Sorry, old man.

His other hand freed his cell phone. Thumbing it

open, he hit an emergency speed-dial button. It was answered immediately.

Gray spoke rapidly, calling a mayday into central command.

'Help's on the way,' his director announced. 'We have you on camera outside the Castle. Seeing lots of blood. Are you injured?'

'No,' he answered curtly.

'Stay put.'

Gray didn't argue. So far no further shots had been fired. No ringing impacts against the sheltering sign. There was a good chance the shooter had already fled. Still, Gray dared not move – not until the cavalry arrived.

Pocketing his cell phone, Gray retrieved the man's coin from the grass. It was heavy, thick, crudely minted. He lifted it and absently rubbed at its surface. Using the dead man's blood on his fingers, he polished the grime off the surface to reveal an image of what appeared to be a Greek or Roman temple, six pillars under a peaked roof.

What the hell?

In the coin's center stood a single letter.

Gray thought it was the Greek letter Σ.

Sigma.

In mathematics, the letter *sigma* represented the *sum* of all parts, but it was also the emblem for the organization Gray worked for: Sigma, an elite team of ex-Special Forces soldiers who had been retrained in scientific fields to serve as a covert military arm for DARPA, the Defense Department's Advanced Research Projects Agency.

Gray glanced to the Castle. Sigma's headquarters were here, buried beneath the foundations of the Smithsonian Castle in former World War II bunkers. It was perfectly situated to take advantage of the proximity to the halls of government, the Pentagon, and the various private and national laboratories.

Focusing back on the coin, Gray suddenly realized his

mistake. The letter was not a Greek Σ – but merely a large capital *E*. In his panic, his eyes had played tricks, seeing what had been forefront in his mind.

He closed his fist over the coin.

Just an *E*.

It wasn't the first time in the past few weeks that Gray had assumed connections that weren't there – or at least that was the consensus among his colleagues. For a solid month, Gray had been searching for some confirmation that a lost friend, Monk Kokkalis, could still be alive. But so far, even utilizing the full resources of Sigma, he had reached only dead ends.

Chasing ghosts, Painter Crowe had warned after the first weeks.

Maybe he was.

Across the way, doors crashed open in the front of the Castle. A dozen black-suited figures fled outward with weapons raised, clutched near shoulders in double grips.

The cavalry.

They moved cautiously, but no one fired shots at them.

They reached Gray's side quickly and flanked around protectively.

One of the men fell to a knee beside the homeless man. He dropped a paramedic's pack, ready to offer aid.

'I think he's gone,' Gray warned.

The medic checked for a pulse, confirming Gray's assessment.

Dead.

Gray climbed to his feet.

He was surprised to see his boss, Painter Crowe, at the side entrance. Jacketless, his sleeves rolled to the elbows, Director Crowe shoved through the door. His expression was stormy. Though ten years older than Gray, Painter still moved like a lean-muscled wolf. The director must have assessed the risk to be minimal. Or maybe, like Gray, he merely sensed that the sniper had already fled.

Still, what didn't the man understand about *desk job*?

Painter crossed to him as sirens sounded from the distance. 'I have local P.D. locking down the Mall,' he said in clipped tones.

'Too little, too late.'

'Most likely. Still, ballistics will narrow down a trajectory radius. Figure out from where the shots were fired. Was anyone following you?'

Gray shook his head. 'Not that I could assess.'

Gray read the calculations in the director's eyes as he surveyed the Mall. Who would attempt to assassinate Gray? On their own doorstep. It was a clear warning, but against what? Gray had not been active in any operation since the last mission in Cambodia.

'We already pulled your parents into security,' Painter said. 'Just as a precaution.'

Gray nodded, grateful for that. Though he could imagine his father was not too happy. Nor his mother. They had barely recovered from a brutal kidnapping two months ago.

Still, with the immediate threat waning, Gray turned his attention to *who* might have tried to kill him – and more important, *why*. One possibility rose to the forefront: his current line of inquiry. Had his investigation into his friend's fate struck a nerve somewhere?

Despite the death here, hope flared in Gray.

'Director, could the assassination—?'

Painter held up a hand as his brows pinched with worry. He sank to one knee beside the homeless man and gently turned his face. After a moment, he sat back on his heel, his eyes narrowed. He looked more worried.

'What is it, sir?'

'I don't think you were the target, Gray.'

Gray glanced to the sidewalk and remembered the sparking strikes at his heels.

'At least not the primary target,' the director

27

continued. 'The sniper may have tried to eliminate you as a witness.'

'How can you be so sure?'

Painter nodded to the dead body. 'I know this man.'

Shock rang through him.

'His name is Archibald Polk. Professor of neurology at M.I.T.'

Gray cast a skeptical eye upon the man's jaundiced pallor, the grime, the scrabbled beard, but the director sounded certain. If true, the fellow plainly had fallen on hard times.

'How the hell did he end up like this?' he asked.

Painter stood and shook his head. 'I don't know. We've been out of touch for a decade. But the more important question: Why would someone want him dead?'

Gray stared down at the body. He readjusted his own internal assessment. Gray should have been relieved to learn he wasn't a target of an assassin, but if Painter was correct, then Gray's investigation had nothing to do with the attack.

Anger surfaced again – along with a certain sense of responsibility.

The man had died in Gray's arms.

'He must have been coming here,' Painter mumbled and glanced to the Castle. 'To see me. But why?'

Gray held out his hand, remembering the man's urgency. The ancient coin rested on his bloody palm. 'He may have wanted you to have this.'

2:02 P.M.

As sirens sounded in the distance, the elderly man walked slowly down Pennsylvania Avenue. He was dressed in a dusty gray suit. He carried a beat-up traveling valise on one side and held the hand of a girl on the other. The nine-year-old child wore a dress that matched the older man's suit. Her dark hair was tied back from her pale face with a red ribbon. The polish on her black shoes was marred by a drying splash of mud from the playground where she'd been playing before being picked up a moment ago.

'Papa, did you find your friend?' she asked in Russian.

He squeezed her hand and answered in a tired voice. 'Yes, I did, Sasha. But remember, *English*, my dear.'

She shuffled her feet a bit at the reprimand, then continued. 'Was he happy to see you?'

He flashed back to the sight through the sniper rifle's scope, the fall of the body.

'Yes, he was. He was quite surprised.'

'Can we go home now? Marta misses me.'

'Soon.'

'How soon?' she asked petulantly and scratched at her ear. A glint of steel flashed through her dark hair where she itched.

He released her hand and gently pulled her arm down from her ear. He smoothed her hair with a pat. 'I have one more stop. Then we'll head home.'

He neared Tenth Street. The building rose on his right, an ugly box built of slabs of concrete that someone attempted to decorate with a row of flags. He turned toward its entrance.

His destination.

The headquarters for the Federal Bureau of Investigation.

3:46 P.M.

A rattling buzzed from inside Gray's locker.

He hurried forward, half slipping on the wet floor. Fresh from the shower, he wore only a towel around his waist. After debriefing Director Crowe on the details of

29

the shooting, he had retreated to the locker room in the lowest levels of Sigma's bunkers. He had already taken one shower, followed by a rigorous hour in the gym working free weights – then showered again. The exertion had helped settle his mind.

But not completely.

Not until he had some answers about the murder.

Reaching his locker, he tugged the door open and caught his BlackBerry as it rattled across the bottom of the metal locker. It had to be Director Crowe. As his fingers closed on it, the vibration ceased. He'd missed the call. He checked the log and frowned. It was not Painter Crowe.

The screen read: R. Trypol.

He had almost forgotten.

Captain Ron Trypol of Naval Intelligence.

The captain had been overseeing the salvage operations at the Indonesian island of Pusat. He had a report due today on his assessment of raising the sunken cruise ship, the *Mistress of the Seas*. He had two navy submersibles on site, searching the wreckage and surrounding area.

But Gray had a more personal interest in the search.

The island of Pusat was where his friend and partner, Monk Kokkalis, had last been seen, spotted as he was dragged under the sea by a weighted net, tangled and caught. Captain Trypol had agreed to look for Monk's body. The captain was a good friend and former colleague of Monk's widow, Kat Bryant. This morning, Gray had gone over to the National Maritime Intelligence Center in Suitland, Maryland, hoping to hear any word. He had been rebuffed, told to wait until after the full debriefing. It was why he had been storming back here, prepared to demand that the director pressure the navy.

Flushed with a twinge of guilt for having set aside his cause, Gray hit the callback button and lifted the phone to his ear. As he waited for the connection to NMIC, he sank to a bench and stared at the locker on the opposite side. Written in black marker across a strip of duct tape was the name of the locker's former owner.

KOKKALIS.

Though Monk was surely dead, no one wanted to remove the tape. It was a silent hope. If only sustained by Gray.

He owed his friend.

Monk had climbed through the ranks of Sigma alongside Gray. His friend had been recruited from the Green Berets at the same time as Gray had been pulled from Leavenworth prison, where he'd been incarcerated after striking a superior officer during his stint with the Army Rangers. They had become quick friends, if not a bit of an odd couple at Sigma. Monk stood only a few inches over five feet, a shaven-headed pit bull compared to Gray's taller, leaner physique. But the true difference lay deeper than mere appearance. Monk's easygoing manner had slowly tempered the uncompromising steel of Gray's heart. If not for Monk's friendship, Gray would have certainly washed out of Sigma, as he had the Army Rangers.

As he waited, Gray pictured his former partner. They'd been through countless scrapes together over the years. Monk bore the puckered bullet wounds and scars to prove it. He had even lost his left hand during one mission, replaced with a prosthetic one. As he sat, Gray could still hear the barking bellow of Monk's laugh . . . or the quiet intensity of his voice, revealing the man's genius-level I.Q., disciplined in forensic medicine and science.

How could someone so large and vital be gone? Without a trace?

The phone finally clicked in his ear. 'Captain Ron Trypol,' a stern voice answered.

'Captain, it's Gray Pierce.'

'Ah, Commander. Good. I had hoped to reach you this afternoon. I don't have much time before my next meeting.'

Gray already heard the dire overtones. 'Captain?'

'I'll get to the point. I've been ordered to call off the search.'

'What?'

'We were able to recover twenty-two bodies. Dental records show none of them to be your man.'

'Only twenty-two?' Even by conservative estimates, that was only a small fraction of the dead.

'I know, Commander. But recovery efforts were already hampered by the extreme depths and pressures. The entire bottom of the lagoon is riddled with caverns and lava tubes, many extending miles in tangled mazes.'

'Still, with—'

'Commander.' The man's tone was firm. 'We lost a diver two days ago. A good man with a family and two children.'

Gray closed his eyes, knowing the ache of that loss.

'To search the caves only risks more men. And for what?'

Gray remained silent.

'Commander Pierce, I assume you haven't heard any more word. No further cryptic messages?'

Gray sighed.

To gain the captain's cooperation, he had related the one message he had received . . . or *possibly* received. It had occurred weeks after Monk had vanished. Following the events that occurred at the island, the only piece of his friend to be salvaged had been his prosthetic hand, a state-of-the-art piece of biotechnology built by DARPA engineers, which included a built-in wireless radio interface. While transporting the disembodied hand to Monk's funeral, the prosthetic fingers had begun to tap out a weak S.O.S. It had lasted only a few seconds – and only Gray had heard it. Then it had gone silent. Technicians had examined the hand and concluded it was most likely a mere glitch. The hand's digital log showed no incoming signal. It was just a malfunction. Nothing more. An electrical ghost-in-the-machine.

Still, Gray had refused to give up – even as week after week passed.

'Commander?' Trypol said.

'No,' Gray admitted sullenly. 'There's been no further word.'

Trypol paused, then spoke more slowly. 'Then perhaps it's time to lay this to rest, Commander. For everyone's sake.' His voice softened at the edges. 'And what about Kat? Your man's wife. What does she have to say about all this?'

It was a sore point. Gray wished he'd never mentioned it to her. But how could he not? Monk was her husband; they had a little girl together, Penelope. Still, maybe it had been the wrong thing to do. Kat had listened to Gray's story with a stoic expression. She stood in her black funeral dress, ramrod straight, her eyes sunken with grief. She knew it was a thin lifeline, only a frail hope. She had glanced to Penelope in the car seat of the black limousine, then back to Gray. She didn't say a word, only shook her head once. She could not grasp that lifeline. She could not survive losing Monk a second time. It would destroy her when she was already this fragile. And she had Penelope to consider, her own *piece* of Monk. True flesh and blood. Not some phantom hope.

He had understood. So he had continued his investigation on his own. He had not spoken to Kat since that day. It was a silent, mutual pact between them. She did not want to hear from him until the matter was resolved one way or the other. Gray's mother, though, spent several afternoons with Kat and the baby. His mother knew nothing about the S.O.S., but she had sensed that something was wrong with Kat.

Haunted, that was how his mother had described Kat.

And Gray knew what haunted her.

Despite what Kat had decided that day, she *had* grasped that lifeline. What the mind attempted to set aside, the heart could not. And it was torturing her.

For her sake, for Monk's family, Gray needed to face a harsh reality.

'Thank you for your efforts, Captain,' Gray finally mumbled.

'You did right by him, Commander. Know that. But eventually we have to move on.'

Gray cleared his throat. 'My condolences for the loss of your man, sir.'

'And the same to you.'

Gray ended the connection. He stood for a long breath. Finally, he stepped over to the opposite locker, placed a palm on its cold metal surface, as cold as a grave.

I'm sorry.

He reached up, peeled a corner of the duct tape, and ripped it away.

Gray was done chasing ghosts.

Good-bye, Monk.

4:02 P.M.

Painter spun the ancient coin atop his desk. He watched the silver flash as he concentrated on the mystery it represented. It had been returned from the lab half an hour ago. He had read the detailed report that had accompanied it. The coin had been laser-mapped for fingerprints, both its metallic content and surface soot had been analyzed with a mass spectrometer, and a multitude of photographs had been taken, including some taken with a stereo-microscope. The coin's spinning slowed, and it toppled to the mahogany desktop. Carefully cleaned, the ancient image on the surface shone brightly.

A Greek temple supported by six Doric pillars.

In the center of the temple rested a large letter.

E

The Greek letter *epsilon*.

On the opposite side was the bust of a woman with the words DIVA FAUSTINA written below it. From the report, at least the origin of the coin was no longer a mystery.

But what did—?

His intercom chimed. 'Director Crowe, Commander Pierce has arrived.'

'Very good. Send him in, Brant.'

Painter pulled the research report closer to him as the door swung open. Gray stepped through, his black hair wet and combed. He had changed out of his bloody clothes and wore a green T-shirt with ARMY emblazoned on the front, along with black jeans and boots. As he entered, Painter noted a shadow over the man's features, but also a certain weary resolve in his gray-blue eyes. Painter could guess the reason. He had already heard from the Office of Naval Intelligence through his own channels.

Painter waved Gray to a seat.

As he sat, the man's attention noted the coin on his desk. A flicker of curiosity flared.

Good.

Painter shifted the coin toward Gray. 'Commander, I know you asked for an indeterminate leave of absence, but I'd like you to take the lead on this case.'

Gray made no move to take the coin. 'May I ask a question first, sir?'

Painter nodded.

'The dead man. The professor.'

'Archibald Polk.'

'You mentioned that he must have been on his way here. To see you.'

Painter nodded. He suspected where the line of questioning was leading.

'So Professor Polk was familiar with Sigma? Despite the top secret clearance for such knowledge, he knew about our organization?'

'Yes. In a manner of speaking.'

Gray's brow crinkled. 'What manner is that?'

'Archibald Polk *invented* Sigma.'

Painter took a small measure of satisfaction in the man's surprise. Gray needed a little shaking up. The man sat up straighter in his chair.

Painter held up a hand. 'I've answered your question, Gray. So now you answer mine. Will you take the lead on this case?'

'After the professor was shot in front of me, I want answers as much as anyone.'

'And what about your . . . extracurricular activities?'

A wince of pain narrowed Gray's eyes. The planes of his face seemed to grow harder as a part of him clenched internally. 'I assume you've heard, sir.'

'Yes. The navy has discontinued its search.'

Gray took a deep breath. 'I've pursued all angles. There's nothing more I can do. I admit that.'

'And do you think Monk is still alive?'

'I . . . I don't know.'

'And you can live with that?'

Gray met his gaze, unflinching. 'I'll have to.'

Painter nodded, satisfied. 'Then let's talk about this coin.'

Gray reached out and took the coin from the desktop. Turning it in his fingers, he examined its freshly cleaned surfaces. 'Were you able to determine much about it?'

'Quite a bit. It's a Roman coin minted during the second century. Take a look at the woman's portrait on the back. That's Faustina the Elder, wife of the Roman emperor Antoninus Pius. She was a patron of orphaned girls and sponsored many women's charities. She also had a fascination with a sisterhood of sibyls, prophetic women from a temple in Greece.'

Painter waved for Gray to turn the coin over. 'That's the temple on the other side. The temple of Delphi.'

'As in the *Oracle* of Delphi? The female prophets?'

'The same.'

The coin's report on Painter's desk included a historical sheet about the Oracle, detailing how these women would inhale hallucinogenic fumes and answer questions of the future from supplicants. But their prophecies were more than just fortune-telling, for these women had a great impact on the ancient world. Over the course of a millennium, the Oracle's prophecies played a role in freeing thousands of slaves, setting the seeds of Western democracy, and elevating the sanctity of human life. Some claimed their words were pivotal at lifting Greece out from barbarism and toward modern civilization.

'But what about the big *E* in the center of the temple?' Gray asked. 'I assume the letter is Greek, too. Epsilon.'

'Yes. That's also from the Oracle's temple. There were a couple cryptic inscriptions in the temple: *Gnothi seauton*, which translates—'

'Know thyself,' Gray answered.

Painter nodded. He had to remind himself that Gray was well versed in ancient philosophies. When Painter had first recruited him out of Leavenworth prison, Gray had been studying both advanced chemistry and Taoism. It was this very uniqueness of his mind that had intrigued

Painter from the start. But such distinctiveness came with a price. Gray did not always play well with others, as he had demonstrated amply these past weeks. It was good to see him focusing on the here and now again.

'Then there was that mysterious *E*,' Painter continued, nodding to the coin. 'It lay carved in the temple's inner sanctum.'

'But what does it mean?'

Painter shrugged. 'No one knows. Not even the Greeks. Historians going all the way back to the ancient Greek scholar Plutarch have speculated at its significance. The current thought among modern historians is that there used to be *two* letters. A *G* and an *E*, representing the Earth goddess, Gaia. The earliest temple at Delphi was built to worship Gaia.'

'Still, if the meaning is so mysterious, why depict it on the coin?'

Painter slid the report across his desk toward Gray. 'You can read more about it in here. Over time, the Oracle's *E* became a symbol for a cult of prophecy. It's depicted in paintings throughout the ages, including Nicolas Poussin's *Ordination*, where it's inscribed above Christ's head as he hands the keys of heaven to Peter. The symbol is supposed to mark a time of great and fundamental change in the world, usually brought about by a single individual, whether that be the Oracle of Delphi or Jesus of Nazareth.'

Gray left the papers on the desk and shook his head. 'But what does all this have to do with the dead man?' Gray lifted the silver coin. 'Was this valuable? Worth killing over?'

Painter shook his head. 'Not especially. It's of moderate value, but nothing spectacular.'

'Then what—?'

The intercom's buzz cut him off. 'Director Crowe, I'm sorry to interrupt,' his assistant said over the speaker.

'What is it, Brant?'

'I have an urgent call from Dr. Jennings down in the pathology lab. He's asking for an immediate teleconference.'

'Fine. Queue it up on monitor one.'

Gray stood, ready to leave, but Painter waved him down, then swung his chair around. His office, buried in the subterranean bunker, had no windows, but it did have three large wall-mounted plasma screens. His private windows on the world. They were presently dark, but the monitor on the left flickered to life.

Painter found himself staring into one of the pathology labs. In the foreground stood Dr. Malcolm Jennings. The sixty-year-old chief of R&D for Sigma was dressed in surgical scrubs and had a clear plastic face-shield tilted atop his head. Behind him spread one of the pathology suites: sealed concrete floor, rows of digital scales, and in the center a body rested on the table, respectfully covered with a sheet.

Professor Archibald Polk.

It had taken a few calls to get his body released to Sigma versus the city's morgue, but Malcolm Jennings was a well-regarded forensic pathologist.

But from the grim set to the man's lips, something was wrong.

'What is it, Malcolm?'

'I had to quarantine the laboratory.'

Painter didn't like the sound of that. 'A contagious concern?'

'No, but there is definitely a concern. Let me show you.' He stepped out of view of the camera, but his voice carried to them. 'From the preliminary physical exam, I was already suspicious. I discovered patches of hair loss, eroded teeth enamel, and burns on his skin. If the man hadn't been shot, I wager he would've been dead in a matter of days.'

'What are you saying, Malcolm?' Painter asked.

He must not have heard. The pathologist stepped back into view, but now he wore a heavier, weighted apron. He carried a device that trailed a black wand.

Gray stood and shifted closer to the monitor.

Dr. Jennings waved the black wand over the dead man. The device in his other hand erupted with a furious clicking. The pathologist turned to face the camera.

'This body is radioactive.'

2

Out in the steaming swelter again, Gray strode down the sidewalk in front of the Smithsonian Castle. The national Mall spread to the left, mostly deserted due to the heat.

Behind Gray, crime tape still marked off the site of the afternoon's murder. The forensics unit had finished its sweep, but the area was still locked down, under the eye of a posted D.C. policeman.

Gray walked east along Jefferson Drive. He was shadowed by a large bodyguard, whom he was doing his best to ignore. He had not asked for any protection, especially this man. He touched the mike at his throat and subvocalized into it. 'I've found a trail.'

The fizzle of a reply rasped out of his wireless earpiece. Cocking his head, Gray seated it better. 'Say again,' he whispered.

'Can you follow the trail?' Painter Crowe asked.

'Yes . . . but I don't know for how long. The readings are weak.' Gray had suggested his current plan of action. He studied the device in his hand, a Gamma-Scout portable radiation detector. Its halogen-filled Geiger-Müller tube was sensitive enough to pick up trace radiation, especially when attuned to the specific strontium 90 isotope detected in Polk's body. Gray had hoped that a residual trace signature might have been left behind, the radiological equivalent of a scent trail. And it seemed to be working.

'Do your best, Gray. Any information on the professor's whereabouts these past days could be crucial. I already have a call in to his daughter, but I've been unable to reach her.'

'I'll follow this as far as I can.' Gray continued down the sidewalk, monitoring the detector. 'I'll report in if I discover anything.'

Gray signed off and continued alongside the national Mall. After another half block, the signal suddenly died on his device. Swearing, he stopped, retreated, and bumped into the bodyguard shadowing him.

'Damn it, Pierce,' the man grumbled. 'I just polished these shoes.'

Gray glanced over a shoulder to the muscled mountain behind him. Joe Kowalski, a former seaman with the navy, was dressed in a sportcoat and slacks. Both fit him poorly. With hair razored to a black stubble and a nose knotted by an old break, he looked more like a shaved gorilla forced into a wrinkled suit.

Kowalski bent down and used the cuff of his sportcoat to polish up his shoe. 'I paid three hundred bucks for these. They're chain stitch Chukkas imported from England. I had to special order them in my size.'

Cocking an eyebrow, Gray glanced up from his Gamma-Scout reader.

Kowalski seemed to realize he might have said too much. His expression turned sheepish. 'Okay. I like shoes. So what? I had a date, but . . . well . . . she canceled.'

Smart lady.

'Sorry about that,' Gray offered aloud.

'Well . . . at least they're not scratched,' Kowalski said.

'I meant *sorry* about being stood up.'

'Oh. Yeah.' He shrugged. 'Her loss.'

Gray didn't bother arguing. He returned his attention to his handheld reader and turned in a slow circle. A step to the right, he caught the radioactive scent again. It angled away from the sidewalk and trailed across the grassy Mall. 'This way.'

The professor's route took them through the Mall's Sculpture Garden across from the Hirshhorn Museum. Gray followed Polk's steps into the shady, sunken oasis, and out again. Beyond the garden, Polk's path continued across the Mall, edging alongside the tents of a Labor Day media event that was still being dismantled.

Gray glanced back to the sunken garden, studying the professor's path. 'He was trying to keep out of sight.'

'Or maybe the guy was just hot,' Kowalski countered, wiping his sweaty brow.

Gray searched around. To the west, the Washington Monument pointed toward the blistering sun; to the east rose the dome of the U.S. Capitol Building.

Needing answers, Gray continued. The digital readout on the Gamma-Scout slowly faded as he crossed the Mall. With each step, he watched the millirems of radiation ticking downward.

Reaching the far side of the Mall, Gray hurried across Madison Drive. He picked up the trail again as it entered another park. The signal grew stronger as Gray neared a shadowy copse of red-twig dogwood and Natchez crape myrtles. A bench stood next to a knee-high bed of hydrangeas.

Gray stepped to the bench.

In the secluded spot, the millirems ticked up higher again.

Had Polk waited here? Was that why the residual radiation trace was stronger?

Gray shifted a flowering branch of a crape myrtle and

found a wide view of the Mall stretching ahead, including a straight-on view of the Smithsonian Castle. Had the professor waited here until he thought it was safe? Gray squinted against the glare of the sun. He remembered Malcolm's diagnosis, the debilitation, the wasting. Polk had been on his last legs. Desperation must have finally drawn him out.

Why?

Gray began to step away when Kowalski cleared his throat. He was on one knee, dusting a shoe, but his other arm reached under the bench. 'Look at this,' he said and stood. Turning, he held a tiny pair of binoculars.

Gray shifted the detector closer to the scopes. The readings spiked higher. 'They're hot.'

Kowalski grimaced and thrust out the binoculars by their neck strap. 'Take 'em, take 'em.'

Gray retrieved the binoculars. His partner's fears were baseless. While there was radiation, it was only moderately worse than the usual background radiation.

Turning, Gray lifted the binoculars and peered through them toward the Castle. The view of the building swelled. He watched a figure pass along the front. Through the scopes, he made out the pedestrian's features. Gray recalled Polk's urgency when they'd neared each other. He'd dismissed it as a panhandler's desperation for a bit of charity. He now suspected Polk had recognized him. Maybe it wasn't solely desperation that had drawn him out. Had he spotted Gray crossing the Mall and come out of hiding to intercept him?

Gray dropped the binoculars into the lead-lined bag hung at his waist.

'Let's go.'

Out of the copse of trees, Gray followed the trail west along Madison Drive to a set of steps.

The trail turned up them.

Gray lifted his head and found himself facing the

44

Mall entrance to one of the Smithsonian's most famous museums: the National Museum of Natural History. It housed a massive collection of artifacts from around the world – ecological, geological, and archaeological – ranging from tiny fossils to a full-scale T-rex.

Gray craned his neck. The museum's dome loomed above a triangular portico supported by six giant Corinthian pillars. Staring upward, he was suddenly struck by how much the museum's facade looked like the Greek temple on the professor's coin.

Could there be a connection?

Before he followed the trail inside, he knew he'd better report in with central command. Stepping off to the side, he leaned on the stone balustrade and switched on his encrypted radio. He reached Director Crowe immediately.

'Have you found something?' Painter asked.

Gray kept his voice to a faint whisper. 'Looks like the professor's trail leads inside the Smithsonian's natural history museum.'

'The museum . . . ?'

'I'll continue the search inside. But was there any connection between him and this place?'

'Not that I'm aware. But I'll check into past associates.'

Gray remembered an earlier snippet of conversation about Dr. Polk's past. 'Director Crowe, one other thing. You never did explain something.'

'What's that, Commander?'

'You said the professor *invented* Sigma Force. What did you mean by that?'

Silence stretched for a bit, then Painter continued. 'Gray, what do you know about an organization called the Jasons?'

Taken aback by the odd question, Gray could not even fathom the context. 'Sir?'

'The Jasons are a scientific think tank formed back during the Cold War. They included leaders in their respective fields, many Nobel Prize winners. They banded together to offer advice to the military elite about technological projects.'

'And Professor Polk was a member?'

'He was. Over the years, the Jasons proved to be of great value to the military. They met each summer and brainstormed on new innovations. And to answer your question, it was during one such meeting that Archibald Polk suggested the formation of a *militarized* team of investigators to serve DARPA, to act as field operatives for the agency.'

'And so Sigma was born.'

'Exactly. But I'm not sure any of this is significant in regard to his murder. From what I've heard so far, Polk's not been active with the Jasons for years.'

Gray stared up at the towering Greek facade. 'Maybe one of his fellow Jasons worked here at the museum? Maybe that's why he came?'

'That's a good point of investigation. I'll look into it, but it might take some time to root out. Over these past few years, their organization has become more and more secretive. Divided among various top secret projects, Jasons don't even know what other Jasons are doing nowadays. But I'll keep making calls.'

'And I'll keep following this trail.' He signed off and waved to Kowalski. 'C'mon. We're going inside.'

'About time we got out of the goddamn sun.'

Gray didn't argue. Stepping through the doors, he appreciated the shadowy, air-conditioned interior. The museum was free to the public, but Gray flashed his glossy black I.D. card to the guard who manned the metal detector.

He was waved through.

Pushing into the main rotunda, Gray was struck by the sheer size of the space. The rotunda was octagonal in shape and rose three stories, each level lined by more pillars, leading to the massive Guastavino-tiled dome. Sunlight streamed through clerestory windows and a central oculus.

Closer at hand, in the center of the rotunda, stood one of the museum's mascots, an eight-ton African bull elephant. It posed with raised trunk and curved tusks amid a field of dry grass. Polk's path led around the elephant and toward a public staircase.

As Gray followed, he noted a banner hung high on the wall to the left. It advertised an exhibit opening next month. It depicted the head of Medusa, her hair wild with twisting snakes, reflected on a circular shield. Staring upward, Gray's feet slowed.

He pictured Polk's strange coin as he read the name of the upcoming exhibit, sensing he was on the right track.

LOST MYSTERIES OF GREEK MYTHOLOGY

6:32 P.M.

In the darkened room, the two men stared through the one-way glass into a child's playroom. They sat in leather club chairs, while behind them climbed four rows of stadium seating, all empty at the moment.

This was a private meeting.

Beyond the mirrored glass, the neighboring room was brightly lit. The walls were painted white, with just the barest hint of sky blue, a color that from psychological statistics was supposed to encourage a calming, meditative state. It held a daybed with a flowered comforter, an open box of toys, and a child-size desk.

The older of the two men sat straight in his seat. At his side was a scuffed valise that held a disassembled Dragunov sniper rifle.

The other man, at fifty-seven years of age, was twenty

years younger than his Russian companion. He slouched in a pressed suit. His eyes were fixed on the girl as she stood in front of a plastic easel and shuffled through a tray of pastel felt markers. She had spent the last half hour meticulously drawing a rectangle in green upon the white sheet of butcher paper attached to the easel. She had run the marker around and around in a hypnotically rhythmic pattern.

'Dr. Raev,' the man said, 'I don't mean to harp, but are you absolutely *certain* Dr. Polk did not have it on his person?'

Dr. Yuri Raev sighed. 'I have spent my life on this project.' *And my soul,* he added silently. 'I will not have it ruined when we are so close.'

'So then where is it? We turned over that cheap motel he stayed in last night. Nothing. It would raise too many questions if it should end up in *unfriendly* hands.'

Yuri glanced at the man in the neighboring seat. John Mapplethorpe, a division chief for the Defense Intelligence Agency, had a long face with sagging jowls and bags under his eyes, as if he were made of candle wax and been left too long in the sun. Even the dye he used on his hair was too dark, too obvious a vanity for his age. Not that Yuri had any right to fault a man for attempting to stem the tide of age. Beneath the sag of his own skin, Yuri's body remained toned, his reflexes sharp, and his mind as quick and agile as it ever had been. Between injections of androgens and growth hormone, along with vigorous exercise, he fought as adamantly as anyone to hold back time. But it was not vanity that drove him.

He stared into the room.

No, not vanity.

Mapplethorpe drummed his fingers on the arm of his chair. 'We must recover what Polk stole.'

'He did not have it with him,' Yuri assured Mapplethorpe more forcefully. 'It is too large to conceal on his person, even under a jacket. I was fortunate to stop him when I did. Before he spoke to anyone.'

'I hope you're right. For all our sakes.' Mapplethorpe turned his attention back to the room. 'And she was able to track him? All the way from Russia.'

Yuri nodded. Fatherly pride entered his voice. 'With her and her twin brother, we may have finally breached the barrier.'

'Too bad she couldn't have been quicker.' Mapplethorpe made a dismissive sound. 'My brother-in-law's daughter has an autistic boy. Did I ever tell you that? But he's not an idiot savant. He can hardly tie his shoes.'

Yuri bristled. 'The preferable term is *autistic* savant.'

The other man shrugged.

Yuri's distaste for the American continued to grow. Like Mapplethorpe, few people really understood autism, even in the medical profession. Yuri knew the disorder intimately. It was in fact a *spectrum* of disorders, characterized by weaknesses in communication skills and social interaction, along with abnormal responses to sensations. This led tragically to children with delayed and compromised language and speech abilities, repetitive motor mannerisms and tics, preoccupation with objects, and often dysfunctional ways of relating to events or people.

But sometimes such a disorder generated miracles.

In rare instances, an autistic child demonstrated an astonishing brilliance in a narrow specialized field, such as mathematics, music, or art. And while 10 percent of autistic children demonstrated some degree of such savant talent, what interested Yuri were those rarest of individuals, known as *prodigious* savants, those few who arose with talent that stretched the very definition of genius. Worldwide, there were fewer than forty such individuals. But even among such exceptional individuals, a handful rose who dwarfed the others.

They arose from one genetic line.

An old Gypsy word echoed in his head.

Chovihanis.

Yuri stared through the window at the dark-haired girl.

Mapplethorpe mumbled beside him. 'We must not let anyone catch a hint of what we're doing. Or the Nuremberg Nazi trials will look like traffic court.'

Yuri didn't respond. Mapplethorpe barely comprehended the full scope of his research. But after the Berlin Wall fell, Yuri had needed new resources to continue his work. It took a full decade to slowly test the waters in America. It seemed hopeless; then the political climate suddenly changed. The global war on terror had forged new alliances and allegiances. Enemies became allies. But more important, the boundaries of propriety were breached. It was a new era, with a new morality. An old catchphrase was now law: *the ends justified the means.*

Any means.

As long as it was for the common good.

Yuri's government had known this all along. It was only the Americans who were late in facing this harsh reality.

'What's that girl doing?' Mapplethorpe asked.

Yuri snapped out of his own reverie. He stood up. Sasha was at the easel, a black felt marker in her hand. Her arm flew up and down the stretch of butcher paper. She stabbed and stroked, very angular. There seemed no pattern. She worked one corner, then another.

Mapplethorpe snorted at the mess. 'I thought you said she was talented in art.'

'She is.'

Sasha continued to work. The rectangle she originally drew in green began to fill with black swirls and swipes. She held her other arm straight out from her body, stiff as a plank, as if she sought to balance herself against some force beyond this world.

Finally both arms fell to her sides.

She turned away from the easel, dropped into a cross-legged crouch, and rocked slightly. Her brow was sweaty. She reached to a discarded toy wooden block and began rhythmically turning it in her fingers, as if she were trying to solve some puzzle known only to her.

Yuri turned his attention to her artwork.

Mapplethorpe joined him. 'What was that all about? It's just gibberish.'

'*Nyet.*' Yuri accidentally slipped into Russian, but he was worried . . . very worried.

He hurried to the door that led into the next room. Mapplethorpe followed. As he entered the child's room, Sasha just rocked and twiddled the block in her fingers. From past experience, Yuri knew she would be shut down for a while.

He also had learned a thing or two about Sasha's talent.

Reaching the easel, he ripped the butcher sheet down.

'What are you doing?' Mapplethorpe asked.

Yuri turned the drawing upside down and clipped it back onto the easel. Sasha sometimes drew in reverse. It was not uncommon among autistic savants. They often experienced the world through very different senses. Numbers had sounds. Words had smells.

Yuri glanced over to Sasha.

Her brilliant blue eyes remained fixed on her toy block.

Yuri turned back and noted Mapplethorpe's amazement. The man drew closer to the drawing. He pointed, wordless with astonishment. Finally words tumbled out. 'Dear God . . . that looks like an elephant in the center.'

Yuri stared, too. His heart pounded in his throat. She shouldn't have been able to do that unless triggered. It had been such sketches that had led them to Dr. Polk – drawings of the Mall, of the Smithsonian Castle – leading them to set up a sniper's nest in an unwatched corner of the Mall. They'd had to move quickly, responding in two hours. There was a limit to Sasha's range.

Mapplethorpe leaned closer. 'The *room* it's in. I think I know that place. I took my grandchild there only two weeks ago. It's the rotunda of the natural history museum.'

Yuri frowned. 'The one on the national Mall?'

Where his quarry had been hiding for so long today.

Mapplethorpe nodded.

Yuri stared toward the mirror and saw only his own reflection. Had Sasha sensed them back there? And more important, had she sensed Mapplethorpe's intense worry about what had been stolen by Dr. Polk?

There was only one way to find out.

Yuri pointed to the picture and spoke to Mapplethorpe. 'I'd suggest you get your men over there. Immediately.'

6:48 P.M.

Gray continued deeper into the museum. Past the central rotunda with its stuffed elephant, Polk's radioactive path led directly to a public stairwell. Gray followed it past the next floor and down farther again. It finally ended at a security door marked MUSEUM PERSONNEL ONLY. NO ADMITTANCE.

Gray tested the door. It was secured with an electronic lock. It required a magnetic employee card to pass through here. Gray frowned. So how did Polk get through here? Gray touched his throat mike and patched a call to central command.

Painter answered immediately. 'Commander?'

'Sir, I need some help.' Gray explained where the trail ended. 'I'll need access past this point.'

'Hang tight, Gray. I'm going to upgrade your I.D. card's clearance to encompass the Smithsonian museums.' Silence stretched for a bit. Gray imagined the director tapping at his computer.

Next to him, Kowalski leaned on the neighboring wall and whistled through his teeth.

'Try it now,' Painter finally said.

Gray swiped his card. He heard the lock's tumblers release. 'Got it. I'll let you know what we find.'

Ending the call, Gray ducked through the door and

set off into the off-limit spaces of the museum. It was not all that different from the rest of the building, if only slightly more utilitarian: marble floors honed to a lustrous sheen by decades of shuffling feet, wan fluorescent lighting, and wooden doors whose frosted glass windows were etched with scholarly enterprises.

ENTOMOLOGY, INVERTEBRATE ZOOLOGY, PALEO-BIOLOGY, BOTANY.

The trail led through the maze – then the readings jostled higher as they approached an unmarked door. Gray waved the Gamma-Scout reader toward its handle. The digital numbers spiked. Stepping back, Gray noted a fainter trail continued down the hall. The hallway ahead ended at a cavernous space, lined on the far side by large steel roll-up doors. The museum's loading docks. Gray stared up and down the hall, picturing a ghostly version of Polk. The professor must have entered the museum through the docks, then continued out the museum's front door.

Had he done that to shake a tail?

Kowalski tried the door handle. 'Unlocked,' he said and proved it by swinging the door open.

The dark space ahead smelled of dust, dry hay, and a hint of cedar.

Gray reached inside and found a light switch. He flicked it on. Racks and shelves filled the back half of a cavernous space. Wooden crates with shipping labels stapled to them were stacked in a pile along one side. Several had been cracked open. Old packing straw and more modern Styrofoam packing peanuts littered the floor.

A storage room.

To the left of the door, a single desk supported a computer and printer. Tables stretched along the other side, crowded with pottery and sections of decorated stone blocks. Someone had been taking inventory. Several larger objects rested on wooden floor pallets deeper in the room: a marble statue of a woman with her arms broken away, a corroded bronze sculpture of a bull's head, a base of a stone pillar.

Gray followed the trail inside, wondering what had led the professor to trespass here. Had he just been hiding from a passing guard? But the professor's path seemed direct. It led straight to one of the objects on the floor pallets, a dome of carved rock. The artifact stood waist-high with a hole on top. It looked like a granite model of a volcano, except it was covered with writing. Gray leaned closer to the inscriptions.

Ancient Greek.

Frowning, Gray tested it with the Gamma-Scout reader.

Polk's trail circled around the pallet.

Gray traced the dead man's footsteps. Why had Polk been fascinated with this artifact?

Before he could contemplate it further, a crash sounded to his left. He turned to see Kowalski backing away from one of the tables. He held the handle of an urn in his fingers. The rest of the vase lay shattered at his toes. 'It . . . it broke.'

The man had a gift for the obvious.

Gray shook his head. He should have left Kowalski out in the hallway. He was like a bull in a china shop – only a bull had better self-control.

'It was wobbly, goddamn it.' Still, he sounded angry more at himself. 'Come over here and see this.' He pointed the broken handle toward the table.

Gray stepped to his side. On the table were stacks of ancient Greek coins. From the gap in the second row, one of the coins was missing. Could it be Polk's coin? Was this where he'd got ahold of it?

'I bumped the base. Tried to catch it.' Kowalski carefully placed the broken handle on the table. 'It came apart in my hands.'

'Don't worry about it. They'll just take it out of your paycheck.'

'Damn it. How much do you think it cost?'

'A few hundred.'

A relieved whistle escaped him. 'Well, that's not too bad.'

'A few hundred *thousand*,' Gray clarified.

'Oh, sweet motherfu—'

Kowalski's reaction was cut off by the rattle of the doorknob. Gray started to turn, but Kowalski's thick mitt of a hand grabbed Gray's upper arm and yanked him back. He shielded Gray with his own body while smoothly pulling a .45-caliber pistol from a shoulder holster.

The slight figure of a young woman entered. She was fumbling with her purse, oblivious of the two in the room. She even swiped blindly for the light switch until she seemed to realize two things at once: the lights were already on and a massive mountain of a man had a pistol leveled at her chest.

She squeaked and backed into the jamb, unable to find the doorway in her fright.

'Sorry,' Kowalski said and shifted his pistol toward the ceiling.

Gray hurried around the befuddled bodyguard. 'It's all right, ma'am. We're museum security. We're investigating a break-in.'

Kowalski pointed his pistol at the shattered vase on the floor. 'Yeah, someone broke that.' He glanced to Gray for confirmation and collaboration as he holstered his weapon.

She clutched her purse to her chest. Her other hand fixed a pair of petite eyeglasses higher on her nose. With her chestnut hair cut in a bob and her small frame, she appeared to be no more than a college sophomore, but from the crinkled pinch of her eyes, bright with suspicion, she was probably a decade older.

'Can I see some identification?' she asked firmly and kept close to the open doorway.

Gray held up his black I.D. pass. It displayed his picture, along with the presidential seal embossed in gold. 'I have a number you can call to confirm who we are.'

She squinted at the pass and seemed to relax slightly, but a tension remained in her shoulders. She stared around the room. 'Was anything stolen?'

'Maybe you can better answer that,' Gray said, hoping she could help. 'I noticed that there seems to be a coin conspicuously missing from the table here.'

'What?' She hurried over, abandoning any hesitation. With one look at the table, her expression fell into a forlorn look. 'Oh, no . . . we had the collection on loan from the Delphi museum.'

Delphi again.

She glanced to the carved dome of rock, the one that seemed to have attracted Polk's attention. It may have been because Kowalski was leaning on it. 'Please don't touch that.'

Kowalski straightened. He looked at his palm, as if it were to blame. He had the decency to blush around the collar. 'Sorry.'

'May I ask what that is?' Gray said casually, nodding to the stone.

Her hands wrung together with worry. 'The prize of the collection. For the upcoming exhibit. Thank God, it wasn't vandalized by the thieves.' She circled it to be sure. 'It's over sixteen hundred years old.'

'But what is it?' Gray pressed.

'It's called an omphalos. Which roughly translates as "navel." In ancient Greece, the omphalos was considered to be the point around which the universe turned. There are many mythologies and stories associated with the omphalos, great powers attributed to it.'

'And how did you acquire it?'

She nodded to the table. 'It came from the same collection as the rest. On loan from the museum at Delphi.'

'Delphi? Where the Oracle of Delphi had her temple?'

She glanced toward Gray, her expression surprised. 'That's right. The omphalos graced the inner sanctum of the temple. Its most holy chamber.'

'And this is that stone.'

'No. Sadly it's only a replica. Until just recently, everyone thought this was the original omphalos, as described in the ancient histories of Plutarch and Socrates. But the sisterhood of Delphic oracles goes back three millennia, and this stone has been dated to half that age.'

'What happened to the original?'

'Lost to history. No one knows.'

She straightened and strode over to a smock hung on a peg by the door. Donning it, she removed her museum identification tag from her shirt and fixed it to the smock.

It was only then that Gray noted the tag. It bore her picture and her name beneath it.

POLK, E.

'Polk . . . ,' he read aloud.

'Dr. Elizabeth Polk,' she said.

A tingle of misgiving iced through Gray. He suddenly knew *why* the professor had come here. 'By any chance do you know an Archibald Polk?'

She fixed him with a more solid stare. 'My father? Why?'

3

'Dead?'

Gray sat on the edge of the desk in the museum's storage room. He knew the pain of what he had to tell her. Elizabeth Polk slumped in the chair, collapsed within her lab coat. There were no tears. Shock locked them away, but she took off her slim eyeglasses, as if readying herself.

'I heard about the shooting on the Mall,' she mumbled. 'But I never thought . . .' She shook her head. 'I've been in the cellars here all day.'

Where there was no cell phone reception, Gray noted silently. Painter had mentioned trying to reach Polk's daughter. And she was right across the Mall the entire time.

'I'm sorry to press you on this, Elizabeth,' he said, 'but when did you last see your father?'

She swallowed hard, starting to lose control. Her voice quavered. 'I . . . I'm not sure. A year ago. We had a falling-out. Oh, God, what I said to him . . .' She placed a hand on her forehead.

Gray read the regret and pain in her eyes. 'I'm sure he knew you loved him.'

Her eyes flashed to him, going harder. 'Thank you for your words. But you didn't know him, did you?'

Gray sensed the tough core hidden behind that mousy, bookish exterior. He faced her anger, knowing it was directed inward rather than at him. Kowalski had retreated to the far side of the room, plainly uncomfortable with the whole scene.

Gray twisted where he sat and pointed to the desktop. The rows of ancient coins still lined a paper blotter there. 'I *know* because we found a coin on your father's body.' Gray recalled what Painter had told him about it. 'A coin with the bust of Faustina the Elder on one side and the temple of Delphi on the other.'

Her eyes widened. She stared down at the gap in the row where the coin once lay.

Gray lifted an arm. 'He came here before he was shot. To your office.'

'It's not my office,' she mumbled, glancing around, as if searching for the ghost of her father. 'I'm doing research for my doctoral dissertation. In fact, it was my father who pulled some strings and got me this graduate position at the Delphi museum in Greece. I'd been out there until a month ago. I'm overseeing the installation of this exhibit. I didn't think my father knew I was here. Especially after our—' She waved away what she was going to say next.

'He must've been keeping tabs on you.'

A few tears did flow, just enough to trickle down one cheek. She brusquely dabbed her face with the sleeve of her lab coat.

Gray gave her a moment. He stared over at Kowalski, who was walking in a bored circle around the stone omphalos, like a slow orbiting moon. Gray knew Elizabeth's father had followed that same orbit. But why?

Elizabeth voiced the same question. 'Why did my father come here? Why did he take the coin?'

'I don't know. But I'm fairly certain your father knew he was being tracked, hunted.' He pictured Polk haunting the edges of the Mall, seeking some way of contacting Sigma in person, staying hidden. 'He might have taken the coin in case he was murdered. The coin was grimy, easy to miss in a pocket if the assailant did a cursory search of the body. But a more thorough exam at a morgue would've revealed the strangeness of the coin. I think he hoped it would lead here. To this office where he would've known you'd report it stolen.'

The woman's tears had dried as he spoke. 'But why would he do that?'

Gray closed his eyes, thinking hard, putting himself in the man's shoes. 'If I'm right about the coin, your father was worried he would be searched. He must've known the hunters were after something. Something he possessed . . .'

Of course.

Gray opened his eyes and stood. He drew Elizabeth up, too. Her eyes studied the room, but not for ghosts this time. Gray saw the understanding in the pinch of her brows. She donned her eyeglasses.

'My father might have hidden here what his murderers were looking for.'

Gray headed to where Kowalski waited beside the conical-shaped stone. 'Your father seemed particularly interested in the temple's omphalos.'

Elizabeth followed with a frown. 'How could you possibly know that?'

Gray briefly explained about the radiation exposure and lifted the Gamma-Scout. 'Your father's trail led here, and for me to get such a strong reading from it, he must have spent some time near the artifact.'

Elizabeth had paled a bit upon hearing of her father's affliction. Still, she waved to Kowalski. 'There's an emergency flashlight plugged into that wall over there.'

He nodded and fetched it.

She approached the stone. 'While it looks solid, it's actually hollow inside. No more than an upended bowl of carved granite.' She pointed to the hole at the top.

Gray understood. Her father could have easily dropped something inside it. He accepted the flashlight from Kowalski, leaned over the stone, and pointed the beam down into the heart of it. It was indeed hollow. At the bottom, the slats of the pallet that supported the stone were illuminated. He shifted the beam around and spotted something off to one side. It looked like a polished stone, roughly the size of a cantaloupe.

'Can't tell what it is,' he mumbled and straightened. 'We need to lift the stone.'

'It's heavy,' Elizabeth explained. 'Took six men to uncrate it. But there's a crowbar among the tools in back. We should be able to tilt it up. But we'll have to be careful.'

'I'll go get it,' Kowalski said.

As he stepped away, the telephone on Elizabeth's desk rang. She crossed toward it and checked the caller I.D. on the handset. 'It's security.' She checked her wristwatch, then glanced to Gray. 'It's already after closing hours. They must be checking on how long I'll be working down here.'

'Tell them at least another hour.'

She nodded and picked up the phone. She confirmed who she was, then listened. Her eyes widened. 'I understand. We'll be right up.' She hung up the phone and turned to Gray. 'Someone called in a bomb threat. Here at the museum. They're evacuating the building.'

Gray remained silent. He knew such a threat, especially now, was no coincidence. He read the same understanding in the woman's eyes. 'Someone knows,' he said slowly. 'After today's shooting on the Mall, no one will dismiss a bomb threat. It's the perfect cover to run a covert sweep of the building.'

He turned to study the omphalos.

Time was running out for delicacy.

Kowalski must have understood this, too. He returned from the back of the storage room. 'I heard,' he said. Instead of the padded crowbar, he hefted a large sledgehammer on his shoulder. 'Get back.'

'No!' Elizabeth warned.

But Kowalski clearly wasn't taking no for an answer. He closed the distance in one stride, raised the hammer over his head, and swung it down.

Elizabeth gasped in fear for the centuries-old artifact.

But instead of hitting the ancient stone, the sledgehammer slammed into the slats of the pallet that supported the omphalos. Wood splintered and broke. Kowalski lifted the hammer again and cracked more slats on the same side.

With half its weight now unsupported, the great stone tilted toward the crushed side of the pallet – then slowly toppled over, upending itself. More slats were pulverized under its weight, but it seemed undamaged from its slow roll.

Kowalski shouldered the hammer.

Elizabeth stared at the man, her expression wavering between horror and awe.

Gray hurried to the pallet and dropped to a knee. The object hidden under the omphalos now rested in plain view. It was not a polished *stone*. Gray lifted his Gamma-Scout reader toward it. It read hot, but no worse than the binoculars they'd found earlier.

Satisfied, Gray retrieved it and stood.

Elizabeth stumbled back as he straightened.

Kowalski's eyes tightened. 'A skull? Is that what this is all about?'

Gray examined it closer. The skull was small and missing its lower jaw. He turned it over. The remaining teeth displayed prominent fangs in a protuberant muzzle.

'Not human,' he said. 'From the size and shape of the cranium, I'd say it's simian. Possibly a chimpanzee.'

Kowalski's expression soured even further. 'Great,' he drawled out. 'More monkeys.'

Gray knew the large man had developed a distaste for all things simian following a previous mission. Something to do with baboons . . . or apes. Gray could never get a straight story from the man.

'But what . . . what's that attached to the skull's side?' Elizabeth pointed out.

Gray knew what she meant. It was hard to miss. Affixed to the temporal bone, just above the opening to the ear canal, rested a curved block of stainless steel.

'I'm not sure,' he answered. 'Maybe a hearing aid. Perhaps even one of the new cochlear implants.'

'For a damn monkey?' Kowalski asked.

Gray shrugged. 'We'll have to examine it later.'

'Why did my father bring that here?'

Gray shook his head. 'I don't know. But someone wanted to stop him. And someone still wants it back.'

'What do we do?'

'We find a way out of here. Before anyone knows we recovered it.'

Gray took a moment to search the rest of the pallet, in case the professor had left anything else here. Like a note explaining everything. One could always hope. He pointed his flashlight into the hollow cavity of the upended omphalos.

Nothing.

As he swung the beam away, the light glanced over the inner surface. Something caught his eye there. It looked like a spiraling groove carved into its surface, starting at the lip and corkscrewing up toward the hole. He reached a finger to it and realized it was a single long line of cursive script. Leaning over, he narrowed the flashlight's beam upon the writing.

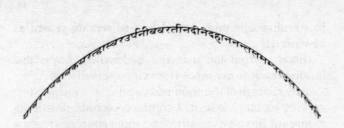

Elizabeth noted his attention. 'Ancient Sanskrit.'

Gray straightened back. 'What's Sanskrit doing on the inside—?'

Kowalski cut him off. 'Does it friggin' matter already?' He pointed a thumb toward the door. 'Remember that bomb scare. Shouldn't we be haulin' ass out of here?'

Gray straightened. The man had a point. They'd wasted enough time. The sweep of the building was probably already—

A muffled shout echoed from the hallway.

Kowalski rolled his eyes in a plain expression of *I told you so*.

'What do we do?' Elizabeth asked.

7:37 P.M.

Painter knocked on the half-open door to the pathologist's office.

'Come in,' Malcolm called out. 'Jones, do you have the data from—?'

Painter pushed the door wider just as Malcolm swung around in his desk chair. The pathologist still wore a set of blue scrubs. His glasses rested atop his head. He was rubbing at the bridge of his nose when he noted who stood in his doorway.

His eyes widened. 'Director . . .' He made a motion

to stand, but Painter waved him to remain seated as he entered.

'Brant alerted me that you had called. I was just heading back to my office from video surveillance.'

'Any footage of the shooter?'

'Not so far. We're still combing records. But it's a mountain of videos to sift. And some sources are slow to respond.'

Since 9/11, surveillance of the capital had been heightened. For a full ten miles in all directions around the White House, multiview cameras monitored every square foot of streets, parks, and public spaces. And over 60 percent of interior spaces, too. Several cameras had picked up pieces of Dr. Archibald Polk's path across the Mall. They confirmed what Gray had assessed with his radiological tracker. But nagging gaps persisted. Though they had footage of Polk collapsing in Gray's arms, no camera caught even a glimpse of rifle flash or any sign of the shooter.

It was worrisome.

Painter was beginning to suspect that the sniper had known about the cameras and had found a hole in the surveillance net in which to hide. Or worse yet, someone could have tampered with the Mall's footage and purposefully deleted any evidence of the assassin.

Either way, such collusion suggested that Professor Polk's murderer might have powerful ties here in Washington. But who and where? If Polk's history as a Jason had anything to do with the murder, then it opened a Pandora's box of possibilities. The Jasons had their fingers in top secret projects of every shade from gray to deep black.

Painter knew he would be getting no sleep tonight.

None of them would.

'Any word from Gray?' Malcolm asked, shifting a pile of papers from a chair and offering a seat to Painter.

'He's searching the natural history museum. Polk's trail led there.'

'Hopefully he'll find something, but that was also why I patched a call to you. I may have discovered more bread crumbs to follow.'

Curious, Painter sank into the chair. Malcolm rotated his computer's flat-screen monitor to a better angle for Painter to view.

'What did you find?' Painter asked.

'Something curious. I don't know really what to make of it, but it might give us someplace to continue the investigation. Knowing the victim was suffering from radiation poisoning, I sought some clue to the source. Initial examination of Polk's gastrointestinal tract and liver showed he didn't ingest anything radiological in nature.'

'So no dinner poisoned with polonium-210 or the like?'

Malcolm nodded. 'From the degree of radiodermatitis burns to his skin, I was fairly certain the radiation came from an environmental source. He must have been in some type of hot zone. Microanalysis of his hair showed the exposure was acute in nature. He'd been poisoned less than a week ago.'

'But where—?'

Malcolm held up a hand for patience and used his other to tap at his keyboard and bring up a map of the world on the monitor. 'Trace amounts of radioactive debris were caught in the deep alveolar pockets in his lungs. Like coal dust in a miner's lung. I ran the sample through a mass spectrograph and was able to determine a rough breakdown of the isotope content.'

He pointed to his screen. The left side of the computer monitor began to scroll with data. 'Such information is often as unique as a fingerprint. It just took tapping into the IAEA database in Vienna.'

Painter noted that the open search window had the

organization's name stenciled at the top: INTERNATIONAL ATOMIC ENERGY AGENCY.

'The agency monitors hot spots around the world: mines, reactors, industrial sources. Despite what some might think, not all radiation is the same. We're talking about material that is constantly decaying, whose isotope content varies, depending on where it might have been mined and how it was processed. The end result is radiation signatures unique to each use-site.'

'And the debris in the professor's lungs?'

'I ran a search through the IAEA database and got a hit.'

'You know where Polk was exposed?'

He nodded to the screen as the scrolling stopped and the world map blew up, zooming into one location in central Russia. A name appeared in a highlighted box, a name synonymous with radiological disaster.

CHERNOBYL

What was Archibald Polk doing at Chernobyl? How had he been exposed to such a lethal level of radiation from the dead reactor site? The reactor was due this week to be sealed with a new Sarcophagus, a massive articulated steel dome. Amid all the new construction, had Polk somehow been exposed to a lethal dose of radiation there?

Before Painter could question Malcolm in more depth, his cell phone vibrated on his belt. He unhooked it and checked who was calling. It was his assistant. Frowning, he flipped it open.

'What is it, Brant?'

'Director, I received an alert from Homeland. There's just been a bomb threat called in to the natural history museum.'

Painter's fingers tightened on his cell phone.

The natural history museum . . . where Gray had been headed.

That couldn't be good.

'Patch me through to Gray's radio.'

He waited, cell phone at his ear. Malcolm stared over at him.

Had Gray called in the threat? Had someone else?

Either way, something was wrong.

He had confirmation a second later.

Brant came back on the line. 'Sir, he's not responding.'

7:56 P.M.

Elizabeth Polk appraised Gray Pierce as they neared the museum's loading docks. Studying him askance, she noted the faded bruising on one side of his face. His sunburned complexion hid most of the contusions. The beating must have taken place a month or so ago. It gave the planes of his face a look of hammered copper and brought out the blue of his eyes. It was those same eyes that chilled her when he spotted the half dozen men clearing the museum's loading dock and turned them back.

'Something's not right here,' he said.

She caught a glimpse of the warehouse space past his shoulder. Lit by flickering fluorescents, the cavernous space was crowded with tall shelves stacked with cleaning supplies and dry goods for the various museum concession stores. A single forklift rested beside a series of pulleys and counterbalances for bringing in larger pieces of an exhibit. A steel roll-up door stood open to the right. Outlined against the waning daylight, a cadre of men in black riot gear had set up a cordon near the exit. Under the klaxon of the evacuation alarm, they were searching each worker and staff member who sought to exit in that direction.

A narrow-shouldered man in a blue suit oversaw it from a few steps away. He was plainly someone high up the food chain.

Gray forced her back down the hallway. He hefted his shoulder bag higher. It bore the museum logo and carried the strange skull her father had hidden in the museum's storage room. At the thought of her father, a dull ache in her chest threatened to melt into sobbing tears. She held it back. She would address her loss at a quieter moment.

Down the hall, in the opposite direction of the docks, a shout echoed out the stairwell ahead, a call to search every room. Boots pounded down the stairs.

Gray stopped and turned to her. 'Is there another way out of here?'

She nodded. 'The service tunnels. Over this way.'

As she led them back again, Gray fixed her with those stormy eyes, questioning her knowledge.

'Some of the staff take their smoking breaks down there.' She glanced to him guiltily. She really needed to quit. Still, the habit had allowed her to bond with a few of the other researchers. A secret smokers' club. And all it cost was the risk of emphysema and lung cancer. 'We're not supposed to smoke within the museum, of course. Fire danger, but it's all stone and steam pipes down there.'

She led them to an unmarked door and keyed open the electronic lock with her card. The stairs on the far side were stained cement with a steel railing along one side. It led down in sharp turns.

Before they could enter, a low growl drew all their eyes back to the docks. A low shape slunk into view of the hallway. Thirty yards away. A German shepherd. It was outfitted with a black vest and was tethered to a man still out of view.

Elizabeth froze.

The dog spotted them and lunged forward, straining against his leash.

'Go,' Gray urged and pushed her through the open stairwell door and followed. His beefy partner crowded in behind them. It was hot and close. The museum's air-conditioning did not extend here. The only light was a caged emergency bulb.

Gray closed the door with the barest click of the lock engaging. The alarm klaxon muffled. He waved them down the tight stairs and squeezed up to join her. 'Do you know where the tunnels lead?'

She shook her head. 'Not sure. I never went any farther than I had to. It's a maze down there, branching in every direction. Rumors say even under the White House. But surely there must be a street exit somewhere.'

Behind them, something heavy hit the door above, followed by deep barks. Shouts echoed, chasing them down the stairs.

'Could it be a bomb-sniffing dog?' Elizabeth asked. 'Maybe the threat is real.'

Gray's partner, Kowalski, snorted. 'Only around Pierce is a *real* bomb threat considered a *good* thing.'

At the bottom of the stairs, they hit a barred gate. Gray cranked the locking bar aside and creaked the gate open. The tunnels stretched in both directions, pitch-black, sweltering, smelling of wet cement and whispering with trickles of water.

'I hope someone brought the flashlight,' Kowalski commented.

Gray swore softly under his breath. He'd left the light back in the storeroom.

Elizabeth fished in her pocket and produced her cigarette lighter. It was an antique silver Dunhill. She flipped it open and rasped a small flame into existence. With practiced skill, she adjusted the flame.

'Nice,' Kowalski said. 'I wish I'd brought one of my cigars.'

'Me, too,' Elizabeth mumbled back.

71

Kowalski did a double take in her direction.

Before he could say anything, light flooded down the stairs behind them. The alarm klaxon rang louder. Their pursuers had gotten through the upper door.

'Hurry.' Gray headed to the right. 'Stay close.'

Elizabeth kept to Gray's shoulder with Kowalski behind her. She held her lighter high. The flickering glow extended only a few yards ahead. Gray trotted down the tunnel. He kept one arm up, his fingertips trailing along the run of pipes overhead. He took the first branch to get them out of direct view of the stairwell exit.

A single low bark echoed to them.

Gray urged their flight into a run.

Elizabeth's lab coat flapped behind her. Her flame burned through a nest of cobwebs as they raced around another turn.

'Where are we going?' Kowalski asked.

'Away,' Gray answered.

'That's your big plan? Away?'

A burst of furious barking erupted. Shouts rang out. Their trail had been found.

'Forget what I said,' Kowalski corrected. '*Away* sounds just fine by me.'

In a tight group, they fled into the maze of tunnels.

Halfway across the city, Yuri sat on a bench under the spread of a cherry tree. It felt good to sit down. His knees ached, and his lower back threatened to spasm. He had dry-swallowed four tablets of Aleve. He had stronger medications back home, but nothing he dared bring into the States. It would be good to return to the Warren.

He stretched a leg and rubbed a knee.

As he rested, the sun was near to setting and cast long shadows across the parkland walkway. Steps away, a low cement wall bordered the path's far side. Children and parents lined the edge and pointed down into the outdoor habitat beyond the wall. A small piece of China's forestland had been re-created: a rocky outcropping sectioned into grottoes, ponds, and misty streams. Shrubs decorated its steep slopes, along with weeping willows, cork trees, and several species of bamboo. The habitat's two occupants, two Giant pandas on loan from China – Mei Xiang and Tian Tian – had captured the delighted attention of the zoo's last few visitors.

Including Sasha.

The girl stood with her arms folded atop the lip of the stone wall. One shoe swung rhythmically to strike the cement. But it was slowing down.

As he had hoped.

Yuri had brought the girl to the National Zoological Park after her performance with Mapplethorpe. From long experience, he knew the calming effect animals had on his charges. Especially Sasha. Yuri had no need to test the BDNF levels in the girl's spinal fluid. After such an intense episode, the hormone levels of 'brain-derived neurotrophic factors' had surely spiked to dangerous levels. He had not been prepared. Caught off guard by her performance, he knew he had to calm her down quickly. Away from her home environment, she would be especially agitated, vulnerable. There was a risk of lasting neural damage. He had seen it before. It had taken them decades to discover the innate relationship between autistic children's mental health and the palliative effect of their interaction with animals.

So while Mapplethorpe executed a search of the natural history museum, Yuri had transported Sasha to the city's famous zoological park. It was as close a facsimile to the Menagerie as he would find here in the foreign city.

Sasha's kicking slowed even further. She was ramping down. Still, the toe of her patent leather shoes had become badly scuffed. But better her shoes than her mind.

Yuri felt a knot between his shoulder blades ease. He would get her on the next flight back to Russia. Once returned to the Warren, he would schedule her for a complete physical exam: blood chemistries, urinalysis, a full cranial CT scan. He had to be sure there was no damage.

But more important, he needed an answer as to how she had induced an episode on her own. That shouldn't have happened. The cortical implant maintained a steady-state level of stimulation, tailored to each child's ability. Sasha's display back at Mapplethorpe's office should not have happened unless her implant was remotely triggered to provoke such a response.

So what had happened? Had there been a malfunction in her implant? Had someone *else* triggered it? Or even more disturbing, was Sasha growing beyond the yoke of their control?

Despite the day's heat and his relief, he still felt cold.

Something was wrong.

A flurry of noise erupted ahead of him. It came from the crowd lining the panda exhibit. Excited murmurs swelled. A flurry of camera flashes sparkled among the crowd. More people were drawn by the commotion. Yuri heard a named called out and repeated.

'Tai Shan . . . Tai Shan . . .'

He sat up straighter with a wince of protest from his back. He recognized the name from the zoo's brochure. Tai Shan was the panda cub born to Mei Xiang a few summers back. The youngster must have wandered into sight.

The crowd jostled for a better view. More people gathered. Children were lifted to parents' shoulders. Cameras flashed furiously. Frowning at the tourists' manic response, Yuri stood up. He had lost sight of

Sasha in the crush of the crowd. He knew she didn't like to be touched.

He stepped across the walkway and pushed into the pack of people. The park would be closing in the next few minutes. It was time to go.

He reached the wall where Sasha had been standing.

She wasn't there.

With his heart thudding, he searched the stretch of walls to either side. No sign of her ebony hair and red ribbons. He stumbled outward again, shouldering and pawing his way through the crowd. Grunted protests met his rude passage. A camera tumbled from someone's hands and cracked against the pavement.

Someone grabbed his shoulder. He was yanked around.

'Mister, you'd better have a goddamn good reason—'

Yuri shook free. His eyes, bright with true panic, met the larger man. 'My . . . my granddaughter. I've lost my granddaughter.'

Anger melted to concern.

With mostly parents in attendance, word spread quickly. It was every mother and father's worst fear. Questions peppered him. *What does she look like? What was she wearing?* Others offered words of support, promising that she'd be found.

Yuri barely heard them, deafened by his own pounding heart. He should have never left her side, never sat down.

The crowd thinned around him, opening views in all directions.

Yuri turned a full circle. He searched, but he knew the truth.

Sasha was gone.

4

'Door!' Kowalski yelled from the rear.

Gray skidded to a stop and glanced behind him. Elizabeth Polk held out her lighter and revealed a small doorway, hidden two steps off the dark tunnel. Gray had rushed past it, too focused on the roof, searching for a street exit from the service tunnels.

Behind them, calls echoed from the searchers. A single harsh bark rang out as the trackers found their trail again. Gray had crisscrossed among tunnels, trying to lose them, but it proved fruitless, and they were losing ground.

Kowalski reached to the door and fought the handle. 'Locked.' He punched the metal surface in frustration.

Coming up to his side, Gray noted an electronic key-lock below the handle. The lighter's flame flickered across a small steel sign stenciled in Art Deco letters:

NATIONAL MUSEUM OF AMERICAN HISTORY

The door was a subterranean entrance to another of the Smithsonian Institution's museums. Closest to the door, Elizabeth swiped her museum security card, but the lock remained dark. To make sure, Kowalski tugged the handle and shook his head.

'My card's only good for the natural history museum,' Elizabeth said. 'But I hoped—'

A fierce bark drew their attention around. The bobbling glow of flashlights lit up the far end of the tunnel.

'Better move it,' Kowalski said and stepped away from the door.

A shotgun blast erupted. Something sparked off the metal surface, striking where Kowalski had stood a second before. The round ricocheted off the door and spun across the cement floor, spitting blue sparks of electricity.

Kowalski danced away from it, like an elephant from a mouse.

Gray recognized the payload: a Taser XREP. Fired from a standard twelve-gauge, the weapon shot out a self-contained, wireless dart that packed a shocking neuromuscular jolt. It could drop a mountain gorilla.

'HOMELAND SECURITY! HALT OR WE'LL FIRE AGAIN!'

'Now they warn us,' Kowalski said and lifted his arms above his head.

Half hidden behind his partner's bulk, Gray twisted around and swiped his black Sigma identification card through the key-lock. A small green light flicked into existence alongside the lock.

Thank God.

'HANDS ON YOUR HEADS. GET ON YOUR KNEES!'

Gray shoved the handle, and the door cracked open. It was dark beyond. Reaching behind him, he grabbed Elizabeth's elbow. She flinched, then saw the half-open door. She, in turn, reached out and grabbed the back of Kowalski's belt. He had his hands on his head and had been bending down to kneel.

He glanced back to them.

Gray shouldered the door open and pulled Elizabeth with him. Yanked off balance, Kowalski stumbled to one knee – then pushed off the floor and dove after them through the doorway.

Gray heard another blast of a shotgun.

Kowalski knocked into them and sent them sprawling across the dark stairs beyond the threshold. His other leg kicked the door shut – and kept kicking. '—oddamn motherfu—!' he wailed between clenched teeth.

Gray spotted the sparking projectile impaled through the shoe of the man's spasming leg. Elizabeth did, too. She climbed over him, pinned his ankle, and crushed the Taser shell under her shoe heel.

Kowalski's leg continued to twitch for another breath, then stopped.

His cursing did not.

Gray stood and held out an arm to help him up. 'You're lucky it hit your shoe. The leather blunted the barbs from penetrating deeply.'

'Lucky!' Kowalski bent and rubbed the stabs through the polished leather. 'Assholes ruined my new Chukkas!'

Muffled shouts approached the doorway.

'C'mon,' Gray urged and headed up.

Kowalski continued to gripe as they ran up the stairs. 'Crowe's buying me a new pair!'

Gray ignored him as he raced up the stairs.

Kowalski's tirade continued. 'Just leave the monkey skull down there. Let 'em have the goddamn thing.'

'*No!*' rang from both Elizabeth and Gray.

Gray heard the anger in the woman's voice. It matched his own. Her father had died to keep the skull from his pursuers. Died in Gray's arms. He wasn't about to give it up.

They hit the upper stairwell door. It was locked, too. Pounding echoed on the door below. It wouldn't take long for someone to secure a pass-key.

'Over here,' Elizabeth said and pointed to the darkened card reader.

Gray swiped his security I.D. and heard the lock release. He glanced behind him as he pushed the door open. Surely word was already spreading. Whoever was hunting them would know they were fleeing into the Museum of American History.

Gray led them out into a lighted hall. It was almost a match to the basement of the natural history museum, except here there were stacks of boxes in the hallway, crowding the way. Gray tested his own radio, but he still had no signal, buried too deeply under the museum.

'This way,' he said and aimed for a stairway that led up.

They almost bowled over an electrician in a work uniform, weighted down with a roll of conduit over his shoulder and a heavy belt of tools. 'Why don't you watch where you're go—!'

Something he saw in Gray's expression silenced him. He backed out of the way and flattened against the wall. They hurried past him and upward. The farther they climbed, the more chaos they encountered: clusters of workmen, stripped walls, tangles of exposed ductwork. Reaching the next landing, they had to dodge around piles of Sheetrock and flats of stacked marble tiles. The growl of motors and whine of saws echoed from the doorway ahead. The air smelled of fresh paint and tasted of sawdust.

Gray recalled that the Museum of American History had been undergoing a massive renovation, updating its forty-year-old infrastructure, all to better showcase its three million historical treasures, from Abraham Lincoln's top hat to Dorothy's ruby slippers. The museum had been closed to the public for the past two years but was due to open next month.

From the look of things as Gray entered the museum's

central atrium, the grand reopening might be delayed. Plastic sheeting draped almost every surface; scaffolding climbed the three-story core of the renovation. Grand staircases swept from the first floor to the second. Directly overhead a massive skylight was still sheeted with paper.

Gray grabbed the nearest worker, a carpenter whose face was half covered by a respirator. 'The exit! Where's the nearest exit?'

The man squinted at him. 'The Constitution Avenue exit is closed. You'll have to climb to the second level. Head out the main Mall entrance.' He pointed to the staircase.

Gray glanced to Elizabeth, who nodded. They walked out as a group. Gray checked his radio again. Still nothing. Something or someone had to be blocking his signal.

They raced to the stairs and pounded up to the second level. It was less chaotic up here. The green marble floor looked freshly mopped, highlighting the silver stars embedded therein. Gray had a clear view from the central atrium to the glass doors of the Mall exit. He needed to make it out before—

Too late.

A knot of men bearing assault rifles swept into view outside the doors. They wore dark uniforms with patches at their shoulders.

Gray forced Kowalski and Elizabeth back.

Behind them, a growled bark echoed up from the first floor. Workers shouted in surprise.

'What now?' Kowalski asked.

From the Mall entrance, a bullhorn blasted. 'HOMELAND SECURITY! THE BUILDING IS TO BE EVACUATED IMMEDIATELY! EVERYONE TO THE MAIN EXIT!'

'This way,' Gray said.

He led them off to the side, toward the largest piece of art on this floor's gallery. The installation

81

was an abstract flag, made up of fifteen ribbons of mirrored polycarbonate.

'We can't keep running,' Elizabeth said.

'We're not.'

'So we're hiding?' Kowalski asked. 'What about their dogs?'

'We're not running or hiding,' Gray assured them.

He passed the shimmering flag. Its mirrored surface reflected a prismatic view of the museum. In bits and pieces, Gray saw the armed detail take up an impenetrable cordon across the only exit.

Passing one of the scaffoldings stacked with supplies and spare coveralls, Gray grabbed what he needed. He passed a few bundles to Kowalski. He kept what he needed himself: a can of paint and a plastic gallon of paint thinner. He headed into the hallway under the abstract flag. Kowalski read the gallery sign at the entrance and whistled under his breath.

'Pierce, what are you planning on doing?'

Gray led the way into the heart of the museum's most treasured exhibits. It was the main reason for the entire renovation. They entered a long darkened hall. Seats lined one side opposite a wall of paneled glass on the other. Even the chaos behind them seemed to muffle under the weight of the historical treasure preserved behind the glass, one of the nation's most important icons. It lay unfurled on a sloped display, a tatter of cotton and wool a quarter the size of a football field. Its dyes had faded, but it remained a dramatic piece of American history, the flag that inspired the national anthem.

'Pierce . . . ?' Kowalski moaned, beginning to comprehend. 'That's the Star-Spangled Banner.'

Gray placed the can of paint on the floor and began to twist open the cap on the gallon of highly flammable paint thinner.

'Pierce . . . you can't mean to . . . not even as a distraction.'

Ignoring him, Gray turned to Elizabeth. 'Do you still have your lighter?'

8:32 P.M.

Sitting in the security office of the National Zoo, Yuri felt the weight of his seventy-seven years. All the androgens, stimulants, and surgeries could not mask the heaviness of his heart. A numbing fear had turned his limbs to aching lead; worry etched deeper lines in his face.

'We'll find your granddaughter,' the head of security had promised him. 'We have the park closed down. Everyone is looking for her.'

Yuri had been left in the office with a blond young woman who could be no older than twenty-five. She wore the khaki safari uniform of a zoo employee. Her name tag read TABITHA. She seemed nervous in his presence, unsure how to cope with his despair. She stood, coming out from behind the desk.

'Is there anyone you'd like to call? Another relative?'

Yuri lifted his head. He studied her for a breath. Her apple-cheeked youth . . . the years ahead of her. He realized he'd been little older than the girl when he'd stumbled out of the rattling truck into the highlands of the Carpathian mountains. He wished he had never found that Gypsy camp.

'Would you like to use the phone?' she asked.

He slowly nodded. *'Da.'* He could not put it off any longer. He'd already alerted Mapplethorpe, not so much to report to him, as to gain the cooperation of the D.C. policing authorities. But the man had been distracted, busy hunting down what had been stolen. Mapplethorpe had mentioned something about Dr. Polk's daughter.

But Yuri no longer cared. Still, Mapplethorpe had promised to raise an Amber Alert for the missing child. All D.C. resources and outlying counties would be alerted. She had to be found.

Sasha . . .

Her round face and bright blue eyes filled his vision. He should never have left her side. He prayed she had just wandered off. But among a park full of wild animals, even that best scenario was not without its dangers. Worse yet, had someone taken her, abducted her? In her current state, she would be pliable, easily suggestible. Yuri was well familiar with the number of pedophiles out there. They'd even had trouble at the Warren with some of their early employees. There had been so many children, too many. Mistakes had happened.

But not all of the abuses had been mistakes.

He shied from this last thought.

Tabitha carried over a portable telephone.

Yuri shook his head and took out his own cell phone. 'Thank you, but it is a long-distance call,' he explained. 'To Russia. To her grandmother. I'll use my own phone.'

Tabitha nodded and backed away. 'I'll give you your privacy.' She stepped into a neighboring office.

Alone, Yuri dialed the number into his international cell phone. A small chip developed by Russian intelligence would bounce the signal off several cell towers, making it untraceable, along with scrambling the communication.

He had dreaded making this call, but he could wait no longer. The Warren had to be alerted, but it was very early in the morning back there. Not even four o'clock. Still, the phone was answered promptly, the voice curt and sharp.

'What is it?'

Yuri pictured the woman at the other end of the line, his immediate superior, Dr. Savina Martov. The two had discovered the children together, begun the Warren as a team, but Martov's ties to the former KGB had pulled her above Yuri in command. There was a saying in Russia: *No one left the KGB.* And despite what Western leaders might think, that did not exclude the current Russian president. The man still surrounded himself with ex-members of Soviet intelligence. Major contracts were still placed in the hands of former operatives.

And Dr. Savina Martov was no exception.

'Savina, we have a major problem here,' he said in Russian.

He imagined her face frosting over. Like Yuri, she had also undergone hormonal, surgical, and cosmetic treatments, but she had fared even better than Yuri. Her hair was still dark, her features hardly blemished. She could pass for forty years old. Yuri suspected why. She did not battle that same knot of guilt that soured his gut. The sureness of her vision and purpose shone out of her face. Only when one looked in her eyes was the deception ruined. No amount of treatments would mask the cold calculation found there.

'You've still not found what was stolen from us?' she asked in harsh tones. 'I've already heard that Polk has been eliminated. So then why—?'

'It's Sasha. She's gone missing.'

A long silence stretched.

'Savina, did you hear me?'

'Yes. I just had a report in from one of the dormitory workers. It's why I'm up so early. They discovered three empty beds.'

'Who? Which children?'

'Konstantin, his sister Kiska, and Pyotr.'

Savina continued her report, how a search was under way across the Warren, but her voice grew hollow, echoing as if out of a deep well as Yuri had fixated on the last name.

Pyotr. Peter.

He was Sasha's twin brother.

'When?' he blurted out. 'When did the three *rebyonka* go missing?'

Savina sighed harshly. 'They were there at the last bed check according to the matron on duty. So sometime in the last hour.'

Yuri glanced to his wristwatch.

Around the time Sasha vanished.

Was it just a coincidence, or had Pyotr somehow sensed his twin sister's danger? Had it set the boy into a panic? But Pyotr had never shown such talent before. His empathic scores were high – especially with animals – but he'd never shown any of his sister's abilities. Still, as twins, they were closer than any brother and sister. In fact, they still shared their own special language, an incomprehensible twin speak.

As Yuri clutched the phone to his ear, he suspected something more sinister was happening, that unknown forces – possibly an unknown hand – were manipulating events.

But whose?

Savina barked at him, drawing back his attention. 'Find that girl,' she ordered. 'Before it's too late. You know what happens in two days.'

Yuri knew that only too well. It was what they had worked decades to accomplish, why they had performed so many acts of cruelty. All in order to—

A door slammed to the side. Yuri twisted around. The head of zoo security had returned. His tanned face was dour, lined with concern and worry.

Yuri spoke into the phone. 'I'll find her,' he said firmly, but the promise was more to himself than to his icy superior. He clicked off the line and faced the tall man, switching to English. 'Has there been any sign of my granddaughter?'

'I'm afraid not. We've swept the park. So far no sign of her.'

Yuri felt a sinking in his gut.

A hesitation entered the security chief's voice. 'But I must tell you. There was a report of a girl matching your granddaughter's description being carried into a van near the south exit.'

Yuri stood up, his eyes widening.

A hand raised, urging patience. 'The D.C. police are following up on that. It might be a false lead. There's not much more we can do.'

'There must be more.'

'I'm sorry, sir. Also on the way back here, I was informed that someone at the FBI has arranged an escort. They should be here any moment. They'll take you back to your hotel.'

Yuri sensed the hand of Mapplethorpe involved with this last arrangement. 'Thank you. For all your help.' Yuri crossed to the door and reached for the handle. 'I . . . I need some fresh air.'

'Certainly. There's a bench just outside.'

Yuri exited the security office. He spotted the park bench, crossed toward it, but once out of view of the office window, he continued past the bench and strode toward the park exit.

Yuri could not put himself into Mapplethorpe's control. Not even now. The fool knew only a fraction of what was going on, just enough to keep the interest of United States intelligence organizations whetted. They had no suspicion how the world would change in the next few days.

He had to find Sasha before Mapplethorpe did.

And there was only one way to do that.

As he exited the park through a cordon of police, he dialed his cell phone, again engaging the encryption. As before, it was answered promptly, this time by an answering machine.

'You've reached the national switchboard for Argo, Inc. Please leave a message . . .'

Argo, Inc. was the cover for the Jasons. The pseudonym – Argo – was selected because it was the name of Jason's ship out of Greek mythology.

Yuri shook his head at such foolishness as he waited for the beep. He had murdered one of their own just hours ago. Now he needed the help of the secretive cabal of American scientists. And he knew how to get it. Going back to the Cold War, the two sides had been waging a clandestine battle for technological supremacy, each side supported by their respective military establishments and intelligence communities. The tools of war were not just intellectual, but also involved more nefarious means: sabotage, coercion, blackmail. But likewise, being men and women of science, each side operated independently of the military. Over the decades, they had come to recognize two things: there was occasionally common ground between them, but more important, there was a firm line neither side would cross.

When such a scenario arose, a means of communication had been established, a panic button. Speaking into the phone, Yuri gave his encrypted cell number, followed by a code word that traced back to the Cold War.

'Pandora.'

8:38 P.M.

Smoke billowed out the hall of the Star-Spangled Banner gallery.

Gray kept his group clustered in the vestibule just off the central atrium of the museum. They had pulled painters coveralls over their street clothes and covered their faces with respirators. Gray had also splashed paint on their clothes.

He leaned and stared back into the flag gallery. Smoke burned his eyes, but he spotted the flames dancing and racing across the pools of paint thinner he'd spilled across the gallery's wood floor. A moment later, emergency sprinklers engaged. Water jetted in a flood from ceiling spigots. An alarm klaxon rang out sharply.

Gray took an additional moment to make sure that the glass-enclosed display for the banner remained dry. He knew the display was an environmentally controlled chamber meant to preserve the icon for generations to come. For now, the case should protect the flag from the smoke and water.

Satisfied the treasure was safe, Gray turned his attention to the central atrium. Fresh shouts and cries echoed as smoke panicked the workers. The contractors were already on edge with the spreading word of a bomb scare.

And now the fire alarm and smoke.

Gray peeked around the vestibule's exit and into the atrium.

Already summoned by the bullhorn to proceed to this single exit, men and women milled and pushed. Many hauled tools and backpacks. Panic surged the crowd toward the doors, where the armed men had been conducting a systematic search of each exiting worker, including being scented by a pair of German shepherds.

'Let's go,' Gray said.

Under the cover of smoke and terror, the three joined the pressing throng. They split up to make it less likely they'd be recognized through their disguises. As they joined the panicked mass, it was like jumping into a storm-swept sea along a rocky coast. Pushed, shoved, jabbed, and jostled, Gray still kept a watch on the others.

The evacuating workers surged toward the doors. Despite the press, the armed men kept some semblance of order outside. Searches continued, but more cursory and swift. The dogs barked and tugged at their leads, aroused by the noise and confusion.

Gray gripped his shoulder bag tighter, hugging its weight to his chest. If need be, he could bull through the armed line, like a linebacker making a rush for the goal.

To the side, Gray spotted Elizabeth being shoved through

a door and into the arms of one of the guards. She was brusquely searched and urged to move on. She passed one of the dogs, who barked and tugged at its lead. But it had not recognized her scent. The dog was merely agitated and confused by the press of people. Fresh paint and smoke also helped mask Elizabeth's scent. She stumbled away from the cordon of men and out into the national Mall's twilight.

Off on the other side, Kowalski hit the line next. To aid in his disguise, he carried a gallon of paint in each hand, which he was mostly using to knock people out of his way. He also was searched. Even the cans of paint were opened.

Gray held his breath. Not good. The panic was not disrupting the search as much as he would have liked.

Passing inspection, Kowalski was waved out into the Mall.

Gray pushed out the door and met the palm of one of the guards.

'Arms up!' he was ordered. The command was bolstered as another guard leveled a weapon at his chest.

Hands searched him swiftly. From head to toe. Luckily, he had stashed his ankle holster and weapon back in the gallery's trash can.

Still . . .

'Open your bag!'

Gray knew there was no way he could resist. He dropped the bag and unzipped it. He pulled out the only thing it held: a small electric sander. The rest of the bag was shaken to make sure it was empty – then Gray was waved out of the way.

As he passed the barking dog, Gray noted a man standing to the side, dressed in a suit. No body armor. He had a Bluetooth headset fixed to his ear. He was barking orders, plainly in charge. Gray also remembered seeing him at the dock of the natural history museum.

Passing him, Gray spotted the credentials affixed to his jacket pocket.

DIA.

Defense Intelligence Agency.

Gray noted the name in bold type: MAPPLETHORPE.

Before his attention was noticed, Gray continued out into the Mall. He circumspectly joined the others well away from the museum and the confusion, just a trio of workers reuniting. Gray retaped his radio's throat mike under his jaw. He attempted to raise Sigma Command.

Finally, a familiar voice responded.

'Gray! Where are you?'

It was Painter Crowe.

'No time to explain,' Gray said. 'I need an unmarked car at the corner of Fourteenth and Constitution.'

'It'll be there.'

As he headed toward the extraction point, Gray held out a hand toward Kowalski.

The large man passed over one of the gallons of paint. 'Just carrying the thing creeps me out.'

Gray accepted the paint can with relief. Submerged at the bottom lay hidden the strange skull. Gray had chanced that no one would explore too closely the depths of the thick latex paint, especially carried by a worker whose coveralls were splashed with the same paint. Once the skull was cleaned, maybe they'd finally have some answers.

'We made it,' Elizabeth said with a ring of relief.

Gray did not comment.

He knew this was far from over.

Halfway around the world, a man awoke in a dark, windowless room. A few small lights shone from a neighboring bank of equipment. He recognized the blink and beat of an EKG monitor. His nose caught a whiff of disinfectant and iodine. Dazed, he sat up too quickly. The few lights swam, like darting fish in a midnight sea.

The sight stirred something buried. A memory.

. . . lights in dark water . . .

He struggled to sit up, but his elbows were secured to the railings of the bed. A hospital bed. He could not even pull his arms free of the bedsheet. Weak, he lay back down.

Have I been in an accident?

As he took a breath, he sensed someone watching him, a prickling warning. Turning his head, he vaguely made out the outline of a doorway. A dark shape stirred at the threshold. A shoe scraped on tile. Then a furtive whisper. In a foreign language. Russian, from the sound of it.

'Who's there?' he asked hoarsely. His throat burned, as if he had swallowed acid.

Silence. The darkness went deathly still.

He waited, holding his breath.

Then a flash of light bloomed near the doorway. It blinded, stung. He instinctively tried to raise a hand to shield his eyes, forgetting his arms were still secured to the bed.

He blinked away the glare. The flash came from a tiny penlight. The shine revealed three small figures slinking into his room. They were all children. A boy – twelve or thirteen – held the light and shielded a girl maybe a year or two younger. They were followed by a smaller boy who could be no more than eight years old. They approached his bed as if nearing a lion's den.

The taller boy, plainly the leader, swung to the younger one. He whispered in Russian, unintelligible but plainly a concerned inquiry. He called the younger boy a name. It sounded like *Peter*. The child nodded, pointed to the bed, and mumbled in Russian with a ring of certainty to his words.

Stirring in the bed, he finally rasped out, 'Who are you? What do you want?'

The taller boy shushed him with a glare and glanced

toward the open doorway. The children then split up and crossed around the bed. The leader and the girl began freeing the straps that bound his limbs. The smaller boy held back, eyes wide. Like his companions, the child was dressed in loose pants and a dark gray turtleneck sweater with a vest over it, along with a matching cable-knit hat. The boy stared straight at him, unnervingly so, as if reading something on his forehead.

With his arms freed, he sat up. The room swam again, but not as much as before. He ran his hand over his head, trying to steady himself. Under his palm, he found his scalp smooth and a prickly line of sutures behind his left ear, confirming this supposition. Had he been shaved for surgery? Still, as his palm ran across the smooth top of his head, the sensation felt somehow familiar, natural.

Before he could ponder this contradiction, he pulled his other hand into view. Or rather tried to. His other arm ended in a stump at the wrist. His heart thudded harder in shock. He must've been in a horrible accident. His remaining hand trailed across the tender sutures behind his ear, as if trying to read Braille. Obviously a recent surgery. But his wrist was calloused and long healed. Still, he could almost sense his missing fingers. Felt them curl into a phantom fist of frustration.

The taller boy stepped back from the bed. 'Come,' he said in English.

From the clandestine nature of his release and furtive actions of his liberators, he sensed some amount of danger. Dressed in a thin hospital gown, he rolled his feet to the cold tiled floor. The room tilted with the motion.

Whoa . . .

A small groan of nausea escaped him.

'Hurry,' the taller boy urged.

'Wait,' he said, gulping air to settle his stomach. 'Tell me what is going on.'

'No time.' The tall boy stepped away. He was gangly,

all limbs. He attempted to sound authoritative, but the cracking in his voice betrayed both his youth and his terror. He touched his chest, introducing himself. '*Menia zavut* Konstantin. You must come. Before it is too late.'

'But I . . . I don't . . .'

'*Da.* You are confused. For now, know your *zavut* is Monk Kokkalis.'

Making a half-scoffing noise, he shook his head. *Monk Kokkalis.* The name meant nothing to him. As he attempted to voice his disagreement, to correct the mistake, he realized he had no ammunition, only a blank where his name normally resided. His heart clutched into a strained knot. Panic narrowed his vision. How could that be? He fingered the sutures again. Had he taken a blow to the head? A concussion? He sought for any memory beyond waking up here in this room, but there was nothing, a wasteland.

What had happened?

He stared again at the EKG monitor still connected to his chest by taped lead wires. And over in the corner stood a blood pressure monitor and an I.V. pole. So if he could name what lay around him, why couldn't he remember his own *name*? He searched for a past, something to anchor him. But beyond waking up here in this dark room, he had no memory.

The smaller of the two boys seemed to sense his growing distress. The child stepped forward, his blue eyes catching the flash of the penlight. Monk – if that was really his name – sensed the boy knew more about him than he did himself. Proving this, the child seemed to read his heart and spoke the only words that would stir him from the bed.

The boy held up a small hand toward him, his fingers splayed, punctuating his need. 'Save us.'

5

'Chernobyl?' Elizabeth asked. 'What was my father doing in Russia?'

She stared across the coffee table at the two other men. She was seated in an armchair with her back to a picture window that overlooked the woods of Rock Creek Park. They had been driven to this location after escaping the museum. Gray had used the words *safe house*, which had done little to make her feel *safe*. It was like something out of a spy novel. But the charm of the house – a two-story craftsman built of clinker brick and paneled in burnished tiger oak – helped calm her.

Somewhat.

She had washed up upon arriving, taking several minutes to scrub her hands and splash water on her face. But her hair still smelled of smoke, and her fingernails were still stained with paint. Afterward, she had sat for five minutes on the commode with her face in her palms, trying to make sense of the last few hours. She hadn't known she was crying until discovering her hands were damp. It was all too much. She still hadn't had a chance to process the death of her father. Though she didn't doubt the truth of it, she had not come to accept the reality.

Not until she had some answers.

It was those questions that finally drew her out of the bathroom.

She eyed the newcomer across a table set with coffee. The man was introduced as Gray's boss, Director Painter Crowe. She studied him. His features were angular, his complexion tanned. As an anthropologist, she read the Native American heritage in the set of his eyes – despite their glacial blue hue. His dark hair ran with a small streak of white over one ear, like a heron feather tucked there.

Gray shared the sofa with him, crouched and sifting through a stack of papers on the table.

Before anyone could answer her question, Kowalski returned from the kitchen in his stocking feet. His freshly polished shoes rested on the cold hearth. 'Found some Ritz crackers and something that looked like cheese. Not sure. But they had salami.'

He leaned to place the platter in front of Elizabeth.

'Thank you, Joe,' she said, grateful for the simple and real gesture amid all the mystery.

The big man blushed a bit around the ears. 'No problem,' he grumbled as he straightened. He pointed to the platter, seemed to forget what he was going to say – then with a shake of his head, retired to inspect his shoes again.

Painter sat up straighter, drawing back Elizabeth's attention. 'As to Chernobyl, we don't know why your father went there. In fact, we ran his passport. There's no record of him visiting Russia, or for that matter, ever reentering the United States. We can only assume he was traveling with a false passport. The last record we have of his travels was from five months ago. He flew to India. That's the last we know about his whereabouts.'

Elizabeth nodded. 'He travels there often. At least twice a year.'

Gray shifted straighter. 'To India. Why?'

'For a research grant. As a neurologist, he was studying the biological basis for instinct. He worked with a professor of psychology at the University of Mumbai.'

Gray glanced to his boss.

'I'll look into it,' Painter said. 'But I had already heard of your father's interest in instinct and intuition. In fact, it was the basis for his involvement with the Jasons.'

This last was directed at Gray, but Elizabeth stiffened at the mention of the organization. She could not hide her distaste. 'So you know about them – the Jasons.'

Painter glanced to Gray, then back to her. 'Yes, we know your father was working for them.'

'Working? More like *obsessed* with them.'

'What do you mean?'

Elizabeth explained how working with the military grew into an all-consuming passion with her father. Each summer, he'd disappear for months at a time, sometimes longer. The rest of his year was devoted to his responsibilities as a professor at M.I.T. As a result, he was seldom home. It strained relations between her parents. Accusations grew into fights. Her mother came to believe her father was having an affair.

The tension at home only drove her father farther away. A rocky marriage became a ruin. Her mother, already a borderline alcoholic, tipped over the edge. When Elizabeth was sixteen, her mother got drunk and crashed the family's SUV into the Charles River. It was never determined whether it was an accident or a suicide.

But Elizabeth knew who deserved the brunt of the blame.

From that day forward, she seldom spoke to her father. Each retreated into their own world. Now he was gone, too. Forever. Despite her loss, she could not discount a burning seed of anger toward him. Even his strange death left so much unanswered.

'Do you think his involvement with the Jasons had anything to do with his death?' she finally asked.

Painter shook his head. 'It's hard to say. We're still early in the investigation. But I was able to discover which classified military project was assigned to your father. It was called Project—'

'—Stargate,' Elizabeth finished for him. She took some satisfaction from the man's startled expression.

Kowalski sat up straighter by the fireplace. 'Hey, I saw a movie about that . . . had aliens and stuff, right?'

'Not that *Stargate*, Joe,' she answered. 'And don't worry, Mr. Crowe. My father didn't breach his top secret clearance. I'd heard my father mention the project by name a couple of times. Then a decade later, I read the declassified reports from the CIA, released through the Freedom of Information Act.'

'What's this project about?' Gray asked.

Painter nodded at the pile of papers on the table. 'The full details are there, going back to the Cold War. It was officially overseen by the country's second-largest think tank, the Stanford Research Institute, which down the line would help develop stealth technologies. But back in 1973, the institute was commissioned by the CIA to investigate the feasibility of using parapsychology to aid in intelligence gathering.'

'Parapsychology?' Gray raised an eyebrow.

Painter nodded. 'Telepathy, telekinesis . . . but mostly they concentrated on remote viewing, using individuals to spy upon sites and activities from vast distances using only the power of their minds. Sort of like telepathy at a distance.'

Kowalski snorted his derision from across the room. 'Psychic spies.'

'As crazy as that might sound, you have to understand that during the darkest days of the Cold War, any perceived advantage by the Soviets had to be matched in turn by our own intelligence. Any technological gap could not be tolerated. The Soviet Union was pulling out all the stops. To the Soviets, parapsychology was a multidisciplinary field, encompassing bionics, biophysics, psychophysics, physiology, and neurophysiology.'

Painter nodded to Elizabeth. 'Like the work your father was performing on intuition and instinct. The neurophysiology behind it.'

Elizabeth glanced at Gray. From the wary look in his eyes, he seemed hardly convinced, but he continued listening silently. So she did the same.

'According to reports by the CIA, the Soviets had begun producing results. Then in 1971, the Soviet program suddenly went into deep-black classification. Information dried up. All we could ascertain was that research continued in Russia, funded by the KGB. We had to respond in kind or be left behind. So the Stanford Research Institute was commissioned to investigate.'

'And what were their results?' Gray asked.

'Mixed at best,' Painter acknowledged.

Elizabeth had also read the declassified reports. 'In truth, there was *little* success with the project.'

'That's not entirely true,' Painter countered. 'Official reports showed that remote viewing produced useful results fifteen percent of the time, which was above statistical probability. And then there *were* the exceptional cases. Like a New York artist, Ingo Swann. He was able to describe buildings in fine detail when given mere longitude and latitude coordinates. His *hits,* according to some officials, rose up to the eighty-five percent range.'

Painter must have read the continuing doubt in both their eyes. He tapped the stack of papers. 'The Stanford Research Institute's results were replicated by testing at Fort Meade and at the Princeton Engineering Anomalies Research Laboratory. In addition, there were several prominent successes. One of the most cited cases involved the kidnapping and rescue of Brigadier-General James Dozier. According to the physicist in charge of the project, one remote viewer ascertained the name of the town where the general was being held, while another described details of the building, all the way down to the bed where he was chained. Such results are hard to readily dismiss.'

'Yet it was,' Elizabeth said. 'From my understanding, the research stopped in the mid-1990s. The program was dismantled.'

'Not entirely,' Painter added cryptically.

Before he could explain, Gray interrupted. 'But back to the beginning, what does all this have to do with the Jasons?'

'Ah, I was just going to get to that. It seems that the Stanford Research Institute, like the Soviets, had begun to broaden the parameters of their research, extending it into other scientific disciplines.'

'Like neurophysiology,' Gray said. 'Dr. Polk's work.'

Painter nodded. 'While the project was deeply classified, they did outsource to two Jasons who were doing parallel research. One of them was your father, Elizabeth. The other was Dr. Trent McBride, a biomedical engineer in brain physiology.'

Elizabeth knew that name. She remembered late-night visits, her father sequestering himself with strangers in his study, including Dr. McBride. He was hard to forget with his loud, boisterous voice, but in a good-hearted way. He also brought her gifts when she was younger. First editions of Nancy Drew.

'I attempted to contact Dr. McBride,' Painter continued. 'Only to learn that no one's heard from him in the last five months.'

Elizabeth felt a cold chill. *Five months*. 'The same time my father flew to India.'

She shared a worried glance with Gray.

What was going on?

9:40 P.M.

Yuri Raev exited the elevator on the subbasement floor of the research facility. After getting the phone call, it had taken him forty-five minutes to reach the Walter Reed Army Institute of Research in Maryland. The building housed half a million square feet of laboratory space, much of it designated for BL-3 biohazard research, meaning it dealt with all manner of infectious diseases.

Yuri had used the panic code – Pandora – to reach the Jasons. It had taken another ten minutes to patch an alert to those he sought, an inner cabal of the organization who had cooperated with the Russians on the project for the *greater good of both nations*. Yuri had hoped to get the Jasons working on his behalf, to keep Sasha out of Mapplethorpe's hands. The Jasons, with their various scientific backgrounds, understood the delicacy it took in handling the child, both physiologically and psychologically.

Mapplethorpe on the other hand was all about brinkmanship, political ambitions, and blind self-interest. Yuri didn't trust the man.

With Sasha missing, Yuri needed allies on American soil.

He'd been instructed to meet Dr. James Chen, a neurologist and a member of the inner circle, to plan a strategy.

They would be joined by another.

Someone who could help, he was cryptically told.

Yuri was given specific directions and clearance to the location of the rendezvous. He started down the hallway. At this hour, all the doors were closed. Few laboratories were down at this level. As he walked, bleach burned his nose and masked a muskier scent. Behind one door, he heard a familiar soft *hoot* of something simian. Here was where the facility must house its live-animal research subjects, deserted of personnel at this hour.

He checked the room number.

B-2 340.

He found the door with a frosted glass panel and knocked. A shadow passed across the pane, and the door opened promptly.

'Dr. Raev. Thank you for coming.'

Yuri barely got a glimpse of the young Asian man as he turned away. He wore a white laboratory coat over blue denim pants. A pair of eyeglasses rested atop his head, as if forgotten there. The room held a utilitarian table along one wall, and a bank of stainless-steel cages filled the opposite side. A few whiskered black noses poked between the bars. The scritch-scratch of tiny nails whispered from the cages. Laboratory rats. Only these were hairless, except for their whiskers.

Dr. Chen led him through an open back door. There he found a cluttered office: a steel desk stacked with journals, a whiteboard jotted with boxed to-do lists, and a bookcase crammed with glass specimen jars.

Yuri was surprised to find a familiar figure hulked behind the desk, a cell phone at his ear. The man, edging toward his midfifties, demonstrated his Scottish heritage in his massive frame, ruddy cheeks, and a red-and-gray beard tidily trimmed close to a jutting jaw. He was the head of the cabal of Jasons assigned to assist the Russians – and also a colleague and longtime friend of Archibald Polk.

Dr. Trent McBride.

'He's just arrived,' the man said into the phone with a nod toward Yuri. 'I'll brief everyone in an hour.'

McBride closed his cell phone, stood, and held out his hand. 'I've been updated on your situation, Yuri.

Considering the girl's fragile state, this is a top priority. We'll do what we can to help find the child.'

Yuri shook his hand and sat down. Although startled, he felt relieved to find McBride here. Beneath his good-natured bravado, the man had a sharp and practical mind.

'So then you understand,' Yuri said, 'how vital it is that we acquire her again? And soon.'

He nodded. 'How many hours can the girl survive without her medication?'

'Thirty-two.'

'And her last injection?'

'Seven hours,' he answered grimly.

That leaves Sasha only a little over a day to be found.

'Then we'll have to move fast,' McBride said. 'As you might suspect, Mapplethorpe had already called me. In fact, that's why I'm here myself.'

'I thought you were in Geneva. Hadn't you decided to keep a low profile? To keep hidden?'

'Just until matters with Archibald settled out.' His eyes hardened slightly at Yuri. 'Which it seems it has. Though the outcome could have been better. He was my friend.'

'You know, as well as I, that Dr. Polk would not have survived another few days. I had to do what was necessary.'

McBride seemed little mollified.

'And if you recall,' Yuri added, 'I voted *against* approaching Dr. Polk in the first place.'

McBride sagged back into his chair with a squeak. 'I truly thought Archibald would be more amenable, especially once he saw the project firsthand. After all, it was an extension of his life's work. And considering the threat he posed, the only other option was—'

Again a sad shrug.

Dr. Polk had been treading too close to the heart of the

103

research project. *Closer than even McBride knew.* It left them only two choices: recruit him or eliminate him.

Recruitment failed . . . disastrously.

Brought to the Warren, the man had ended up escaping with valuable intelligence. They had no choice but to hunt him down.

'I'm sorry about Archibald,' Yuri said.

And he truly was. Dr. Polk's death, while a tragic necessity, was still a profound loss. On his own, the professor had accomplished so much, even coming close to exposing what the Russians had been keeping secret from the Americans. Ultimately both sides had underestimated Dr. Polk's resourcefulness.

Both prior to kidnapping him and afterward.

Yuri continued. 'In regards to the missing girl—'

McBride interrupted. 'I presume she is one of your Omega subjects.'

He nodded. 'Tested at the ninety-seven percentile range. She's vital to our project. To *both* our work. I fear Mapplethorpe doesn't understand the delicate balance needed to keep an Omega subject alive and functioning.'

McBride rubbed the bridge of his nose. 'During my phone conversation with him, Mapplethorpe did happen to suggest that we might want to *acquire* the child ourselves.'

'I suspected he would try something like that.'

Behind Yuri, the door to the outer office opened. He heard Dr. Chen greet someone, stiff and formal.

Yuri swung around, shocked to see the subject of their discussion appear at the door. Mapplethorpe's sagging features looked even more dour than usual. A chill of misgiving spiked through Yuri.

McBride stood. 'John, we were just talking about you. Did your team have any luck acquiring the augmented skull?'

'No. We've scoured both museums.'

'Odd,' McBride said with a worried frown. 'And what word on the girl?'

'We have helicopters sweeping the entire city grid, section by section, radiating out from the zoo. Still no hits on the tracking device.'

Yuri fixed upon this last bit of information. 'Tracking . . . what tracking device?'

McBride stepped around the desk. He held out a closed fist toward Yuri – then opened his fingers and exposed a tiny object resting on his palm.

Barely larger than the head of a pin.

Yuri had to lean closer to even see it.

'Wonders of nanotechnology,' McBride said. 'A passive microtransmitter with burst-pulse attenuator, all housed in a sterile polymer sleeve. While on my last visit to the Warren, I had all the children injected with them.'

Yuri knew nothing about such implantations; then again, he wasn't kept abreast of everything. 'Did Savina approve such trackers?'

He glanced up to see McBride lift one eyebrow at him. *Surely you're smarter than that, Dr. Raev,* he seemed to imply.

Yuri realized what the American was insinuating. Savina knew nothing about the matter. It *was* McBride who had injected the children – in secret, without anyone's knowledge. He'd had plenty of access to the children, but always while being monitored. Yuri studied the size of the microtransmitter. It was small enough to have been delivered in a hundred different ways.

Why would McBride—?

Yuri's mind quickly cascaded through the possibilities, implications, and consequences. McBride must have placed trackers in all the children. Once he had the children implanted, all he had to do was set up the proper scenario that would require one or more of the children to leave the nest.

Yuri pictured Archibald Polk's face. The realization struck him like a blow to the solar plexus.

'It was a ruse all along,' Yuri gasped out. 'Dr. Polk's escape . . .'

McBride smiled his agreement. 'Very good.'

Mapplethorpe's shadow fell upon him like a physical weight.

Yuri had been played the fool. He glared over at McBride. '*You* were at the Warren when Archibald escaped. *You* helped him escape.'

A nod. 'We needed some way to lure one of your Omega subjects out into the open.'

'*You* used Dr. Polk like bait. Your own friend and colleague.'

'A necessity, I'm afraid.'

'Did he . . . did Archibald know he was being used?'

McBride sighed with a tired ache in his voice. 'I think he might have suspected . . . though he didn't have much choice. Die or run the gauntlet. Sometimes you have to be a patriot whether you want to or not. And I must say he did well. He almost crossed the goal line.'

'All this, to kidnap one child?'

McBride rubbed the bridge of his nose. 'We suspected you Russians were hiding something, yes?'

Yuri kept his face passive. McBride was right, but he had no idea of the breadth of what was hidden.

'We will use this child,' he continued, 'to start our own program here in the United States. To study in greater detail what you've done to the child. Despite our repeated inquiries, your group has not been forthcoming with a full account. You've been holding back key data from the start.'

And they had – not just data, but also future plans.

Yuri asked out loud, 'What about Sasha's medications?'

'We'll manage. With your cooperation.'

Yuri shook his head. 'Never.'

'I was afraid you'd say that.'

A flick of McBride's eye drew Yuri's attention over his shoulder.

Mapplethorpe held a gun in his hand.

He fired at point-blank range.

9:45 P.M.

Gray was not one to stomach coincidences. Two scientists on the same project go missing at the same time – then one turns up in Washington, irradiated and on death's door.

Gray massaged an ache behind his temples. 'Elizabeth, all this has to somehow tie back to your father's original research.'

Painter nodded. 'But the question is *how*? If we knew more details . . . perhaps something not in your father's records.'

The question hung in the air.

Elizabeth glanced down to her lap. Her hands were clutched tightly together. She seemed to finally note the tension there and unlatched her fingers, stretching them a bit.

She mumbled dully. 'I don't know. These last years . . . we weren't talking much. He wasn't happy I was going into anthropology. He wanted me to follow in his . . .' She shook her head. 'Never mind.'

Gray reached out, poured a mug of hot coffee, and passed it to her. She accepted it with a nod. She didn't drink it, just held it between her palms, warming them.

'Your father must not have been *too* unhappy with your career choice,' Gray offered. 'He obtained that research position for you with the museum in Greece.'

She shook her head. 'His assistance wasn't as altruistic as it sounds. My father had always been interested in the Delphic Oracle. Such prophetic women tied into his studies about intuition and instinct. My father came to believe there was something inherent in these women, something they shared. A genetic commonality. Or a shared neurological abnormality. So you see, my father got me that position in Delphi only so I could help with *his* research.'

'But what sort of research was he doing exactly?' Gray said, encouraging her. 'Anything you know might help.'

She sighed. 'I *can* tell you what started my father's obsession with intuition and instinct.' She glanced between them. 'Do either of you know of the earliest experiments the Russians did involving intuition?'

They shook their heads.

'It was a horrible experiment, but it meshed with my father's own line of neurophysiology. A couple decades ago, the Russians separated a mother cat from her kittens. They then took the litter down in a submarine. While monitoring the mother cat's vital signs, the Russian submariners killed one of her kittens. At the exact moment this happened, the mother's heart rate spiked, and her brain activity registered severe pain. The cat became agitated and confused. They repeated it with the other kittens over the next few days. Each time with exactly the same results. Though separated by distance, the mother seemed to sense the death of her kittens.'

'A form of maternal instinct,' Gray said.

Elizabeth nodded. 'Or intuition. Either way, to my father, this was verifiable proof of some biological connection. He focused his research to seek a neurological basis for this strange phenomenon. Eventually he teamed up with the professor in India, who was studying similar abilities among the yogis and mystics of that country.'

'What abilities?' Painter asked.

Elizabeth took a sip of the hot coffee. She shook her head slightly. 'My father began reading up on anecdotal stories of people with special mental talents. He weeded out crackpots and charlatans and sought out cases with some measure of verifiable proof, those rare cases substantiated by real scientists. Like by Albert Einstein.'

Gray did not mask his surprise. 'Einstein?'

A nod. 'At the turn of the century, an Indian woman named Shakuntala was brought to universities around the world to demonstrate her strange abilities. She had no more than the equivalent of a high school education, but she had an inexplicable skill with mathematics. Doing massive calculations in her head.'

'Some form of savant talent?' Painter asked.

'More than that, actually. With chalk in hand, the woman would begin writing the answer to a question *before* it was even voiced. Even Einstein bore witness to her skill. He posed to her a question that took him three months to solve, involving an intricate number of steps. Again before he could finish even asking the question, she was chalking out the answer, a solution that covered the width of the blackboard. He asked her how she was able to do that, but she didn't know, claiming that figures just started to appear before her eyes and she simply wrote them down.'

Elizabeth stared over at them, plainly expecting disbelief. But Gray simply nodded for her to continue. His acquiescence seemed to irritate her, as if Gray dismissing such stories would somehow vindicate something inside her.

'There were other cases, too,' she continued. 'Again in India. A boy who pulled a rickshaw in Madras. He could answer mathematical questions without even hearing the question. His explanation was that he would be overcome with a sense of anxiety when someone with a mathematical question was near him. And the answer would appear lined up in his head "like soldiers." He was eventually taken to Oxford, where he was tested. To prove his skill, he answered mathematical questions that were unsolvable at the time. Oxford recorded his results. Decades later, when higher levels of mathematics were developed, his answers were proven correct. But by that time, the boy had died of old age.'

Elizabeth set down her mug of coffee. 'As astounding as these cases were, they also frustrated my father to no end. He needed *living* test subjects. So, as he continued to collate anecdotal evidence, he found many of the most intriguing cases clustered in India. Among their yogis and mystics. At the time, other scientists were already discovering the physiological basis for many of the yogis' amazing skills. Like withstanding extreme cold for days by adjusting the flow of blood to their limbs and skin. Or fasting for months by lowering their basal metabolic rate.'

Gray nodded. He had studied many of such yogis' teachings. It all came down to a matter of mental control, of tapping into bodily functions that were considered to be involuntary.

'My father immersed himself in Indian history, language, even with the ancient Vedic texts of prophecy. He sought out skilled yogis and began to test them: blood tests, electroencephalograms, brain mapping, even taking DNA tests to track the lineage of the individuals with the most talent. Ultimately he sought to scientifically prove that there was an organic basis in the brain for what the Russians had demonstrated with the mother cat.'

Painter sank back into the sofa. 'It's no wonder he was tapped for the Stanford project. His research certainly dovetailed with their objective.'

'But why would my father be murdered over this? It's been years.' Her eyes met Gray's. 'And what does that strange skull have to do with any of this?'

'We don't know yet,' Painter answered, 'but by morning, we should know more about the skull.'

110

Gray hoped he was right. A team of experts had been called into Sigma to examine the strange object. It was with some reluctance that Gray allowed the skull to be couriered over to central command. Sensing it was the key to the mystery, he hated to have it out of his sight.

A knock at the door ended further discussion.

Painter craned around; Kowalski stood up, one of his shoes in hand.

Gray climbed to his feet, too.

Two plainclothed guards had been posted outside the house. If there was any problem, they would have radioed. Still, Gray unsnapped his holster and slipped out his semiautomatic pistol. Outfitted with radios, why would one of the guards be knocking?

He waved the others back and approached the front entry. He kept to the side and crossed to a small video monitor split into four views, each a live feed from exterior cameras. The upper left featured a view of the porch.

Two figures stood there, a few steps from the door.

A wiry man in a red Windbreaker held the hand of a small child. A girl. She fidgeted with a ribbon in her hair. Gray read no overt threat in the man's manner. In his other hand was a thick sheet of paper. Maybe an envelope. The figure bent down to the bottom of the door.

Gray tensed, but it was just a sheet of yellow paper. The man slid it under the door. The sheet skittered across the waxed wooden floor of the entrance hall. It sailed to Gray's toes.

He stared down at a child's scrawl in black crayon. In crude but deliberate strokes, it depicted the main room of the safe house. Fireplace, chairs, sofa. Exactly as the room was laid out. Four shapes were drawn there, too. Two sat on the sofa, one on a chair. A larger figure leaned by the hearth with a shoe in his hand and had to be Kowalski.

It was a child's picture of their room.

Gray stared back at the video monitor.

Movement drew his attention to the other feeds from the three exterior cameras. Men stepped into view, also in Windbreakers. Gray watched one guard, then the other appear, held at gunpoint.

Kowalski stepped to Gray's side, having crossed silently on his stocking feet. He also studied the screen, then sighed.

'Great,' Kowalski commented. 'What do you all do? Post the addresses for your hideaways on the Internet?'

Outside, the guards were forced to their knees.

The house was surrounded.

They were trapped.

On the other side of the world, the man named Monk sought his own path to freedom.

As the three children stood guard at his hospital room door, Monk struggled into a pair of thick denim coveralls, dark blue to match the long-sleeved shirt he wore. It was difficult with only one hand. All that remained on the chair were a black cable-knit wool cap and a pair of thick socks. He tugged the cap over his shaved head and pushed into the heavy socks, then into boots that were a bit snug, but the leather was worn and broken in.

The privacy allowed Monk to gather his wits about him, though it had done little to fill in the blanks of his life. He still couldn't remember anything beyond waking up here. But at least the exertion of dressing helped steady his feet.

He joined the oldest of the boys, Konstantin, at the door, which was steel and had a locking bar on the outside. The stoutness of the door confirmed he'd been a prisoner and that this was an escape.

The youngest of the trio, Pyotr, took Monk's hand and tugged him down the hall, away from the glow of a nurse's station. He remembered the boy's earlier plea.

Save us.

Monk didn't understand. From what? The girl, who he had learned was named Kiska, led the way to a back stairwell, lit by a red neon sign. Passing under it to the stairs, Monk stared up at the sign's lettering.

Cyrillic.

He had to be in Russia. Despite his lack of memory, he knew he didn't belong here. His thoughts were in English. Without a British accent. That meant he had to be American, didn't it? If he could recognize all that, why couldn't he—

A cascade of images suddenly blinded him, frozen snapshots of another life, popping like camera flashes in his head—

. . . a smile . . . a kitchen with someone's back turned to him . . . the steel head of a sharp ax flashing across blue sky . . . lights rising from deep in dark water . . .

Then it was gone.

His head pounded. He tried to catch himself on the stair railing and instinctively grabbed out with his stumped arm. His scarred forearm slid along the railing. He barely caught his balance. He stared down at his stump and recalled one of the flashes of memory.

. . . the steel head of an ax flashing across blue sky.

Was that how it had happened?

Ahead, the children rushed down the stairs. Except for the youngest boy. Pyotr still held his one good hand. He stared up at Monk with eyes so blue they were almost white. Tiny fingers squeezed his own, reassuring. A gentle tug urged him onward.

He stumbled after the others.

They encountered no one on the stairs and exited out a back doorway and into a moonless, overcast night. The air had a chill to it and hung still and damp. Monk took in deep breaths, slowing his hammering heart.

The massive hum of a generator filled the space.

Monk studied the size and breadth of the hospital, sprawling out in low wings and encompassing two five-story towers.

'Come. This way,' Konstantin said, taking the lead now.

They hurried down a dark cobblestone alleyway between the hospital and a wall that climbed two stories on their left. Monk looked up, trying to get his bearings. A few lamps glowed beyond the wall, highlighting the tile roofs of hidden buildings. They reached a corner and slipped behind the walled enclosure. The ground became raw rock, slippery with dew. There were no lights here on the back side. All Monk could make out was the wall they followed, built of concrete blocks. His palm ran along it as they ran. From the rough mortaring and uneven lay of the bricks, it must have been hastily constructed.

Monk heard an eerie yowl echoing over the wall. This was followed by muffled barks and stifled sharper cries.

His feet slowed. Animals. Was this some form of zoo?

As if the tall boy ahead had read his thoughts, Konstantin glanced back and mouthed the word *menagerie* and waved him onward.

Menagerie?

They reached the far corner, and the path sloped steeply downward from there. From the vantage of their height, Monk stared across a bowled valley and a picturesque village of cobbled lanes and cottages with peaked roofs and flower boxes. Ornate black streetlamps flickered with gas flames. A three-story school filled one corner of the village, surrounded by ball fields and an open amphitheater. The small village clustered around a central square, where a tall fountain's spray danced and glittered.

On the far side of the village rose row after row of industrial-looking apartment buildings, each five stories, squared and laid out in a practical grid. Dark and lightless, it had a dilapidated, deserted feeling to it.

Unlike the village below.

People milled in confusion below. Shouts echoed. He saw children gathered in nightclothes, mingling with adults, some similarly attired, woken from their beds. Others wore gray uniforms and stiff-brimmed hats. Flashlights danced through the narrow streets.

Something had roused the place.

He heard names called, some beckoning, some angry.

'Konstantin! Pyotr! Kiska!'

The children.

A flaming red flare arced upward from the town center, lighting up the sleepy little village, laying stark the buildings beyond, dancing fire over the concrete walls and hollow-eyed windows.

Monk's gaze tracked the flare as it reached its zenith, popped out a tiny parachute, and floated downward.

Monk's attention remained above.

The sky . . . it wasn't just *moonless.*

It wasn't there at all.

The ruddy glow of the flare revealed a massive dome of rock, stretching overhead in all directions, swallowing up the entire place. Monk gaped, stumbling around in a stunned circle.

They hadn't made it *outside.*

They were inside a giant cavern.

Possibly man-made from the blasted look of the roof and walls.

He stared down at the perfect little village, preserved in the cavern like a ship in a bottle. But there was no time for further sightseeing.

Konstantin tugged him down behind a limestone outcropping. A trio of jeeps quietly hummed up a steep road toward them, passed them, and headed toward the hospital complex. The vehicles appeared to be electric-powered and were manned by men in uniforms, bearing guns.

Not good.

Once the jeeps were out of sight, Konstantin pointed away from the village, toward the darkness of the deeper cavern. They traversed the rocky landscape and came upon a thin path, seldom used from the looks of it.

They skirted the subterranean village, sticking to the upper slopes of the cavern. Monk noted a yawning tunnel on the far side, lit by electric lights, sealed by giant metal doors wide enough that two cement trucks could have entered, side by side. It marked a roadway that exited the cavern.

But the children led him in the opposite direction.

Where were they taking him?

Behind, a loud alarm erupted, deafening as an air raid siren in the enclosed space. All four of them turned. A red light flashed and whirled atop the hospital complex.

The villagers had come to realize another truth.

It wasn't just the children who had gone missing.

Monk attempted to herd the kids down the path, but the loud noise had incapacitated them. They covered their ears and squeezed their eyes shut. Kiska looked sick to her stomach. Konstantin was on his knees, rocking. Pyotr hugged tight to Monk.

Hypersensitive.

Still, Monk urged them onward, carrying Pyotr, half dragging Kiska.

Monk glanced back toward the flashing siren. He may have lost his memory – or more precisely, had it *forcibly* extracted – but he knew one thing for dead certain.

He would lose much more than his memory if caught again.

And he feared the children would suffer even worse.

They had to keep going – *but to where?*

6

September 6, 5:22 A.M.
Kiev, Ukraine

Nicolas Solokov waited for the cameras to be set up. He had already been prepped and still wore a collar of tissue paper tucked into his white starched shirt to keep the makeup's cake from staining his shirt and midnight blue suit. He had retreated for a private moment of introspection into one of the back hospital wards. The international news crews were still preparing for the morning broadcast out on the steps of the orphanage.

In the back ward of the Kiev Children's Home, sunlight streamed through high windows. A single nurse moved quietly among the beds. Here the worst cases were hidden away: a two-year-old girl with an inoperable thyroid tumor in her throat, a ten-year-old boy with a swollen head from hydrocephalus, another younger boy whose eyes were dulled by severe mental retardation. This last boy was strapped down, all four limbs.

The nurse, a squarish Ukrainian matron in a blue smock, noted his attention.

'So he doesn't hurt himself, Senator,' she explained, her eyes exhausted from seeing too much suffering.

But there had been worse cases. In 1993, a baby had been born in Moldova with two heads, two hearts, two

117

spinal cords, but only one set of limbs. There was another child whose brain was born outside his skull.

All the legacy of Chernobyl.

In spring of 1986, reactor number four of the Chernobyl Nuclear Power Plant had exploded during the middle of the night. Over the course of ten days, it spewed radiation that was the equivalent of four hundred Hiroshima bombs in a plume that circled the globe. To date, according to the Russian Academy of Medical Sciences, over one hundred thousand people had died from radiation exposure and another seven million were exposed, most of them children, leaving an ongoing legacy of cancers and genetic abnormalities.

And now the second wave of the tragedy was beginning, where those who had been exposed at a young age were having children themselves. A 30 percent increase in birth defects had been reported.

For that reason, the volatile and charismatic leader of the lower house of the Russian parliament had come here. Nicolas's own district of Chelyabinsk lay a thousand miles away, but it had similar concerns. In the Ural Mountains of his district, most of the fuel for Chernobyl had been mined, along with the plutonium for the Soviet weapons program. It remained one of the most radioactive places on the planet.

'They're ready for you, Senator,' his aide said behind him.

He turned to face her.

Elena Ozerov, a trim raven-haired woman in her early twenties with a smoky complexion, wore a black business suit that hid her small breasts and turned her into something androgynously asexual. She was stern, taciturn, and always at his side. The press referred to her as Nicolas's Rasputin, which he did not discourage.

It all went along with his political plan to be seen as the bold reformer, while simultaneously harkening back to the former czarist glory of the old Russian Empire. Even his namesake, Nicolas II, the last czar of the Romanov dynasty, had been imprisoned and killed in Yekaterinburg, where Nicolas was born. While the czar had been a failed leader during his life, after his death he had been canonized by the Russian Orthodox Church. The bishops built the gold-domed Cathedral of the Blood over the home where the family had been murdered. The construction marked a symbolic rebirth of the Romanovs.

Some claimed the forty-one-year-old Senator Nicolas Solokov, with his lankish black hair and curled short beard, was the czar himself reborn.

He encouraged such comparisons.

As Russia sought to rise again on shaky legs – burdened by debt and poverty, rife with graft and corruption – it needed a new leader for this new millennium.

Nicolas intended to be that leader.

And much more.

He allowed Elena to pinch away the ring of tissue paper from around his neck. She looked him up and down, then nodded her approval.

Nicolas stepped toward the lights waiting for him outside.

He pushed through the doors, followed circumspectly by Elena. The podium sat up at the top of the stairs, framed with the name of the orphanage behind him.

He marched to the bristle of microphones at the podium and held an arm high against the barrage of questions. He heard one reporter shout a question about his former ties to the KGB, another about his family's financial connections to the vast mining operations out in the Ural Mountains. As he rose in power, so did the voices of those who sought to pull him down.

Ignoring the questions, he set his own agenda.

Leaning toward the microphones, he let his voice boom out over the nattering questions. 'It is time to shut these doors!' he shouted, pointing back toward the entrance to the orphanage behind him. 'The children of the Ukraine, of Belarus, of all of Mother Russia, have suffered from the sins of our past. Never again!'

Nicolas let his anger ring out. He knew how it looked on camera. The hard face of reform and outrage. He continued his impassioned plea for a new vision of Russia, a call for action, a call to look forward while not forgetting the past.

'Two days from now, the number four reactor at Chernobyl will be sealed under a new steel dome. The new Sarcophagus will mark the end of a tragedy and be forever a memorial to all the men and women who gave their lives to protect not only our Motherland, but also the world. Firemen who stood firm with their hoses while radiation burned away their futures. Pilots who risked the toxic plume to haul in concrete and supplies. Miners who came from across the country to help build the first shield to entomb the reactor. These glorious men and women, fierce with nationalistic pride, are the *true* heart of Russia! Let us never forget them, nor their sacrifice!'

The crowd behind the reporters had grown as Nicolas spoke. He was heartened by the cheers and claps as he paused.

This was the first of many speeches he would be giving, leading up to the ceremony at Chernobyl itself, where the new Sarcophagus would be rolled over the toxic core of the dead reactor. The original concrete shield was already crumbling, meant only as a short-term fix, and that was twenty years ago. The new Sarcophagus weighed eighteen thousand tons and stood half as tall as the Eiffel Tower. It was the largest movable structure on the planet.

Other politicians were already capitalizing on the event with similar events and speeches. But Nicolas had been the loudest and most vocal, a champion for nuclear reform, for cleaning up the radiological hotbeds around the country. Many sought to stifle his rhetoric due to the extreme cost. Members of his own parliament ridiculed and lambasted him in the press.

But Nicolas knew he was right.

As they all would see one day.

'And mark my words!' he continued. 'While we put an end to one chapter of our history, I fear we've only put our finger in a hole in the dike. Our nuclear past is not done with us yet . . . nor the world. When such a time comes, I hope we all prove to have the same stout hearts as those brave men and women who gave up their futures on that tragic day. So let us not squander the gift they've given us. Let us bring about a new Renaissance! From fire, a new world can be born.'

He knew his eyes glinted as he spoke these last words. It was the slogan of his reform.

A new Renaissance.

A *Russian* Renaissance.

All it needed was a little push in the right direction.

Elena leaned toward him, touched his elbow, wanting a word. He tilted toward her as the crack of a rifle blasted from the park across the street. From the corner of his eye, he caught the flash of muzzle fire a fraction of a second before something ripped past his ear.

Sniper.

Assassin.

Elena pulled him down behind the podium as cries and screams erupted from the crowd. Chaos ruled for a breath. Nicolas used the moment to brush his lips across Elena's. His hand combed through her long hair; one finger traced the curve of cold surgical steel that hugged the back of her ear.

He whispered into their kiss.

'That went well.'

121

Painter joined Gray near the front entry and stared at the video feed. He studied the guards held at gunpoint.

The shadowy man on the stoop called through the door, as if sensing their presence. 'We mean no harm,' he said, his accent sharp, marking him as Eastern European.

Painter stared at the stranger on the screen. Then to the girl who stood beside him, holding the stranger's hand. She was staring straight into the hidden camera.

The man called again. 'We are allies of Archibald Polk!' He sounded unsure of himself, as if he didn't know if those in the house would know what that meant. 'We don't have much time!'

Elizabeth hovered behind Painter. They shared a look. If there were to be any answers about the fate of her father, a risk had to be taken. But not too large of a risk. Painter hit the intercom button and spoke into it.

'If you are allies, then you'll free our men and drop your weapons.'

The man on the porch shook his head. 'Not until you prove you can be trusted. We have risked much to bring the girl here. Exposed ourselves.'

Painter glanced to Gray. He shrugged.

'We'll let you inside,' Painter said. 'But only you and the girl.'

'And I will keep your men out here to ensure our safety.'

Kowalski grumbled next to them. 'One big happy family.'

Painter motioned Gray to take Elizabeth around the corner.

Painter kept his body to the side of the door. Kowalski flanked the other side, standing in his stockings. The large man raised his only weapon: the shoe in his hand.

That would have to do.

Painter undid the bolt and cracked the door open. The stranger lifted his palm to show it was empty. The girl held his other hand. She appeared no older than ten, dark-haired in a checkered gray-and-black dress. The man had an olive complexion with a heavy five-o'clock shadow. Maybe Egyptian or Arabic. His eyes, so brown they appeared black in the porch light, smoldered with wary threat. He wore jeans and a dark crimson Windbreaker.

The stranger turned his head, but his gaze never wavered from the open doorway. He barked to his men. Painter didn't understand the language, but from the tones it sounded like a command to stay alert.

'He's a Gypsy,' Kowalski mumbled.

Painter glanced to the large man.

'Had a family down the street from mine.' Kowalski thumbed at the stranger. 'That was Romani he was speaking.'

'He is right,' the stranger said. 'My name is Luca Hearn.'

Painter pulled the doorway wider and motioned the man inside.

The stranger stepped across the threshold cautiously, but he nodded a greeting to Painter and Kowalski. '*Sastimos.*'

'*Nais tuke,*' Kowalski answered. 'But just so you know, that's about *all* the Romani language I remember.'

Painter led Luca and the child back to the main living room. She moved with a slight tremble to her limbs. Her face gleamed with a feverish cast to it.

Luca noted Gray to the side, holding a pistol.

Painter waved for Gray to holster the weapon. He sensed no direct threat from the man. Only an unwavering caution.

Elizabeth stepped forward. 'You mentioned my father.'

Luca crinkled his brow, not understanding.

Painter explained, 'She is Archibald Polk's daughter.'

123

His eyes widened. He bowed his head in her direction. 'I am sorry for your loss. He was a great man.'

'What do you know about my father?' she asked. 'Who is this girl?'

The child pulled free of the man's hand and crossed to the table. She sat down on her knees next to it and rocked back and forth.

'The girl?' Luca said. 'I don't know. A mystery. I received a message from your father. A frantic voice mail. It was chaotic, spoken in a rush. He ordered us to buy a dozen Cobra Marine receivers from Radio Shack and to tune them to a certain wavelength. He sounded crazy, babbling off numbers. He wanted us to stake out the national Mall. To watch for a *package* that set off the receivers.'

'Package?' Painter asked.

Luca glanced down to the child. *'Her.'*

'The girl?' Elizabeth asked, shocked. 'Why?'

Luca shook his head. 'We owed your father. We did as he asked. We were even on the Mall when he was shot, though we didn't know it was your father until later. But we did pick up the trail of the child.'

Painter studied the girl. There must be a bug, a microtransmitter somewhere on her person.

'We followed her to the zoo, where we were able to collect her without anyone knowing.'

'You kidnapped her?' Painter asked.

He shrugged. 'The last words on the message were to *steal the package* and bring it to something or someone named Sigma.'

His words jolted Painter.

'The message cut off abruptly,' the Gypsy said, 'with no further direction or explanation. Once we had the girl, we had to move fast. We feared others would come looking for her. Someone able to track her like we did. Especially with an Amber Alert raised across the district.

124

But we had no idea what the professor meant by Sigma. As we raced around, trying to figure it out, the girl began to draw furiously.'

He pointed to the child, who had gained her feet and walked to a blank wall. She bore a piece of charcoal from the fireplace in her fingers and drew on the wall in a haphazard manner, jerkily, starting in one place, then moving to another.

'She wouldn't stop,' Luca continued. 'She drew a silhouette of a park with trees and a picture of Rock Creek bridge.' He nodded out the window. 'Then after that, a house, set in the same woods. We had to circle the entire park, looking for it, believing it was important. By the time we found this place, she had drawn the picture that I slid under the door.'

Luca stared at them. 'A picture of all of you. Friends and family of Dr. Polk. So I must ask you, do you know this Sigma?'

Painter slipped out a glossy black identification card. It had his photograph fixed with the presidential seal. Etched into its surface was a holographic Greek letter.

Luca examined it, angling it to study the holograph. His eyes widened as he recognized it.

While they had talked, Gray had crossed to the girl. He sat on his haunches, studying the girl's work. He rubbed his chin. Something had drawn his attention. Gray lifted a finger, half hidden between his knees, like a catcher signaling a pitcher. He pointed toward the girl.

Her face shone brighter. Her head lolled slightly to one side. Her eyes were open, but they were not following the path of her scrabbling piece of charcoal. As disturbing as her manner was, it was not what Gray had indicated.

Painter had noted it, too. Her hair, damp with fever sweat, had parted slightly behind her ear. A glint of steel shone through. The shape was unmistakably the same as the device attached to the strange skull.

Only here it was on a *living* subject.

What had Archibald delivered to them?

As Painter's mind spun on possibilities, Elizabeth hung farther back in the room. She pointed toward the wall. 'Come see this,' she said, her voice quavering with an edge of fear.

Painter retreated to her side. She pointed to the artwork forming on the wall. From this far away, what looked like mindless scribbles had begun to take form. He watched the transformation unfold over the course of four long silent minutes.

Elizabeth stuttered her amazement. 'That's . . . that's . . .'

'. . . the Taj Mahal,' Painter finished.

In the silent wonder that followed, a distant sound reached them.

—*whump, whump*—

A helicopter, flying low, coming closer.

Gray straightened and reached for the girl. 'Someone's found us!'

Nicolas rolled off of Elena and onto his back.

The hotel room fan cooled his sweating body. His lower back ached and his shoulders bore deep scratches that still burned. Elena rolled smoothly to her feet, with an easy swing of her hair, tangled to midback. The curving rise and fall of her buttocks as she strode toward the shower came close to arousing him again. He stirred, but he knew he had another interview in a half hour.

News of the failed assassination had already spread far and wide. He would be on every international newscast. He'd already learned that the sniper, shot by the police, had died before reaching the hospital.

With the death, no one would suspect that it had all been preplanned. Even the sniper – a mine worker from Polevskoy whose brother had been killed in an industrial accident last year – never knew how artfully he'd been manipulated into the assassination scheme.

It had all unfolded with technical precision. Elena had timed her touch perfectly. A skill of hers. When primed, she could calculate probabilities to the nth degree. Her statistical analyses of business spreadsheets rivaled the world's best economists. And having studied the technical specifications on most pistols and light arms, she had only to see how a weapon was held and pointed to calculate its precise trajectory.

Trusting this, he had put his life in her hands this morning.

And survived.

At that moment, behind the podium, he'd never felt such a total lack of control, his very survival at the mercy of another. After a lifetime of control, to release that grip even for a moment had quickened his pulse. Afterward, he could not return to the hotel fast enough.

Elena stepped wet from her shower and leaned naked in the doorway. The lust in her eyes slowly died – trailing the last spark of erotic stimulation from her augment's neural array. The fiery lioness was becoming a sleepy kitten. Still, Nicolas studied that last ember of fire – an arousing blend of need and hatred – but even that would fade to a simple cold obedience.

Such stimulation of her implant was necessary – not only to make the coupling intense, but also to trigger the proper physiological response to increase the chance of fertilization. Nicolas had read the studies. And his mother wanted children from him, even approved of the union of Nicolas and Elena. It was a perfect match: his will and her cold calculation.

Nicolas had done his best to make his mother happy this morning.

And he had the bruises and scratches to prove it.

However, his mother might not have approved of him allowing Elena to tie him to the bedposts and whip his thighs with a scrub brush. But as his mother always told him when he was growing up:

The ends always justify the means.

Ever practical, his mother.

The phone rang at his bedside table. Elena strode over, answered it, then held the receiver out for him.

'General-Major Savina Martov,' Elena said formally, gone cold again. 'For the senator.'

He took the receiver with a sigh. As usual, the woman's timing was impeccable. She must have heard about the failed assassination attempt. She would want a full debriefing and must have wondered why he hadn't already reported in. The schedule in the next days would tighten to an unbreakable knot – at both their ends – leading up to the formal sealing of Chernobyl. Nothing could go wrong.

Nicolas shifted his weight off his bruised buttock with a wince.

The caller spoke before he could. 'We have a problem, Nicolas.'

He sighed. 'What is it, Mother?'

10:50 P.M.
Washington, D.C.

Gray cradled the girl in his arms and hurried across the front yard. The crisp September night contrasted with the feverish heat of the child. He felt the burn of her skin through his shirt. Her fever had spiked while laboring on her artwork. She had collapsed when Gray had pulled the charcoal from her fingers. She was conscious, but her eyes stared blankly, and her limbs were oddly stiff and wooden, as if he were carrying a life-size doll. Her waxy features heightened the comparison.

Gray touched her face, noting the fine delicacy of her tiny eyelashes.

Who could do this to a child?

They had to get her to safety.

Out in the yard, Gray searched the skies. A single black helicopter – military design – swept low down the street. Another idled higher at the other end of the block. And a third circled the park behind them.

Triangulating in on their position.

Their sedan still stood in the driveway. Luca and his men had three identical Ford SUVs parked down the street. The Gypsy clan leader had already gathered his men. He barked orders in Romani and pointed his arms out in various directions, instructing them to split up. Three men took off on foot toward the park, where they would divide again. Another two ran across the street and disappeared between two houses. A dog barked at their passage.

Ahead, Kowalski marched with Elizabeth toward the

Lincoln Town Car in the driveway. She had her cell phone to her ear.

Painter headed toward a small car parked at the curb, a Toyota Yaris that belonged to one of the security guards. Gray followed him. The guard was already behind the wheel after being freed by Luca's men.

Painter opened the backseat and turned to Gray and held out his arms. Gray passed him the child.

'She's burning up,' Gray said.

He nodded. 'Once safe, we'll get her medical attention. I've already called Kat and Lisa to report to command.'

Lisa was Dr. Lisa Cummings, an experienced medical doctor with a PhD in physiology. She was also the director's girlfriend. Captain Kat Bryant was Sigma's expert in intelligence services and coordination. She would oversee the field operation.

'But first,' Painter said, his eyes on the skies as he ducked into the backseat with the child, 'we have to break this cordon.'

Off to the side, one of the Ford SUVs shot straight down the street with its headlights off; the other swung sharply around and flew in the opposite direction, zipping past Painter's idling Toyota.

'Let's hope this works,' Gray said.

Before leaving, Painter had Luca bring in one of the Cobra receivers that they'd used to track the girl at the national Mall. As the director had hoped, the devices were actually transceivers – capable of both receiving *and* transmitting. Painter had showed Luca how to switch the radios from receiving a specific signal to *broadcasting* it. Luca had all his men do the same. They were now scattering in all directions, transmitting the girl's signature signal, creating a dozen different trails to follow – and most likely broadcasting louder than the girl's small microtransmitter. Under the cover of such confusion, Painter hoped to escape with the girl to the subterranean bunkers of Sigma's central command. There, he could isolate her signal and protect her.

Gray stepped in the other direction, toward the waiting Town Car. Kowalski already was revving the engine, impatient. They were headed for Reagan International Airport. Gray pictured the charcoal sketch of the Taj Mahal. The famous mausoleum was located in India, the very country where Dr. Polk had last been seen. Even before the girl's arrival, Gray had decided to extend the investigation to India, to follow Dr. Polk's trail out there. The mysterious drawing only added to his determination.

In India, there remained one person who could cast a better light on Archibald Polk's research and his whereabouts prior to his disappearance.

Elizabeth stood by the open door, studying the skies nervously. She clicked her cell phone closed as Gray reached her side.

'I was able to reach Dr. Masterson,' she said. 'My father's colleague at the university of Mumbai. But he wasn't in Mumbai. He was in *Agra*.'

'Agra?' Gray asked.

'The city in India where the Taj Mahal is located. He was *there* when I called. At the site.'

Gray stared over at the Toyota as it swung from the curb and glided down the streets. *What is going on?*

Overhead, the helicopters wavered. The birds began to drift in opposite directions, drawn off by decoys.

Gray tried one last time. 'Elizabeth, you would be safer staying here.'

'No, I'm coming with you. As you'll find out, Dr. Masterson is not the most forthcoming. But he knows me. He's expecting me. To get the professor's cooperation, I'll need to be there.'

Elizabeth's gaze met Gray's. He read a mix of emotions in her face: determination, fear, and a bone-deep grief.

'He was my father,' she said. 'I have to go.'

'And besides,' Kowalski called over from the driver's side of the car. 'I'll keep an eye on her.'

A shadow of a smile dimmed the raw edge of her emotion. 'That's not a good thing, is it?' she mouthed to Gray.

'Not by a long shot.'

He waved her into the car. He didn't argue too firmly against her coming. He suspected they would need her expertise before this was all over. Her father had specifically gone to her temporary office at the Museum of Natural History. He had gotten her that position at the Greek museum. Somehow all this tied back to Delphi – but how?

Luca had joined them by now. He had heard the last part of the conversation. 'I am coming, too.'

Gray nodded. Painter had already made that arrangement, to buy Luca's cooperation with the girl's escape. Which was fine with Gray. He still had a slew of questions for the man, mostly concerning his relationship with Dr. Polk. The Gypsy leader also seemed dead determined about something. Gray saw it in the shadows behind his dark eyes.

With the matter settled, Gray slid into the front passenger seat. Luca and Elizabeth piled into the back.

'Hang tight!' Kowalski called to them as he hauled the car into reverse, pounded the gas, and sent them squealing out of the driveway and into the street.

Overhead, the *thump-thump* of the helicopters receded into the night.

Gray's thoughts drifted to questions about the girl.

Who is she? Where did she come from?

Monk followed the three children. They were trailed by another who joined them at the lower hatch.

But she was not a child.

Monk felt those dark eyes on his back.

As a group, they climbed a spiral staircase drilled through raw limestone. The rock walls dripped with water, making the steps slippery. The stairway was narrow, utilitarian, plainly a service stair. It had proved to be a long climb. Monk half carried Pyotr now.

Earlier, while the siren blared, the kids had led Monk down a path that skirted the cavern and ended up at a small hatchway. The door opened into the stairway they were now climbing. Down below, Monk had been introduced to the last and strangest member of their party.

Her name was Marta.

'Here!' Konstantin called from ahead, bearing their only flashlight. He had reached the top of the stairs. Monk gathered the other two children and joined him. The older boy folded his lanky form and crouched beside a pile of packed gear. Ahead, a short tunnel ended at another hatch.

Konstantin pushed a pack into Monk's arms. Monk carried it toward the hatch and placed his palm on the door. It felt warm.

He turned as the last member of their party climbed into the tunnel from the stairs. Weighing eighty pounds and stooped to the height of three feet, she knuckled on one arm. Her body was covered in soft dark fur, except for her exposed face, hands, and feet. The fur around her face had gone a silvery gray.

Konstantin claimed the female chimpanzee was over sixty years old.

The reunion between the children and the ape at the lower hatchway had been a warm one. Despite the siren's blare and the wincing sensitivity of the children, the chimpanzee had taken each child under her arm and given them a reassuring squeeze, motherly, maternal.

Monk had to admit that her presence had helped calm the kids.

Even now, she shuffled among them, leaning, subvocalizing quietly.

The youngest, Pyotr, was the one who got the most attention. The pair seemed to have a strange way of communicating. It wasn't sign language, more like body language: gentle touches, posturing, long stares into each other's eyes. The young boy, exhausted by the climb, seemed to gain strength from the elderly ape.

Konstantin crossed to the hatch. He held out a small plastic badge toward Monk and showed him how to attach it to his coverall.

'What is it?' Monk asked.

Konstantin nodded toward the sealed doorway. 'Monitoring badge . . . for radiation levels.'

Monk stared over to the door. Radiation? What lay beyond that door? He remembered the heat he'd felt when he'd laid his palm on the hatch. In his head, he painted a blasted landscape, a terrain turned to ruin and slag.

With everyone ready, Konstantin crossed to the hatch and yanked hard on the lever that secured it. The door cracked and opened.

A blinding blaze of light flooded in, like staring into a fiery blast furnace. Monk shielded his eyes with his forearm. It took him another two breaths to realize he was merely facing a rising sun. He stumbled outside with the children.

The landscape had not been blasted to slag, as he had feared.

If anything, the opposite was true.

The hatch opened out onto a ledge of a heavily wooded slope, thick with birches and alders. Many of the trees had gone fiery with the change of seasons. To one side, a creek tumbled over mossy green rocks. Low mountains stretched off into the distance, dotted by tiny alpine lakes that shone like droplets of silver.

They had climbed out of hell into paradise.

But hell wasn't done with them yet.

From the tunnel behind them, a strange yowling cry echoed out to them. Monk remembered hearing the same howl coming from the walled complex that neighbored the hospital.

The Menagerie.

A second and third cry answered the first.

He didn't need Konstantin's urging to keep moving.

Monk recognized what he was hearing – not from memory, but from that buried part of his brain where instinct of predator and prey were still written.

Another howl echoed.

Louder and closer.

They were being hunted.

7

She remained a mystery in a very small package.

Painter studied the girl through the window. She had finally fallen asleep. Kat Bryant kept vigil at her bedside, a copy of Dr. Seuss's *Green Eggs and Ham* open in her lap. She had read to the girl until the sedatives had relaxed the child enough to sleep.

The child hadn't said a word since they'd arrived at midnight. Her eyes would track things, plainly registering what was going on around her. But there was little other response. She spent most of her time rocking back and forth, stiffening when touched. They had managed to get her to drink from a juice box and eat two chocolate-chip cookies. They'd also run some initial tests: blood chemistries, a full physical, even an MRI of her entire body. She still ran a low-grade fever, but it wasn't as elevated as earlier.

During the physical exam, they'd also found the microtransmitter embedded deep in the girl's upper arm. The chip would require surgery to remove, so they decided to leave it in place. Besides, the signal was insulated here, blocked. There would be no tracking it.

Kat stirred and stood up. The woman was dressed

137

casually, her auburn hair accented against a white cotton broadcloth shirt that was worn loose over tan slacks. She had been called to central command from home to oversee field operations, but with Gray's team still in the air, she found herself more useful here. Having a young daughter herself, Kat had brought in the copy of Dr. Seuss. Though the child remained unresponsive, she warmed up to Kat. Her rocking slowed.

Painter was happy to see Kat Bryant back at work. After the loss of her husband, Monk, she'd been adrift for many weeks. Yet now she seemed to be recovering, moving forward again.

Stepping out of the room, Kat closed the door softly and joined Painter in the neighboring observation room. High-backed chairs surrounded a conference table.

'She's asleep.' Kat sank into one of the chairs with a sigh.

'Maybe you should, too. It will be a few more hours until Gray's plane lands in India.'

She nodded. 'I'll check with the sitter who's watching Penelope, then crash for a couple of hours.'

The door to the outer hall opened. They both turned to see Lisa Cummings and the center's pathologist, Malcolm Jennings, enter the room. The two, dressed in matching white laboratory smocks and blue scrubs, were in an animated but whispered conversation. Lisa had her hands shoved in the pockets of her smock, pulling the coat tight to her shoulders, a sign of deep concentration. She had put her long blond hair up into a French braid. The pair had spent the last hour in the MRI suite, going over results.

From their heated, excited chatter – full of medical jargon beyond Painter's comprehension – they had come to some conclusions, though not necessarily a consensus.

'Neuromodulation of that scale without glial cell support?' Lisa said with a shake of her head. 'The stimulation of the nucleus basalis, of course, makes sense.'

'Does it?' Painter asked, drawing their attention.

Lisa seemed to finally see Painter and Kat. Her shoulders relaxed, and her hands left her pockets. A whispery smile feathered her features as her gaze met his. One of her hands trailed across Painter's shoulders as she passed and took one of the seats.

Malcolm took the last remaining seat. 'How's the child doing?'

'Asleep for the moment,' Kat said.

'So what have we learned?' Painter asked.

'That we're moving through a landscape both new and old,' Malcolm answered cryptically. He slipped on a pair of glasses, tinged slightly blue for reading computer screens with less eyestrain. He settled them in place and opened a laptop he'd carried under one arm. 'We've compiled the MRI scans of the child and my analysis of the skull. Both devices are the same, though the child's is more sophisticated.'

'What are they?' Kat asked.

'For the most part, they're TMS generators,' Malcolm answered.

'Transcranial magnetic stimulators,' Lisa elaborated, though that didn't help much.

Painter shared a confused expression with Kat. 'Why don't you start at the beginning?' he asked. 'And use small words.'

Malcolm tapped the side of his head with a pen. 'Then we'll start here. The human brain. Composed of *thirty billion* neurons. Each neuron communicates to its neighbors via multiple synapses. Creating roughly *one million billion* synaptic connections. These connections, in turn, create a very large number of neural circuits. And by *large,* I mean in the order of ten followed by a million zeros.'

'A million zeros?' Painter said.

Malcolm looked over the edge of his glasses at Painter.

'To give you some scale. The *total* number of atoms in the entire universe is only ten followed by *eighty* zeros.'

At Painter's shocked reaction, Malcolm nodded. 'So there's a vast amount of computing power locked in our skulls that we're only beginning to comprehend. We've just been scratching the surface.' He pointed toward the window. 'Someone out there has been delving much deeper.'

'What do you mean?' Kat asked, her expression showing worry for the girl.

'With our current technology, we've been making tentative strides into this new frontier. Like sending probes into space, we've been slipping electrodes into brains. All input into the brain is via electrical impulses. We don't see with our eyes. We see with our brains. It's why cochlear implants work to return hearing to the deaf. The implant turns sounds into electrical impulses, which are passed to the brain via a microelectrode inserted into the auditory nerve. Over time, the cortex learns to reinterpret this new signal, and like learning a new language, the deaf begin to hear.'

Malcolm waved to his laptop. 'The human brain – being electrical, being malleable to new signals – has an innate ability to connect to machines. In some regards, that makes us perfect natural-born cyborgs.'

Painter frowned. 'Where are you going with all this?'

Lisa placed a hand atop his. 'We're already there. The division between man and machine is already blurred. We now have microelectrodes so small that they can be inserted into individual neurons. At Brown University in 2006, they inserted a microchip into a paralyzed man's brain, linked by a hundred of these microelectrodes. Within four days of practicing, the man – *through his thoughts alone* – could move a computer cursor on a screen, open e-mail, control a television, and move a robotic arm. That's how far we've breached the frontier.'

Painter glanced to the window. 'And someone's gone farther than that?'

Both Lisa and Malcolm nodded.

'The device?' Painter asked.

'A step above anything we've seen. It has nanofilament electrodes so tiny that it's hard to say where the device ends and the child's brain begins. But the basic function is well known. From studies done at Harvard University on rats, we know that TMS devices promote the growth of neurons – though, oddly, only in areas involved with learning and memory. We still don't understand why. But what we do know is that magnetic stimulation can also turn on and off these neurons like a switch. Children are especially pliable in this manner.'

'So if I understand this all correctly, someone has wired such a device to the child, stimulated nerve growth in a specific area, and now controls its functioning like a switch.'

'Generally speaking, yes,' Malcolm said. 'They've tapped deep into that vast neural network I described. Only with the magnetic-stimulation of new neurons, they've expanded that network even farther. And if I'm right, I'd say they've focused that expansion in a very narrow area.'

'What makes you say that?'

'There's a law in neurology. Hebb's law. That basically states *nerves that fire together, wire together*. By stimulating one site in the brain, they are reinforcing it harder and harder.'

'But to what end?' Painter asked.

Malcolm shared a worried glance with Lisa. He wanted her to explain.

She sighed. 'I spoke to the psychologist, Zach Larson, who examined the girl when she was first brought in. From her nonresponsiveness, repetitive behavior, and sensitivity to stimulation, Zach is certain the girl is autistic. And from the behavior you described at the safe house, probably an autistic savant.'

Painter had read Larson's report, too. It had been put together quickly, but it had been thorough. He had run a small battery of psychological tests, including a genetic study for some of the typical markers for autism. The last was still pending.

He'd also included fact sheets on the subject of autistic savants, those rare individuals who – though compromised by their disorder – have amazing islands of talent. A skill that is deep and narrow. Painter remembered the character played by Dustin Hoffman in the movie *Rain Man*. His ability was to do lightning calculations. But this was only *one* of the savant talents on Larson's list. Others included calendar calculations, memorization skills, musical talent, mechanical and spatial skills, exquisite discrimination of smell, taste, or hearing, and also art.

Painter pictured the drawing of the Taj Mahal. It had been sketched in minutes, handsomely drawn to scale, with perfectly balanced perspective. The girl was certainly talented.

But was it more than that?

The last on Larson's list of savant talents was a rare and controversial report of some autistic savants who displayed extrasensory skills.

Painter could not dismiss that the girl's drawings had led the Gypsies unerringly to their safe house. He recalled the earlier discussion with Elizabeth, about her father's work on intuition and instinct, about his connection with a deep-black government project involved in remote viewing.

Lisa continued, 'We think the device is meant to stimulate that area of the brain where the savant talent lies. It's known that most savant talent arises from the right side of the brain, the same side where the device is attached on both the skull and the girl. Even using today's technology, it would not take much effort to localize the region regulating this talent. And once found, the magnetic stimulation could both amplify that area *and* control it.'

Painter stood with dawning horror. If Lisa and Malcolm were correct, someone was harnessing this child's abilities. He crossed toward the window.

Who did this to the girl?

Kat had joined Painter and pointed through the window. 'She's awake.'

And she was drawing again.

The girl had found a notepad and black felt pen on the bedside table. She scratched across it, not quite as frantically as before, but she was still bent with concentration over the page.

Kat headed to the door. Painter followed.

The girl did not acknowledge them, but as they stepped through, both pad and pen dropped to her bedsheet. She went back to rocking.

Kat stared down at the artwork, then fell back a step with a small gasp. Painter understood her reaction. There was no mistaking what was drawn in ink and paper, a portrait.

It was her husband, Monk.

Monk helped Pyotr along a fallen log that forded a deep stream, churning over jumbled rocks. Moss grew heavy on the log, along with a few fat white mushrooms. The entire place smelled damp.

Kiska was already on the other side, standing with Marta, holding the old chimpanzee's paw. Monk wanted to be across the next rise and into the neighboring valley. Hopping off the log, he stared behind him. They were crossing a dense birch forest, whose white-barked trunks looked like dried bone. The green foliage was already flamed in patches.

Monk picked one of the red leaves, rubbing it between his fingers. Still soft, not dried out. Early fall. But the changing leaves promised a cold night among the low mountains here. But at least there should be no snow. He dropped the crushed leaf.

How did he know all this?

He shook his head. Such answers would have to wait. Still, he found it disturbing how quickly he was growing accustomed to the disconnect between his lack of memory and his knowledge of the world. Then again, they were being hunted. They had to move quietly, sound carried far in the mountains. Through whispers and hand signals, they communicated.

Monk searched the far side of the stream. They had been on the run for the past three hours. He had set a hard pace, trying to put as much distance between them and where they'd exited the subterranean world. He didn't know how long it would take for the hunters to realize the escapees had abandoned the cavern and to pick up their trail out here.

Monk waited at the stream's edge.

144

Where was Konstantin?

As if beckoned by his thought, the taller boy came dancing down the far slope, as lithe and firm footed as a young buck. His face, though, was a mask of fear as he ambled, arms out, across the slippery log.

'I did it!' he said. Wheezing heavily, he jumped and landed next to Monk. 'I took your hospital nightshirt and dragged it to the stream in the other valley.'

'And you threw it in the water?'

'Past that beaver dam. Like you said.'

Monk nodded. His hospital nightshirt had been soiled with blood and sweat. One of the kids had stolen it from his room after he'd changed. It was smart thinking. If they'd left the shirt, his captors would have known he'd changed.

It also came in handy in laying a false trail. He had further soiled the shirt by wiping sweat from his brow and underarms. He had done the same with the kids and the chimpanzee, too. The riper garment should leave a stronger trail, a false trail. Hopefully the scent would send the hunters searching in the wrong direction.

'Help me with this,' Monk said to Konstantin and leaned down to the log they'd used to cross.

Together, the two got the log rocking, but they still couldn't dislodge it. Monk then felt a huff at his cheek. He turned to see Marta shouldering into the log. With a single heave, the chimpanzee rolled the fallen log into the stream. She was strong. The log fell with a heavy splash, then bobbed and teetered down the waterway. Monk watched it float away. The more ways they could break their trail, all the better.

Satisfied, Monk headed out.

Konstantin kept up, but Kiska and Pyotr struggled. The way was steep. Monk and Marta both helped the smaller children, hauling them up the harder patches. Finally, they reached the top of the rise. Ahead, more hills spread in all directions, mostly wooded with a few open meadows. Off to the left, not too far away, a wide patch of silver marked a large lake.

Monk stepped in that direction. With a lake like that, there should be people, someone who could help them.

Konstantin grabbed his elbow. 'We can't go that way. Only death lies that way.' His other hand squeezed the badge affixed to his belt, a radiation monitor.

In such verdant surroundings, Monk had forgotten about that danger. He flipped his badge up. Its surface was white, but as the radiation levels rose, it would begin to turn pink, then red, then dark crimson, then black. Sort of like a drugstore pregnancy test—

Photo-flashes of memory cracked across his vision.

—a laughing blue eye, tiny fingernails—

Then nothing again.

His head throbbed. He fingered the tender suture line through his wool cap. Konstantin looked at him with narrow, concerned eyes.

Kiska, who Monk had learned was Konstantin's sister, hugged her arms around her belly. 'I'm hungry,' she whispered, as if fearful of both being heard and of showing weakness.

Konstantin frowned in his sister's direction, but Monk knew they all should eat to keep their strength up. After their panicked flight, they needed a moment to regroup, to plan some strategy beyond running. Monk stared toward the lake while fingering his badge.

Only death lies that way.

He needed to better understand their situation.

'We'll find a place to shelter and eat quickly,' Monk said.

He crossed down into the next valley. A series of small ponds cascaded through a set of terraced ledges. The place sparkled with a dozen waterfalls and cataracts. The air smelled loamy and damp. Halfway down, a fern-strewn cliff side had been eroded into a pocket with an overhang. He led the children to it.

They hunkered down and opened packs. Protein bars and bottled water were passed around.

Monk searched his pack. No weapons, but he did find a topographic map. He unfolded it on the ground. The header was in Cyrillic. Konstantin joined him, chewing on a peanut-butter-flavored bar. Monk noted the mountainous landscape was marked with scores of tiny Xs.

'Mines,' Konstantin said. 'Uranium mines.' He ran a finger along the Cyrillic header, then waved an arm to encompass the area. 'The Southern Ural Mountains. Chelyabinsk district. Center of old weapons factories. Very dangerous.'

The boy tapped all around the map where radiological hazard symbols dotted the terrain. 'Many open mines, old radiochemical and plutonium plants. Nuclear waste facilities. All shut down, except for one or two.' He waved to indicate a far distance away.

Monk mumbled with a shake of his head, staring down at all the hazard symbols. 'And all I wanted to know was where we were.'

'Very dangerous, *da*,' Konstantin warned. He pointed an arm in the direction of the large lake, now out of sight. 'Lake Karachay. Liquid waste dumping ground for old Mayak atomic complex. You stand one hour by the lake and you will be dead a week later. We must go around.'

Konstantin leaned closer to the map and tapped in the center of a cluster of mines and radiation plants. 'We come from here. The Warren. An old underground city – Chelyabinsk 88 – where thousands of prisoners were housed who worked the mines. One of many such places.'

Monk pictured the industrial-looking buildings he

had seen in the cavern. Obviously someone else had found a new use for the abandoned place.

Konstantin continued, 'We must go around Lake Karachay – but not too near.' He glanced up to Monk to make sure he understood. 'Which means we must cross the Asanov swamp to reach here.'

The boy held his finger over another mine opening on the far side of the lake.

Monk didn't understand. Weren't they seeking to escape, to get to someone who could help them?

'What's there?' Monk asked, nodding to the mine marker.

'We must stop them.' Konstantin glanced to Pyotr, who cradled with Marta on a bed of moss.

'Stop who?' Monk remembered the young boy's words to him.

Save us.

Konstantin turned back to Monk. 'It is why we brought you here.'

11:30 A.M.

General-Major Savina Martov glowered at the assembled children. They were in the school's main auditorium. A photograph of the American glowed from a large LCD screen behind her.

'Has anyone seen this man lurking around early this morning? He may have been wearing a hospital gown.'

The children stared blankly at her from banks of wooden seats. They'd all been rousted early from their dormitories. More than sixty children sat in tiers, designated by the color of their shirts. The white-shirted sat at the back, those who carried the genetic markers but showed little talent. The grays sat in the middle, mildly talented, but not remarkable.

Unlike the ten who shared the front seats.

These last wore uniforms with black shirts. Omega class. Those rare few who displayed astounding talents. The dozen best, selected to serve Savina's son, Nicolas, in the hard times to come, to be his inner council with Savina as its head.

Nicolas was a sore point for Savina, a disappointment. He'd been born a white shirt. A loss of the genetic dice. Savina had impregnated herself via artificial insemination from one of the first generation. She'd been rash and paid dearly for it. She'd acted before they fully understood the genetics. There had been complications during the birth. She could have no other children. But she had developed a new purpose for Nicolas, one that would bring about true and lasting change. It became her life's work after Nicolas was born.

And they were so close.

She stared at the row of black shirts.

And the two empty seats in the Omega-class section.

One child had vanished last night.

Pyotr.

His sister had vanished at the same time from a zoo in America. Savina still had heard no update on the girl's status from Yuri. The man had gone strangely silent, not even responding to a transmitted emergency code.

Something was happening.

She needed answers. Her voice grew sharper. 'And no one saw Konstantin, Kiska, or Pyotr leaving their dorm rooms? *No one!*'

Again the blank stares.

Motion at the back of the room drew her eye. A toadish-looking man stepped into the room and nodded to her. Lieutenant Borsakov, her second in command. He was dressed in his usual gray uniform, including a stiff black-brimmed cap. He'd found something.

At last.

She turned to the trio of teachers standing to the side. 'Confine them to their dormitories. Under close guard. Until the matter is settled.'

She climbed the stairs and exited the auditorium, drawing Borsakov in her wake. Pock-faced and scarred, he stood only as high as her shoulders, which she preferred. She liked men shorter than herself. But he was bulky with muscle, and sometimes she caught him staring at her with a flicker of hunger. She preferred that, too.

He trailed a step behind her as they crossed through the school to the exit. Once outside, she found two of his men. One had a chained Russian wolf at his side. It growled and rumbled, curling back lips to expose sharp teeth. The guard yanked on the lead, scolding it.

Savina gave the creature a wide berth. A mix of Russian wolfhound and Siberian wolf, its muscular form stood almost to Borsakov's chest. The beast came from their animal research facility – nicknamed the Menagerie. It was where they experimented with new augments and tested various applications, using all manner of higher mammals: dogs, cats, pigs, sheep, chimps. It also served as a macabre petting zoo for the village. They'd found over the years that the children bonded with the animals and the relationship helped stabilize them psychologically. And maybe the bond wasn't entirely human-animal, but also augment to augment, a shared commonality.

Even the wolf bore a surgical steel device.

The augment capped the base of the dog's skull, attached via titanium screws and wired in place. With the touch of a button on the radio-transmitter, they could feed pain or pleasure, enhance aggression or docility, dull senses or stimulate arousal.

'What have you found, Lieutenant?' she asked.

'The children are not in the cavern,' he said.

She stopped and turned.

'We searched the entire village, even the deserted apartment complex, but when we circled wider, we discovered a scent trail along a back wall, behind the animal facility. It led to one of the service hatches to the surface.'

'They went outside?'

'We believe with the American from the hospital. The children's trail came *from* the hospital.'

So that at least answered one question. The American hadn't escaped, then kidnapped the children. It seemed it was the other way around. The children must have helped him escape.

But why?

What was so important about the man?

It was a question that had nagged Savina since the man had first arrived. Two months ago, Russian intelligence had been alerted about a plague ship that had been pirated in the Indonesian seas. Intelligence services around the world were looking for it. She had been tasked to see if her subjects could find it. A test. One she had passed. Primed, the twelve Omegas had pinpointed the island where the ship was being held. A Russian submersible was sent to investigate and came upon the lagoon just as the ship was sinking.

It was victory enough – until Sasha had begun scribbling with a fervor that almost burnt her augment out. A dozen pictures, from a dozen views, of a drowning man, being dragged down by a net. Believing this was significant – and being curious herself – Savina had alerted the Russian submariners. They already had divers in the water.

They found such a man, barely conscious, tangled in a net. They rushed up in diving sleds, forced a respirator into his mouth, and rescued him back to their submersible.

Savina had ordered the man brought here, believing he must be significant. But once at Chelyabinsk 88, he claimed to be just one of the cruise ship's electricians. During their interrogation, the man had not seemed especially bright to her, just a scarred and shaven brute of a man with a coarse vocabulary and missing one hand. Likewise, Sasha had showed no interest in him. Neither did any of her fellow Omega-class subjects.

It made no sense, and the man proved to be a nuisance, caught one day tapping into a surface broadcast trunk, wired to his prosthetic cuff. They did not know what he was doing nor what type of signal he had sent out, but in the end, it had no repercussions. For security's sake, they had the cuff surgically removed.

Over the weeks, Savina had grown to believe that the girl's intensity had just been a childish fear for the drowning man's life. Done with the matter, she had turned the American over to the care of the laboratory group at the Menagerie. They were studying memory, and a living human subject was raw material not to be wasted.

Savina had sat in on his surgery.

What they had done to him . . .

It still made her shudder.

But now he was gone – vanished with the brother of Sasha, who was also missing. What game were these children playing?

She didn't know, and this late in her own plans, she didn't have time to figure it out.

'Your orders, General-Major?'

'Search the surface.'

'I'll bring all the dogs,' his voice snapped.

She stopped him. 'Not just the dogs.'

Borsakov stared at her, his eyebrows pinched questioningly. But he knew what she wanted done. 'General-Major? What about the children?'

She strode away. Now was not the time for subtle actions. She still had ten children. That would be enough.

She confirmed her order. 'Loose the cats, too.'

Pyotr sat between Marta's legs. Her strong, warm arms wrapped around him. He didn't like to be touched, but he let her. The sweet earthy smell of her damp fur swelled around him. He heard the *hush-hush* of her breathing, felt the beat of her large heart in his own spine. He had known Marta all his life. He had known these arms. After Pyotr's first operation at the age of five, she was brought to his room.

He remembered her large hand. It had scared him, but she lay there for most of the day, her head resting on the edge of his bed, staring at him. Finally, one of his hands had drifted to hers. His fingers danced along the wrinkled lines of her overturned paw, curious. She had stared at him with large brown eyes, moist and knowing. Long fingers wrapped around his.

He knew what it was.

A promise.

Others would play with her, cry in her arms, sit long nights with her . . . but Pyotr knew a truth that morning. She had secrets that were his alone. And his secret was hers.

In those arms, he stared out at the strange woods. They were allowed up here sometimes, to wander the forest with a teacher, to sit in the quietness. But it still frightened Pyotr. A wind whispered through the forest, knocking limbs and shedding twirling falls of leaves. He watched them and knew something was coming.

He was not like his sister.

But some things he knew. He leaned deeper into Marta, away from the leaves. His heart beat faster and the world faded, all except for the leaves. Drifting, twirling, dancing . . . terrifying . . .

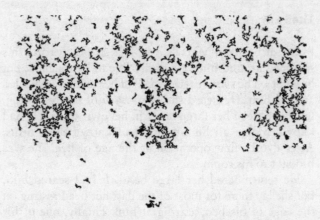

Marta hooted quietly in his ear. *What is wrong?*

He trembled and quaked. His heart was in his throat, pounding a warning as more and more leaves fell. He searched in the spaces among the leaves. Konstantin had once told him how he could multiply so fast in his head.

Every number has a shape ... even the biggest, longest number is a shape. So when I calculate, I look to the empty space between those two numbers. The gap also has a shape, formed by the boundaries of the other two numbers. And that empty shape, too, is a number. And that number is always the answer.

Pyotr didn't fully understand. He could not do math like Konstantin, nor could he solve puzzles like Kiska, nor could he see far like his sister. But Pyotr knew no one else who could do what he could do.

He could read hearts ... all sorts of hearts.

Great and small.

And something was coming, something with a dark, hungry heart.

Pyotr searched among the falling leaves as his own small heart hammered. He filled in the emptiness one space at a time.

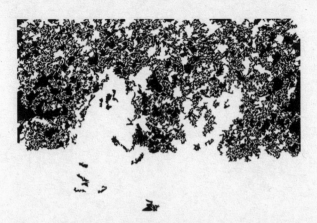

Sweat beaded on his forehead. The world was just falling leaves and the dark spaces between, swirling and churning, reaching for him. In the distance, he heard Konstantin shout his name.

Marta's arms tightened around him – not protecting him against the others, but holding him safe. She knew his heart, too.

He had to see.

Had to know.

Something was coming.

He filled the spaces with ink and shadow, with the teeth and growl, with the pound of pad on hard ground. He saw what was coming.

SECOND

8

Two hours until touchdown.

Gray stared out the windows of the Bombardier Global Express XRS. The day wore rapidly onward as the private jet streaked across the sky. During the course of their journey, the sun had risen on a new day, climbed over their heads, and had begun to fall again behind them. They would be landing on fumes, traveling at a squeak over supersonic speeds. The modified corporate jet had been gifted to Sigma by the billionaire aeronautics financier Ryder Blunt for past services rendered. Two U.S. Air Force pilots pushed the engines to get them to India by midafternoon local time.

Gray turned his attention back to the group assembled around a teak table. He had allowed everyone to sleep for six hours, but most looked exhausted. Kowalski still had his chair reclined flat, snoring in time with the engines. Gray saw no reason to disturb him. They all could use more sleep.

Focused on the dossier in front of her, the only person who showed no weariness was the newcomer to their small group. With expertise in neurology and neurochemistry, the same disciplines as Archibald Polk, it was no wonder Painter had assigned this member of Sigma to join their band.

Dr. Shay Rosauro was a little over average height, her complexion a cinnamon mocha, and her dark amber eyes sparked with flecks of gold and a fierce intelligence. Her shoulder-length black hair was bound back from her face with a black bandanna. She had served in the air force, and from her records, she could have piloted the Bombardier herself. She even wore a uniform blouse top with a wide black belt over khakis and boots.

And while Gray had never worked with her before, it seemed she had met Kowalski. She had done a double take when the large man had stepped into view. Kowalski had grinned, given her a bear hug of a greeting, then passed to climb into the plane. As she followed, she had stared back at Gray with an expression that read *you've got to be kidding*.

With everyone rested, Gray wanted to get his team on the same page by the time they were wheels down in India, especially in regard to whom they were meeting. 'Elizabeth, what can you tell us about Dr. Hayden Masterson? In what capacity was your father working with this professor from Mumbai?'

She nodded, stifled a yawn with a fist, then more firmly balanced her glasses on her nose. 'He's originally from Oxford, actually. Trained as a psychologist and physiologist, specializing in meditative techniques and brain function. He's been in India for the past thirty years, studying the country's yogis and mystics.'

'A line of research parallel to your father's.'

Elizabeth nodded.

'I know of Masterson's work,' Rosauro said with mild surprise. 'He's brilliant, but eccentric, and some of his theories are contentious. He was one of the first researchers to advocate for the plasticity of the human brain, controversial at the time but now readily accepted.'

'What do you mean by plasticity?' Gray asked.

'Well, until the past few years, neurology stuck by an old tenet that the human brain was *hardwired*, that each section of the brain served one purpose only. One location, one function. For the last two decades, neurology's goal has been to map out what each part of the brain does. Where speech rises from, which section of the brain handles hearing, which neurons make you feel your left hand, or control balance.'

Gray nodded.

'But now we understand that the brain is *not* hardwired, that these brain maps are changeable, alterable. Or in other words, *plastic*. It is such fluidity of function that explains how many stroke victims are able to regain function of paralyzed limbs after a portion of their brains are destroyed. The brain rewires itself around the damage.'

Elizabeth nodded. 'Dr. Masterson was extending his research to studies with yogis. Through such mystics' abilities to control their own metabolism and blood flow, he sought to show how the brain is not only changeable – but *trainable*. That the brain's plasticity is *moldable*.'

Rosauro leaned back. 'With the possibilities of harnessing this plasticity, it's a Brave New World out there for neurologists. Increasing intelligence, helping the blind to see, the deaf to hear.'

Gray pictured the device found on the skull. *The deaf to hear*. The device *had* looked like some form of cochlear implant.

Gray asked Elizabeth, 'Did Dr. Masterson say when he last saw your father?'

'The professor said he'd tell me more, but he first wanted to talk to the people who had hired my father. He sounded scared. I couldn't get anything else out of him.'

'Hired him?'

Luca Hearn, the final member of their group, spoke,

his Romani accent thicker from his exhaustion. 'That would be our clan. We hired Dr. Polk.'

Gray turned to the man. Before landing, Gray had intended to discuss the role of the Gypsies in Dr. Polk's story. Much had been left unanswered after their flight from the safe house. Such as, why Polk had chosen to contact Luca rather than anyone else? Had it been paranoia? Had the professor believed he could trust no one else? Considering his murder was followed by the suspicious sweep by agents of his own government, maybe Dr. Polk had been right.

'How did you get involved with the professor?' Gray asked.

'He approached us two years ago. He wanted to collect DNA samples from certain members of our clans. Those who practiced *pen dukkerin*.'

'*Pen* what?'

Kowalski answered from his sprawl on his bed. He had stopped snoring, but his eyes were still closed as he spoke. '*Dukkerin*. Fortune-telling. You know, palm reading, gazing in a crystal ball.'

Luca nodded. 'It is a tradition among our people, going back centuries, but Dr. Polk didn't want anyone who was performing *hokkani boro* – the great trick.'

'Fakers,' Kowalski added. 'Tricksters.'

'Dr. Polk knew there were those among our clans who we ourselves respected for their skill in this art. The rare ones. True *chovihanis*. Those with the gift. Those were who he sought.'

Elizabeth shifted straighter. 'My father was doing the same with yogis of India. Taking DNA samples, looking for some commonality.'

Gray remembered how her father sought out those rare cases of documented yogis and mystics, those who demonstrated heightened abilities of intuition or instinct. The fortune-telling and tarot-card reading of

162

the Gypsies would fit that mold. But the genetic angle was new.

It raised another question in Gray's mind. 'Why the sudden switch from studying yogis to Gypsies? What's the connection?'

Luca stared at him as if he were dense. 'Where do you think the Romani clans come from?'

Now it was Gray's turn to be baffled. He actually didn't know much about the nomadic Gypsy clans, certainly not their origins.

Luca noted his confusion. 'Not many know our story. When our clans first moved into Europe, we were thought to have come from Egypt.' He rubbed the back of his hand across his burnished face. 'Because of our dark skin, dark eyes. We were called *aigyptoi* or *Gyptians*, which later became the word *Gypsies*. Until only recently, even our clans were unsure of our origins. But linguists recently discovered that the Romani tongue has its roots in Sanskrit.'

'The language of ancient India,' Gray said, surprised, but he was beginning to understand the connection now.

'We arose from India. That is *amaro baro them*, our ancestral homeland. Northern India, to be precise, the Punjab region.'

'But why did you migrate away?' Elizabeth asked. 'From what I understand of your history, you had a hard time in Europe.'

'Hard time? We were persecuted, hunted, killed.' Fire entered his voice. 'We died by the hundreds of thousands at the hands of the Nazis, forced to wear the Black Triangle. *Bengesko niamso!*' This last was plainly a curse at the Nazis.

Elizabeth glanced away from his vehemence.

Luca shook his head, calming himself. 'Not much is known about our early past. Even historians can't say for certain *why* the clans left India. From old records, we know the Romani clans fled India sometime in the tenth century, passing through Persia to the empire of Byzantium and beyond. War plagued northwest India during that time. Also India had come to adopt a strict caste system. Those left at the bottom, classified as casteless, were deemed *untouchable*. These included thieves, musicians, dishonored warriors, but also *magicians*, those whose abilities were considered heretical by the local religions.'

'Your *chovihanis*,' Gray said.

Luca nodded. 'Life became unbearable, unsafe. So the casteless banded together into clans and left India, headed west, for more welcoming lands.' He snorted bitterly. 'We are still searching.'

'Let's get back to Dr. Polk,' Gray said, redirecting the conversation. 'Did you cooperate with the professor's request? Did you supply him with those samples?'

'We did. A payment in blood. In exchange for his help.'

Gray studied the man. 'Help in doing what?'

His voice fired up again. 'To find something stolen most brutally from us. The very heart of our people. We—'

The plane bumped violently. Glasses rose in the air, as did Kowalski. He scrabbled from his blanket with a shout of surprise. Gray, belted in his seat, felt his stomach climb into his throat. They lost elevation fast.

The pilot came on over the intercom. 'Sorry about that, folks. Hard air ahead.'

The whole plane shook.

'Buckle in tight,' the pilot continued. 'We'll have you on the ground in another hour. And, Commander Pierce, we have a land-to-air call for you coming from Director Crowe. I'll patch it back to you.'

Gray motioned everyone into their seats. Kowalski had raised his seat back and was already snugging his belt tight.

Swiveling his own chair away from the others, Gray removed the phone from his armrest and lifted it to his ear.

'Commander Pierce here.'

'Gray, I thought I'd brief you on what Lisa and Malcolm learned about the device attached to the skull.'

As Gray listened to the director explain about microelectrodes and autistic savants, he stared out the window. He watched the sun settle to the west as the jet screamed to the east. He pictured the girl's small face, her fragility, her innocence.

At least she was safe.

But a question nagged at Gray.

Are there others like her out there?

12:22 P.M.
Southern Ural Mountains

Monk ran with Pyotr in his arms alongside the streambed. The boy clung to him. His eyes were still glassy, his face damp with both sweat and tears. Kiska raced ahead, following the long lope of Marta, who knuckled with both arms. Konstantin kept to Monk's side.

'How do we know what Pyotr saw was real?' Monk gasped out to Konstantin. 'Tigers? Maybe it was just a daydream, a waking nightmare.'

The older boy turned slightly and pulled his wool cap up. He combed back his hair to reveal a shiny curve of steel behind his ear. 'You were not the only one operated on.' He pulled down his cap and nodded to Pyotr. 'What he saw was no dream.'

Monk struggled to comprehend. Konstantin had already explained how Monk had ended up here, rescued

165

from a sinking cruise ship, based on a drawing done by Pyotr's sister. It made no sense.

Maybe *he* was the one dreaming.

Konstantin continued, 'There are two Siberian tigers kept at the Menagerie. Arkady and Zakhar. The soldiers sometimes hunt with them in the deep forest. Wild boar and elk. They are very smart. Not easy to fool.'

'How far away?' Monk asked.

Konstantin spoke in Russian to the boy.

Pyotr answered in the same tongue. As he spoke, his voice grew firmer, coming more fully out of his trance.

Konstantin finally nodded. 'He does not know. Only that they are coming. He can taste their hunger.'

Monk hurried them down the stream to where it emptied into a wider river. He heard the rush of water before seeing the course. It dug a deep channel. If they could get across—

Something screamed into the air. High overhead and farther back up the narrow valley. It kept on wailing, piercing like a siren. It made his teeth ache and vibrated his bones. The children dropped flat to the ground, covering their heads and rolling in agony. Marta hooted and trotted a protective ring around them.

Cringing against the noise, Monk peered up between spruce branches. Something wafted down into the back half of the valley. It drifted on a red parachute, like a flare, but it carried a round metal object the size of a baseball. The piercing wail came from it. Some sort of sonic flare. Climbing on a boulder, Monk spotted other red pinpricks in the distance. More flares.

He hopped down.

They must be blindly strafing in all directions.

A frantic crashing erupted on the far side of the stream.

Monk caught a flash of tawny fur. His heart thudded in panic.

Tiger.

Instead, two roe deer smashed into view, and with a flash of dancing hooves, they darted away. Monk forced his heart out of his throat and crossed to the children. The sonic blast had flattened them. The hunters knew of the kids' hypersensitivity and were trying to immobilize them.

Monk scooped Pyotr up with his stumped arm and tossed him across his shoulder. He dragged Kiska to her feet and supported her around the waist, hiking her up. Burdened, Monk crossed to Konstantin, intending to kick the boy into action.

They dared not stop.

Marta intervened. She nosed under Konstantin's chest and pulled one of his arms over her back. Supporting him with her shoulders, she sidled down toward the river below. The boy's legs dragged behind her.

Monk followed with the other two children. While deafened by the sonic flare, Monk still felt the boy's trembling moans of agony. He hobbled faster and reached the river's course.

The water flowed through a steep-banked channel, a full four meters wide. It churned and gurgled, loud enough to dull the sharper ranges of the sonic flare.

Monk waved to Marta. He pointed downriver. She swung in that direction. They continued, following the twisting course. After a few turns, the steep ridges blocked more and more of the wailing.

Kiska stirred first. She knocked free of Monk's arm and gained her own feet. She still covered her ears with her hands. Konstantin soon followed, freeing Marta, who panted and gasped, knuckling on both arms.

As they fled from the screams, Monk kept a watch behind him.

Expecting at any moment to see a pair of tigers loping after them.

Distracted, he ran into Kiska, who had stopped. Tangled, he toppled to his knees, dropping the boy to the ground.

Konstantin had also halted at his sister's side, frozen in place with Marta. It seemed they had more to fear than just the hunters behind them.

Beyond the pair, a massive brown bear rose up from the riverbank. It had to weigh six hundred pounds, damp from the river and plainly tense from the caterwauling of the flares. Black eyes stared back at their party. It rose up on its hind limbs, stretching eight feet tall, bristling, growling, baring yellow teeth.

The Russian grizzly.

The symbol of Mother Russia.

With a roar, it fell and charged straight at them.

6:03 A.M.
Washington, D.C.

The old man woke into brightness. It stung his eyes and pounded into his skull. He groaned and turned his head away. Nausea spilled burning gorge up into his throat. He choked it back down with a gasp.

He blinked away the glare and found himself strapped to a bed. Though a sheet covered him, he knew he was naked. The room was stark white, clinical, sterile. No windows. A single door with a small barred window. Closed.

A figure sat in a chair beside the bed, in a suit, the jacket hung on the seat back, sleeves rolled up. His legs were crossed, his hands folded primly on his lap.

He leaned forward. 'Good morning, Yuri.'

Trent McBride smiled down at him without a trace of warmth.

Yuri glanced down to his chest, remembering being shot by a tranquilizer dart. He searched around, still confused, dazed.

'You've been given a counterstimulant,' McBride said. 'Must have you alert, since we have much to discuss.'

'*Kak . . . ya . . .* ,' he choked out, his tongue pasty and thick.

McBride sighed, reached to a bedside table where a glass with a straw rested, and offered Yuri a sip.

He did not refuse. The lukewarm liquid burned like the finest vodka. It pushed back the shadows at the edges of his thoughts and washed the paste from his tongue.

'Trent, what are you doing?' Yuri tugged at the straps that bound down his arms.

'Filling in the blanks.' McBride pressed an intercom button at the head of the bed. 'As I mentioned, you've not been forthcoming with all the details of your research at Chelyabinsk 88. We must correct that oversight.'

'How do you mean?' Yuri tried to sound innocent, but he failed miserably as his voice shook. He wished he were a stronger man.

'Hmm,' Trent said. He leaned forward and stripped the sheet covering Yuri. 'I suppose we might as well get the ugly part over with so we can speak like true colleagues.'

Yuri stared down at his naked body. His pale skin was dotted by tiny suction cups, each the size of a dime, topped by a pea-size knot of electronics sprouting a thread-thin antenna. They lined his legs from toe to groin, his arms from fingertip to shoulder. His chest was a chessboard grid of the sticky cups.

Before he could question what they were, the door to the room opened and a slender figure entered. Yuri had to struggle a moment to remember his name, though he had just met the man. Dr. James Chen. They had used the researcher's office for the meeting at Walter Reed.

The door clamped shut, soundproofed.

Chen crossed to them. He carried a laptop open in his arms. 'We're all calibrated.'

As the man settled into a seat and rested his laptop on the bedside table, Yuri caught a glimpse of the computer screen before it was swung away. It had a stylized figure of an outstretched man dotted with small glowing circles.

'Electroacupuncture,' McBride said and waved a hand over the array of suction cups. 'Microelectrodes inserted into acupuncture points along the prime meridians. I don't purport to understand it fully. This is Dr. Chen's line of expertise. He's made remarkable progress using this technique to alleviate pain, allowing battlefield surgery without general anesthesia. Brilliant work and why he became a Jason. I then recruited him to our joint investigation because of his innovative use of microelectrodes. Microelectrodes like you used with your own test subjects.'

McBride tweaked one of the antennas with a finger. Yuri felt a stinging stab. 'We've learned that what can be used to deaden pain in the right circumstances, can also be used to *amplify* it.'

'Trent . . . don't . . . ,' Yuri begged.

McBride ignored him, turned to Chen, and pointed to one of the cups near his knee, then to a second one near his groin.

The researcher lifted a stylus and drew a line on the computer screen.

Yuri's leg blistered with fiery pain. A scream burst from his throat. It was as if someone had dug a scalpel from knee to groin, cutting down to the bone. Then it ended just as quickly.

Gasping, Yuri searched down. He expected to see blood flowing, flesh smoking. But there was only pale skin.

McBride waved again across the field of tiny cups. 'We can do the same across any of these points. In any pattern. We can flay you alive without harming a hair. A virtual operation with *all* the pain.'

'Wh-why?'

McBride stared down at him again. While his face

was mild, his eyes were fierce. 'I will have answers, yes? Let's start with what you've been keeping secret about the children.'

'I don't—'

McBride turned to Chen.

'No!' Yuri shouted out.

McBride leaned back to him. 'Then let's not play games. We've been able to replicate your augments without any difficulty. The schematics that your team provided were very thorough and precise. But in the end, not all that innovative. Merely a sophisticated TMS device. We attempted to duplicate your results, using a pair of autistic savant children in Canada. Our experiments were . . . well, let's just say disappointing.'

Yuri inwardly cringed. So the Americans were closer than even Savina had suspected. They'd already come to recognize how unique the situation was at Chelyabinsk 88.

'So,' McBride asked again, 'what have you been keeping secret from us?'

Yuri hesitated too long. A fiery slash cut across his chest. His muscles spasmed, his back arched from the bed. He screamed so loudly that no sound came out.

As the pain cut off, Yuri trembled and quaked with aftershocks. He tasted blood on his tongue. Still he dared not wait. What did it matter if the Americans found out? It was already too late.

'DNA,' he gasped out. 'It's their DNA.'

McBride hovered closer. 'How do you mean?'

Yuri swallowed, gulping for air. 'The secret lies in the subjects' genetics. We only discovered this ourselves twelve years ago.'

Yuri explained in fits and starts, questioned repeatedly by McBride. He related the discovery in 1959 of a cluster of exceptional savant talent, a group of Gypsy children. A genetic line that ran through the history of the Gypsies.

The *chovihanis*. The clans kept this line secret and attempted to preserve it through inbreeding, resulting in genetic aberrations. He told how the Russians had stolen this genetic heritage for study, for incorporation into their own research into parapsychology.

'But it was nothing mystical,' Yuri explained. 'The children were merely savants . . . though savants of a *prodigious* level. We tried to heighten their ability – first through breeding, then through bioengineering. But over the years, as genetic testing grew more refined, we were able to pinpoint what made the children unique.'

McBride leaned closer.

'Autism is triggered by a mix of environmental factors coupled with a variable number of ten genes. What we discovered was that the strongest of the savants – our Omega-class subjects – carried a specific *three* genes. Three genetic markers. When they appeared in just the right sequence, coupled with mild to moderate autism, an amazing savant talent would arise.'

'Which you in turn augmented further,' McBride said. 'Creating a perfect storm of genetics and bioengineering.'

Yuri nodded.

'Brilliant. Truly brilliant. Then it was just as well we used Archibald to lure one of your Omega subjects out into the open. And all the more reason for us to get hold of that girl.'

Yuri startled. Concern rang through him. 'You don't have Sasha?'

McBride frowned and tilted back to his chair. 'No, but in the past hour, we've determined where she is likely being kept. And it seems the same group has sent a team to follow in Archibald's footsteps. Luckily we have taken measures to erase those footsteps completely.'

'Who . . . who has Sasha?'

'You want to know?' McBride glowered down at Yuri. It was plainly a sore spot for the man. 'I'll show you.'

He motioned to Chen.

No!

Yuri's chest lit with fire, streaking in jagged lines across his chest, linking point to point, forming a crooked symbol on his chest, a letter, a fiery Greek letter.

McBride growled through Yuri's agony. 'They won't be a problem for long.'

2:04 P.M.
Agra, India

Despite her father's fascination, Elizabeth had never been to India. She stared out the taxi van as it swept away from the airport. The windows were down but offered little relief from the heat, well over a hundred degrees.

Traffic moved at a snail's pace, snarled amid rickshaws pulled by both bicycles and even one camel. She was close enough to a neighboring taxi, whose windows were also open, that she could smell the driver's thin cigar as he chewed on its end. The smoke cut like a knife through the density of the city's mélange of curry, filth, and cooking grease. The neighboring driver huffed at the traffic and pounded the heel of his hand on his horn.

The blare was barely heard above the chaos, made worse by a festival under way ahead, bright with the sounds of cymbals. All around, pedestrians packed the sidewalks and walked through the creeping cars, fighting for space with bicycles and motorcycles.

Elizabeth found her breathing growing heavier, her chest constricting – not from the humidity and heat but from the press of humanity. She wasn't normally claustrophobic, but the noise, the unending vibrancy, the hawk and holler of so many people, blanketed her, squeezed her. Her hands formed fists on her knees.

Finally, through judicious use of his own horn, the taxi driver broke through a gap and pushed for the next intersection. He turned the corner, and the way opened to a wider thoroughfare that aimed straight for the heart of the city.

Elizabeth sighed in relief.

'Finally,' Kowalski said next to her, echoing her sentiment. 'We should've rented a van. I could've gotten us there faster.'

The large man was crammed against her side, but he seemed to sense her distress and tried to keep back, which didn't help the other passenger sharing their row.

Beyond Kowalski, Shay Rosauro elbowed the large man for more room. Her face shone with a sheen of sweat. She had used the time stuck in traffic to undo the black bandanna that bound her hair and refold it into an efficient head scarf that tucked behind her ears.

Gray, who sat in the front passenger's seat of the van, leaned toward the driver and pointed. The driver nodded. Gray settled back into place.

The final member of their company sat in the back row of the van. Luca Hearn wore an inscrutable expression, but his dark eyes seemed to watch everything. He had strapped two daggers to wrist sheaths before leaving the plane, prepared for an unwelcome homecoming to the land of his people.

Gray twisted in his seat. 'We'll be at the hotel in another ten minutes,' he called back to them.

The taxi sped to where the road ended at the Yamuna River. Its waters glinted like blue steel in the bright sunlight, lined by palms. To the left rose a massive fort built of red sandstone, with high parapets and thick walls. Reaching the river, they turned away from the fort and followed the curve of the waterway.

Traffic slowed again, but in only a few minutes, the view opened to the left, revealing an expansive parkland of meadows, gardens, reflecting pools, and patches of forest. The greenbelt hugged the banks of the river, but the true wonder seemed to float above it all, a cloud of white marble set against the shimmering blue sky.

The Taj Mahal.

The mausoleum was an engineering wonder and an architectural marvel. But at the moment, it appeared more like a dream, aglow and drifting in the heavens. Built over three centuries ago by the Mughal emperor Shāh Jāhan, to mark the final resting place of his beloved wife, it was to many a testament to the eternity of love.

But it was not their destination.

The taxi van skirted to the side and pulled up to a five-story white building, lined at each level by large arched windows, the Deedar-e-Taj Hotel. It was here they were to meet Dr. Hayden Masterson.

'The restaurant is on the top,' Elizabeth said as they piled out. She checked her watch. They were half an hour late.

Gray paid the driver, and they all crossed past a dancing fountain into the hotel lobby, gloriously air-conditioned.

'Kowalski,' Gray said and pointed to the front desk, 'you and Luca secure our rooms. We'll head up.' He nodded to Elizabeth and Rosauro.

Kowalski sighed heavily, but he mumbled something about a cold shower. He hovered a moment near

Elizabeth as Gray turned toward the elevator. 'Are you okay?' he mumbled to her.

'Me?'

'Back in the taxi. I thought maybe . . . you looked sort of . . .' He shrugged.

'Just the heat . . . maybe nerves,' she mumbled.

'I have just the ticket.' He leaned conspiratorially over to her and parted his suit jacket enough to reveal two cigars in an inner pocket. 'Cubans. From the duty-free shop at the airport.'

She smiled at him. She could almost kiss him right now.

Before she could say anything, the elevator chimed behind her. Gray called for her to hurry.

Kowalski straightened and patted his jacket. He winked at her as he turned away. Actually *winked*. Who still winked? Still, her smile did linger on her lips as she turned to join Gray and Rosauro.

Gray ushered her inside and punched the button for the top floor. 'Is there anything else we should know about Dr. Masterson?' he asked her.

'Just don't mention Manchester United,' she mumbled.

'The soccer team?'

'Trust me, or you'll never hear a word about my father or his research. Also, don't push him. Let him get to the point in his own time.'

The elevator doors whisked open upon a strange sight. A large restaurant filled the roof level, sparsely occupied at this hour. Tables were set with linen and fine china. The smell of curry and garlic lingered tantalizingly in the air.

But what was unusual was that the entire restaurant slowly *rotated*. It spun through a panoramic view of the city, including the Taj Mahal.

At a table by one of the windows, a tall man unfolded from his seat. He lifted an arm, then lowered it, and tapped at his wristwatch.

Elizabeth smiled and crossed toward him, stepping onto the turning platform. It was a bit disconcerting at first, but she led the others forward through the nests of empty tables. A few servers in gold vests nodded a greeting to them.

It had been several years since she had last seen Dr. Masterson. He still wore his characteristic white suit, formal, colonial, with a wide-brimmed Panama hat that rested on a neighboring table. A cane leaned there, too, with a hooked ivory handle carved in the shape of a white crane. His hair, worn long to the shoulder, had also gone white to match, which she was sure did not entirely displease him. His face was craggy, leathery, tanned to a deep bronze that by now probably never faded.

Elizabeth made formal introductions. Dr. Shay Rosauro expressed what an honor it was to meet him, which went a long way to turning his irritated frown into something that bordered on welcoming. Women were a weakness of Hayden's, especially the attention of someone as long-limbed and lithe as Dr. Rosauro. Elizabeth's father had once hinted at *why* the professor had remained at the University of Mumbai, versus Oxford or Cambridge. It seemed to involve a sticky matter concerning an undergraduate student.

Hayden waved them all to their seats, making sure Dr. Rosauro was positioned next to him. By the time they were situated, the restaurant had rotated to a stunning view of the Taj Mahal.

Hayden noted their attention. 'The mausoleum to Mumtaz Mahal, wife of the Shāh Jāhan,!' he said with a bluster. 'That dear wife of the emperor extracted four promises from the bloke.' He ticked them off with his fingers. 'To build a great tomb to her, of course. Second, that he *would* marry again. Now that's a wife! Third, that he'd be forever kind to their children. And lastly, that Jahan would visit her tomb each year on the anniversary of her death. Which he did honor, until the day he was buried in the Taj with his dear wife.'

'True love,' Rosauro said, staring out at the beauty of the mausoleum.

'And what's a love story without a little spilled blood?' Hayden said and patted Rosauro's hand. He left his palm resting there. 'It is alleged that Jahan had the hands of all his artisans chopped off upon completion of the tomb, to ensure that they could never again build a monument with such grace as the Taj Mahal.'

At Hayden's other side, Gray stirred, plainly anxious to bring the discussion to bear on the reason they'd all traveled halfway around the globe. Elizabeth brushed her toe against Gray's, warning him.

His eyes met hers.

Don't push him, she silently communicated.

As she faced around, Hayden's right ear blew away with a spray of blood – at the exact time a sharp *chime* rang out like struck crystal.

Gray and Rosauro both moved while Elizabeth was still frozen in place. Rosauro yanked Hayden down to the floor; Gray tackled into Elizabeth. She caught a glimpse of a perfect hole in the pane of glass behind Hayden, radiating cracks.

As she fell, more holes appeared with ringing *cracks* – then she hit the floor, Gray on top of her.

'Stay down!'

She cringed flat as a barrage of gunfire ripped through the restaurant, coming from some sniper on a neighboring rooftop. Crystal glassware shattered. One of the servers twisted around, as if kicked, and fell flat. Blood poured out onto the tile floor.

Gray urged her to crawl. But Elizabeth was too afraid to move. The sniper couldn't shoot her if she remained where she was. Gray corrected her of this misconception.

'He's pinning us down!' he hollered to both Elizabeth and Hayden, who also seemed unwilling to move. 'Trying to hold us here!'

Elizabeth understood what that implied. She gained her hands and knees. They had to move. Now.

More gunmen were on their way here.

9

As the bear charged, the large man shoved Pyotr down the steep riverbank. Arms out, he struck hard and rolled. Branches poked, something scraped his cheek. Pyotr tumbled toward the river, scrabbling amid the wet ferns and slippery beds of pine needles. He didn't know how to swim. Water terrified him.

Sharper screams cut through the bear's roar.

His friends.

Konstantin and Kiska.

Pyotr's knee struck a rock with a pain that shot to his spine. He landed flat on the riverbank's edge. Water swirled past his nose.

He cringed back from his reflection in the dark waters. His image swam and churned, sunlight glinted and sparked as a strong gust stirred the branches overhanging the river.

Pyotr hung there in that scintillating moment of terror, suspended above the dark, dazzling water.

He'd had no warning of the brown bear until it rose up before them. Its gentle heart had been overshadowed by the hunger that hunted them, its steady beat muffled by the strident siren behind them.

181

Still, Pyotr's terror spiked higher.
Not because of the water.
Not because of the bear.
Light and dark swirled under him. Oil on water.

Not the bear.
Not the bear.
He panted in dread.
The bear was not the danger.
Something else . . .

Monk raised his pack, his only weapon, as the bear pounded down upon him. He had shoved Pyotr toward the water and the other two children into the underbrush on the other side. Marta leaped to a low branch and swung down toward Pyotr.

Monk hollered and swung his pack high in the air.

The bear barreled straight at him. Monk flung the pack hard and leaped to the side. Too late. As he flew, the bear struck his legs like a freight train, flipping Monk sideways. The pack bounced uselessly off its furry shoulders.

Monk hit the trunk of a larch tree broadside and crumpled to its base. With the wind knocked from him, he gasped and fought to his feet, his arms up to protect his face and head.

But the bear ignored him and charged onward down the deer track.

Monk stumbled back to the path. Forty yards away, the bear bowled into two shadowy shapes lurking there. Two tall wolves, long limbed and snarling. The bear swatted a massive paw and sent one wolf flying, end over end. The other leaped for the bear's throat but found only yellow teeth and a fierce bellow of rage. The wolf howled, but still fought.

Monk noticed the cap of steel on the back of the wolves' skulls. Hunters from the underground city. Scouts. There could be more.

Monk quickly gathered Konstantin and Kiska. Marta appeared, with Pyotr riding her back. Monk collected the boy and pointed.

'Run!' he whispered.

They took off together. If there were other hunters on the trail behind them, they would have to get past the bear. It offered some protection.

Monk glanced back as the battle continued amid

roars and howls. The bear had reacted with swift and deadly aggression, responding with a blind hostility that bordered on fury. Did the bear have experience with these wolves? Had the soldiers hunted the woods with them? Or was it something more fundamental, a reaction to an affront against nature. Like a lioness swiftly killing off a deformed cub.

Either way, it bought Monk and the children some extra leeway.

But for how long?

2:28 P.M.
Agra, India

Gray herded everyone across the shattered restaurant. Without a clear target, the continual barrage from the sniper had died down to bursts, enough to keep them pinned low.

Moving in a crouch, Gray aimed for the fire exit. The stairwell opened beside the elevator. They dared not use the lift. Whoever arranged this ambush surely had people posted in the lobby, watching the front exit and elevator bay. To call for the lift would only alert any men posted below. They'd be trapped. The only hope was to use the stairs to reach another level of the hotel and hole up in one of the rooms and regroup.

Their route to the stairwell was confounded by the rotation of the floor, but Gray knew the motion had also saved Dr. Masterson's life. That first bullet had been meant for the back of the professor's skull. The rotation of the floor must have thrown off the sniper's aim, turning a fatal shot into a grazing wound.

Gray had to give the old guy some credit. After the initial shock, he seemed hardly fazed. He pressed a cloth napkin against his ear, already soaked with blood. He had somehow managed to grab his white hat and had it perched aslant on his head. Rosauro kept to his side, bearing the man's ivory-handled cane.

Gray and Elizabeth reached the stationary lobby of the restaurant, followed a step behind by Rosauro and Masterson. 'The stairs,' Gray said.

'On it.'

Rosauro dashed across the lobby in two running strides, then slid low to the door like a baseball player stealing home. She smoothly slipped a Sig Sauer semiautomatic from an ankle holster. Staying on her knees, she reached up, yanked the handle, and used her shoulder to nudge the door open, just wide enough to cover with her pistol and observe the stairs.

Gray heard it immediately. Boots pounded up the tile stairs. Many boots.

'Seven to ten,' Rosauro assessed.

They were too late.

'Hold them back,' Gray ordered and rolled over to the elevator.

Noting his destination, Elizabeth reached for one of the call buttons, but Gray blocked her before she could press it. According to the lighted display above the doors, the cage was still waiting at the lobby level. It was surely under watch.

Gray scooted over to one of the restaurant's service stations and found a carving knife and an armful of folded tablecloths. He returned to the elevator and slipped the knife between the doors. He levered the blade enough to get his fingers and the tip of a boot through the gap. With a single heave, he shoved the doors open.

As he did so, the *crack* of a pistol blasted – followed by a cry of surprise and pain from the stairwell. A short spat of gunplay followed. But Rosauro had the higher ground. Gray didn't know how long that advantage would hold out. If they rushed her post, she'd be swamped.

They had to move fast.

Beyond the open doors, the elevator shaft was pitch dark. Two oily cables dangled. There was also a metal service ladder to one side.

They'd never have time to climb.

Gray passed the tablecloths to Masterson and Elizabeth. He showed them how to bundle them between their hands. 'It's only a short step,' he assured them and pointed to the cables. 'Hang tight and brake with your shoes. Try not to make too much noise when you get to the cage below. Wait for us there.'

He got a worried nod from Elizabeth and a roll of the eyes from Masterson. But the gunfire discouraged any dissent. Elizabeth pressed forward first. She reached out with her wrapped hands and leaped to the cables. With a small cry, she slid down the shaft.

Once she disappeared into the gloom, Masterson followed, securing his cane under his pant belt, like a sword in a scabbard. He was tall and long-limbed enough to reach the cables by stretching his arms out.

Down he went.

'Go!' Rosauro called to him. She did not turn but fired two quick shots. 'I'll be right behind you.'

'The elevator latch—'

'Go, Pierce!'

Gray knew better than to argue with a woman . . . especially one with a gun. He bundled his hands, leaped, and mounted the cable. He slid down with a shout back to Rosauro.

Before he even finished his yell, she appeared at the lip overhead, limned against the brightness. She swung to the service ladder, yanked the inside latch, and closed the elevator doors. Darkness swallowed Gray as he slid down the cable. He felt the line shake as Rosauro joined him.

Gray's eyes quickly grew accustomed to the gloom. Weak light filtered through each level's doors. As he slid past the floors, counting them down, he made out the shadowy elevator car below. Two figures huddled together at one corner.

A tiny flicker of flame ignited below.

Elizabeth's cigarette lighter.

Gray braked his descent and landed lightly atop the elevator.

A moment later, Rosauro dropped next to him.

Gray found the service hatch. He removed his own weapon and opened the hatch enough to peek through. The cage was empty below, the doors closed. He motioned the others to remain on top.

Gripping the edge of the hatchway with one hand, Gray swung down and dropped into a crouch, his weapon up. He reached for the button that opened the doors. He heard shouts and panic coming from the lobby. The gunfire had stirred the sleepy hotel into a beehive.

Just as well.

The chaos could serve them.

Gray hit the button, and the doors parted. He darted out as soon as there was enough space and ducked to the left, where a waist-high planter supported a dwarf palm tree.

The lobby churned and milled with people. Management yelled in both Hindi and English.

Steps away, Gray immediately picked out two people who looked too calm, wearing jackets despite the heat. Hands in pockets. He noted earpieces in place.

They spotted him, too.

But his sudden and unexpected appearance caught them off guard. Despite the crowd, Gray had no choice but to react quickly. A prolonged firefight would only threaten more lives.

With his weapon already raised through the palm leaves, he squeezed the trigger and dropped the first man with a headshot. Pivoting on his toe, he squeezed twice more in rapid succession, knowing his aim was not as fixed. The first shot struck the man's shoulder, spinning him back. The second went wide and buried itself into the plaster wall.

The gunman fired through the pocket of his jacket, but Gray dropped to the floor as plaster blasted behind him. Lying on his shoulder, arms extended, he fired again, a few inches from the floor. The assailant's ankle exploded, and he toppled face forward and hit the marble floor hard with his chin, shattering bone. He didn't move again.

Gray turned to the elevator in time to see the cage doors slip closed.

The bystanders in the lobby, stunned for a breath, emptied in all directions with screams and shouts.

Gray stabbed the button.

Nothing.

He glanced up to the lighted display. The elevator had been called.

It was headed *up*.

Up toward the gunmen in the rooftop restaurant.

Crouching atop the elevator, Elizabeth heard the lift pulleys engage. With a lurch, the car began to rise. The elevator had been called.

'*Mierda* . . . ,' Rosauro swore next to her.

Elizabeth stared up to the dark shaft. 'What are we going to do?' she asked. She still held her lighter, flickering with a tiny flame. She felt helpless, and she hated how her hands shook.

'You're going to stay here,' Rosauro said and leaned forward and blew out the flame. 'In the dark. Not a word. Not a sound.'

The woman sat on the lip of the hatch, then dropped down into the elevator.

'Close the door,' she called quietly up to them. 'But keep it unlocked. Just in case.'

In case of what?

Still, Elizabeth obeyed. She swung the hatch almost closed, holding it ajar with her pinky. Her last sight of Rosauro was as the woman readied her weapon.

Biting back a curse as the elevator lifted away, Gray ran for the stairs. He knocked a few people aside and leaped over a couple huddled low on the stairs, covering their heads. He mounted the stairs three at a time, racing around and around, pausing only long enough to make sure the car hadn't stopped. If he could get above it and hit the call button, then he could stop the elevator before it reached the roof.

He missed it on the second level and sprinted.

Shouts called from above, deep-throated and brusque. It sounded like the assault team was headed back down. Gray burst onto the third floor to check the elevator and ran smack into a wall – or rather, the human equivalent of it.

Kowalski stood at the elevator bay, finger on the button.

'Gray!' he said, rubbing his stomach. 'Ow, what the hell, man?'

The elevator chimed open.

Rosauro leaped out, her pistol pressed into Kowalski's face.

'Hey!' He bumped back a step.

'*You* called the elevator?' Gray asked.

'Yeah, I was going up to the restaurant, find out what all the commotion was.'

Gray didn't know which was Kowalski's greatest asset: his thickheadedness or his laziness.

'Everybody out!' Gray yelled.

Rosauro was already in motion, helping Elizabeth and Masterson down through the hatch. Gray led them back to the stairs. Kowalski brought up their rear.

Rosauro moved alongside him as they fled down the stairs. 'I heard them speaking English. No British accents. American.'

Gray nodded.

Mercenaries from the look of the pair in the lobby.

Still, he pictured the man he'd spotted outside the Museum of American History. With the name badge from the Defense Intelligence Agency. Mapplethorpe. Someone knew they'd be here.

They reached the deserted lobby. Gray urged everyone toward the open door – but before they could reach it, a figure stepped into view. He shouldered a snub-nosed M4 carbine assault rifle. Additionally, strapped to his back, he bore a long-barreled M24, fitted with a sniper's scope.

It was the gunman from the neighboring rooftop.

The barrel of his weapon pointed at Masterson's nose.

The sniper didn't intend to miss *this* shot.

Then the gunman's head snapped backward. He dropped to his knees like a puppet with its strings cut. Then fell face forward with a clatter. At the base of his skull, the shiny steel handle of a throwing dagger protruded.

Beyond the body, Luca stood outside by the dancing fountain. The Gypsy had another dagger ready in his hand. Gray kicked away the loose rifle, which Kowalski retrieved. Luca rushed up to them and yanked out his knife.

'Thanks,' Gray said.

'I was outside smoking when the gunfire began,' the man explained and waved to the courtyard. 'Tracked its source across the street. Went over there. I was going up when he came down, so I hid and followed him back here.'

Gray clapped the man gratefully on the shoulder. He'd saved all their lives. Gray pointed to the door. 'Everybody out. We need to get out of this city. Fast.'

They hurried out to the street.

'*Fast* might be a problem,' Kowalski said. He stood with one hand on his hip, half hiding the snubbed assault rifle under his suit jacket.

Gray stared up and down the street and along the neighboring service alley. Every direction was packed with taxis, rickshaws, wagons, trucks, and cars.

All stopped dead. Not moving.

A chorus of horns and music blared, along with singing and chanting. A festival was in full swing down the street. The commotion had helped to mask the chaos at the hotel, but not completely.

Distantly, Gray heard a siren wailing. City police. Responding to the gunfire. He also heard shouts echo out of the lobby. The assault team headed down.

Rosauro turned to him. 'What do we—?'

A scream of motorcycle engines cut her off. Gray turned. To the left a few blocks back, three black bikes zigzagged through the logjam. Too fast, too intent. They barreled through people, knocking them aside. They sped straight toward the hotel. Each bike bore an additional rider with a rifle. More commandos.

Gray pulled everyone into the service alley, out of direct view. He turned to Masterson and snatched the white hat from his head. 'Your coat, too,' he ordered as he crammed the hat on his own head.

'What do you intend, sir?' Masterson asked as he climbed out of his white jacket.

'That sniper targeted you first, Dr. Masterson. You're the primary target.'

'Pierce . . . ,' Rosauro said warningly.

Gray hiked into the loose jacket. 'I'm going to lead those bikes away,' he explained and pointed to the crowded street. He aimed his other arm down the narrow alley. 'You take the others that way. We'll regroup at the fort we saw coming into town.'

Rosauro paused to digest his plan, then quickly nodded.

'I'm coming with you,' Kowalski said. He stepped from beside Elizabeth and raised his weapon. 'You'll need backup.'

Rosauro nodded. 'He's better with you than me. I'll have enough on my hands protecting the civilians.'

Gray didn't have time to argue. He could use a little muscle and firepower. 'Go!' he said.

'Mr. Pierce!'

Gray turned back. Masterson tossed his cane at him. He caught it, completing his ensemble.

'Just don't lose it! That's an eighteenth-century ivory handle!'

Gray hurried out into the streets with Kowalski in tow. He ran in a feigned stumble, waving his cane, shouting with a British accent. 'Someone help! They're bloody trying to kill me!'

He headed down the street toward the festival, running among the stalled cars and idling wagons. Behind them, the motorcycles choked and bobbled as they reached the hotel – then whined back up into a full scream.

Coming after them.

Kowalski followed. 'They've taken the bait.'

6:33 A.M.
Washington, D.C.

A knock on the door startled Painter. He had been close to dozing off, seated in his chair, elbows on the desktop, a pile of notes and test results from Lisa and Malcolm beneath his face. Earlier, he had ordered Kat to take a nap in one of the medical center's spare beds. Up all night himself, he should've taken that same advice.

He pressed the lock release under his desk, and the door swung open. He'd been expecting Lisa or

Malcolm. Painter sat straighter in surprise and gained his feet.

A tall, wide-shouldered man entered, dressed in a blue suit. His red hair had gone mostly a whitish gray, combed neatly back.

'Sean?'

Sean McKnight was the director of DARPA and Painter's immediate superior. He'd also been the man to recruit Painter into Sigma over a decade ago, when Sean had sat in Painter's chair. McKnight had been the visionary first director of Sigma, taking Archibald Polk's concept and turning it into reality. But more important, Sean was a good friend.

The man waved Painter back into his seat.

'Don't get up for me, son,' he said. 'I'm not about to take *that* chair again.'

Painter smiled. On his first day as director, Sean had sent Painter a crate of antacids. He had thought it was a good gag gift – but a couple of years later, Painter had gone through half the crate.

'Something tells me, Sean, *your* job isn't any lighter.'

'Not today it's not.' Sean sank into a chair across the desk from him. 'I've been checking into that man Commander Pierce saw outside the museum. Mapplethorpe. John Mapplethorpe.'

'So it wasn't a false I.D. he'd spotted?'

'On the contrary. Mapplethorpe is a division chief for the Defense Intelligence Agency. His oversight is the Russian Federation and its splinter states.'

Painter recalled Malcolm's initial assessment about where Polk had been fatally exposed to radiation. Chernobyl. What was Mapplethorpe's role in all of this?

'The man has powerful allies among intelligence agencies,' Sean continued. 'Known for his ruthlessness and manipulation. But he's also known as someone who can get results. A valuable commodity in Washington.'

'So how is he involved in all of this?'

'I've read your update. You know all about the declassified Project Stargate. How it was discontinued in the middle 1990s.'

'But it wasn't,' Painter said. 'In its final years, it vanished into the Defense Intelligence Agency.'

'That's correct. It became Mapplethorpe's project. He was approached in 1996 by a pair of Russian scientists – who were running the Soviet Union's version of Stargate. They were strapped for funds and sought our aid. We agreed to help – for our mutual benefit in this new world of borderless enemies. So a small cabal of Jasons was assigned to work jointly with the Russians. That's when the whole project went deeply classified. Vanished. Only a handful of people were even aware of its continuing existence.'

'Until Archibald came stumbling to our doorstep,' Painter said.

'We believe he sought to expose them. To bring out evidence.'

'Of the atrocities being committed in the name of science.'

'In the name of *national security*,' Sean corrected. 'Keep that in mind. That's the oil that greases the wheels in Washington. Do not underestimate Mapplethorpe. He knows how to play this game. And he believes himself a true patriot. He's also gone a long way to establish himself as such in the intelligence communities. Here and abroad.'

Painter shook his head.

Sean continued, 'Mapplethorpe has got every intelligence agency in the country looking for that skull you acquired. Every combination of initials imaginable. CIA, FBI, NSA, NRO, ONI . . . I wager he's even employed the network of retired spies with the AARP.'

Sean tried to smile at his own joke, but it came out

tired. 'I can't keep a lid on this much longer. Archibald was shot right on your doorstep. His ties to the Jasons, to Sigma, will not go unnoticed for long. And after last year's government oversight on our operations, there are many classified trails that lead here.'

'So what are you saying?' Painter asked.

'I think it's time that the skull made a reappearance. The wolves are circling closer. I can broker the skull through another intelligence agency, so it doesn't leave a trail back to Sigma.' He met and held Painter's gaze. 'But that'll buy you only a half a day grace period with the girl. If Gray and his team don't have answers before then, we may be forced to give her up.'

'I won't do that, Sean.'

'You may have no choice.'

Painter stood. 'Then you meet her first. You look at her, what was done to her. And you tell me how I can hand that girl over to Mapplethorpe.'

Painter saw his mentor balk. It was easier to condemn the faceless. Still, Sean nodded and stood. He never shied from the difficult. It was why Painter respected the man so much.

'Let's go say hello,' Sean said.

They exited together and descended the two levels to where the child was being kept.

As they reached the lower floor, Painter spotted Kat and Lisa at the end of the hall near the door to the girl's room. Kat seemed frantic. Painter knew the woman had been upset after seeing the child draw a picture of her husband, Monk, but Kat had eventually calmed down. She had admitted opening her wallet to show the girl pictures of her own daughter, Penelope, as a baby, hoping to establish a bond with the child. She'd had a picture of Monk among the photos.

But I'm sure she didn't see it, Kat had said. *At least I'm fairly certain.*

The only other explanation, as wild as it might be, was that the girl had somehow plucked Monk's image out of Kat's head, someone close to the woman's heart.

Either way, Kat had calmed down and agreed that it was best she take a nap. Exhaustion had put her on edge.

Spotting the men now, Kat came down the hall to meet them, plainly too anxious to wait.

'Director,' she said in a rush, 'we were about to call you. The girl's fever is spiking again. We have to do something. Lisa thinks . . . thinks she's dying.'

2:35 P.M.
Agra, India

Gray hurried down the street. The closer he got to the major intersection ahead, the worse the traffic snarled. Pedestrians were now packed shoulder to shoulder, slowly flowing through the creeping vehicles. The festival closed off the major thoroughfare. Traffic was diverted to secondary roads.

Horns blared, bicycle bells rang, people yelled and cursed.

Behind them, the scream of the motorcycles had wound down to a deep-throated growl. Even the hunters had become mired in this bog of humanity. Still, Gray made sure to stay low.

Kowalski shoved closer to him, ducking under the nose of a horse-drawn wagon. 'Some of 'em are on foot now.'

Gray glanced back. The three black motorcycles had been slowly losing ground. The cycles' passengers had abandoned the bikes and now followed through the crowd behind them. Two flanked the road, and one came down the center of the street.

Three threats had become six.

'Don't like those odds,' Gray mumbled. He came up

with a fast plan and told Kowalski what to do and where to meet. 'I'll take the high road. You take the low.'

The large man crouched in front of a truck. He stared at the muck of droppings from horse, donkey, and camel underfoot. 'How come I have to take the low road?'

'Because I'm wearing white.'

With a shake of his head, Kowalski dropped even lower, one hand on the asphalt. In a crouch, he shuffled *back* toward the hotel.

Holding the Panama hat atop his head, Gray leaped to the trunk of the taxi ahead and fled across the top of it toward the festival. His boots pounded a timpani across the taxi's rooftop and hood – then he bounded over to the next car in line and continued down the street, leaping and clambering across the tops of cars, taxis, and wagons. Shouts followed him, and fists shook in his wake. But in the bumper-to-bumper traffic, the high road was the faster mode of travel.

Gray glanced over a shoulder. As he'd hoped, the hunters had spotted him. In order not to lose him, the three on foot had mounted the high road, too. They came after him from three different directions, but at least they were too unbalanced to risk a shot at him.

Crouching low, using Masterson's cane for balance and support, Gray leapfrogged his way toward the noisy, boisterous festival. He had to lure the three footmen away from the motorcycles.

Divide and conquer.

Sliding across the roof of a van, Gray surveyed the congested sea of humanity behind him. Only this sea had a new shark in its waters now. Gray could not spot Kowalski, but he witnessed the man's handiwork. Farther back, the lead motorcycle edged alongside a truck. When it reached the front, the cyclist suddenly jerked upright, his body shaking. Gray heard a distant *pop-pop-pop,* like the celebratory firecrackers that echoed from the festival.

The driver and cycle sank into the churning sea.

Kowalski remained hidden. With the hunters' eyes on Gray's flight, it was easy for the large man to drop back, lie in wait, then jab his stolen M4 carbine into the rider as he passed. Point-blank, muffled.

But the shark wasn't done hunting these seas.

Gray left the large man to his bloody work and continued toward the confusion and chaos that was the festival. It sang, danced, cheered, laughed, and screamed. Music blew from horns and rang out with the clash of cymbals. It was the festival of Janmashtami, a celebration of the birth of Krishna.

From his vantage, he spotted patches of folks dancing the Ras Lila, a traditional Manipuri dance representing Krishna's early, mischievous years when he had dalliances with milkmaids. The packed crowds were also dotted with piles of young men forming human pyramids, striving to reach clay pots strung high across the street. The pots, called *dahi-handi,* were filled with curd and butter. The game reenacted Krishna's childish exploits, when he and his boyhood friends used to steal butter from neighbors.

Gray heard the traditional chant of support.

'*Govinda! Govinda!*'

Another name for Krishna.

Gray raced across the top of vehicles toward the festival. With the road ahead blocked off and traffic diverted, Gray's high road ended at the street party. He leaped off the hood of the last taxi and into the crowd.

As he landed amid the mass of revelers, he shed the white hat and coat, removing his disguise and blending into the crowd. He kept the cane in one hand and his pistol pressed to his thigh as he pushed through the masses of people. He aimed for the edge of the festival where shops and food wagons crowded with patrons lined the street square.

The plan was to regroup with Kowalski at the northwest corner of the square. They dared not continue to the rendezvous at the fort until they knew they'd shaken their tail. Gray reached a building with a fire escape. The metal ladder was pulled down, the balconies crowded with people enjoying the festival below. Gray climbed to the second floor for a good vantage place to observe the crowds and watch for Kowalski.

Reaching the level, Gray spotted one of his pursuers as he leaped from the hood of a truck into the mass of the festival. His other two compatriots were already in the mix, readily discernible by their black helmets. One bent down and lifted a soiled, trampled white hat. He threw it away in disgust and frustration.

Gray hoped they'd realize the hopelessness of their situation and retreat. But nothing was ever that easy.

Kowalski burst into the crowd. His suit jacket was a rumpled ruin. His hands were empty, his cheek bloody. But his worst feature was his height. The man stood a head and shoulder higher than the average partier. He surveyed the crowd with a hand shielding his eyes against the glare as he pushed through the sea of revelry.

Only this time, Kowalski wasn't the shark in the waters.

One of the helmeted men pointed in the big man's direction, recognizing him. They closed in on him from all directions.

Not good.

Gray turned, but the balcony had grown even more crowded, the ladder jammed up with people. He'd never reach the center of the crowd in time.

Twisting back around, Gray mounted the top of the balcony's railing, then leaped off it – *straight up*.

Overhead, a thick, oily wire was strung from the balcony above and across the square. Gray swept his arm high and hooked the ivory handle of the cane to the wire. His momentum and swing of his legs sent him skating along the wire, weighted down in the center by one of the large clay *dahi-handi* pots. He clutched the cane and swung his other arm straight down.

As his heels passed over the head of one of the helmeted hunters, Gray fired between his legs. The impact pounded the man to the ground, the helmet shattering like a walnut shell.

Then Gray hit the top of the human pyramid that was climbing for the clay pot. He knocked the topmost man down a peg and took his place at the top. As he scrabbled to keep from falling, the cane went toppling down the side of the pyramid – along with Gray's pistol.

Faces stared up at him.

Including the remaining two gunmen.

Weaponless, Gray balanced on the shoulders of the man below him and shoved up. He grabbed the bottom of the large clay pot, unhooked it, and with a silent prayer to Krishna, he lobbed it down at the nearest gunman.

His prayer was answered.

The heavy pot hit the man square in his upraised face, exploding with a wash of shards and butter. He went down hard.

The third gunman lifted his arm, cradling a pistol. As the crowd screamed, he fired two shots at Gray – but Gray was no longer there. The human pyramid crumpled under him. Bullets whined past the top of his head as he fell.

He landed in a tangle of limbs.

Gray struggled around, trying to find a footing. The gunman stalked toward the human dog pile, his gun raised. Before he could fire, a flash of white blurred in front. The man's head cracked back, struck in the face by the ivory handle of Masterson's cane. Kowalski had wielded the recovered cane like a batter swinging for the bleachers.

Blood spurted, and the man fell straight-backed to the pavement.

Kowalski snatched up the man's pistol and extended

the cane across the tangle of limbs and men. Gray grabbed the handle, and Kowalski pulled him free.

'Death by butter,' the large man said. 'Not bad, Pierce. Puts new meaning to watching your cholesterol.'

All around, the square had erupted in chaos. People fled in all directions. Uniformed police tried to wade against the human tide. Gray and Kowalski, now huddled low, allowed themselves to be dragged by the current out of the square and into the neighboring streets.

After a few harried minutes, the massive bulk of the red sandstone fort rose ahead of them, perched on the banks of the Yamuna River. They crossed toward the ancient walled structure – Akbar's Fort – a major tourist attraction of the city, second only to the Taj Mahal.

Taxis, vans, and limousines lined the avenue before it.

'Pierce!' a shout called to him.

Shay Rosauro waved from beside one of the limousines, a long white whale. He marched over to her. Luca stood at the open door. Masterson and Elizabeth were already inside.

'Not exactly inconspicuous,' Gray said, eyeing the vehicle.

'Should hold all of us,' Rosauro explained – then offered a sly smile. 'Besides, who says we can't pimp our ride a little?'

'Lady knows what she's talking about,' Kowalski said and strode toward the front. 'Maybe they'll let me drive it.'

'No!' echoed from both Gray and Rosauro.

With a wounded frown, Kowalski returned and ducked into the back of the limo. Rosauro followed.

Before joining them, Gray searched the sidewalks, the streets. No one seemed to be paying attention. Hopefully they'd shaken their tail completely. He craned around and stared across the curve of the river.

Off in the distance, the white marble of the mausoleum

glowed with sunlight, peaceful and eternal, slumbering beside the bright water.

Gray turned his back on the Taj Mahal.

Only the dead slept so peacefully.

As he entered the back of the limousine, Masterson let out a gasp of outrage. 'What did you do to my cane?'

Gray fell into his seat. The eighteenth-century ivory handle was bloody. The fine detail of the carved crane had been ground smooth from its ride across the braided wire.

'The cane is the least of your worries, Professor,' Gray said.

Masterson glowered at him as the limo pulled from the curb.

Gray pointed to the man's bandaged ear. 'Someone's trying to kill you. The question, Dr. Masterson, is *why*.'

10

'Loose ends,' Trent McBride explained. 'There are too many of them.'

Yuri saw the man glance in his direction, but he didn't flinch. Let them kill him. It did not matter. Yuri sat in an office chair. They'd allowed him to dress again after removing the electrodes. His fiery torture had continued for another twenty minutes. Yuri had not held back. He'd divulged much, confessing more details about the genetics of the children, the secret he and Savina had kept from the Americans.

He even admitted why the Russians had not objected to Dr. Archibald Polk's recruitment. Yuri admitted that Polk had been getting too close to the heart of the genetic secret. Savina had already planned to orchestrate an accident while the man was at the Warren, to silence him.

But in this game of scientific brinkmanship, neither he nor Savina imagined that Polk's own colleague and friend would arrange his escape, all to lure one of their children out into the open.

And Savina had taken the bait. She cared little that Polk had escaped with the skull, which McBride had given him. It was the genetic secret he held that had panicked Savina

203

into sending Yuri and Sasha into the hunt for the man. She had fallen cleanly into the American's trap.

'Loose ends?' Mapplethorpe asked, drawing back his attention. He shook his head, unconcerned. 'I see only three. The girl, the skull, and Polk's trail in India. The last is already being handled. And I've heard rumblings through intelligence channels that our missing skull might mysteriously turn up.'

'How did you manage that?' McBride asked.

'Get waters boiling just right, and you'll be surprised what will come to the surface.'

'And the girl?'

Yuri paid more attention. Mapplethorpe's gaze flicked to him. Yuri knew the only reason he was still alive was because of Sasha. Mapplethorpe needed him, knew about her medical condition, about a problem seen in all the children. The stress of the mental manipulation was not without physical consequences to the subjects. In fact, few lived far into their twenties, especially those with the most savant talent. It was a problem that required harvesting eggs and sperm to keep the strongest genetic line viable.

Mapplethorpe sighed. 'We should have the girl before the sun sets . . . if not sooner.'

And you'll still be too late, Yuri thought.

So simple these Americans, so quick to assume that what was tortured testimony was the whole story. While Yuri had not lied, he had committed one sin: *a sin of omission*. In fact, McBride hadn't even known the question to ask, so secure was he in his superiority and his sadistic trust in the power of pain.

Yuri kept his face stoic. They sought to break him with their tortures, but he was an old man, one used to keeping secrets. All they'd accomplished was to harden his core for what was to come. In the past months, Yuri had started to have reservations about Savina's plan.

It was only natural.

Millions would die in horrible ways.

All for a new world to be born.

A new Renaissance.

Yuri stared at Mapplethorpe's self-satisfied smirk and at McBride's bright-eyed confidence.

All hesitation died inside him.

Savina was right.

It was time for the world to burn.

2:55 P.M.
Southern Ural Mountains

General-Major Savina Martov knew something was wrong. She felt it in her bones, a nonspecific anxiety. She could no longer remain in her office. She needed reassurances.

With a radio held to the side of her face, she led two soldiers through the dark and abandoned streets that cut through the old Soviet-era apartments that filled the back half of the Chelyabinsk 88 cavern. The featureless concrete blocks that rose to either side were the original housing for prisoners who worked the mines and refinement plants. The men had traded life sentences in the gulags for five years' work here. Not that any of them ever saw that fifth year. Most died from radiation before the end of their first year.

A foolish gamble, but then again, hope could turn any rational man desperate. This was the legacy she had inherited. It served as a reminder.

Others thought her cruel, but sometimes necessity could wear no other face. The children were well fed, their needs attended. Pain was minimized as much as humanly possible.

Cruelty?

She stared around at the hollow-eyed apartments, cold, dark, haunted.

All she saw was necessity.

The radio fritzed at her ear as Lieutenant Borsakov came back online. So far she had heard only negative reports from the second in command. He was still searching the surrounding mountains and foothills for the children. He'd been led astray by several false trails, discovering a discarded hospital shirt.

'We found two dead dogs,' Borsakov said. 'By the river. They'd been torn to shreds. Bear attack. But we've picked up a strong trail.'

'And what about the cats?' she asked, speaking into a radio.

Silence stretched for a moment.

'Lieutenant,' she said more firmly.

'We were holding off sending them until we had a clear trail. Didn't want to risk the dogs with the tigers ranging the hills.'

He kept his voice practical, but Savina recognized the strained edge behind his words. The lieutenant was not so much concerned with the dogs as he was the children.

Why did she always have to be the hard one?

She spoke crisply. 'You have a strong trail now, do you not, Lieutenant?'

'Yes, General-Major.'

'Then do not disappoint me again.'

'No, General-Major.'

She clicked off the line. She may have been harsher than she intended, but she'd already heard disturbing news in the past hour.

A maintenance worker from the neighboring town of Ozyorsk had discovered one of the Warren's decommissioned trucks, one once used to transport waste from a uranium enrichment plant near the shore of Lake Karachay. Inside, the worker had found a fake badge with Dr. Archibald Polk's face.

It answered the mystery of the professor's escape.

He'd had help.

And it didn't take much contemplation to figure out *who* had assisted in his escape. It had to be Dr. Trent McBride. What game were the Americans playing? With Yuri's continuing silence, she could only imagine that he and the girl had been captured. In fact, the escape might have been staged to accomplish just that end.

If so, Savina had to respect McBride for such an effort.

Like her, he understood *necessity*.

In retrospect, she should have never engaged in a partnership with the United States. But she'd had little choice at the time. In the turmoil following the breakup of the Soviet Union, her project had lost all funding. It was only through such a union that her work was allowed to continue.

The United States supplied the interim cash, seeking new ways to expand their ability to gather intelligence. Her project offered such a promise. But her project also offered one thing more. She supplied the American government with *plausible deniability,* similar to the secret CIA-financed torture camps in Europe. In this new world, the lines of acceptable conduct – whether military or scientific – had become blurred.

Not on our soil was the new American credo.

And she'd been happy at the time to exploit that.

Still, the loss of Yuri and the child was not insurmountable. It only required accelerating her timetable. Her operation – titled Saturn – was supposed to follow Nicolas's actions in Chernobyl by a week. Now the two would commence on the same day.

Tomorrow.

The two operations – Uranus and Saturn – were named after two strategic offenses during World War II, when Soviet forces defeated the Germans in the Battle of Stalingrad, the bloodiest battle in human history. Close to two million were killed in that battle, including vast numbers of civilian casualties. Still, the Germans' defeat was considered the turning point of the war.

A glorious victory for the Motherland.

And as in the past, Operation Uranus and Saturn would once again free Russia and change the course of world history.

And likewise, not without casualties.

Necessity was a cruel master.

Savina reached the far wall of the cavern. A tunnel opened, framed by thick lead blast doors, miniature versions of the same doors that closed the main tunnel into Chelyabinsk 88.

Just inside the mouth of the tunnel rested a train and bumper stops. The electrified tracks carried a single train back and forth between the Warren and the heart of Operation Saturn, on the far side of Lake Karachay. The old tunnel went under the toxic lake, allowing for fast transport between the two sites without risk of exposure to the lake's hot radiological soup of strontium 90 and cesium 137.

The train was already waiting for her.

Savina climbed into one of the lead-lined cabs. There were only two enclosed cars, one on either end of the train. The remaining four sections were open ore cars for hauling supplies, mining gear, and rocks.

As the train sidled out with a *clack* of wheels and sizzle of electricity, the blast doors sealed behind her. The tunnel went dark. She stared up as the train began the five-minute journey. As it accelerated, Savina pictured the weight of water overhead, insulated by a quarter mile of rock.

The region above was the heart of the Soviet Union's uranium and plutonium production. Mostly now defunct, the facility had once had seven active plutonium production reactors and three plutonium separation plants. It was all sloppily run. Since 1948, the production facilities had leaked *five* times more radiation than Chernobyl and *all* of the world's atmospheric nuclear tests *combined*.

And half that radiation was still stored in Lake Karachay.

The radiation level on the lake's shore measured six hundred roentgens per hour. Sufficient to deliver a lethal dose in one hour.

Savina remembered where the maintenance worker from Ozyorsk had found Dr. Archibald Polk's abandoned truck.

On the shore of that lake.

She shook her head. There had been no need to hunt down Dr. Polk. He'd been dead already.

Light appeared ahead.

It glowed with the hope for a brighter future.

The heart of Operation Saturn.

3:15 P.M.

'They're planning on doing *what*?' Monk said, a bit too loudly as he walked alongside the riverbank.

He and the kids had been walking alongside the churning river for the past hour. It was not the same waterway as where they'd encountered the bear. Monk had forded that turbulent stream by using a series of boulders and followed it down to this larger river, buried in a dense fir forest. Monk had studied the topographic map several times. It seemed they were following along the watershed that drained the eastern slopes of the Ural Mountains. On the western side, the Urals shed their rainwater and snowmelt into the Caspian Sea; on this side, it all flowed into a region of massive rivers and hundreds of lakes, all of which eventually emptied into the Arctic Ocean.

What the Russians were planning . . .

Shock had rung in his voice.

Konstantin winced at his sharpness.

'I'm sorry,' Monk said more quietly, knowing voices traveled far in the mountains. He had been the one to warn the children to speak only in whispers. He obeyed his own rule now, though his voice was still strained. 'Even with the hole in my memory, I know what they're planning is madness.'

'They will succeed,' Konstantin countered matter-of-factly. 'It is not difficult. A simple strategy. We' – he waved to Pyotr and Kiska, then in a general motion behind him, indicating the other children like him at the underground compound – 'have run scenarios and models, judged probable outcomes, analyzed statistical global data, studied environmental impact, and extrapolated end results. It is far from madness.'

Monk listened to the boy. He sounded more like a computer than a teenager. Then again, Monk remembered the cold steel behind Konstantin's ear. They all had them. Even Marta bore a thumb-size block of surgical steel buried in the fur behind her ear. During the past hour, Konstantin had also used the time to demonstrate his skill at calculations. The mental exercise had seemed to calm him. Kiska showed him how she could identify a bird's song and mimic it in perfect pitch.

Only Pyotr seemed shy about his abilities.

'Empath,' Konstantin had explained. 'He can read someone's emotions, even when they're hiding it, or acting contrarily. One teacher said he was a living lie detector. Because of this, he prefers the company of animals, spends much of his time at the Menagerie. He's the one who insisted we bring Marta.'

Monk stared at where the boy walked with the elderly

210

chimpanzee. He had been studying the boy, watching how he interacted. The two seemed to be in constant communication, silent glances, a pinch of brow or pucker of lip, a swing of arm.

He watched Pyotr suddenly stiffen and stop. Marta did, too. Pyotr swung to Konstantin and spoke in a rush, a frightened babble, first in Russian, then English. His small eyes turned up to Monk, searching for some miraculous salvation.

'They're here,' the boy whispered.

Monk didn't have to ask *who* Pyotr meant. It was plain from the raw terror in his voice.

Arkady and Zakhar.

The two Siberian tigers.

'Go!' Monk said. They ran down the riverbank. Konstantin led the way. His sister, Kiska, as fleet-footed as a gazelle, followed behind him. Monk allowed Konstantin to pick the best path through the blueberry bushes, scraggly brush, and boulders that lined the riverbanks. Monk kept a watch on their back trail. He had to be careful. Streams of straw-yellow spruce needles flowed from the thick forest to the river's edge and created patches as slick as ice underfoot.

Pyotr slipped on a patch and landed hard on his backside. Marta scooped him under a hairy arm and got him back on his feet. Monk herded them forward. Konstantin and Kiska widened the distance ahead of them.

They ran for five minutes, but exhaustion quickly began to slow them. Even adrenaline and terror fired you for only so long. Ten minutes more and they were slogging at a stumbling half trot.

The group closed together again.

There remained no sound of pursuit, no crash of branches or snap of twigs. No sign of the tigers.

Konstantin, panting and red-faced, glared at Pyotr

and spoke harshly in Russian, plainly berating the boy for the false alarm.

Monk waved Konstantin off. 'It's not his fault,' he gasped out.

Pyotr wore a wounded yet still terrified expression.

Marta hooted softly, bumping Konstantin.

Kiska also scolded her brother in Russian.

Monk had been warned that Pyotr could not judge distances well, only intent. He had to trust that when the tigers got really close—

—Pyotr went ramrod stiff, his eyes huge.

He opened his mouth, but terror choked him silent.

No words were necessary.

'Now!' Monk screamed.

Turning as one, they all ran – straight for the swift-flowing river as planned. Monk grabbed Pyotr, hugged him tight, and leaped from the bank. He heard twin splashes as Kiska and Konstantin hit the water downstream a few yards.

Monk surfaced in the icy-cold flow with the boy clinging like a vine to his neck. He twisted in time to see Marta swing up into the branches of a tree, climbing fast.

Deeper in the forest . . . motion . . . swift . . . a flash of fiery fur . . .

Monk kicked for the deepest and fastest current. He spotted Marta leaping from one tree to another in the dense forest. Chimpanzees could not swim and had no natural buoyancy. She had to take another path.

Forest shadows shattered as a huge shape burst into view, low, muzzle rippling, paws wide, striped tail high and stiff.

The tiger leaped straight from the riverbank at Monk.

He back-paddled and kicked, dragged by the weight of his pack and the boy. Pyotr tightened his arms, strangling him.

The tiger flew, legs out wide, black claws bared, a scream of feral fury.

Monk could not swim fast enough.

But the river's flow made up for it.

The tiger crashed into the water a few yards away, missing its prey.

Monk angled into a swift channel between two boulders. He got dumped into a churning hole, thrown down deep, then back up again.

Pyotr choked and coughed.

Monk twisted and spotted the tiger thrashing upriver. It spun in an eddy of current. Despite the myths of cats and water, tigers were not averse to water. Still, the beast paddled for the shore. It was not how cats hunted.

Cats were all about the ambush.

The tigers had plainly stalked them, following them quietly through the forest as they fled away, driven by Pyotr's initial warning. The boy had been right. Following age-old instincts and cunning, the pair had tracked them, waited until their prey had tired before charging. Tigers were sprinters, not long-distance runners. They timed their charge so they could strike at the perfect moment.

Along the river's edge, another tiger appeared, stalking back and forth, thwarted. The first cat hauled out of the river, waterlogged and drenched. It shook its laden pelt and sprayed water.

Monk got a good look at the pair. Though still muscular, they looked emaciated, starved. Their fur had a ragged appearance. He noted matching steel skullcaps, like on the wolves. One tiger's ear was gnarled, shredded from an old hunting injury. Zakhar, according to Konstantin's description. Born siblings, it was the only way they could be told apart.

In a single smooth motion, as if responding to a silent whistle, the pair turned and vanished into the darkness.

Monk knew it wasn't over.

The hunt was just beginning.

He twisted and saw Konstantin and Kiska disappear around a bend in the river. Monk sidestroked after them. Pyotr shivered against him. Monk knew the boy was not trembling from the cold, nor even from fear of the tigers. His huge, panicked eyes were not on the riverbank, but on the flow of water all around him.

What was terrifying him?

3:35 P.M.

Pyotr clung to the large man. He kept his arms tight around his neck, his legs around his waist. Water flowed all around him, filling his world. He tasted it on his lips, felt it in his ears, smelled its sweetness and green rot. Its ice cold cut to his bones.

He could not swim.

Like Marta.

He searched the far bank as it swept past, searching for his friend.

Pyotr knew much of his fear of water came from her heart. Deep water was death to her. He had felt the quickening thud of her heart when they crossed on the boulders earlier today, saw the tightening of her jaw, the glassy wideness to her eyes.

Her terror was his.

Pyotr clasped tighter to the man.

But the true heart of Marta's terror lay deeper than any sea. He had known it from the moment she had come to his bedside, laying a lined paw upon his sheets, inviting friendship. Most thought she had come to comfort him as he recovered from his first surgery.

But in that long breathless moment, staring into her caramel-brown eyes, Pyotr had known her secret. She had come to him, seeking comfort for *herself,* reassurance from him.

From that moment, terror and love had bonded them equally.

Along with a dark secret.

4:28 P.M.
New Delhi, India

'Did you know man can see into the future?' Dr. Hayden Masterson asked as he tapped at the computer.

Gray stirred from studying the depths of his coffee. The group shared one of the private rooms at the Delhi Internet Café and Video. Kowalski leaned against the frosted glass door, ensuring their privacy. He picked at an adhesive bandage on his chin. Elizabeth had tended to the man's scrapes and was now stacking the pages coming out of the laser printer beside the workstation. It was just the four of them. Rosauro and Luca had gone out to rent them a new car for the journey ahead.

Though Gray still wasn't sure where they were going.

That all depended on Masterson – and he wasn't in a talking mood. The professor had spoken hardly a word since they'd escaped from the attack at the hotel. Attempts to draw the man out, to get him to reveal *why* he might be the target of assassination, had only seemed to make him withdraw.

He just continued to study the marred ivory handle of his cane. His eyes glazed – not with shock, but in deep concentration.

Elizabeth had given Gray a quiet shake of her head.
Don't press him.

So they'd driven north out of Agra, aiming for the capital of India, New Delhi. During the ninety-mile trek, Gray had them change vehicles twice along the way.

Once they reached the teeming outskirts of the city,

Masterson had given only one instruction: *I need access to a computer.*

So here they were, in a cramped back room of an Internet café. The professor had promptly logged on to a private address on the University of Mumbai's Web site, requiring three levels of code to access it.

'Archibald's research,' Masterson had explained and had begun printing it all out. He had remained silent until this cryptic statement about mankind seeing the future.

'How do you mean?' Gray asked.

Masterson pushed back from his workstation. 'Well, many people don't know this, but it's been scientifically proven in the last couple of years that man has the ability to see a short span into the future. About three seconds or so.'

'Three seconds?' Kowalski said. 'Lot of good that'll do you.'

'It does plenty,' Masterson replied.

Gray frowned at Kowalski and turned back to the professor. 'But what do you mean by *scientifically* proven?'

'Are you familiar with the CIA's Stargate project?'

Gray shared a glance with Elizabeth. 'The project Dr. Polk worked on for a while.'

'Another researcher on the project, Dr. Dean Radin, performed a series of experiments on volunteers. He wired them up with lie detectors, measuring skin conductivity, and began showing them a series of images on a screen. A random mix of horrible and soothing photos. The violent and explicit images would trigger a strong response on the lie detector, an *electronic wince*. After a few minutes, the subjects began to wince *before* a horrible image would appear on the screen, reacting up to three seconds in advance. It happened time and again. Other scientists, including Nobel Prize winners, repeated these tests at both Edinburgh and Cornell universities. With the same statistical results.'

Elizabeth shook her head with disbelief. 'How could that be?'

Masterson shrugged. 'I have no idea. But the experiment was extended to gamblers, too. They were monitored while playing cards. They began showing the same pattern, reacting seconds *before* a card would turn over. A positive response when the turn was favorable, and negative when it wasn't. This so intrigued a Nobel-winning physicist from Cambridge University that he performed a more elaborate study, hooking such test subjects to MRI scanners in order to study their brain activity. He found that the source of this premonition seemed to lie *in* the brain. This Nobel Prize winner – and keep in mind, not some bloody quack – concluded that ordinary people *can* see for short spans into the future.'

'That's amazing,' Elizabeth said.

Masterson fixed her with a steady stare. 'It's what drove your father,' he said gently. 'To determine *how* and *why* this could be. If ordinary people could see for three seconds into the future, why not longer? Hours, days, weeks, years. For physicists, such a concept is not beyond comprehension. Even Albert Einstein once said that the difference between the past and future is only *a stubbornly persistent illusion*. Time is just another dimension, like distance. We have no trouble looking forward or backward along a path. So why not along *time*, too?'

Gray pictured the strange girl. Her charcoal sketch of the Taj Mahal. If man could look through time, as Dr. Masterson reported, then why not across great distances? He remembered Director Crowe's statement about the successes the CIA project had with remote viewing.

'All it would take,' Masterson said, 'would be to find those rare individuals who could see farther than the ordinary. To study them.'

Or exploit them, Gray thought, still thinking of the girl.

Elizabeth passed the last page from the printer to the stack. She handed it to Masterson. 'My father . . . he was looking for these rare individuals.'

'No, my dear, he wasn't looking for them.'

Elizabeth's eyes pinched in confusion.

Masterson patted her hand. 'Your father *found* them.'

Gray perked up. 'What?'

A knock on the door interrupted the professor before he could explain. Kowalski shifted, checked who it was, and opened the door.

Rosauro poked in her head and passed to Gray a heavy set of rental keys. 'All done in here?'

'No,' Gray answered.

Masterson bowled past him with an armload of papers under his arm. 'Yes, we are.'

Gray rolled his eyes and waved to the others. 'C'mon.'

He followed, mentally strangling the irascible professor.

Kowalski kept to Gray's side. 'He's just getting even,' the large man said and nodded to the walking stick under Masterson's other arm. 'For what you did to his cane.'

They exited the Internet café and found Luca Hearn leaning on the hood of a pewter-colored Mercedes-Benz G55 SUV. It looked like a tank.

Rosauro circled around to the front. She already had a hand raised against his objections. 'Okay, it's not inconspicuous. I know. But I didn't know where we were going *or* how fast we might need to get there.'

Kowalski grinned much too widely. 'Or how many Hondas we might need to run over.'

'It's got four-wheel drive, almost five hundred horses . . . and . . . and . . .' She shrugged. 'I liked it.'

Kowalski passed her to inspect the car. 'Oh, yeah, from now on, Rosauro picks out all our transportation!'

Gray sighed and stepped toward Dr. Masterson. 'Where to now?'

The professor was studying the stack of papers and waved his cane toward the north, plainly irritated. Gray waited for more details, but got none.

Elizabeth's warning echoed in his head. *Don't press him . . .*

Giving up, Gray pointed to the SUV. He had no time to argue. They'd been in one place too long already. He wanted to keep moving, even if he didn't know exactly where. If anyone had put a tracer on the University of Mumbai's Web site, they could be zeroing in on them right now.

'Load up,' Gray ordered.

Kowalski cupped his hands for the keys.

Gray tossed them to Rosauro instead.

Kowalski glowered at him. 'You are just plain evil.'

5:06 P.M.

Elizabeth could wait no longer. Going against her own advice, she turned to Dr. Masterson. 'Hayden, enough of your games. What did you mean when you said my father *found* those people?'

'Just what I said, my dear.'

The professor sat in the center of the SUV's middle row, flanked by Elizabeth and Gray. Pen in hand, Hayden had been sifting through the printouts for the past ten minutes. Rosauro glanced back at them from the driver's seat. Kowalski sulked in the passenger seat with his arms stubbornly crossed.

Luca stirred behind them and leaned forward to listen.

Hayden explained, 'Your father spent the past decade collecting and comparing DNA samples from the most promising yogis and mystics of India. He traveled far and wide, from north to south. He collated reams of data, cross-referenced genetic code. He ran a statistical model analyzing mental ability versus genetic variance.'

'He tested Luca's people, too,' Elizabeth said.

The Gypsy made a noise of agreement.

'Because they rose from the Punjab region,' Hayden said.

'Why is that important?' Gray asked.

'Let me show you.' The professor searched the stack for half a minute, then pulled out one sheet. 'Your father, Elizabeth, was a true genius, vastly underappreciated by his peers. He was able to pinpoint three genes that seemed to be common to those who showed the strongest traits. Like many scientific breakthroughs, such a discovery was equal parts brilliance and luck. He came upon these genes when he noted that many of the most talented individuals seemed to show signs of autism in varying degrees.'

'Autism?' Elizabeth asked. 'Why autism?'

'Because the debilitating mental condition, while compromising social functioning, can often produce some astounding savant abilities.' Hayden patted her knee. 'Did you know that many of the key figures in history displayed autistic tendencies?'

Elizabeth shook her head.

He ticked names off, using his fingers. 'In the arts, that included Michelangelo, Jane Austen, Emily Dickinson, along with Beethoven and Mozart. In science, you have Thomas Edison, Albert Einstein, and Isaac Newton. In politics, Thomas Jefferson. Even Nostradamus was believed to be autistic to some degree.'

'Nostradamus?' Gray asked. 'The French astrologer?'

Hayden nodded. 'Such individuals have changed history, improved mankind, moved us forward. There's a line Archibald loved to quote. From Dr. Temple Grandin, a bestselling writer with autism. "*If by some magic, autism had been eradicated from the face of the earth, then men would still be socializing in front of a wood fire at the entrance to a cave.*" And I believe she was right.'

220

'And my father?'

'Most definitely. Your father came to believe that there was a direct connection between autism and his own studies into intuition and presentiment.'

'And he found this connection?' Gray said.

The professor sighed. 'While we don't know the exact cause for autism, most scientists agree that there are ten different genes that potentially contribute to the appearance of the condition. So Archibald ran these ten genes through his statistical model and discovered three of these genes were common among *all* those with high talent. It was the breakthrough he had been looking for. With these three genetic markers, he began to trace geographically the frequency of these markers in the general population. He came up with a map.'

The professor passed Elizabeth the sheet of paper on his lap. It was a map of India. Across the breadth of it were hundreds of small dots.

Elizabeth studied it, then handed it to Gray.

Hayden explained, 'Each dot represents an individual bearing the genetic marker. But if you look closely, you'll see how many dots appear around major cities, like Delhi and Mumbai. Which only makes sense, since there are many people living in those cities.'

'But what about up here?' Gray asked and pointed toward the north.

Elizabeth knew what Gray was asking about. A large number of dots – *more than anywhere else* – clustered to the north, where no major city was marked.

'Exactly. Archibald wondered the same.' Hayden took the map back and tapped the cluster to the north. 'He concentrated the last three years of his life in that area. He sought to discover why this dense cluster appears up there.'

'What's there?' she asked.

'The Punjab.' The answer came from behind Elizabeth. From Luca Hearn. 'The original homeland of the Romani.'

'Indeed. It is why Archibald contacted the Gypsy clans in Europe and the United States. He found it rather coincidental that such a rich history of prophecy and fortune-telling would arise from the same spot and spread to Europe and beyond. He sought to see if his genetic marker could be found among the Gypsies.'

'Was it?' Elizabeth posed the question to both Hayden and Luca.

Hayden answered, 'Yes, but not in the concentrations he was suspecting. It disappointed your father.'

Luca made a noncommittal noise.

She turned to him. 'What?'

'There was a reason,' Luca said.

Gray twisted around. 'What do you mean?'

'It was why we hired Dr. Polk.'

Elizabeth remembered that the Gypsy clan leader had never fully elaborated on the matter. He'd started to explain on the airplane, but they had been interrupted.

'As I told you before, Dr. Polk sought to collect blood samples from our most gifted *chovihanis*. Not fakers, but real seers. But there were few among us who still met this criteria.'

'Why?'

'Because the heart of our people was stolen from us.'

Slowly and in a grim voice, Luca continued, telling a tale of a deep secret among his clans, one that went back centuries. The secret concerned one clan among all the others, one that was most cherished. It was forbidden even to speak of them to *gadje,* to outsiders. The clan was kept separate, hidden, protected by the other clans. It was the true source of the Gypsies' heritage of prophecy. On rare occasions, some of these *chovihanis* would move and live among the other clans, sharing their talents, taking husbands or wives. But mostly they remained insular and apart. Then nearly fifty years ago, the clan was discovered. Every man and woman was slaughtered, butchered, and buried in a shallow, frozen grave.

Luca's words grew especially bitter. 'Only in that mass grave, there were no bones of any children.'

Elizabeth understood the impact. 'Someone took them.'

'We never discovered who . . . but we never stopped looking. We had hoped that Dr. Polk with his new way of tracking – by DNA – might find a trail that had long gone cold.'

'Was he successful?' Elizabeth asked.

Luca shook his head. 'Not that he ever revealed. He did send one odd query a few months ago. He wanted to know more about our status as *untouchables,* the casteless of India.'

Elizabeth didn't know what that meant. She glanced to Hayden, but the professor shrugged. Still, she noted something in his expression, a narrowing of his eyes. He knew something.

But instead of explaining, he marked a small *x* on the map with his pen.

'What's that?' Elizabeth asked, noting how it lay in the middle of the cluster of dots in the Punjab region.

'It's where we must go next if we want answers.'

'And where's that?' Gray pressed.

'To the place where Archibald vanished.'

11

Nicolas crossed through the ghost town's amusement park.

Old yellow bumper cars sat in pools of stagnant green water, amid waist-high weeds. The roof of the ride had long since collapsed, leaving a frame of red corrosion arched over it. Ahead, the park's giant Ferris wheel – the Big Dipper – rose into the late-afternoon sky, limned against the low sun. Its yellow umbrella chairs hung idle from the rusted skeleton. A symbol and monument to the ruin left behind in the wake of Chernobyl.

Nicolas continued on.

The park had been built in anticipation of the celebrations of May Day back in 1986. Instead, a week prior to the celebration, the city of Pripyat, home to forty-eight thousand workers and their families, was killed, smothered under a veil of radiation. The city, built in the 1970s, had been a shining example of Soviet architecture and urban living: the Energetic Theater, the palatial Polissia Hotel, a state-of-the-art hospital, scores of schools.

The theater lay now in ruins. The hotel had birch trees growing out of its roof. The schools had become crumbled shells, piled with moldy textbooks, old dolls, and wooden toy blocks. In one room, Nicolas had seen piles of discarded gas masks, lying in limp heaps like the scalped faces of the dead. The once vibrant city had been reduced to broken windows, collapsed walls, old bed frames, and peeling paint. Weeds and trees grew wild everywhere, cracking apart what man had built. Now only tours came here, four hundred dollars a head to explore the haunted place.

And the cause of it all . . .

Nicolas shaded his eyes and stared. He could just make out on the horizon a hazy bump, two miles off.

The Chernobyl power plant.

The explosion of reactor number four had cast a plume that wrapped the world. Yet here, the evacuation order was delayed for thirty hours. The forest around the city turned red with radioactive dust. Townspeople swept their porches and balconies to keep them clean while plutonium fires burned two miles away.

Nicolas shook his head, mostly because he knew a news crew followed him, rolling B-roll footage for the evening news. Nicolas strode through the amusement park. He had been warned to stay on the fresh asphalt strip that crossed the ruins of the abandoned town. The radiation levels spiked higher if you tread out into the mossy stretches of the urban wasteland. The worst zones were marked off with triangular yellow signs. The new asphalt path had been laid to accommodate the flood of dignitaries, officials, and newspeople that were descending on Chernobyl in anticipation of the installation of the new steel Sarcophagus over its decaying concrete shell.

By this evening, the showplace Polissia Hotel would return to a tarnished bit of its former glory. The hotel's ballroom had been hastily renovated, cleared, and cleaned to host a formal black-tie party tonight. Even the birch trees growing out of the roof had been cut down for the event.

Nothing but the best for their international guests. There would be representatives from almost every nation, even a handful of stars from Hollywood. Pripyat would shine for this one night, a bright gala in the center of a radiological ruin.

Both the Russian president and prime minister would be in attendance, along with many members from the upper and lower house of Federal Assembly. Many were already here, making halfhearted assertions of change and reform, attempting to churn political currency from this momentous event.

But no one had been more vocal and vehement for a true change than Senator Nicolas Solokov. And after this morning's assassination attempt, he had the spotlight shining him full in the face.

As the cameras taped him, Nicolas stepped off the asphalt walkway and crossed to a neighboring wall. Upon its surface had been painted a stark black shadow of a pair of children playing with a toy truck. It was said a mad Frenchman had spent months in Pripyat. His shadow art could be found throughout the city, haunting and disturbing, representing the ghosts of the lost children.

His own personal shadow, Elena, remained upon the asphalt walk. She had already chosen this particular piece of art to be the most poignant. Earlier she had scouted the zone with a dosimeter to make sure the radiation levels were safe.

It was all about showmanship this evening.

Nicolas leaned a hand on the wall. He traced the children's form with a finger. He pressed the back of his wrist to one eye. Elena had already dabbed the sleeve of his suit jacket with drops of ammonia. The sting drew the required tears.

He turned to the cameras, his fingers still on the cheek of the shadow child. 'This is why we must change,' he said and waved his hand to encompass the city. 'How can anyone look across this blasted landscape and not know that our great country must move into a new era? We must put all this behind us – yet never forget.'

He wiped his cheek and hardened his countenance – a few tears were fine, but he did not want to appear weak. His voice growled toward the microphones. 'Look at this city! What man has ruined, nature consumes. Some have called this place Chernobyl's Garden of Eden. Is it not a handsome forest that has taken over the city? Birds sing. Deer roam in great abundance. But know that the wolves have also returned.'

He stared toward the darkening horizon. 'Do not be fooled by the beauty here. It still remains a *radioactive* garden. We all crossed through the two military checkpoints to enter the thirty-kilometer-wide Chernobyl Exclusion Zone. We all passed the two thousand vehicles used to put out Chernobyl's radioactive blaze. Firetrucks, aircraft, ambulances, still too hot to get near. We all wear our dosimeter badges. So do not be deceived. Nature has returned, but it will suffer for generations. What appears healthy and vital is *not*. This is not rebirth. Only false hope. For a true rebirth, we must look in new directions, toward new goals, toward a new Renaissance.'

He turned again to the shadowy children. He shook his head.

'How could we not?' he finished sadly.

Someone along the roadway clapped.

Faced away from the camera, Nicolas smiled. As camera flashes captured his thoughtful and resolute pose, his own shadow consumed the children's shapes. After a long moment, he turned away and went back to the asphalt walkway.

He marched back toward the hotel. Elena trailed him. Rounding a turn, he saw a commotion at the front of the Polissia Hotel. A stretch black limousine pulled to the entrance of the hotel, surrounded by a sleek fleet of bulletproof sedans. Men in dark suits piled out, forming a thick cordon. The arriving dignitary climbed from the limousine, an arm raised in greeting.

Camera and video lights spotlighted the figure, outlining the newcomer's profile.

There was no mistaking that silhouette.

The president of the United States.

Here to support a vital nuclear pact between Russia and the United States.

The major reason Pripyat had been cleaned up and sanitized was so it could host such dignitaries.

Not wanting to be upstaged, Nicolas waited for the entire party to vanish into the hotel's lobby. Once the way was clear, he headed out again.

Everything was in place.

He glanced to the Chernobyl plant as the sun sank toward twilight.

By this time tomorrow, a new world would be born.

5:49 P.M.
Southern Ural Mountains

Monk stood on a ridge and stared out across the low mountains. With the sun sinking, the valley below lay in deep shadows.

'We have to cross that?' he asked. 'There's no other way around?'

Konstantin folded the map. 'Not without going hundreds of miles to circle it, which would take many days. The mine we must reach on the far side of Lake Karachay lies only twelve miles away if we cross here.'

Monk stared down at the swampy valley. The river they'd floated down dumped over this last ridge and fed into the wide valley below. Many other creeks and streams did the same. In the slanted sunlight, waterfalls and cataracts shone like flows of quicksilver. But shadowed by the low mountains, the valley floor was all drowned forests and wide stretches of open black marshes rimmed by reeds and grasses. It would be difficult to cross, and once it got dark, it would be easy to get lost.

He sighed heavily. They had no choice but to cross the swamplands. He turned to where Kiska and Pyotr sat on a log. The kids still looked like a pair of half-drowned kittens. They had ridden the river for a quarter mile until the chill drove them to shore. Monk had them exit on the opposite side of the river from the hunting cats. The water should break their trail, and the river only grew wider the farther down the mountains it flowed. The tigers would have to brave a stiff river crossing to pick up their scent.

And for the past two hours, Pyotr had remained silent, plainly worried about Marta. But at least the boy showed no panic, no sign he sensed the tigers nearby.

Once out of the water, Monk had everyone remove their clothes, twist them as dry as possible, and redress. The two-hour hike during the warmest part of the day had helped dry most of their clothes. But now they would get wet again, and the sun was setting. It would be a cold night.

But Konstantin was right. They had to keep moving for now. It was not safe to remain on solid ground with two tigers stalking these highland forests. The swamp would at least offer some shelter.

Monk picked a path down the steep ridge. He helped Pyotr, while Konstantin held his sister's hand. The two youngest children were fading fast. As a group, they sank out of the warmer sunlight and into the chillier shadows.

Trees grew heavier here, mostly pines and birches. But along the maze of creeks that flowed into the bog, willows draped with sullen shoulders, the tips of their branches sweeping the waters.

Monk headed out, forcing a path. The underbrush was a tangled mix of juniper bushes and berries. But the way grew clearer as the ground grew muddier. Soon they were stepping from moss clump to moss clump, which was not difficult, considering how well the mosses flourished here. The fuzzy green carpet covered rocky outcroppings and climbed up the white trunks of birches, as if trying to drag them beneath the earth.

Their pace began to slow, literally *bogged* down as the patches of stagnant water rose around them.

A piercing call drew Monk's eyes up. An eagle swept past with wings as wide as Monk's outstretched arms.

Hunting.

It reminded Monk of the dangers behind them.

He increased their pace. For once, the small children seemed better suited for the terrain. Their lighter bodies floated over the sucking mud, whereas Monk had to watch each step or lose a boot.

For the next hour, they moved sluggishly, traversing less than a mile by Monk's calculation. He spotted snakes that slithered from their path and caught a flashing glimpse of a fox as it hopped from hillock to hillock and vanished. Monk's ears strained for every noise. He heard things lumbering through the swamps. A heavy set of antlers marked the passage of a massive elk.

Before they knew it, they were ankle-deep in water, moving in a zigzagging pattern from island to island. The cold air smelled dank with algae and mold. Insects buzzed with a continual white noise. The passage grew darker as the sun continued to fall behind the mountains.

Monk's steps slipped to a plodding pace.

Konstantin moved alongside Monk's flank. He still held Kiska's hand. The girl was nearly asleep on her feet.

Pyotr stuck close to Monk's hip. Monk had to hike

the boy onto his shoulders whenever they crossed through deeper water.

Pyotr suddenly grabbed Monk's hand, clamping hard.

Something crashed through the trees, coming right at them.

Oh, no . . .

Monk yelled, knowing what was coming. 'Go! Run!'

Monk snatched up the boy, who struggled and cried out. Konstantin splashed away, his knees high, dragging his sister behind him. Monk's left foot sank to his calf. He tugged, but he could not free his limb. It was as if it had sunk into cement.

The rip and snap of branches aimed for them.

Monk tossed Pyotr ahead of him and twisted around to face the charge. He heard the boy splash into the water. But instead of running away, Pyotr scrabbled back to Monk.

'No! Pyotr, go!'

The boy continued past him as a large shadow leaped out of the trees and landed heavily into the water with a splash. Boy and shadow fell upon each other in a warm greeting.

Marta.

Monk fought the hammering in his heart. 'Pyotr, next time . . . some warning.' He wormed his foot slowly out of the muck.

The chimpanzee hugged the boy and lifted him bodily out of the shallow water. Konstantin and Kiska splashed back to them. Marta let Pyotr go and gave each child a tight squeeze. She came next to Monk, arms up and wide. He bent down and accepted a hug from her, too. Her body was hot, her breath huffing in his ear. He felt the tremble of exhaustion in her old body. He returned the hug, knowing how hard she must have fought to rejoin them.

As Monk straightened, he wondered how Marta *had*

found them. He did understand how she had overtaken them. While they had slogged through mud and water, she had swept through the bog's trees, closing the distance. But still, how had she tracked them?

Monk stared back into the dark fen.

If she could follow them . . .

'Let's keep moving,' he said and waved toward the heart of the swamps.

Together again, they traversed the swamplands. The reappearance of Marta invigorated the children, but the weight of the bog soon had them all heaving and struggling again. Konstantin drifted farther ahead. Pyotr hovered next to Monk, while Marta kept mostly to the trees, swinging low, her toes skimming the waters.

Slowly, the sun vanished behind the mountains, leaving them in dark twilight. Monk could barely make out Konstantin. Off to the left, an owl hooted in a long hollow note as full night threatened.

Konstantin called softly back to them out of a denser copse of willows, sounding urgent. 'An *izba*!'

Monk didn't know what he meant, but it didn't sound good. Hauling after the boy, Monk found the water growing less deep.

He pushed through a drape of willow branches and saw that one of the ubiquitous tiny islands rose ahead. But it wasn't empty. Atop the low hillock squatted a tiny cabin on short pylons. It was constructed of rough-hewn logs and topped by a moss-covered roof. The single window was dark. There was no sign of life. No smoke from the chimney.

Konstantin waited at the edge of the island among some tall reeds.

Monk joined him.

The tall boy pointed. 'A hunter's berth. Cabins like this are all over the mountains.'

'I'll check it out,' Monk said. 'Stay here.'

He climbed up onto the island and circled the cabin. It was small, with a chimney of stacked stone. Grasses grew as high as his waist. It didn't look as if anyone had been here in ages. There was a single window, shuttered closed from the inside. Monk spotted a short pier, empty of any boats. But a flat-bottomed punt – a raft with a pointed prow – had been pulled into some neighboring reeds. Moss covered half the raft, but hopefully it was still serviceable.

Monk returned to the front of the cabin. He tried the door. It was unlocked, but the boards had warped, and it took some effort to tug it open with a creaking pop from its rusted hinges. The interior was dark and smelled musty. But at least it was dry. The log cabin had only one room. The floor was pine with a scatter of hay over most of it. The only furniture was a small table with four chairs. Crude cabinets lined one whole wall, but there was no kitchen. It appeared that all the cooking was done at the fireplace, where some cast-iron pans and pots were stacked. Monk noted a stack of dry wood.

Good enough.

Monk stepped to the door and waved for the kids to come inside.

He hated to stop, but they all needed to rest for a bit. With the window shuttered, Monk could risk a small fire. It would be good to dry out their clothes and boots, have a warm place for the coldest part of the night. Once rested and dry, they could set out before dawn, hopefully using that raft.

Konstantin helped him get a fire started while the two children sat on the floor, leaning on Marta. The older boy found matches in a waxen box, and the old dry wood took to flame with just a touch of kindling. A fire stoked quickly, snapping and popping. Smoke vanished up the chimney's flue.

As Monk added another log, Konstantin searched the

cabinets. He discovered fishing tackle, a rusted lantern with a little sloshing kerosene, a single heavy bowie-style knife, and a half-empty box of shotgun shells. But no gun. In a closet, he found a few curled, yellow magazines sporting naked women, which Monk confiscated and found a good use for as kindling. But on the top shelf, four heavy faded quilts had been folded and stacked.

As Konstantin handed out the quilts, he pointed to Monk's discarded pack. Monk glanced over. The boy indicated his radiation monitor. No longer white, it now had a pink hue to it.

'Radiation,' Monk mumbled.

Konstantin nodded. 'The processing plant that poisoned Lake Karachay.' He waved toward the northeast. 'It also slowly leaked down into the ground.'

Contaminating the groundwater, Monk realized. And where did all the runoff from the local mountains end up? Monk stared toward the shuttered window, picturing the bog outside.

He shook his head.

And he thought all he had to worry about was man-eating tigers.

7:04 P.M.

Pyotr sat naked, huddled in a thick quilt before the fire. Their shoes were lined up on the hearth, and their clothes hung out to dry on fishing line. The line was so thin it was as if his pants and shirt were floating in the air.

He enjoyed the flickering flames as they danced and crackled, but he didn't like the smoke. It swirled up into the chimney as if it were something alive, born out of the fire.

He shivered and shifted on his backside closer to the bright flames.

235

The matron at the school used to tell them stories of the witch Baba Yaga, how she lived in a dark forest in a log cabin that moved around on chicken legs and would hunt down children to eat. Pyotr pictured the stilts he'd seen outside that held up their cabin. What if this was the witch's cabin, hiding its claws deep beneath the ground?

He eyed the smoke more suspiciously.

And didn't the witch have invisible servants to help her?

He searched around for them. He didn't see anything move on its own. But then again, the flames danced shadows everywhere, so it was hard to tell.

He moved closer again to the warmth of the flames. Still, he kept his eyes on the swirling curls of smoke.

He rocked slightly in place to reassure himself. Marta came up and slid next to him, curling around him. He leaned into her. A strong arm pulled him even closer.

Do not fear.

But he did fear. He felt it itching over the inside of his skull like a thousand spiders. He watched the smoke, knowing that was where the danger truly lay as it swept up the chimney, possibly warning Baba Yaga that there were children in her house.

Pyotr's heart thudded faster.

The witch was coming.

He knew it.

His eyes widened upon the smoke. He searched for the danger.

Marta *hoo-hoo-ed* in his ear, reassuring him, but it did no good. The witch was coming to eat them. They were in danger. Children in danger. The fire popped, scaring him into a small jump. Then he knew.

Not children.

But child.

And not them.

But another.

Pyotr stared hard at the smoke, pushing through the darkness to the truth. As the smoke curled to the sky, he saw who was in danger.

It was his sister.

Sasha.

11:07 A.M.
Washington, D.C.

'D.I.C.,' Lisa explained at the bedside of the girl.

Kat struggled to understand. She stood with her arms tight to her belly as she stared down at the tiny slip of a

237

girl, so thin-limbed in her hospital gown, lost amid the sheets and pillows of the railed bed. Wires trailed from under her sheets to a bank of equipment against one wall, monitoring blood pressure and heart rate. An intravenous line dripped a slurry of saline and medicines. Still, over the past hours, her pale skin had grown more ashen, her lips a hint of blue.

'Disseminated intravascular coagulation,' Lisa translated, though she might as well have been speaking Latin.

Monk, with his medical training, would have known what she was talking about. Kat shook this last thought out of her head, still rebounding from seeing the child's picture. She had plainly drawn it for Kat. They had formed a bond. Kat had seen it in the child's eyes when she read to her. Mostly the girl's manner was flat and affected, but occasionally she would turn those small eyes up at Kat. Something shone there, a mix of trust and almost recognition. It had melted Kat's heart. With a new baby herself, she knew her maternal instincts and hormones were running strong, her emotions raw with the recent loss of her husband.

'What does that mean?' Painter asked Lisa.

He stood on the opposite side of the bed beside Lisa. He had just returned after taking a call from Gray in India. His team had been attacked and was now headed to the northern regions. Painter was already investigating who had orchestrated the ambush – the assassination attempt on the professor could not have been coincidence, someone *knew* Gray had been flying out there. Despite needing to follow up on the mystery, the director had taken time to come down here to listen to Lisa's report.

Dr. Cummings had finished a slew of blood tests.

Before Painter's question could be answered, Dr. Sean McKnight entered the room. He had taken off his suit coat and tie. He had his sleeves rolled to the elbow. He had gone to make some calls following Gray's debriefing. Painter turned to him, an eyebrow raised in question, but Sean just waved for Lisa to continue. He sank into a bedside chair. He had kept a vigil there for the past hour. Even now he rested a hand on the bedsheet. Kat and Sean had talked for a long while. He had two grandchildren.

Lisa cleared her throat. 'D.I.C. is a pathological process where the body's blood begins to form tiny clots throughout all systems. It depletes the body's clotting factors and leads contrarily to internal bleeding. The causes are varied, but the condition arises usually secondary to a primary illness. Snake bites, cancers, major burns, shock. But one of the most common reasons is meningitis. Usually a septic inflammation of the brain. Which considering the fever and . . .'

Lisa waved to the device attached to the side of the child's skull. Her lips thinned with worry. 'All tests confirm the diagnosis. Decreased platelets, elevated FDPs, prolonged bleeding times. I'm certain of the diagnosis. I have her on platelets, and I'm transfusing her with antithrombin and drotrecogin alfa. It should help stabilize her for the moment, but the ultimate cure is to treat the primary disease that triggered the D.I.C. And that remains unknown. She's not septic. Her blood and CSF cultures are all negative. Might be viral, but I'm thinking something else is going on, something we're in the dark about, something tied to the implant.'

Kat took a deep, shuddering breath. 'And without knowing that . . .'

Lisa crossed her own arms to match Kat's pose. 'She's failing. I've slowed her decline, but we must know more. The initials – D.I.C. – have another connotation among medical professionals. They stand for *Death Is Coming*.'

Kat turned to Painter. 'We must do something.'

He nodded and glanced to Sean. 'We have no choice. We need answers. Maybe with time we could discern the pathology here, but there are certain individuals who know more, who are current with this biotechnology and know specifically what was done to this girl.'

Sean sighed. 'We'll have to tread carefully.'

Kat sensed a discussion had already occurred between Sean and Painter. 'What are you planning?'

'If we're going to save this child' – Painter stared at the fragile girl – 'we're going to have to get in bed with the enemy.'

11:38 P.M.

Trent McBride strode down the long deserted hallway. This section of Walter Reed was due for renovation. Hospital rooms to either side were in shambles, walls moldy, plaster cracked, but his goal was the mental ward lockdown in back. Here the walls were cement block, the windows barred, the doors steel with tiny grated cutouts.

Trent crossed to the last cell. A guard stood outside the door. They weren't taking any chances. The guard stepped to the side and offered a jangling set of keys to Trent.

He took them and checked through the small window in the door. Yuri lay sprawled fully dressed in the bed. Trent unlocked the door, and Yuri sat up. For an old man, he was wiry and spry, plainly he had been juicing up on a strong cocktail of androgens and other anti-aging hormones. How those Russians loved their performance-enhancing drugs.

He swung the door wide. 'Time to go to work, Yuri.'

The man stood up, his eyes flashing. 'Sasha?'

'We shall see.'

Yuri crossed to the door. Trent didn't like the resolute cast to the man's expression and grew suddenly suspicious. Rather than beaten, Yuri had an edge of steel to him, like a sword's blade pounded and folded to a finer edge. Maybe all the old man's strength didn't just come from injections into his ass cheeks.

But resolute or not, Yuri was under his thumb.

Still, Trent waved for the guard to follow with his sidearm. Trent had planned to walk Yuri back himself. Well over six feet and twice the man's weight, Trent hadn't been worried about needing an escort. But he did not trust the cast to Yuri's eye.

They headed out.

'Where are we going?' Yuri asked.

To put a final nail in Archibald Polk's coffin, he answered silently. Trent had orchestrated the death of his old friend, but now he was planning on putting an end to one of Archibald's shining successes, his brainchild, a secret organization that the man had dreamed up while serving the Jasons.

A team of killer scientists.

Basically Jasons with guns.

But after murdering the professor, Trent must now destroy the man's brainchild. For his own work to continue, Sigma must die.

12

As the sun sank into the horizon, Gray admitted that Rosauro's choice of vehicle proved to be a wise decision. In the passenger seat, he kept a palm pressed to the roof to keep him in his seat as their SUV bumped along a deeply rutted muddy road. They'd left the last significant town an hour ago and trekked through the rural back hills.

Dairy farms, sugarcane fields, and mango orchards divided the rolling landscape into a patchwork. Masterson had explained that Punjab was India's abundant breadbasket, the Granary of India, as he described it, producing a majority of its wheat, millet, and rice.

'And someone has to work all these fields,' Masterson had said as he gave them directions from the backseat.

Kowalski and Elizabeth shared the row with him. Behind them, Luca sat in the rear, polishing his daggers.

'Take that next left track,' Masterson ordered.

Rosauro hauled on the wheel, and the SUV splashed through a watery ditch, almost a creek. Small downpours had dumped on them throughout the trip up here. *Punjab* was Persian for 'land of five rivers,'

243

which was one of the reasons it was India's major agricultural state.

Gray checked the twilight skies as night approached. Clouds rolled low. They'd have more rain before the night was over.

'Up ahead,' Masterson said. 'Over that next hill.'

The vehicle slogged up the slope, churning mud. At the top of the rise, a small bowl-shaped valley opened, ringed by hills. A dark village lay at the bottom, a densely packed mix of stone homes and mud huts with palm-thatch roofs. A couple of fires glowed at the edge of the town, stirred by a few men standing around with long poles. Burning garbage. A bullock cart stood beside one fire, stacked high with refuse. The single horned bull stirred at the approach of their vehicle down the hill.

'The other side of India,' Masterson said. 'Over three-quarters of India's population still live in rural areas. But here we have those who live at the bottom of the caste system. The Harijan, as Gandhi renamed them, which means "people of God," but they are mostly still derided as *dalit* or *achuta,* which roughly translates as *untouchable.*'

Gray noted Luca had sheathed his daggers and turned a more attentive ear. *Untouchables.* These could be the same roots as his clans.

Lit by flames, the village men gathered with scythes and poles, wary of the approaching strangers.

'Who are these people?' Gray asked, wanting to know more about whom they faced.

'To answer that,' Masterson said, 'you have to understand India's caste system. Legends have that all the major *varnas* – or classes of people – arose from one godlike being. The Brahmans, which include priests and teachers, arose out of the mouth of this being. Rulers and soldiers from its arms. Merchants and traders from

244

its thighs. The feet gave rise to laborers. Each has its own pecking order, much of it laid out in a two-thousand-year-old collection known as the Laws of Manu, which details what you can and can't do.'

'And these untouchables?' Gray asked, keeping an eye on the gathering men and boys.

'The fifth *varna* is said *not* to have risen from this great being at all. They were outcasts, considered too polluted and impure to mix with regular people. People who handled animal skins, blood, excrement, even the bodies of the dead. They were shunned from higher-caste homes and temples, not allowed to eat with the same utensils. Not even their shadows were allowed to touch a higher caste's body. And if you should break any of these rules, you could be beaten, raped, murdered.'

Elizabeth leaned forward. 'And no one stops this from happening?'

Masterson snorted. 'The Indian constitution outlaws such discrimination, but it still continues, especially in rural areas. Fifteen percent of the population still falls into the classification of untouchable. There is no escape. A child born from an *achuta* is forever an *achuta*. They remain victims of millennia-old religious laws, laws that permanently cast them as subhuman. And let's be honest. Like I said before, someone has to work all these fields.'

Gray pictured the vast rolling farmlands and orchards.

Masterson continued, 'The untouchables are a built-in slave class. So while there is some progress made on their behalf, mostly in the cities, the rural areas still need workers – and the caste system serves them well. Villages such as this one have been burned or destroyed because they dared to ask for better wages or working conditions. Hence the suspicion here now.'

He nodded to the welcoming party carrying farm instruments.

'Dear God,' Elizabeth said.

'God has nothing to do with this,' Masterson said sourly. 'It's all about economy. Your father was a strong advocate for these people. Lately he was having more and more trouble gaining the cooperation of yogis and Brahman mystics.'

'Because of his association with untouchables?' she asked.

'That . . . and the fact that he was looking for the source of the genetic marker among the untouchable peoples. When word spread of that, many doors were slammed in his face. So much for higher enlightenment. In fact, after he disappeared, I was convinced he'd been murdered for that very reason.'

Gray waved Rosauro to stop at the edge of the glow from the burning garbage fires. 'And this village? This is where Dr. Polk was last seen?'

Masterson nodded. 'The last I heard from Archibald was an excited phone call. He'd made some discovery and was anxious to share it – then I never heard from him again. But he sometimes did that – would vanish for months at a time into the remote rural areas, going from village to village. Places that still have no name and are shunned by those of higher castes. But after a while, I began to fear the worst.'

'And what of these people?' Gray asked. 'Do we have anything to fear from them?'

'On the contrary.' Masterson opened his car door and used his cane to push to his feet.

Gray followed him. Other doors opened, and everyone exited. 'Stay near the truck,' he warned them.

Masterson traipsed toward the fire with Gray in tow. The professor called out in Hindi. Gray understood a few phrases and words from his own studies of Indian religion and philosophy, but not enough to follow what the man was saying. He seemed to be asking for someone, searching faces.

246

The men remained a solid wall, bristling with weapons.

The ox lowed its own complaint beside the wagon, as if sensing the tension.

Finally Masterson stood between the two smoking pyres. The air reeked, smelling of fried liver and burning tires. Gray forced himself not to cover his mouth. Masterson waved back to the truck and continued to speak. Gray heard Archibald Polk's name followed by the Hindi word *betee*.

Daughter.

All the men turned their gazes toward Elizabeth. Weapons were lowered. Chatter spread among them. Arms pointed at her. The wall of men parted in welcome. A pair of the boys, their voices raised in a happy shout, ran back down a narrow alleyway between two stone houses.

Masterson turned to Gray. 'The *achuta* in this area hold Archibald in high esteem. I had no doubt the presence of the respected man's daughter would be met with hospitality. We have nothing to fear from these people.'

'Except for dysentery,' Kowalski said as he reached them with the others.

Elizabeth elbowed him in the ribs.

Gray led them into the village, sensing they had more to worry about than just upset bowels.

8:02 P.M.

Elizabeth crossed between the two fires. Beyond their glow, the village roused. Someone started to clank loudly on a makeshift drum. A woman appeared, her face half covered in a sari. She motioned them toward the village center.

As she turned, Elizabeth caught a glimpse of scarred, sagging flesh, hidden under the thin veil. Masterson noted Elizabeth's attention.

247

She leaned toward him. 'What happened to her?'

The professor answered softly and nodded to the woman. 'Your father mentioned her. Her son was caught fishing in a pond of a higher-caste village. She went to scold him off, but they were caught. The villagers beat the child and poured acid on the woman's face. She lost an eye and half her face.'

Elizabeth's body went cold. 'How awful.'

'And she considers herself lucky. Because they didn't rape her, too.'

Shocked, Elizabeth followed the woman, galled by such an atrocity, but at the same time, awed by her strength to survive and persevere.

The woman led them along a maze of crooked alleys to the village center. Another fire blazed there. People gathered at a few wooden tables around a well pump. Women swept the tables free of leaves or carried out food. Young children ran all around, barefoot, mostly shirtless.

As Elizabeth passed, several men bowed their heads, sometimes even at the waist as she walked. Plainly in respect for her father. She had never known much about what he'd been doing out here.

Masterson motioned with his cane toward the men. 'Archibald did much good for the local villages. He exposed and disbanded a militia that terrorized these parts, even got better wages for the villagers, better medical care and education. But more important, he respected them.'

'I didn't know,' she mumbled.

'He won their trust. And it was in these hills that he concentrated his genetic testing.'

'Why here?' Gray asked on the professor's other side.

'Because just as Archibald devised that map I showed you, he also did a more detailed schematic of the Punjab region. A trail of genetic evidence pointed to these hills, but I think it was something more.'

Elizabeth frowned. 'Like what?'

'I'm not sure. His interest in the region spiked about two years ago. He stopped testing broadly across India and began concentrating here.' The professor glanced back to Luca. 'And with the Gypsies.'

Elizabeth thought back two years. She had been finishing her PhD program at Georgetown. She'd had little contact with her father during that time. Nor patience. Their occasional phone conversations were usually short and terse. If she had known what he was doing beyond his own field of study, maybe things could have been different.

Reaching the heart of the village, they were greeted with smiles and urged to come to the table. Food was already piling high – roti flatbread, rice dishes, steamed vegetables, small plums and fat dates, bowls of buttermilk – simple but heartfelt fare. A woman on her knees stirred a lentil stew on a horseshoe-shaped oven. Her daughter carried a bucket of cow dung to feed the flames beneath.

Kowalski joined Elizabeth, stepping close. 'Not exactly Burger King.'

'Maybe because they worship cows.'

'Hey, I worship them, too. Especially grilled rare with a nice baked potato.'

She smiled. How did that infernal man always get her to smile? She was suddenly too conscious of how close he stood and stepped away.

Off to the side, one of the villagers began plucking the strings of a sitar, accompanied by a man with a harmonica and another with a tabla drum.

A tall newcomer stepped up to them all. He appeared to be in his midthirties, his hair cropped short, olive skinned. He was dressed in a traditional dhoti kurta, a spotless wrap of rectangular cloth that hung from waist to ankle, along with a tunic buttoned over a long-sleeved shirt. Atop his head, he wore an embroidered knitted cap called a kufi. He bowed deeply and spoke in English with a crisp British accent.

'I am Abhi Bhanjee, but I would be honored if you would call me Abe. We Indians have a saying: *At ithi devo bhava*. It means "Our guests are like gods." And none more so than the daughter of Professor Archibald Polk, a dear friend of mine.' He waved them to the table. 'Please join us.'

They obeyed, but it did not take long for his smile to dim as the man learned about her father.

'I had not heard,' he said softly, his face a mask of pain. 'It is a loss most tragic and sad. My condolences, Miss Polk.'

She bowed her head in acknowledgment.

'He was last seen here at your village,' Gray added and nodded to Masterson. 'He called the professor, said he was coming here.'

Masterson cleared his throat. 'We hoped you might be able to cast a light on where Archibald went.'

'I knew he should not have gone alone,' the man said with a shake of his head. 'But he would not wait.'

'Go where?' Gray asked.

'It was wrong to take him there to begin with. It is a cursed place.'

Elizabeth reached and touched the man's hand with her fingertips. 'If you know something . . . anything . . .'

He swallowed visibly and reached to a pocket inside his tunic. He slipped out a tiny cloth bag that clinked. 'It all started when I showed your father these.' He fingered the bag open and upended the contents onto the table. 'We find them occasionally when we till the fields of these lands.'

Old tarnished coins, nearly black with age, rattled and danced. One rolled to Elizabeth. She stopped it with her palm, then picked it up. She examined the surface, rubbing some of the grime with her thumb – until she realized what she was holding.

Upon the surface, abraded but still distinct, was the face of a woman, her cheeks framed by a tangle of small snakes. It was the Gorgon named Medusa. Elizabeth knew what she was holding.

'An ancient Greek coin,' she said with surprise. 'You found these in your fields?'

Abe nodded.

'Amazing.' Elizabeth turned the coin toward the firelight. 'Greeks did rule the Punjab for a while. Along with Persians, Arabs, Mughals, Afghans. Alexander the Great even fought a great battle in this region.'

Gray picked up another coin. His expression darkened. He held out the coin toward her. 'You'd better look at this, Elizabeth.'

She took it and studied it. Her fingers began to tremble. Upon its surface, a Greek temple had been minted. And not just any temple. She stared at the three pillars that framed a dark doorway. Prominent in that threshold stood a large letter *E*.

'It's the Temple of Delphi,' she gasped out.

'It looks like the same coin your father stole from the museum.'

She struggled to understand, but she could not think. It was as if someone had short-circuited her brain. 'When . . . when did you first show my father these coins?'

Abe frowned. 'I'm not certain. About two years ago. He told me to keep them safe and hidden, but since he is dead and you are his daughter . . .'

She barely heard him. Two years ago. The same time her father had arranged for her to work at the Delphi museum. She sensed she was holding the coin that had bought her the museum position. Too busy here himself, her father must have wanted her to follow up on this mystery. A spark of anger fired through her, but she was also too aware of the villagers around her and how they'd been treated. Maybe her father couldn't leave, couldn't abandon them.

Still, he could have told her something.

Unless . . . maybe he was protecting her?

She shook her head, filled with questions. What was going on here? She sought answers on the other side of the coin. The surface was black with a large worn symbol that did not appear to be Greek.

Abe noted her confused expression. He pointed to the coin, having studied it before. 'That is a chakra wheel. An ancient Hindu symbol.'

But what's it doing on a Greek coin? she wondered.

'May I see?' Luca asked. He crossed around the table to stare over her shoulder. His body stiffened, and his fingers tightened on the table's edge. 'That . . . that symbol. It's also on the Romani flag.'

'What?' Elizabeth asked.

He straightened, his brow crinkled with confusion. 'The symbol was chosen because the Sanskrit word *chakra* means "wheel." It is said to represent a Gypsy's wagon wheel, symbolic of our nomadic heritage, while still honoring our Indian roots. But there were always rumors that the symbol had deeper, more ancient roots among the clans.'

As the others discussed the significance, Elizabeth studied the coin in silence, beginning to sense at least one truth.

Gray leaned toward her, reading something on her face. 'What is it?'

She met his steely gaze. She held up the coin and pointed to the temple side. 'My father pulled strings to get me that position at the Delphi museum shortly after finding this.' She flipped the coin to the chakra side. 'At the same time, he started to investigate the Gypsies and their connection to India. Two sides of a coin, two lines of inquiry.'

Elizabeth turned the coin on edge. 'But what lies between the two? What connects them?'

She turned to Abhi Bhanjee. He had not told them everything.

'Where did my father go?' she asked with a bite to her voice.

A shout from one of the villagers answered her. A man came running from the outer fires. The music died away – but a distant drumming continued, a heavy beat that thumped to the chest.

Gray jerked up.

Elizabeth stood, confused, and stared out toward the hills, trying to discern the direction of the noise, but it seemed to come from everywhere – then three lights speared out of the overcast sky.

Helicopters.

'Everyone back to the SUV!' Gray shouted.

Abe yelled in Hindi, barking hard orders. Men and women fled in all directions. In the tumult, Elizabeth got separated, spun by passing bodies. Disoriented, she fought to follow their group.

Like diving hawks, the helicopters swept toward the village, then split wide to circle. With her eyes on the skies, she stumbled, but a thick arm caught her. Kowalski scooped her around the waist and lifted her to her toes, urging her faster.

'C'mon, babe.'

He forded through the chaos, a rolling rock.

At the edges of the village, the helicopters settled to a hover. Ropes slithered out from open side doors. Even before their ends reached the ground, dark forms slid down the lines, heavy with helmets and gear.

They would never make it to the SUV.

8:38 P.M.
Pripyat, Ukraine

Nicolas snapped his cell phone closed. *So that was one less problem to worry about.* He crossed down the hallway toward the gala. Music wafted, a traditional Russian composition from the nineteenth century, 'Snegúrochka,' 'The Snow Maiden.'

He drew his palm down the lines of his tuxedo. While others dressed in modern couture, Nicolas had handpicked his outfit in Milan, a single-button Brioni cashmere jacket with a peaked lapel and shawl collar. It was classic and elegant, chosen because the Duke of Windsor had worn such suits in the 1930s and 1940s. It had a vintage look that melded with Nicolas's rhetoric, but he had updated his appearance by replacing the traditional bow tie – which never looked good with his trimmed beard – with a silk pleated tie, accented by a diamond tack set in Russian silver.

Knowing how well he looked, he entered the ballroom.

New marble floors shone under the light of a dozen Baccarat crystal chandeliers, a charitable donation by the company for this event. Tables circled an empty dance floor. But the true dancing had already commenced. The crowd mingled and swirled in eddies of political power, vying for the right nod, a moment alone with the right potentate, a whispered deal.

Russia's prime minister and the U.S. president

created the largest pools. Each was vying for support in regard to how to handle sanctions against burgeoning nuclear threats. An important summit on the matter was scheduled in St. Petersburg after the ceremony here. The sealing of Chernobyl was the symbolic start of that meeting.

Nicolas stared over at the pair, surrounded by a sea of people. He intended to wade into those waters. With his growing popularity as the spokesman for nuclear reform, those seas would easily part for him.

He should at least shake the hands of the two men he planned to kill.

But before he waded into those waters, he headed over to Elena. She stood by one of the arched windows. Heavy silk drapery framed both the window and the woman. She cut a stately figure in a black dress that flowed like oil over her lithe form, a Hollywood matinee idol brought back to life. She carried a flute of champagne in one hand, as if forgotten. She faced the darkness beyond the window.

He joined her.

Beyond the ruins of the city, bright lights twinkled near the horizon. Work crews would labor throughout the night to ready the viewing stands and ensure that the installation of the new Sarcophagus over the shell of Chernobyl went smoothly. The eyes of the world would be on the event.

He touched her arm.

She was not startled, having noticed his reflection in the mirror.

His voluptuous Rasputin.

'It is almost over,' he said and leaned to her ear.

According to his man, the concussion charges had already been secured in place. Nothing could stop them.

Gunfire erupted before Gray could reach the edge of the village. Screams and shouts echoed. Helicopters thumped overhead. He flattened himself against a stone wall. Beyond the pair of garbage fires, the Mercedes SUV rested at the edge of the glow.

A soldier in black gear ran low across the open ground, assault rifle at his shoulder. Others had to be already solidifying positions around the village, locking the place down. Then they'd close in for the kill, sweeping through the maze of the village.

Gray knew the only hope for the villagers was for his team to flee, to draw off the hunters. They had to make their escape before the village was secured.

He stretched an arm back to Rosauro. 'Keys.'

They were slapped into his hand, but Rosauro had more bad news. 'Kowalski. Elizabeth. They're not here.'

Gray glanced back. In the mad rush through the twisted alleys, he'd failed to notice. 'Find them,' he ordered Rosauro. 'Now.'

She nodded and dashed away.

Gray stared hard at Luca. 'Guard the professor. Stay out of sight.'

The Gypsy nodded. Two daggers glinted in his fingers.

Gray could wait no longer.

Crouching low, he ran out of hiding and into the open.

Elizabeth fled with Kowalski down a crooked alley. A sewage trench lined one side, reeking and foul.

'Follow that,' she urged. 'It has to lead out of here.'

Kowalski nodded and took the next corner. He had a pistol clenched in a meaty paw. She kept to his shoulder.

'Do you have another gun?' she asked.

'You shoot?'

'Skeet. In college.'

'Not much difference. Targets just scream a bit more.'

He reached under his jacket to the small of his back and slipped out a small blue steel Beretta and passed it blindly back to her.

Her fingers tightened hard on the grip, drawing strength from the cold steel.

They set off. The alleyway was deserted, but gunfire spat from the outskirts as villagers defended their homes and lives.

One of the helicopters swept low overhead. The wash from its rotors scattered leaves and bits of garbage. They ducked out of sight into a mud hut. Elizabeth caught a glimpse of children huddled behind a low cot.

After the helicopter flew past, Kowalski tugged her toward the door – but then piled back into her. A soldier in black dashed past the opening. The war must be moving into the village proper. Kowalski peeked out, waved for her, then led her back outside.

'We'll strike for the hills,' he said.

They zigzagged through two more turns and reached a straight shot toward open hills. Bodies lay on the street ahead, blood sluicing into the sewage drain. At least one of them wore black camouflage. Kowalski kept close to one wall and hurried forward. He led with his pistol up.

A spat of automatic fire chattered beyond the village.

How would they get past that?

Kowalski paused at the soldier's dead body. He tugged off the man's helmet.

Maybe a disguise, Elizabeth thought. Not bad thinking.

But as Kowalski yanked, the soldier's head came off with the helmet. Shocked and horrified, he fell back into her. Tangled, they both stumbled to the ground.

A dark shadow appeared behind them.

Another soldier.

She raised her pistol and shot wildly. The rounds cracked stones and ricocheted, missing the target but driving him back around the corner. Kowalski's weapon blasted behind her, sounding like a cannon in the narrow alley. She risked a glance over her shoulder and saw two more soldiers at the end of the street.

They were pinned down and outgunned.

Gray ducked out of the alley and into the open. He dove under the bullock cart that still stood by the pyres of burning garbage. Sliding on his stomach, he edged even with one of the fires. Shielded by the cart, he reached out to the edge of the bonfire. If the gunshots and helicopters didn't spook the ox from its post, then Gray would have to light a fire under its tail.

Literally.

Snatching up a chunk of burning tire from the pyre's edge, Gray flipped it into the oily pile of refuse still stacked atop the cart. It didn't take long for the flames to catch and spread. With a burning branch in his other hand, he crawled fully under the cart and goosed the ox in the hind end.

It roared a loud bellow and kicked back at him, knocking the cart a good blow. Gray snatched the front board of the wagon as the ox took off, lowing angrily. It shot straight for the hills, dragging the cart, leaving behind a trail of flaming garbage.

Bumped and jarred underneath the cart, Gray kept a hard clamp on the front board and made sure to stay clear of the heavy wheels. The ox and cart reached the hills and bounced across a runoff ditch.

Gray let go and sank into the watery mud and muck.

The cart continued off into the hills, a fiery meteor sailing to points unknown. Gray hoped any eyes in the sky would keep watching that flaming trajectory.

In the dark, Gray swam and pushed along the muddy ditch as it circled the village. He reached the far side of the Mercedes and waited for the nearest helicopter to drift farther away – then lurched out of the gully and ran low to the ground, keeping the SUV between him and the village.

He'd have to get inside the vehicle quickly. The SUV's dome light would illuminate when he opened the door. Keys in hand, he took a deep breath.

He could wait no longer.

Pinned in the alleyway with soldiers at both ends, Elizabeth searched for an escape. She found one. An open window. A step away.

She nudged Kowalski and pointed.

'Go!' he growled.

She dove through the opening. Cradling her pistol, she landed in a rough tumble. The room was empty, just a dirt floor. Kowalski came barreling in after her. She barely got out of the way in time. Gunfire strafed at his heels. Boots pounded toward them from both directions.

'Door,' she called.

On the opposite side from the window, a low archway led into another alley. Together they fled outside—

—and right into a clutch of another four soldiers.

With surprise on all sides, they scrambled with weapons. But before a shot could be fired, flashes of flailing steel rained down upon the soldiers. Elizabeth and Kowalski backed together. One man pointed his pistol out at the attackers, but steel snapped and sliced his hand from his arm. Another fell to his knees, his throat slashed open.

In a heartbeat, all four men lay dead, torn apart.

Their rescuers were three men.

Abe and two of the villagers.

Their weapons were unique to the country. *Urumi*. The infamous whip-swords of India. Each sword was a flail of four flexible blades, each an inch wide and five feet long – yet so thin that the steel coiled like a whip. Elizabeth's father had shown her demonstrations of the fighting known as Kalaripayattu. With a flick of the wrist, the blades unfurled and cleaved flesh with more force than any standard sword.

'Come!' Abe said. 'Your friends are this way.'

He led them back into the village. They followed a circuitous path both around and through village homes and huts. Abe lashed out with the sword occasionally, striking even around corners to blind and maim. Then he'd jump out to finish the job with his men.

Kowalski's eyes gleamed in the darkness as he watched the slaughter. 'With a weapon like that, no wonder they're called untouchable. I have to get me one of those.'

Coming around another corner, Abe slashed out – then jerked his arm back with a glint of thrashing steel. A cry of surprise sounded from around the corner.

'So sorry,' Abe said.

Rosauro appeared. She held a hand across her cheek. Blood seeped from under her fingers. But her eyes widened when she saw who accompanied the swordsman.

'Thank God I found you,' she said. 'Hurry!'

As a group, they fled after her.

After a flurry of confusing turns, a familiar pair of fires glowed at the end of an alley. Crouched between two mud huts, Luca waved to them. Elizabeth spotted the professor, huddled deeper in the shadows.

Where was Gray?

As answer, a heavy engine roared to life beyond the village.

'Get ready!' Rosauro growled at them, blood running down her face.

Ready for what?

Gray shifted into drive and floored the gas pedal. All four tires catapulted him forward. The SUV lunged as one of the rear-side windows splintered. He shot past the twin garbage fires.

A helicopter swooped into view ahead. It had no mounted gun, but it did have someone hanging from its side door with a machine gun.

Gray pounded the brakes. Bullets strafed through the mud just past his front bumper. He threw the truck into reverse, hit the gas, and hightailed it backward with the strength of five hundred horses.

Yanking the wheel, he whipped around his back end, lifting up on two wheels. Landing on four tires, he shot back toward the alley and hit the rear hatch release. A warning light flashed on the dash as the back hatch swung open on hydraulic hinges. He crashed between the two fires, scattering flaming garbage.

He braked to a stop, nearly striking Rosauro in the thighs as she rushed at him with the others. They clambered and dove into the back cabin. People fell in a tangle in the middle row, making room. He spotted a familiar shaved bulldog's head. They'd found Kowalski.

And Elizabeth, too.

Presently crushed under the large man.

Rosauro called from the rear, 'Go!'

Gray kicked the gas and punched the hatch release to close the door.

Ahead, two helicopters aimed toward him from opposite directions. Twin lines of bullets chewed through the mud.

Gray swerved, juking one way, then the other.

The helicopters matched his moves.

A torrent of fresh gunfire erupted from the village behind him – aimed at the birds in the sky. The barrage was impressive, even laced with fiery tracer rounds. A few of the villagers must have confiscated some of the assault team's automatic weapons.

One of the snipers in the helicopter fell from his perch. Its searchlight shattered and went dark.

The other bird veered. Gray ducked past its hail of fire and reached the hills. He kept the gas floored. With his headlights off, he followed the path of the bullock cart, hoping whatever path the ox took would be passable with the four-wheel drive.

He shot away from the bright fires of the village and out into the rolling darkness. Two helicopters followed, chasing them with searchlights. The third lowered at the edge of the village, dropping lines to the ground, collecting stray men.

Rosauro leaned forward. 'They're Russians!'

'Russians?'

'I think so,' she explained. 'The commandos were carrying AN-94s.'

Russian military assault rifles.

In the rearview mirror, Gray caught a worried glimpse on Masterson's face. First an American mercenary team, *now Russians* . . . How many people wanted this guy dead? Answers would have to wait for the moment.

Gray could see that the helicopters, reflected in his mirrors, continued to close the distance. While Gray had succeeded in his plan – getting the team clear of the village and drawing off the assault team – now what?

'Turn right at the bottom of the next hill!' a voice called behind him with a British accent. Gray glanced back and saw they had a stowaway.

Abhi Bhanjee.

Rosauro explained, 'He knows a way to shake our tail!'

Hitting the bottom of the slope with a splash of water, Gray took a hard right and followed the muddy valley.

'Now left past that next fencerow!' Abe yelled.

What fencerow?

Gray leaned forward. Without headlights, it was too dark to see. If only he had more lights . . .

A helicopter swept past, its searchlight blazing. It was not exactly what Gray had been hoping for. Still, with the better illumination, he spotted a fence of stacked stones ahead. Unfortunately the beam also spotted them. Brilliant light swamped the SUV.

A salvo of gunfire erupted, peppering the water, pinging his back end.

With no time to spare, Gray reached the fence and yanked to the left. Even with the four-wheel drive, the back end fishtailed in the water and mud. But the tires finally gripped, and they fled up a short rise and out of the water.

The helicopter swept wide. But its spotlight pivoted smoothly and kept fixed to them, tracking their passage below.

Shooting over the top of the next rise, the SUV lifted into the air for a breath, then struck down hard enough to knock Gray's teeth together. Cries rose from the rear.

At the bottom of the slope and to the right, a black sea divided the gray landscape ahead. It was not water, but a vast forest.

'Mango orchard!' Abe said. 'Very old farm. Very old trees. My family has worked many generations there.'

Gray shot toward that dark orchard.

The spotlight followed. Gunfire rained at them, but Gray kept a slaloming, unpredictable course. Not a single bullet touched them.

With a final roar of the engine, they barreled into the orchard. Trees towered in straight rows. Branches arched into a continuous canopy, cutting off the glare of the spotlight. Gray slowed as the light vanished and darkness fell around him. Still, he made several turns, running perpendicular to their original path. The thumping of the helicopter's blades faded. Gray fled deeper, like an escaped prisoner running through a dark cornfield.

'How large is this orchard?' he asked, calculating how well they'd be able to hide here.

'Over ten thousand acres.'

That's one big cornfield.

As the danger ebbed, everyone settled themselves more comfortably into their seats.

Rosauro leaned forward. 'There's another reason Abe insisted he come along.'

'Why's that?'

She lifted a coin into view. It was the Greek coin with the chakra wheel on the back. She pointed to the temple.

'He knows where this is.'

Gray glanced into the rearview mirror. He spotted Abhi Bhanjee seated in the back row next to Luca. Even through the gloom, Gray recognized the man's terror. He remembered the Hindu man's description about where Archibald Polk had been headed when he'd vanished.

A cursed place.

13

Monk kept guard.

In dry clothes and with his bones warmed by the hearth, Monk circled the cabin. He creaked around as quietly as possible, stepping carefully. He wore his boots, though the laces were untied. He had all the children redress and put on their shoes before curling up in their quilts. If they had to leave suddenly, he didn't want them fumbling with clothing.

Konstantin and Kiska huddled together, each cocooned in their blankets. They seemed smaller in sleep, especially Konstantin. His sharp attention and mature speech patterns made him seem older. But with his body relaxed, Monk realized he could be no older than twelve.

Stepping past them, Monk moved extra softly. By now, he knew which floorboards creaked the loudest and avoided them. Pyotr lay curled in the embrace of the old chimpanzee. She sat on the floor, her head hung to her chest, breathing deeply in sleep. Pyotr had panicked earlier, scared for his twin sister. Monk trusted the boy's instinct, but there was nothing they could do. It took a full hour to get Pyotr to finally relax, but the day's trek had worn the boy to a thread. He finally succumbed to his exhaustion and drifted to sleep, guarded over by Marta.

No matter how softly Monk tread, she would lift her head toward him as he passed. Bleary, warm eyes stared up at him, then the lids drifted down along with her head.

Keep watching over him, Marta.

At least someone loved these children.

Monk returned to his seat beside the door. He had upended the table across the threshold and had positioned a chair in front of that. He sank to it with a sigh.

He listened to the night noises of the swamp: the gurgle of water, the croaking of frogs, the buzz of crickets, and the occasional soft hooting of a hunting owl. He had been startled earlier by something large moving past the cabin, but a peek through the shutters revealed a muddy boar, grubbing around.

Monk let the creature roam, serving as a tusked sentinel. But eventually it moved on.

The rhythms of the swamp lulled him. Before long, his own chin sank toward his chest. He'd only close his eyes for a few minutes.

—You're late again, Monk! Get moving!

His head snapped back up, cracking against the underside of the upended table. Pain lanced through his skull – not from his knock against wood, but from deeper down. For a moment, he tasted . . . tasted *cinnamon,* spiced and warm, along with a whispery brush against his lips. A scent filled him, stirred him.

It faded quickly.

Just a dream . . .

But Monk knew better. He sat straighter as the icy spike of pain melted away. He fingered the sutures behind his ear.

Who am I?

Konstantin had described a sinking cruise liner, a weighted net, and his rescue at sea. Had he worked on

266

the ship? Had he been a passenger? There was no answer inside him, only darkness.

Monk gazed across the room and found a pair of eyes staring back at him. Pyotr hadn't moved. He just looked at Monk. The knock of his head against the table must have woken the boy.

Or maybe it was something else.

Monk met the boy's gaze. He read a well of sorrow in the child's eyes, too deep for one so young. It scared Monk a little. It was no simple grief or fear. Hopelessness shone in his tiny face, a despair that had no place in any child's eyes. The boy shivered, stirring Marta.

She hooted softly and looked over her shoulder at Monk.

He stood and crossed to them. The boy's face gleamed brightly in the firelight. Too brightly. Monk checked his forehead.

Hot. Feverish.

That's all he needed was a sick child.

Couldn't he catch even a small break?

His silent question was answered by a feral scream. Close. It started as a throaty growl, and then pitched into a full scream. It reminded Monk of someone yanking on the cord of a chain saw.

A second cry answered from the opposite side of the domicile.

The feral screams jerked both Konstantin and Kiska to their feet.

There had been no warning.

Monk had heard no sign of the cats' approach. Even the boy had remained unaware. Maybe it was the fever or simple exhaustion. Monk had hoped for some notice.

The cabin was not secure. From what he saw on the riverbank earlier, each tiger weighed around seven hundred pounds, most of it toughened muscle. The cats could tear through the door or claw through the roof in seconds. But for now, they circled, growling, sizing up the place.

Konstantin had expressed another concern. Even if the tigers didn't storm the cabin, they were surely being followed by hunters on two legs. They could not let the cats trap them here.

So with no choice, they moved quickly.

Monk slipped the spear-point bowie knife they'd found in the cabin from his belt and clenched the wooden handle between his teeth – then he crossed to the stone hearth and pulled a flaming brand out of the fire. Earlier, using the knife, he had chopped a three-foot-long branch from a scraggly pine outside. The resin was highly combustible and had fueled the stick into a fiery torch.

Monk hurried around the room. He tapped the torch to the underside of the thatch roof. Long neglected, it was as dry as tinder. He had also emptied the kerosene from the rusty lantern into some rags and stuffed them in the roof.

Flames spread quickly.

The cats yowled into higher octaves, splitting the night.

Behind Monk, Konstantin lifted two pine boards from the floor. Monk had already pried out the old nails with the same knife and loosened the boards. Raised on short stilts, the cabin had a low crawl space beneath it, open on all sides. It was too low-roofed for Monk, but not for the children or Marta. He prayed the cats could not shimmy under there also.

Opposite the door, Kiska unlatched the shutter from the cabin's window and dropped it open.

At the same time, Monk kicked the table aside from the door.

Ready and running out of time, he waved the kids below as smoke filled the upper half of the cabin and heat blazed down.

Marta helped Pyotr under the floorboards. Kiska

268

went next. Konstantin followed. The older boy nodded to Monk, no longer a *boy,* but a dour young man again. 'Be careful,' Konstantin warned.

With the dagger between his teeth, Monk returned his nod.

Konstantin dropped away and vanished.

Monk had to keep the cats distracted. The roof fire and smoke should confuse them. He had to add to it. With the torch in his hand, he counted to ten – then kicked the warped door with all his strength. Boards cracked, and the door smashed wide.

A tiger crouched three yards away. Startled, it curled into a long menacing hiss. One claw swiped at the empty air in his direction.

The feline equivalent of *fuck you.*

Monk gaped a half second at its sheer size. Thirteen feet long. Eyes glowed with reflected firelight as the cabin's roof burned. Lips rippled back, pink tongue arched deep inside a cage of long fangs.

Monk swung the torch in a fiery arc. His heart pounded a primal drumbeat that traced back to mankind's prehistoric roots huddled in dark caves.

Still, as he'd hoped, the loud bang of the door drew the second cat. It came ripping around the corner on the left, low to the ground, a blur of striped fur and massive paws. Monk shoved his torch in the cat's face as it lunged at him.

Fur burned, and the cat screeched and rolled away.

Monk caught a glimpse of the tiger's gnarled left ear, marking this one as Zakhar.

His brother Arkady howled and charged, defending his littermate.

Monk knew the cat intended to bowl into him, torch or not.

So Monk hiked his arm back and hurled the fiery brand like a javelin. It speared through the air and struck the tiger square in its open mouth. The cat shot straight up, spitting and writhing in midair.

Monk grabbed the knife from his teeth, pivoted on his toe, and lunged back into the cabin. As he turned, from the corner of his eye, he spotted Zakhar pounding straight at him.

Gasping in terror, Monk sprinted across the smoky interior of the cabin. Like tear gas, the heat and sting of soot blinded him. He ran on instinct. The open window lay directly opposite the door. Blinking tears, he made out a darker square set against the blurry wall.

He dove straight at it, stretching his arms ahead of him.

His aim was sure – until a claw snagged his pant leg. Cloth ripped free, but his body jerked. His shoulder hit the window's edge with an arm-numbing blow. His momentum enabled him to tumble out the window. He landed hard with the wind knocked out of him. The knife flew from his fingertips into high weeds.

Behind him, Zakhar slammed into the wall, unprepared for the mouse hole through which Monk had escaped. The impact shook the entire cabin; flames danced higher. A howl of raw fury chased Monk back to his feet.

He stumbled a step, caught himself, then sprinted away from the cabin toward the water. It was that stumble that doomed him.

2:20 P.M.
Washington, D.C.

'Her condition is a form of meningitis,' Dr. Yuri Raev admitted.

Painter sat across the dining table from the older Russian scientist. Dr. Raev was flanked by John Mapplethorpe, who Painter recognized from a dossier

Sean McKnight had prepared – and a surprising guest, Dr. Trent McBride, the supposedly missing colleague of Archibald Polk.

It seemed he had been found.

Painter had a thousand questions for the man, but the meeting here at the Capital Grille on Pennsylvania Avenue had been tightly negotiated across intelligence channels. The limit and scope of their discussions had been ironed out. Any discussion of Dr. Polk was off the table. At least for now. The only matter open for dialogue was the health of the girl.

As such, Painter had brought his own experts to the roundtable. On his side of the table sat Lisa and Malcolm. The pair had the medical knowledge and background to weigh the validity of the information offered.

Across the table, the Russian looked ill at ease. He was not the monster Painter had envisioned in his mind when he'd negotiated this roundtable. The man looked like a kindly grandfather in his rumpled dark suit, but there was a haunted quality to his eyes. Painter also read the crinkled concern as he talked about the child. The lines on his face had deepened and spread when he glanced through the medical file Lisa had slid across the table. Painter suspected the only reason the man was cooperating was a true fear for the girl's life.

'Her deterioration is a result of her augment,' Yuri continued. 'We don't completely understand why. The device's microelectrodes are composed of carbon-platinum nanotubules. We believe that the more a subject utilizes their talents, the faster they deteriorate. Has Sasha been drawing while you've had her in your custody?'

Painter remembered all her feverish sketches: the safe house, the Taj Mahal, a picture of Monk. He slowly nodded. 'Exactly what is she doing when she draws?'

Mapplethorpe lifted a hand. There was an oiliness to

his voice, well suited to slide around the truth. 'You know that is beyond the scope of discussion here. You're treading on thin ice, Director Crowe.'

Yuri spoke over Mapplethorpe's objection, which Painter found interesting. 'She is a prodigious savant,' he said, ignoring glares from either side. 'Her natural talents blend keen spatial dynamics with artistic talent, and when augmented, these abilities cross to — '

'That's enough,' Mapplethorpe barked. 'Or we end matters here and walk away. You can send us the girl's body after she's dead.'

Yuri's face darkened, but he went silent.

Lisa encouraged him back on track. 'Why does utilizing her abilities accelerate Sasha's deterioration?'

Yuri spoke softly, with a trace of guilt. 'When stimulated, the interface between the organic and inorganic begins to leak.'

Malcolm stirred. 'What do you mean by "leak"?'

'Our researchers believe that nanoparticles break away from the ends of the microelectrodes and contaminate the cerebral spinal fluid.'

Lisa stirred. 'No wonder our cultures came back negative. The meningitis wasn't bacterial or viral, but a contamination of foreign particles.'

Yuri nodded.

'And to cure her, we must treat that contamination?' she asked.

'Yes. It has taken us many years to devise a system of preventative medicine. At the core, we employ a modified version of a chemotherapeutic drug used to treat bladder cancer. Cis-platinum. The monoatomic platinum acts as a binder for the stray nanoparticles and helps flush them out. The exact cocktail and dosage of drugs necessary to facilitate such a treatment will require an examination of the girl and immediate access to fresh blood tests.'

Painter noted the corners of McBride's lips harden. It

seemed there was some dissatisfaction with this dependency on Dr. Raev. But if the Russian was telling the truth, he was vital to the girl's survival.

Under the table, Lisa's hand rested on Painter's knee. The long linen tablecloth hid her attention. They were seated in the Fabric Room of the Capital Grille steakhouse, neutral ground, a restaurant known for the number of deals struck across the fine china and linen. They had the private dining hall to themselves. The rest of the restaurant was notably empty. Most likely arranged by Mapplethorpe to assure further privacy.

Lisa's fingers tightened on his knee, signaling that she believed Dr. Raev. Painter also noted the division between the Russian and the other two men. Was there a way of utilizing that to his advantage?

McBride spoke. 'We have Dr. Raev's pharmacy of medicines. If you'll bring the girl to a hospital, we can get her treatment started immediately. Perhaps Walter Reed Army Medical Center.'

Painter shook his head.

Nice try, bud.

Lisa supported him. 'She's too fragile to move. We're barely managing her D.I.C. as it is. Any additional stress could destabilize her beyond recovery.'

'Then I must go to her,' Yuri said.

Painter knew they'd come to the prickly point of these negotiations. The child was a political and scientific hot potato. He had left her in the care of Kat and Sean. Sean, as the director of DARPA, was also wielding his skill behind the scenes. The roundtable here was just the tip of the political iceberg.

Painter had no choice but to bring Yuri to the girl, breaching Sigma security – but unfortunately, Mapplethorpe knew this, too. And from their reactions here and the obvious friction between them, Mapplethorpe would never allow Yuri to go alone.

'I will allow one person to accompany Dr. Raev,' Painter said.

Mapplethorpe misinterpreted his restriction. 'We know where Sigma command is located, if that's what you fear revealing. Beneath the Smithsonian Castle.'

Though Painter shouldn't have been startled, his gut still clenched. Mapplethorpe had his fingers tangled throughout the intelligence web of Washington. Sean had warned that it would not take the man long to determine who was involved and where they were located. Still, with all his political power, Mapplethorpe could not gain access to Sigma's inner sanctum. Behind the scenes, the man was surely still attempting to storm their gates. Sean's goal was to keep those gates barred tightly.

Painter kept his features stoic. 'Be that as it may, I'll allow only one person to accompany Dr. Raev.' He glanced between the two men.

McBride lifted a hand. 'I'll go. I can be of use to Yuri.'

From the Russian's slight roll of his eyes, it seemed Dr. Raev did not agree.

Mapplethorpe stared hard at Painter, then slowly nodded. 'But we'll want a concession for our cooperation,' he said.

'What's that?'

'You may keep the girl – but from here on out, you'll grant free access to her once she's recovered. She is a resource we'll not let slip away. Our national security is at stake.'

'Don't wave the flag at me,' Painter said. 'What you cooperated in to produce this girl is beyond all conventions of human decency.'

'We only financed and offered scientific counsel at the end. The project was already well established. If we hadn't *cooperated*, as you say, our country would be at serious risk.'

'What a crock! When you cross such a line, you

damage all of us. What nation are we trying to protect, if that nation advocates the brutality necessary to produce this girl?'

'Are you truly that naive, Crowe? It's a new world out there.'

'No, it's not. Last I checked, it's the same planet circling the same sun. The only thing that's changed is how we're reacting, what lines we're willing to cross. We have the ability to stop that.'

Mapplethorpe glowered at him. Painter saw the resolution in the man's eyes. The man truly believed what he was doing was necessary, saw no fault in it. Here was a level of zealotry that brooked no argument. Painter wondered where such certainty came from – was it just patriotism or did he wrap himself in such dogma to protect himself from the atrocities he committed, crimes he knew in his heart were too horrible to justify any other way?

Either way, they were at an impasse.

'Do we have a deal?' Mapplethorpe asked. 'Otherwise, we'll move on. There are always other children.'

Painter studied his adversary. To cure the child, he had no choice but to get into political bed with him. Painter could not let the girl die. He'd have to deal with the political fallout afterward.

Painter slowly nodded. 'When can you be ready?'

McBride spoke up. 'I'll need an hour to collect Dr. Raev's medicines.'

'We'll be waiting,' Painter said and stood, ending the summit.

Mapplethorpe followed him up and held out his hand, as if they'd just completed a real estate sale. And maybe they had. Painter was about to sell a part of his soul.

Still, with no choice, he shook the man's hand.

Mapplethorpe's palm was cold and dry, his grip firm with certainty.

A part of Painter envied that level of unwavering conviction. But did the man sleep as well at night? As they departed through the wood-paneled restaurant and out under the blue-green awning, Painter was troubled by one statement by Mapplethorpe, a disturbing aside.

There are always other children.

Who was he talking about?

10:42 P.M.
Southern Ural Mountains

He had to get away.

Monk sprinted toward the open water. Behind him, a tiger's scream sliced through the night, coming from the flaming cabin.

Zakhar.

The cat fought to climb through the window.

Monk increased his pace.

Ahead, he spotted a small raft out in the water. Earlier, Monk had hauled the old punt out of the reeds. He'd scraped away most of the moss and found the raft still floated. Unfortunately, there were no oars, so Monk had fashioned a long pole out of the trunk of a sapling.

Out in the deeper water, Konstantin stood in the stern of the raft and leaned hard on the makeshift pole. The raft drifted farther away. At least they had made it.

As planned, the children had crawled out from under the cabin while Monk had distracted the cats. The raft waited for them a yard offshore. They were to hop on board, shove off, and head for the deepest water.

Monk was supposed to have joined them – but his exit from the cabin had not gone as smoothly as he'd hoped.

The delay gave time for the second tiger – Arkady – to tear around the flaming cabin with a hiss of fury and charge straight at Monk.

The drum of heavy pads trampled behind him. Monk fought for the water's edge. Without a weapon, escape was his only hope.

Gasping, he stretched his stride.

The landscape jittered.

A low growl closed on him.

Footfalls pounded.

No breath.

Heartbeat in his ears.

A sharper hiss . . . ready to pounce.

The glint of water.

Too far.

Hopeless, he turned and dropped, skidded on his backside.

The cat hunched to spring with its last stride, but—out of the high weeds, a dark shadow leaped and struck the cat in the side. Monk caught a flash of silver. Then the shadow hurdled the tiger, hit the ground, and bounded headlong into a thick patch of willows and vanished.

Marta.

The chimpanzee hadn't left with the kids.

Arkady, caught off balance in midlunge, had been knocked on his side. The tiger thrashed back to his paws as Monk crabbed backward on hands and feet. Staggering, the tiger yowled a coarse, strangled sound.

Blackness poured down the cat's throat, erasing stripes into shadow.

Blood.

Impaled under his jaw, the handle of a knife protruded.

The bowie knife from the cabin.

Monk had lost it when he fell.

The chimpanzee had recovered it, used it, saved his life.

Monk remembered – and he couldn't say how he remembered – that chimps were natural tool users. With twigs, they fished termites out of nests. With sharpened

277

branches, they stabbed African bush babies out of holes in trunks.

And Marta was no ordinary chimp.

Arkady trembled all over, his yowl drowning in blood.

Another took up his cry.

Zakhar screamed with a violence that set Monk's jaw to aching.

Monk shoved and fled toward the water. Reaching the muddy bank, he dove straight out and landed on his belly in the shallows. He kicked and lunged for the deeper water.

Zakhar's howl swelled with outrage.

Monk splashed and paddled far enough to dive completely underwater. The cold cleared the panic, but even underwater, he heard the tiger's scream. Holding his breath, Monk stroked and frog-kicked out into the deeper water.

As his lungs grew to burning, he surfaced quietly.

Treading water, he stared back toward the cabin. Flames cast high into the darkness. Limned in the firelight, Zakhar circled his brother. The other tiger did not move.

Monk heard Marta sweeping through the trees. He craned and saw her swing free and drop heavily to the raft. It lay ten yards away.

Monk swam to it and hauled himself atop it. He sprawled on his back, out of breath, panting.

On his left, Marta lay curled on her side, tucked tight, rocking slightly. A low moan flowed from her. Pyotr sprawled atop her, comforting her, holding her.

Monk lifted to an elbow, glanced to the cabin, then back to Marta.

As Zakhar continued to scream, Monk reached out a hand and rested it on the chimpanzee's shoulder. Her body trembled, bent in a posture of grief.

It had to be done, he willed to her.

Arkady had been tortured, abused, driven half mad. The cat had become more a monster than one of God's creatures.

Death was a blessing.

Still, Marta moaned.

Killing was never easy.

At the stern, Konstantin heaved on the long pole and sent them floating toward the heart of the swamp.

Monk sat up. Something caught his eye. Before they had settled in for the night, he had stored everyone's packs on the raft. His gaze focused on a badge hanging from a zipper. The radiation monitor.

In the reflected firelight, it was plain to see.

The pink color had grown darker.

And with it, so did their hopes.

4:31 P.M.
Washington, D.C.

Yuri adjusted the flow of the drip line from the I.V. bag. His fingers trembled as he worked. He was too conscious of Sasha in the bed, lost amid the blanket and sheets. She was worse than he'd feared.

He silently cursed the hour he'd lost, waiting on McBride and Mapplethorpe. It was time he could've used to initiate Sasha's treatment. Instead, he'd been locked up at the FBI building while the other two had gone about some private business. McBride finally returned with all of the medications from Yuri's hotel room.

On foot, they had then crossed the Mall, where they were met outside the Smithsonian Castle and escorted down a private elevator to the secure facility below. They were searched, scanned, and blindfolded. Led by hand, Yuri had quickly lost his bearings in the subterranean maze of the facility. They finally reached a room, a door closed behind them, and the lock clicked.

Only then was his blindfold removed.

Yuri found himself in a small hospital room. One wall was mostly mirrored, surely two-way glass. Two people stood guard over the child: a tall auburn-haired woman who introduced herself as Kat Bryant and Dr. Lisa Cummings, whom he'd met at the restaurant. Lisa held out a stack of medical reports.

'We're at your service,' Lisa said. 'Tell us what must be done.'

Yuri set to work. He read all the reports, reviewed the latest blood chemistries. It took him another ten minutes to calculate the dosages. McBride tried to help, watching over his shoulder.

Yuri had growled at him, 'Stay out of my way.'

The Americans did not know the alchemy in preserving the children. Yuri intended to keep it that way, and the method was too complicated to torture out of him. But he could not let Sasha die without trying to save her, so he had to let McBride watch. But once Sasha was safe . . .

Kat interrupted his reverie, standing behind him. 'Will she be okay?'

Yuri tapped the drip. Satisfied with the flow, he turned and found the woman's eyes upon him. Her hair was braided back from her face, revealing the worry in the hard edges around her eyes and mouth.

He sighed and offered her the truth. 'I've done all I can. We'll need hourly renal tests, urine specific gravities. It will give us some idea of the progress, but it will take five or six hours before we know if she'll survive.'

His voice cracked with his last words. He turned away, embarrassed to show weakness to these strangers. He found McBride staring back at him, a callous glint to his eyes. The man had retreated to a chair by the door. He sat smugly with his legs crossed.

'All we can do is wait,' Yuri mumbled and found a seat beside the bed. A child's book lay open atop it.

Kat reached down and collected it. 'I was reading it to her.'

Yuri nodded. On the plane ride here, Sasha had leaned her head on Yuri's arm while he quietly read her Russian fables. He smiled softly at the memory. They were trained not to grow attached, but she was special.

His hand drifted to where one of her fingers poked from the sheets. A blood pressure monitor was clamped to it. He ran his finger down the thin digit, so like a porcelain doll's.

Finally he leaned back into his chair. It would be a long wait. McBride tapped his shoe on the floor. Machines *shushed* and beeped. After a few minutes, Dr. Cummings slipped from the room to discuss matters with the group's pathologist. Kat settled into a chair on the opposite side of the bed.

As the first hour slowly passed, Yuri noted a pile of papers on the bedside table. A corner of a sheet caught his eye. It was heavily scribbled with a black marker. Glimpsing just the edge, Yuri recognized Sasha's work. He shifted through various sheets, not comprehending their meaning. But on the last sheet, Yuri found a familiar face. He stiffened in his seat with surprise.

It was their prisoner back at Chelyabinsk 88.

Yuri kept the picture flat. McBride knew nothing about the capture of the American. He'd never been told. Still, Yuri must have stared too long at the picture.

'My husband.' Kat spoke up from the opposite side of the bed. 'Sasha drew it. I think she saw his picture in my wallet.'

He slowly nodded and covered the picture.

Her husband . . . ?

'Why would she do that?' Kat asked. She stared at him with a bit more focused intent. 'Draw such a picture.'

Yuri stared back at the girl. His heart pounded harder, and his vision narrowed. It was Sasha's drawings that had saved the man's life. And now here was the same man's wife. It was beyond coincidence, outside probable chance. What was going on?

'Dr. Raev?' the woman pressed.

He was saved from having to answer by the flutter of tiny lashes. Sasha's eyes opened, revealing their watery blue depths. Yuri scooted closer. The woman stood up.

Sasha remained groggy, her gaze unfocused. But her heart-shaped face turned toward Yuri. *'Unchi Pepe . . . ?'*

That name.

Yuri's blood pounded in his ears and iced through him. He flashed to a dark aisle in a cold church, to a child clutching a rag doll before a stone altar, staring up at him with the same blue eyes.

Here were the same words. The same accusation.

Unchi Pepe . . .

The pet name for Josef Mengele, the Butcher of Auschwitz.

He took Sasha's hand, knocking loose the blood pressure monitor.

No, he promised to her. *Not ever again*.

Tears blurred his vision.

Her tiny fingers clamped weakly to him. Her lids fluttered. 'Papa . . . Papa Yuri . . . ?'

'Yes,' he whispered. 'I'm here, baby. I won't leave you.'

Her lips moved as she faded back to sleep. Her fingers relaxed and slipped from his. 'Marta . . . Marta's scared . . .'

11:50 P.M.
Southern Ural Mountains

The body was still warm, but the blood was cold.

The kill was an hour or so old.

Lieutenant Borsakov lifted his palm from the flank of the dead tiger. He reached to the head, grabbed an ear, and tugged up. The other ear matched the first, marking this cat as Arkady.

He dropped it and stood.

In his other hand, Borsakov carried his sidearm, a Yarygin PYa. He kept it raised, wishing it was chambered in something stronger than 9 mm. He searched for Zakhar. There was no sign of the cat.

Behind him, the old *ibza* still smoked and smoldered.

Impressed at the escape, he crossed back to the airboat. A pilot and two other soldiers sat aboard, bearing assault rifles, covering him. The headlamp of the swamp boat speared out into the darkness. The giant fan at the back of the craft slowly spun as the pilot idled its engine.

Borsakov climbed back aboard and waved them out into the dark swamp. The engine whined, the fan spun to a gale, and they sailed away from the glowing ruins of the hunter's lodge and headed back out into the night. The hunt would have been easier if they'd had the use of infrared scopes or night-vision goggles, but Borsakov had discovered someone had sneaked into the supply shed sometime during the past day and damaged their limited equipment.

Either the American or the children.

They'd known they would be hunted.

'Should we not report in with General-Major Martov?' his second in command asked and reached to the team's radio.

Borsakov shook his head.

The general-major did not take setbacks well.

The airboat flew through the swamp.

He would call when the American was dead.

As they fled, Borsakov glanced back to the island, to the smoldering ruins and dead cat. He pictured the American and what he had accomplished.

Who was this man? And where did he get his training?

6:02 P.M.
Washington, D.C.

Trent McBride lifted the phone's receiver to his ear. They'd allowed him to use a wall phone and patched his call to Mapplethorpe's office. Trent was under no illusion that the conversation would be private. Someone was surely monitoring.

But that wouldn't stop him from calling in a status report.

After a few cursory exchanges with Mapplethorpe, Trent said, 'It looks like the girl may survive.'

If she had died, then there would be no reason to proceed.

'Very good,' Mapplethorpe answered. A short and significant pause followed; then he spoke. 'How long until we know for sure?'

Trent checked his watch and calculated how much time he'd need. 'To be certain. Six hours,' he said.

Middle of the night.

It would take coordination, but then they'd have everything.

Mapplethorpe growled with satisfaction. 'Then that's very good news indeed.'

14

'We can go no farther,' Abhi Bhanjee said.

Gray didn't argue. The Mercedes SUV was up to its axles in mud. Exhausted, his nerves stretched to a piano-wire tautness, he drove the truck up to a stonier piece of ground.

For the past two hours, rain had dumped heavily out of low skies. It seemed impossible for clouds to hold such volumes of water. They had left the mango orchards thirty miles ago and trekked through a landscape just as wooded, but here the terrain was wild. The rolling hills had given way to a broken escarpment of steep hills and cliffs. With the rain, creeks swelled and surged throughout the landscape. It was as if the entire world wept.

But at least the torrent of rain had drowned away the helicopters. The hunters had given up the chase after losing their prey among the thousands of acres of property. Abe knew the lands around here well and had guided them along a steep-walled valley out of the orchards and into this inhospitable terrain.

No one comes here, the man had said. *Not good for farming.*

That was an understatement.

'We are not far,' Abe assured them as Gray braked to

287

a stop. 'Less than a kilometer. But we must walk from here.'

Gray hid the SUV under the draping boughs of a banyan tree. Turning off the engine, he stared out at the cliffs and pictured the temple on the Greek coin. Abe claimed such a structure lay out among these lands. It was where Dr. Polk had been headed the day he disappeared. Only a few local villagers knew of this place. It was a site both revered and feared by Abe's people, sacred ground for the *achuta*.

Why had Dr. Polk come out here? What had so excited the professor?

Water sluiced over the windshield, blurring the view.

'Perhaps it's best if we wait for a break in the weather,' Masterson suggested. 'We can look for this temple after it stops raining.'

Gray checked his watch. It was nearing midnight. He didn't want to be anywhere near here by morning. Come daylight, the helicopters would be out searching again. The tank-size Mercedes SUV would be easy to spot in the open hills. Gray had already taken measures and disabled the truck's GPS unit, fearing that was how the Russians had tracked them from Delhi.

He had many unanswered questions in his head, but he knew one thing for certain. If they were going to track the last steps taken by Dr. Polk, they'd better do it now.

He swung around to address the passengers. 'I'm going with Abe. But the rest of you might want to stay with the vehicle.'

Elizabeth raised her hand. 'I'm going with you. If there's some lost temple out there, you may need my help.'

Kowalski nodded. 'And where she goes, I'm going.'

Elizabeth glanced to him with a look that started out annoyed but melted into something less sure.

'We should stay together,' Rosauro said, grabbing their pack of gear.

Luca nodded.

Masterson rolled his eyes. 'It looks like we're all going to get wet.'

With the matter decided, they piled out of the SUV and into the rain. After a couple of steps, Gray was soaked to the skin. His clothes seemed to have gained twenty pounds.

Kowalski cursed and glanced longingly back toward the SUV, but once Elizabeth moved, he followed in her footsteps.

'Over this way,' Abe said and pointed to a shattered cliff that rose up into ragged plateaus covered in trees. Roots tangled out of the sandstone walls, like the gnarled faces of old men, worn from the cliffs by rain and wind. Lightning crackled across the sky, booming with thunder.

The storm worsened.

Bone tired, Gray began to have further doubts about his plan. Since leaving Delhi earlier in the day, he'd been unable to contact Sigma. They'd lost the team's satellite phone during the assault at the hotel. The prepaid cell phone he'd purchased in Delhi had no reception in this remote area.

They were on their own. And while Gray normally preferred to operate with as little oversight as possible, he had the civilians to consider.

Abe set out toward a narrow ravine cut into the cliff. A creek flowed down the center of it, chugging leadenly with runoff. A narrow path bordered it, with sheer walls rising to either side.

Gray followed Abe to the path. Once in the canyon, the rains lessened, as the winds were blocked. Still, water poured down the walls. The creek's rumble, trapped in the ravine, grew louder.

They continued single file.

The canyon zigzagged like a thunderbolt, growing narrower and taller as it cut into the high hills.

Abe narrated as he walked. 'Our people sometimes retreat here during times of persecution. My great-grandfather told stories of purges, where entire villages were destroyed. Those who escaped fled here to hide.'

No wonder the achuta *keep this place secret,* Gray thought.

'But these walls do not guarantee protection,' Abe added cryptically. 'Not forever.'

Gray glanced to him, but Abe stepped ahead to where the canyon split into two courses. Abe ran his hand along one wall, as if assuring himself of something – then continued onward to the left.

Gray fingered where Abe had touched. There was writing inscribed into the wall, barely visible through the rain, just shadows on the rock.

Elizabeth studied the writing closer. 'Harappan,' she said, surprised, and stared around her. 'We must be in the outer edges of the Indus Valley. A great civilization once made their home here.'

Masterson agreed with a nod. 'The Harappans lived along the Indus River five thousand years ago, leaving behind the ruins of sophisticated cities and temples. You can find them throughout the region. Perhaps our young Hindu friend mistook one of the old Harappan ruins for the temple inscribed on the strange coin.'

Gray continued onward. 'There's only one way to find out.'

After another two turns, the canyon suddenly widened

into a small bowl. Water tumbled into it on the far side, dumping over a short cliff and into a pool that fed the creek they'd been following.

Abe stopped and waved an arm around the bowl. 'We are here.'

Gray frowned. The canyon was empty – then lightning crackled with a brilliant display that lit the basin. Silvery light bathed the cliffs and reflected off the central pool.

All around the bowl, the sandstone walls had been dug out into notched tiers. Each level sheltered cliff-dwelling homes. They climbed from floor to the lip that overhung the valley. Sections of homes had broken away over the centuries into boulders and rubble. It reminded Gray of the cliff dwellings of the Anasazi Indians. But from the style of architecture, no *Indians* – neither Native Americans nor the peoples of India – had built these dwellings.

Gray stepped forward and turned in a circle. The facades of the homes were white marble, stark against the darker stone. The cliffs, composed of softer sandstone, had long been worn down by centuries of wind and rain. The homes looked like they grew straight out of the walls. The white marble reminded Gray of fossilized skeletons jutting out of a cliff face.

Despite being half swallowed by the storm-melted walls, the basic architectural elements of the marble structures were still evident. Low triangular roofs supported fluted columns. Carvings and sculptures, long softened by age, decorated pediments and cornices.

There was no doubt as to the source of the architecture.

'It's Greek,' Elizabeth said with awe. She stared around, water streaming down her face. 'A Greek temple complex. Hidden here.'

Masterson stood beside her. He had his sodden hat in hand and combed his fingers through his soaked white hair. 'Simply amazing. Archibald, you old fool, you could've told me . . .'

Gray also gaped, wonder washing away his exhaustion.

Elizabeth pointed. 'That's a temple *in antis*, one of the simplest Greek architectural units. Over there's a later-era prostyle structure. And look at that rounded facade of columns. It must mark a tholos, a circular temple, burrowed into the cliff.'

While she spoke, Gray's attention focused upon a structure on the far side of the bowl. His heart beat harder. A temple lay halfway up the cliff face. Boulders were strewn at the foot of it, marking where a part of the canyon's lip had cracked and fallen. Rainwater flowed through the upper crack and streamed across the front of the temple, giving it a watery, illusory appearance.

But there was no mistaking it.

Six columns supported a triangular roof and framed a dark doorway.

'Just like on the coin,' Rosauro said, noting his attention.

Abe headed toward the tall temple. 'That is not all.'

Straining with curiosity, Gray followed and dragged the wet party with him.

Once they reached the pile of boulders, Abe crossed to one side and waved them to follow. He mounted the stack of boulders and clambered higher. He seemed to know a path up the rubble.

Climbing single file, they followed the Hindu man.

Elizabeth and Masterson continued an ongoing dialogue. 'Why do you think they built the temple complex here? And in such an odd manner?'

'They were clearly hiding,' Masterson said. 'It's a bloody hard place to find, especially buried into these walls. But I've seen similar cliff-dwelling arrangements among the Harappan ruins deeper in the Indus Valley. Perhaps these builders took over an old Harappan site, modified it to their tastes.'

'That could be. It was common for one civilization to build atop another.'

As they talked, Gray stared at the temple. Closer now, he saw that what he'd thought were black shadows on the marble columns were actually old scorch marks. Finer details emerged. Cracks and fissures marred the facade; one large section of the upper pediment had broken away.

Gray suspected the damage was not from age alone. It looked like an ancient battle had been fought here.

Ahead, Abe jumped off the top boulder and climbed between two pillars. Gray went next and shimmied onto the marble floor of the temple, finally out of the rain. The six support columns stood a yard from the building they fronted, creating a small porch.

He stood to make room for the others. Kowalski and Luca helped Elizabeth and Masterson. Rosauro came last, burdened with a pack. With everyone gathered, Gray headed to the door, but Abe knelt for a moment and whispered a prayer. Gray waited, sensing to do otherwise would be like trespassing.

Abe stood and nodded.

Gray took out a small flashlight and flicked it on. He entered first, his light blazing into the dark interior.

The chamber was large and perfectly square, twenty feet on a side and again as tall. More columns lined the walls, several broken into rubble. Dug out of the center of the floor was a fire pit, deeply blackened. To either side, arched openings led into side chambers, like chapels in a church.

Gray noted something piled in the smaller rooms. He shifted for a closer look as the others entered the temple. Abe kept to the side, his arms crossed nervously. He didn't follow.

As Gray pointed his flashlight, he understood the Hindu man's reluctance. Bones filled the room, stacked like cords of wood, topped by hundreds of skulls. All human. From the rotted appearance and yellowing, the skeletons were ancient.

Gray pictured the scorch marks on the building.

Abe spoke. 'We were told stories, passed from father to son, mother to daughter. Of a great battle here. A thousand years ago. It is told how our ancestors found this place full of bones. In honor of the dead, we gathered their remains and interred them in these temples.' He waved toward the bowl outside. 'There are many more bones out there.'

Gray turned away from the room. Someone had discovered these people and massacred them. He remembered Abe's cryptic words from earlier.

These walls do not guarantee protection. Not forever.

The fate of the original inhabitants was a warning to Abe's people. It was a good place to hide, but one could not escape the world forever.

Gray stepped over to the only other feature in the room.

Like the temple facade, this feature was also depicted on the coin.

Gray crossed to the back wall and shone his light across its surface. The wall of creamy marble had been inset with stark black stone, forming a familiar symbol, climbing twenty feet tall.

'A chakra wheel,' Elizabeth said, mystified. She pulled out a pocket-size digital camera and began taking pictures. 'Like the other side of the coin.'

Luca ran a hand along the wall. Gray could read his

thoughts. *Was this the ancient symbol that was the source of the Romani emblem?*

Had Archibald Polk wondered the same?

Kowalski sighed, clearly not impressed with the room. 'What a letdown.'

'What are you talking about?' Elizabeth chided. 'This is the archaeological and anthropological discovery of a lifetime.'

He shrugged. 'Yeah, but so what? Where's all the gold and jewels?'

Gray hated to admit it, but he agreed with Kowalski. He stepped away. He swung the flashlight in a full circle around the chamber. Something *was* missing, but it wasn't gold or precious gems.

Rosauro joined him. 'What's wrong?'

'Something's not here,' he mumbled.

'What?'

Others heard them in the confined space. They stared over.

Gray made one more circle. 'On the coin . . . there was that prominent *E*? The Greek letter *epsilon.*'

'He's right,' Elizabeth said.

Gray wiped drips of rain from his face. 'Everything on the coin is found here – the temple facade, the chakra wheel – so where is the Greek letter?'

'It's one minor detail,' Masterson said. 'What does it matter?'

'It's not *minor*,' Elizabeth argued. 'Someone had gone to a lot of trouble to mimic the temple complex at Delphi. What we saw outside . . . the temple *in antis* was the shape of the Delphi's treasury buildings, the round tholos temple looked like a fair facsimile of the one built to worship Athena at Delphi. And this place here. The exterior and interior are how the Oracle's temple was laid out. And the *E* was one of its most prominent decorations.'

Gray recalled his discussion with Painter, about how the Delphic *E* grew to symbolize a cult of prophecy, a code trailing throughout history in art and architecture.

Luca stepped forward. 'I may also know of this letter.'

Gray turned to the Gypsy clan leader.

'I told you of the children who were stolen from us,' he said. 'Those of my people who first came upon the massacred camp spoke of a stone church there. The door had been broken open, but upon the shattered planks a large bronze *E* was found. No one knew what it meant. The only ones who knew were buried in that mass grave. The secret died with them. Perhaps this is the same *E*?'

Marking the chovihanis, Gray thought. *Gypsy fortune-tellers. Another cult of prophecy.*

'All well and good,' Masterson persisted, plainly growing tired, too. 'But what does it matter if the *E* is missing *here*?'

'Maybe nothing,' Gray admitted, but he said it with little conviction. He turned to Abe. 'When did you first show Dr. Polk this site?'

He shrugged. 'I took Dr. Polk here the first time a year ago. He looked around, took notes, and left.'

Elizabeth's eyes looked wounded. 'He didn't tell me anything about this discovery.'

'Because he respected our secrets,' Abe said stiffly. 'He was a good man.'

Gray studied Masterson's sour expression. The professor had initially been surprised by the discovery, but after the shock faded and he found no real worth to his own line of research, his interest had waned. Had Dr. Polk experienced the same? The archaeological discovery was significant, but because he couldn't connect it to his own research, he'd respected the *achuta's* secret and had kept quiet about it.

If so, why the sudden urgency to come out here just before he disappeared? He must have discovered some new connection, something bearing on his own line of study.

Gray asked Abe, 'Was there anything that triggered Dr. Polk's sudden need to come here? Anything unusual that led up to that day?'

The man shook his head. 'He came to visit the village. Like he had done many times. We were talking about an upcoming election where an *achuta* candidate was up for a mayoral position. I had found a new coin and showed him, but he asked to see the one with the temple on it again. He glanced at it without too much interest, even spinning it on the table as we spoke. Then suddenly his eyes got huge, and he jumped up. He wanted to immediately come here, but I had obligations with the election. I asked him to wait until I returned . . .'

His voice trailed off and was picked up by Elizabeth. 'My father was not known for his patience.'

Masterson nodded. 'That was the day I got the frantic call from him. He claimed that he had discovered something that would shake our understanding of the human mind once it was known.'

As an idea jangled through him, Gray turned to Rosauro. 'Let me see that coin again.'

She passed it over.

Gray examined it: temple on one side, chakra wheel on the other. 'Elizabeth, you said your father obtained that position for you at Delphi so you could explore how it might connect to his own research. What did you end up telling him about Delphi's history?'

'Just the basics,' she said. 'He was less interested in the history than he was in the discovery of ethylene gases near the temple site. My father wanted more details into the Oracle's rituals, looking again for physiological support for her intuitive powers.'

'So if he wasn't interested in the history, when did he learn about the significance of the Greek letter *epsilon*?'

'I sent him a paper on it.'

'When?'

'About a month before he—' Her eyes suddenly widened.

Gray nodded. He knelt on the marble floor and placed his flashlight down. Propping the coin up on its edge, Gray flicked it and sent it spinning on the floor, lit by the flashlight beam.

He leaned down, studying it.

The spinning coin formed a blurry, silvery globe. The *E*, positioned in the center of the coin, now rested at the core of the whirling globe. Gray sensed the symbolism. Painter had said that the *E* may have had its roots in the earliest worship of the Earth mother, Gaia. Now it rested at the *center* of the silvery sphere, like Gaia herself in the physical world. But the letter also represented human's intuitive potential, rising out of the *core* of the human body, out of the brain.

Gray let his own mind relax, seeking significance.

What had Archibald Polk realized?

The coin spun, a silvery mystery, hiding an ancient secret.

But what—?

Then Gray knew.

Reaching out, he slapped the coin flat against the marble. *Of course!*

11:35 P.M.
Pripyat, Ukraine

'The Americans have Sasha,' Nicolas said sharply as he stepped into the bedroom. He was naked under an open robe, but his anger kept him warm.

Elena lay draped across the bedspread, nude. She had one leg up, and an arm draped to the side, waiting for him. They had returned from the gala to their hotel outside the Chernobyl Exclusion Zone, where many of the dignitaries were being housed prior to tomorrow's event.

Nicolas had spent the past half hour on a scrambled satellite phone, making sure every last detail was addressed before the morning. A call to his mother at the Warren revealed the latest bit of upsetting news. With her ties to former operatives in the KGB, she had heard the rumblings coming out of Washington's intelligence communities. The city had been in turmoil over the past twenty hours, searching for a girl. It must be Sasha. Then things had gone deathly quiet. Even Yuri went silent. Both he and his mother knew what that implied.

Someone had found her.

And Nicolas suspected who it was.

His fingers clenched into a fist.

It was likely the same organization that had been plaguing him in India, dredging up Dr. Polk's research, stirring something that Nicolas had thought had ended with the man's death. One attempt to quash that trail had already failed. But maybe it was just as well.

He'd had one communication, brief, after the failure.

It seemed the team in India was closing in on a secret that Dr. Polk had kept from everyone. Something vital to the professor's research. Something significant about the children. But what?

Elena stirred on the bed and lifted to an elbow. Concern rang in her voice. 'What will you do about little Sasha?'

Nicolas knew all the children grew close. Raised together in the Warren, the older children often took on parental roles with the younger ones. Elena had been especially fond of little Sasha and her brother.

The pair was important to Nicolas, too.

He sank to the bed, and she curled into him, worried and angry. One of her hands slid up under his robe and rested on his thigh. Her skin was hot, feverish. He had kept her waiting too long.

Then long fingernails suddenly clamped onto his thigh, stabbing deeply.

Elena stared up at him. Fire burned behind her eyes, waiting to be unleashed. A trickle of blood ran down Nicolas's inner thigh, as exciting as the tip of a hungry tongue.

A hard certainty entered Elena's voice. It brooked no argument, demanding, commanding. 'Nothing must happen to little Sasha.'

Her fingers tightened yet again, sending pain shooting to his groin.

He gasped and promised her. 'Measures are already under way. All we need—'

Nails dragged up his leg, trailing pain.

—is something to trade.'

11:45 P.M.
Punjab, India

As thunder boomed and lightning lit up the temple chamber, Elizabeth followed Gray to the giant chakra wheel on the wall. He laid his palm there. Since spinning the coin, he had clearly come to realize something.

But what?

Gray spoke as he stared upward. 'From my studies of Indian philosophy, the center of a chakra wheel usually holds a Sanskrit letter, representing one of the energy centers. *Muladhara*, the root chakra at the base of the spine. *Manipura*, in the region of the solar plexus. *Anahata*, the heart.' He stared upward. 'This one is empty. Blank.'

'The same on the coin,' Elizabeth said tentatively, not understanding where this was leading.

'Exactly.' Gray had collected the coin and passed it to her now. 'But flip the coin over. If you could stare through the center of the chakra wheel to the other side of the coin, what's positioned there?'

Elizabeth turned the coin back and forth. The capital *epsilon* lay in the center of the temple, in the exact position as the axle of the chakra wheel on the other side. 'It's the *E*,' she mumbled.

'It stands on the reverse side of the wheel.' Gray turned to Masterson. 'May I borrow your cane?'

The professor passed it reluctantly.

Gray stepped back, reached up, and pushed on the edge of the center circle of black marble. His muscles strained, and the small circle shifted out of place, pivoting around a vertical axis, like a valve in a pipe.

'A secret door,' Masterson exclaimed.

Gray waved to Kowalski. 'Give me a leg up.'

Kowalski crossed, dropped to a knee, and laced his fingers. Gray stepped into his grip and climbed high enough to shove the balanced slab of marble wider open. The lower edge of the secret door stood ten feet off the ground. With Kowalski's boost, Gray wiggled through the opening.

'There're stairs!' he called back as his legs vanished. 'Leading down! Cut into the sandstone back here!'

Elizabeth could hardly wait. She crossed to Kowalski. 'Help me.'

She stepped to his knee, but he grabbed her by the waist and lifted her up. She squeaked a little in surprise. He was strong. She grabbed the edge of the opening to steady herself and blindly sought for a foothold to push through the door.

'Ow, that's my nose,' Kowalski griped.

'Sorry.'

He grabbed her ankle and shifted it to his shoulder. She shoved and fell the rest of the way through. She found Gray down a few steps, shining his light over the walls. Writing decorated all the surfaces, a mix of shapes and letters.

'Harappan again,' she said with a strain, and gained her feet.

'And look at this,' Gray said. He swung his flashlight and shone it on the reverse side of the black marble door. A large capital *epsilon* had been carved deep into the stone.

He'd been right.

Elizabeth freed her camera and took several pictures while Rosauro and Luca joined them, crowding the stairs.

Gray leaned out. 'Dr. Masterson?'

Through the opening, Elizabeth saw the professor back away.

'Such clambering is for younger folk than I,' he said, clearly exhausted, limping back with his cane. 'Just let me know what you find.'

'I'll remain here, too,' Abe added, but his voice sounded more scared than tired. Elizabeth had noted how nervous he had grown the closer they got to here.

Gray called down. 'Kowalski, stay here. In case we get into trouble.'

'Fine by me,' he answered. 'Doubt I could fit through there anyway.'

Kowalski's eyes flicked to Elizabeth. He nodded, silently warning her to be careful.

Thunder again rumbled, felt in the stones.

'Let's go,' Gray said.

He led the way down with his flashlight. Elizabeth followed, trailed by Rosauro and Luca. Her fingers traced the wall. Harappan script flowed down the stairwell. The ancient language had never been deciphered, mostly because of the scarcity of the script that survived. Archaeologists were still searching for the Rosetta stone for this language, some codex that would allow them to crack their ancient code.

She gazed around her. *This could be it.*

Thrilled and amazed, her heart thumped in her chest. She was surprised no one else could hear it. At the same time, she pictured her father following these same footsteps. She imagined his heart had thundered the same as hers. In this moment, she felt a strange intimacy, a closeness they'd never shared in life. And never would. Her throat closed a bit as emotion racked through her.

The stairwell was not long and ended in a small chamber, cut from the sandstone. Water gurgled and echoed on the far side. A natural spring poured out of a knee-high hole in the wall and flowed through a crack in the floor, then vanished out the opposite wall.

'A Harappan well cave,' Elizabeth said, recognizing the configuration. 'Living alongside the Indus River, the civilization grew skilled at irrigation.'

Gray shone his light around the space. It was crudely circular. Cut into the stone floor was another chakra wheel. But the center of this one wasn't empty. A large egg-shaped stone rested there.

'It's a copy of the omphalos,' Elizabeth said.

She and the others were drawn to it. It stood as high as her midriff and was twice as large as the one from the Delphi museum. The dome's outer surface was carved with trees and leaves.

Elizabeth swallowed hard and stared around her. 'Someone has re-created the original adytum, the inner sanctum of the Oracle, where she cast her prophecies.'

Elizabeth stepped over to a toppled bronze chair. It had three legs. 'Here's a tripod. The classical seat of the Oracle.'

'Or *oracles*.' Gray had wandered a few steps away. He pointed his flashlight to more toppled chairs.

Five total.

Elizabeth snapped several pictures. What was this place? What was it doing here?

Rosauro called from the wall, hiking up her pack. 'You might want to see this,' she said.

Luca stood farther down the wall. His arm was raised to the surface, but not touching. Even in the shadows, Elizabeth noted how his hand shook.

Elizabeth crossed to Rosauro. A mosaic, nearly black with age, covered the wall. Several tiles littered the floor, fallen away. Someone had wiped sections of the mosaic down, removing centuries of mold and grime. It looked hastily done. Elizabeth imagined her father swabbing a cloth over the artwork, seeking what lay beneath.

She stared at what was revealed.

From floor to ceiling, it depicted a siege on a temple set amid mountains. 'Parnassus,' Elizabeth mumbled. 'Under attack by Romans. It's showing the downfall of the Temple of Delphi.'

The next section revealed a room not unlike the one they were in, even with an omphalos in the center – but the stone was shown in cross section. Hidden beneath its dome crouched a small girl, cradled in the arms of a young woman, curled tight together as a Roman soldier searched for them.

Elizabeth glanced to the stone behind her. *It couldn't be . . .*

She stepped along the wall. The next tableaux revealed a caravan of horses, donkeys, and carts. At the head of the train, the same slender woman led the child. The long caravan climbed up and over a mountain. The last cart was hauled by two fiery stallions, clearly representing the steeds who drew Apollo's sun chariot across the skies. But they were not dragging the sun here. In the back of the cart rested the same stone that had protected the woman and child. The omphalos of Delphi.

Elizabeth turned and faced the stone behind her. She trembled all over. 'That's not a *copy*,' she said with a shudder. 'That's the original omphalos. The one spoken of in the histories of Plutarch and Socrates.'

'And see this,' Rosauro said.

The woman drew Elizabeth to the next scene. It was a picture of the canyon, a joyous scene of the Greeks building temples into the cliffs. The adytum was also depicted, but instead of one Oracle seated atop a tripod, there were five. They circled the omphalos, which smoked like a volcano from the hole at its top. The smoke formed a figure of a young boy with outstretched arms. His eyes were fire, and flames climbed from his open palms.

Was the boy indicative of prophecy in general or something more specific?

Either way, Elizabeth found those fiery eyes staring back at her.

At her shoulder, Gray had also followed the story. He waved an arm along the wall, encompassing the tale.

'The last Oracle, the child, must have been spirited away after the downfall of the temple. In secret, the Greek temple guardians and supporters fled the Roman persecution and settled here, where they rebuilt among these Harappan ruins, and stayed hidden.'

Elizabeth remembered Abe's story of this place. 'They remained safe for seven hundred years, perhaps intermingling with the local tribes in secret. And after so many generations, the Greeks were slowly absorbed into the Indian culture.'

'Then they grew afoul of religious persecution and the growing Indian caste system,' Gray said. 'All the bones. A massacre occurred here.'

Luca spoke at the end of the wall. 'And they fled again,' he said.

They joined him. He stood a step from the churning

spring. The art here was not mosaic tiles, but someone had painted a hurried frieze. It was done in black paint, showing the attack of the temples. People fled in all directions, but one group, highlighted by radiant streaks, escaped in a caravan of tall wagons with large wheels. It faded smaller and smaller across the wall, heading far away.

Luca placed his fingers gently to the wagons. His voice cracked with emotion. 'These are our people,' he said. 'The Romani. This is where we came from. This is our origin.'

Gray shifted back. He stared across the wall, his face stunned.

The Greek guardians escaped with the last child and the omphalos, hiding in this valley and absorbing over the span of seven centuries into Indian culture, then that same culture persecuted them and sent them wandering once again, but under a new name.

Gypsies.

Gray waved an arm to encompass the wall. 'The story depicted here must trace a genetic line that has been preserved throughout history. Flowing from Greece, to here, and out again. A genetic line of savant power.'

'This is why we wander,' Luca said, still staring at the caravan. 'As the Hindu man said, no place is safe forever. So we kept moving, trying to protect the secret held within the heart of our clans.'

'Until the secret was stolen from you,' Gray said.

'A secret that trails all the way back to Delphi,' Elizabeth added.

She pictured the child back in Washington. Could she truly be a descendant of the last Oracle of Delphi?

Rosauro stepped to the fresco and pointed to the lines of other figures fleeing the besieged complex in various directions. 'These refugees,' she said to

Elizabeth. 'This must be why your father found all the genetic trails led to this region, why the markers are so concentrated in this area, especially among the lower castes. It's where the refugees were absorbed into the populace.'

As they talked, Gray had crossed down the wall one more time, studying each image more closely. He came to the last mosaic, the one with the fiery boy. 'There's writing below here,' he said.

Elizabeth stepped closer. There were three lines. The topmost was a handsome line of Harappan script, the next line Sanskrit, the last Greek. Below the lines rested another chakra wheel.

'I can't read the Harappan hieroglyphics,' she said. 'No one can. And below that, I can make out only the first few words of the Sanskrit and Greek. The rest has been worn away. What I can translate, reads "*the world will burn . . .*"' She took some snapshots, especially of the fiery figure. 'The rest is lost.'

Gray leaned lower and touched the chakra wheel inscribed below the lines. 'This must be important. It's repeated over and over.'

He straightened and turned toward the larger chakra wheel carved into the floor. The omphalos rested at its center. Elizabeth could almost read Gray's mind. *If the chakra was important, then what lay at its center must be doubly so.* The man's eyes narrowed as he stalked over to the stone. They'd only given it a cursory glance.

'Your father hid the skull *inside* the stone at the museum. Maybe there was a reason.'

Gray climbed on top of the domed omphalos.

'Be careful,' Elizabeth squeaked out, fearful of marring the piece of ancient history. She circled the stone and noted the bottom rim was inscribed with three languages again: Harappan, Sanskrit, and Greek.

She took more pictures.

Balancing on top of the omphalos, Gray shone his light down through the hole and into its hollow heart.

'What do you see?' she asked.

'Gold . . . in the shape of two eagles.'

Elizabeth's breath shortened. 'Are they facing away from each other?'

Gray glanced back to her. 'Yes.'

'It's another lost artifact from Delphi, representing Zeus's eagles. According to mythology, the pair was sent in opposite directions from his shoulders to pinpoint the center of the world. They came to roost at Delphi, marking the navel of the world.'

'Your father surely must have found them, too.' Gray reached inside. 'Maybe there's some reason they're hidden here, the same reason your father hid the skull in the omphalos at the museum.'

As he strained, Elizabeth edged around the stone, continuing her translation of the three lines.

'I think I can reach them . . . ,' Gray said.

Elizabeth mumbled the words found there, tracing each letter with her finger. ' "*Greed and blasphemy bring doom to all.*" '

Elizabeth stopped.

Oh, no!

'Got it,' Gray said as he reached the golden idols.

Elizabeth snapped straight. 'Don't!'

Startled, Gray slipped.

Something loud thumped inside the stone, followed by a thunderous crack underfoot. A low roar followed, coming from the rear of the chamber, growing in volume, like a freight train barreling toward them.

Everyone froze for a breath, then Gray shoved an arm toward the stairs. 'Everybody out!' he screamed.

Too late.

From the spring's hole, an explosion of water blasted out with the power of a fire hose – in a column two feet thick. Fissures skittered across the wall, radiating out from the opening.

A man-made flash flood.

The water smashed against the far wall and swept into the room, knocking them all off their feet with the force of its current.

Elizabeth tangled into the others as the room swelled rapidly with icy water. Gray nabbed her elbow and dragged her toward the stairs.

'A trap . . .' She coughed in shock. 'Pressure switch! My father . . . tried to warn us . . .'

Gray cried, 'Out! Out!'

She climbed the first few stairs on hands and feet. Behind her, Gray fished Luca out of the water and shoved him toward the stairs. The level had already climbed to the top of her thighs and rose higher with every breath. Gray remained below, braced in the stairwell opening, searching the small cave.

Elizabeth knew why.

Where was Rosauro?

Gray had lost sight of her. She had been closest to the spring when it blew. The blasting water swirled like a whirlpool in the cavern and reflected his flashlight's beam. He could not see beneath the surface. By now, the water had climbed to his waist. Still, Rosauro should be able to stand, and even if knocked out, her body should be buoyant enough to reveal her location.

Unless . . .

Gray turned to Luca and held out his arm. 'Your dagger!'

With a flash of silver, a blade appeared in the Gypsy's hand. He slapped the grip into Gray's palm. In turn, Gray tossed him the flashlight.

'Hold the beam underwater!' he ordered and dove out into the growing lake.

309

The current grabbed him and whipped him around the edge of the room. He didn't fight it. He let the force churn him to the far side of the cave. He knew when he'd reached it, sensing the raw power of the jetting spring below. He twisted and kicked toward the opposite wall.

Conscious or not, only one thing could be holding Rosauro down beneath the water.

Pressure.

Gray dove to where the spring had drained out of the cavern. In the dim light of the flashlight, he spotted a struggling form trapped in the drainage slot. Rosauro had been sucked tight against the hole, one arm swallowed down its throat. Gray heard of people drowning, pinned to swimming pool drains. This was a force a hundred times as fierce.

Gray grabbed her free arm and pulled himself down to her. He braced his legs to either side of the trough. She stared up at him. Even in the weak light, he saw the raw panic on her face.

Gray slashed out with the dagger. He'd lost one teammate to drowning – he wasn't about to lose another. The blade sliced through the straps of Rosauro's backpack. Half the bag had been sucked into the hole, holding her trapped. Once cut free, Gray dropped the dagger, grabbed her around the chest, and heaved with his legs.

For a moment, she remained stuck. Then the pack shifted deeper into the hole, weakening the pressure enough for Gray to pop her out. He tumbled back with her in his arms. He let the spin of the current carry them toward the light and the stairwell.

The water had risen to within a foot of the roof.

A grinding *boom* of stone echoed. The current suddenly slammed harder as the cavern wall gave way behind him.

Surging forward, Gray kicked off the bottom and up into the flooded stairwell.

Gasping, he surfaced into Luca's arms. Luca helped Gray haul Rosauro up the stairs. She coughed and choked. Water spilled from her lips. But she took deep gulping breaths between.

She used one breath to spit out a curse in Spanish that would burn even the hairs off Kowalski's ears.

Behind them, the chamber flooded to the roof, and the water level suddenly churned up after them.

'Time to go,' Gray said.

He pulled Rosauro to her feet and waved Elizabeth and Luca ahead. Rosauro was weak-kneed, but with water surging at their heels, she steadied enough to run on her own. Still, she cradled her left arm, strained from the suction.

They fled upward, chased by a flume of rising floodwaters.

Reaching the top, Elizabeth slithered backward out the opening, hung from her hands, then dropped to the floor below.

'Go!' Gray called to Luca when the man hesitated.

Luca obeyed and disappeared.

Gray helped Rosauro through the black marble door. She dangled from her good arm, then dropped. Gray followed her as water flooded the last step and washed over him in a wave.

He leaped away, clearing his fingers a second before the surge of water struck the door and slammed it closed. He landed and stared up. With the marble door cut at an angle, it could only rotate in one direction. The water pressure now held it closed.

Self-sealing.

Turning, he heard a roar echoing from the canyon. Lightning flashed. Churning white water flowed across the valley floor. The canyon was flooding, too, but this was a natural flood – not the consequence of Gray's ham-fisted fumbling.

He stared at the volume of water coursing through the canyon.

No wonder these buildings had been built into the cliffs.

Gray realized one other thing.

Luca had noted it, too, and whispered, 'Where is everyone?'

As if hearing his question, Masterson limped into view by the door, leaning on his cane. He'd been out of sight on the porch outside. Probably keeping an eye on the flooding waters with the others.

'Thank God,' the professor said. 'You'd been down there bloody long enough. What did you find?'

Elizabeth stepped forward, excited. 'The answers to everything! It was amazing.'

'Is that right?'

Behind Masterson, more figures rushed into view.

Others flooded in from the two side rooms. They all wore black, bristling with assault weapons ready at their shoulders.

The Russian commandos.

'You'll have to tell me all about it,' Masterson said. 'Since your father refused to.'

Kowalski was shoved into view at the outer door, hands on his head. His right eyebrow was split, bleeding down his face. Soldiers forced him to his knees.

'They killed Abe,' he growled out. 'Shot him like a dog.'

Masterson shrugged. 'And why not? He was *achuta*. Dogs are treated better in India.'

The soldiers spread out around them.

Elizabeth stared at the professor, stunned, hardly able to speak. Still, heat fired through her words, realizing the depth of the betrayal here. 'It was you! You betrayed my father!'

'I had no choice, Elizabeth. He'd been getting too close to the truth.'

Gray went cold. He understood the game that had been played out here. Masterson had been paid to keep an eye on Dr. Polk's research, to feed his data to his superiors . . . but once Elizabeth's father got too close, he had to be taken out of the game.

Who was behind it all?

Masterson must have recognized the icy fury in Gray's eyes. He backed a step away, though there was nothing Gray could do. Masterson waved his cane. 'Commander Pierce, it seems for now you and the others are needed alive. But maybe not the big fellow here.'

He pointed his cane at Kowalski.

'Kill him.'

Kowalski's eyes got huge.

Gray lunged forward, but three rifle barrels butted against his chest.

Elizabeth shouted out, 'Please, Hayden, *no*! I beg you!'

Gray heard the catch in her voice, so did Masterson.

The professor glanced between Elizabeth and Kowalski – then rolled his eyes. 'Fine. Only because I owe your father. But at the first sign of trouble from any of you, we start shooting.'

Masterson stared over to Gray. 'You wanted to know where Archibald went?' He turned and headed away. 'You should be careful what you wish for.'

THIRD

15

Monk poled through the swamps as best he could with one hand. But they dared not stop. They'd been hunted throughout the night. Stabilizing the oar-pole in the crook of his stumped arm, he pulled and shoved with his good hand. The raft glided silently across the drowned landscape.

Over the course of the night, his eyes had adjusted to the wan light from the moon. He had grown skilled at maneuvering the raft. They had several close calls as an airboat searched the swamps for them. The whining noise of its fan and its bright searchlight gave Monk plenty of warning to seek shelter. Also thick mists hung low over the water, which helped keep them hidden.

Still, they'd almost been caught once, when Monk had misjudged a sluggish current and struck a tree with a loud crack. The airboat had heard and come rushing over. He tried his best to hide under the branches of a willow, but they were sure to be spotted if the searchers looked too closely.

Their salvation came from an unexpected place.

As the airboat slowed and throttled down, Kiska had folded her hands over her mouth, took a deep breath, then let out a low bleating complaint of an elk cow. They'd heard the calls periodically throughout the night. Monk remembered how the girl had demonstrated her talent, an ear for perfect pitch and mimicry, mirroring birdcalls with an uncanny accuracy. The hunters had still searched, but less thoroughly, and moved onward after a minute.

Still they could not count on such luck forever. And worse yet, Monk knew they were slowly being herded closer toward Lake Karachay and its pall of radioactivity. The airboat swept the safer regions of the swamp, which only left them one recourse: to stray closer and closer in the direction of the lake.

Every hour, Monk risked lighting a single match to check the color of their dosimeters. The pink warning had darkened to full red. Konstantin had informed Monk matter-of-factly that one full day at that dosage was lethal. As Monk poled through floating rafts of weed and algae, his skin itched with the grainy sense that he was slowly being poisoned.

And the children were even more susceptible.

The trio slept fitfully, curled with Marta on the raft. An edge of terror kept them jumping at every croak and hoot from the nighttime swamp. Marta had finally taken to the trees. She had done so periodically, even drawing off the hunters once by hooting and luring the airboat in the opposite direction. Her diversion bought them a full hour of reprieve.

She was one smart ape.

Monk prayed she was as smart as he hoped – for a danger greater than the threat of radiation poisoning loomed.

To the east, the dark skies paled with the approach of dawn. Without the cover of night, they would quickly be discovered. To survive, they had to find a way of escaping their tail.

That meant leaving a trail of bread crumbs.

Konstantin and Kiska had shredded the wrappings from their protein bars and gathered their empty water bottles. As Monk churned a path through the weeds, disturbing a clear track through the vegetation, the two children had dropped bits and pieces of garbage into the water.

'Not too much,' Monk warned in a whisper. 'Spread them farther apart.'

Monk had spent the last hour searching for the perfect spot in the dark swamp. He'd finally found it: a long curving course, lined by dense willow groves and black patches of fir trees. Their timing had to be perfect. They would have only one shot. But with the far shore still a good two miles away and dawn fast approaching, they were doomed if they didn't take the risk.

The final member of their party, Pyotr, sat in the middle of the raft, his arms wrapped around his legs. As he rocked in place, he stared toward the stern of the raft, as if watching his friends spread their bread crumbs, but Monk knew the boy's gaze stretched much farther.

Reaching the end of the watery course, Monk swung the pole to the front and prodded it deep. He bolstered it with his shoulder and stopped the raft. This is where they'd make their stand.

Borsakov sat next to the airboat's pilot. The seats were perched high above the flat-bottomed aluminum hull. Ahead of them crouched two of his soldiers; one manned the searchlight at the boat's prow, the other kept a rifle ready at his shoulder.

After five hours of searching, Borsakov's ears ached from all the noise. Behind him, the engine rumbled as the giant fan spun. The broken metal guard over the blades rattled and banged with every turn. The propwash that propelled the craft shook reeds and branches behind the boat.

319

The pilot wore the only set of earphones. He rested one hand on the steering stick, the other on the throttle. The smell of smoke and diesel fuel masked the mossy dampness of the swamp. They idled through a shallow section of open water. The searchlight swept the reeds that rimmed the edges.

Over the course of the night, they'd seen wild boar and elk, scared eagles from nests, glided past beaver dams and through clouds of insects. Their searchlight had reflected off thousands of smaller eyes, denizens of the swamp.

Still, they'd seen no sign of the escapees.

And on their last tank of fuel, they had until—

A simian scream cut through the engine's rumble. It came from the right. The soldiers at the prow heard it, too. Both searchlight and rifle swung in that direction. Borsakov touched the pilot's shoulder and pointed.

In the flash of light, something large swung across a narrow gap in the treeline, then disappeared into the forest. Borsakov knew one of the laboratory animals had also vanished with the children. A chimpanzee.

The engine roared louder as the pilot pushed the throttle stick forward. The boat sped toward the gap, gliding up on a cushion of air. The craft slowed as they reached the edge of the open water. The reeds here were bent, where someone had pushed through to reach a side channel.

Finally . . .

Borsakov pointed ahead.

Past the gap, a narrow channel snaked ahead, lined by willows and choked by floating patches of weed. The craft sped up. The searchlight swept to all sides, piercing through the darkness. The rifleman reached down to the water and scooped up an empty plastic water bottle.

Someone had definitely been through here.

Borsakov waved the pilot to a faster clip, sensing his

320

targets couldn't be far. The course ambled in gentle curves. The boat followed swiftly, sweeping right and left.

The searchlight revealed more debris floating in the water, bits of trash and more bottles. Too much. Something was wrong here. Their prey had never been this foolish. Suspicious, Borsakov reached to the pilot and squeezed his shoulder. He motioned him to slow down.

Monk heard the engine's roar lower to a rumble.

Crouched with the children, he watched the airboat glide into view around the last bend in the channel, plainly throttling down, going too slowly.

Not good.

The searchlight speared forward, gliding across the water straight at them. They would be spotted in a second. Their only hope—

—from out of the dark forest to the left, a dark shadow leaped headlong over the boat. It flew high, clearing the blades, but from its clenched feet, a handful of dark objects were tossed at the boat.

They struck the giant fan like bomb loads.

The shotgun shells from the cabin.

Monk heard them *pop* against the blades. The fan sliced through the plastic casings, which didn't ignite, but which still exploded outward with stinging birdshot.

Cries erupted, half surprise and half pain as the crew was struck by flying pellets. The pilot, high in his seat, ducked and dropped in fear. He hit his stick, and the engine roared to life. The boat kicked forward like a stung jackrabbit, off kilter by the turn. The pilot wrested the control stick.

The searchlight blazed down the channel and swept over them, highlighting them in its brilliance. Monk saw the copilot scream and point.

Too late, buddy.

The two soldiers in front were suddenly flung backward. They struck the others. Tangled in a group, they hit the metal guard at the rear of the boat. The airboat jackknifed into the air and barrel-rolled.

Monk heard a scream of agony and a stuttered grind of blades. Blood and bone sprayed out of the back of the fan like a contrail – then the boat struck the water upside down, landing hard with a gasp of diesel smoke and a drowning choke from its engine. The searchlight still glowed out of the murky water.

Monk turned away. Earlier, with the children's help, he had braided fishing line from the cabin into a translucent rope as thick as his finger – then he rigged it shoulder-height across the channel. It had clotheslined the crew and flipped the unstable boat.

From out of the trees above the raft, Marta dropped and landed leadenly to the planks. Pyotr was immediately in her arms. She sat on her haunches, gasping, panting. Still, she hugged Pyotr. Her eyes, though, were fixed on Monk, glassy and bright in the moonlight.

Monk nodded to her, grateful, yet at the same time, slightly unnerved.

He had needed the airboat to fly up the channel, drawn by the sure trail of their prey. Marta's bombardment had been intended only as a distraction to keep them from seeing the rope strung across the channel.

She had done her job brilliantly.

Pyotr clung to her. After explaining the plan earlier, the boy had sat with Marta and held out the shotgun shells. He spoke slowly to her in Russian, but Monk suspected the true understanding between the pair arose from much deeper. In the end, she had taken the shells in the toes of her feet, leaped into the trees, and vanished.

Monk poled out across the next channel. Here a sluggish current propelled them onward. Toward the distant shore. Though relieved that his trap had worked,

Monk knew with certainty that they were sweeping toward even greater danger.

But he had no choice.

Millions of lives were at stake.

Still, Monk studied Marta and the three children. To him, with no memory of another life, they were his world. They were all that mattered. He would do all he could to protect them.

As he urged the raft along the current, he recalled the painful flashback at the cabin as he had half drowsed.

The taste of cinnamon, soft lips . . .

What life had been stolen from him?

And could he ever get it back?

12:04 A.M.
Washington, D.C.

Just after midnight, Kat hung up the phone and stood up from the table. She glanced toward the window into the neighboring hospital room. She had finished a conference call with Director Crowe and Sean McKnight. The two were up in Painter's office, waging an interdepartmental war from their bunker. Both men were engaged in a power struggle across the various intelligence agencies.

All over the fate of the girl.

Kat, with her own background in the field, had offered what counsel she could, but she could do no more. It was up to the two of them to find some way to thwart John Mapplethorpe.

Kat knew where she could do the most good.

She crossed toward the door that led into the hospital room. It was guarded by an armed corpsman. She paused by the window of one-way glass and stared into the room.

Propped by pillows in the bed, Sasha sat with a coloring book in her lap and a box of Crayola crayons.

With an intravenous line still in her arm, she worked on a page, her face intent but calm.

Sasha suddenly glanced up from her work and stared straight at Kat. The glass was mirrored on the other side; there was no way the child could see that she was there. But Kat could not shake the sense that the girl was looking at her, could see her.

To one side, Yuri sat in a chair. He had pulled Sasha from the brink of death, proving his skill. He seemed as relieved as Kat at the girl's recovery. Satisfied and exhausted, he sat slumped in his seat, chin on his chest, lightly drowsing.

Kat turned and nodded to the guard. He had already unlocked the door and swung it open for her. She crossed into the room. McBride still sat in the same chair. He had only moved to make a few phone calls and to use the restroom, always under guard.

On the other side of the bed from Yuri, Lisa and Malcolm stood, both with charts in hand. They compared notes and numbers, as cryptic as any code.

Lisa smiled at her as she joined them. 'Her recovery is remarkable. I could spend years just studying the treatment regimen.'

'But it's only a stopgap,' Kat said and she nodded to Yuri. 'Not a cure.'

Lisa's expression sobered and she turned back to the girl. 'That's true.'

Yuri had related the long-term prognosis for Sasha. Her augment shortened her life span. Like a flame set to a candle, it would burn through her, wear her away to nothing. The greater the talent, the hotter the flame.

Kat had asked how long Yuri expected the child to live. The answer had turned her cold. *With her level of talent, another four or five years at best.*

Kat had balked at such a pronouncement.

Contrarily, McBride had seemed relieved, expressing

his assurances that American ingenuity could surely double that life span, which still meant Sasha would not reach her twentieth birthday.

Lisa continued, 'The only hope for her is to remove the implant. She would lose her ability, but she'd also survive.'

McBride spoke up behind them. 'She might survive, but in what state? The augment, besides heightening her savant talent, also minimizes the symptoms of her autism. Take the augment away, and you'll be left with a child disconnected from the world.'

'That's better than being in the grave,' Kat said.

'Is it?' McBride challenged her. 'Who are you to judge? With the augment, she has a full life, as short as that might be. Many children are born doomed from the start, given life sentences by medical conditions. Leukemia, AIDS, birth defects. Shouldn't we seek to give them the best *quality* of life, rather than *quantity*?'

Kat scowled. 'You only want to use her.'

'Since when is mutual benefit such a bad thing?'

Kat turned her back on him, frustrated with his arguments and justifications. It was monstrous. How could he rationalize any of this? Especially with the life of a child in the balance.

Sasha continued to work in her coloring book. She drew with a dark green crayon. Her hand moved rapidly across the page, filling in one spot, then another, totally at random.

'Should she be coloring?' Kat asked.

Yuri stirred, roused by their talking. 'Some release is good after such an episode,' he mumbled, clearing his throat. 'Like opening a pressure valve. As long as the augment is not activated remotely, triggering her, such calm work will ease her mentally.'

'Well, she does seem happy,' Kat admitted.

As she worked, Sasha's face was relaxed with a faint

ghost of a smile. She straightened and reached a small hand to Kat. She spoke in Russian and tugged at her sleeve with her tiny fingers.

Kat glanced to Yuri.

He offered a tired grin. 'She said you should be happy, too.'

Sasha pushed her book toward Kat, as if she wanted Kat to join her in coloring the pages. Kat sank into a seat and accepted the book. She frowned when she saw the girl had not been filling in lines but had been working on a blank page. With amazing clarity, she had drawn a scene. A man poled a wooden raft through a dark forest with a faint suggestion of other figures seated behind him.

Kat's hands began to tremble. She saw who manned the raft. She struggled to understand. It looked like Monk. But she had no memory of Monk ever being on a raft. Why would the girl draw such a thing?

Sasha must have sensed her distress. Her smile wilted to confusion. Her lips trembled, as though fearful she had done something wrong. She stared from Yuri to Kat. Tears glistened. She mumbled in Russian, apologetic and scared.

Yuri scooted closer and reassured her with the soft voice of a grandfather. Kat forced down her reaction – for the child's sake. Still, her heart pounded. She remembered seeing Yuri stiffen when he saw the child's earlier picture. At the time, for a split second, she had thought maybe he had recognized the face on the paper, but that was impossible.

McBride climbed out of his chair and approached the bed, plainly curious.

Kat ignored him. It was none of his business. Instead, her gaze fixed on Yuri. The man met her stare over the top of Sasha's head. Like the child, he wore an apologetic expression.

Why would—

A muffled explosion rocked through the facility, echoing down from above. Alarm bells rang out. All eyes turned toward the ceiling, but Kat leaped to her feet. She was a fraction of a second too slow.

McBride lunged out and grabbed Dr. Lisa Cummings by her blond French braid. He pulled her toward him while he backpedaled to the wall. Kat Bryant grabbed for him but missed. He slammed back into the corner, out of direct sight line from the door and the window.

His other hand pulled his cell phone from his jacket pocket. He pressed a button on its side, and the top half flipped in his fingers, revealing a small barrel. He shoved it hard against Lisa's throat, pointing it up toward her skull.

'Don't move,' he whispered in her ear.

Cell phone guns had become the scourge of security forces. But the device Mapplethorpe had given him was state-of-the-art. He could even take calls on it. It had passed through the security search and scanner without a blip of concern. Chambered in .22-caliber rounds, there was unfortunately a limit to the weapon.

'I have five bullets!' he shouted to the stunned room. 'I will kill the doctor first – then the child.'

A guard leveled a weapon at him, but he kept shielded behind Lisa's body.

'Drop your gun!' he boomed at the man.

The guard kept his position, weapon never wavering.

'No one has to die!' McBride said. He nodded his head upward. 'We only want the child. So put down your pistol!'

Kat straightened from her tumbled grab. She had come close to nabbing him. He would have to watch her closely. In turn, she eyed him, studying him like a book. Still, the woman motioned for the guard to lower his weapon.

'Drop it and kick it over here!' McBride ordered.

With another nod from Kat, the sidearm skittered over to his toes.

McBride's mission was simple: to secure the child until Mapplethorpe and his forces arrived.

'All we have to do is wait!' he said. 'So no sudden moves, no heroes.'

As the explosion rocked through the subterranean bunker, Painter instinctively turned to the wall monitor on his left. The large screen displayed a live feed from Sasha's room.

Painter shot to his feet. His heart pounded, and his vision narrowed with fury. He brought up the sound with a blind punch to his keyboard.

'No sudden moves, no heroes!'

Sean rose on the other side of the desk. Gunfire echoed

down to them. Painter brought up the camera feed from the top level of Sigma and displayed it on the screen behind his desk. He tore his eyes away from Lisa and checked the other monitor. Smoke filled the passageway. Helmeted figures in Kevlar vests and face masks ran low through the pall, rifles on their shoulders.

'I can't believe the bastard's goddamn nerve,' Sean said.

There was no need to guess who he meant.

Mapplethorpe.

'They're going for the girl,' Sean growled out.

A bullhorn echoed from the topmost level of Sigma. *'EVERYONE DOWN ON THE FLOOR! ANY RESISTANCE WILL BE MET WITH DEADLY FORCE!'*

Sean crossed to Painter. 'There's no way this is sanctioned. We would have been issued a stand-down order first. The bastard's gone rogue.' Sean turned toward him. 'You know what you have to do.'

Painter's attention returned to Lisa. He saw the weapon pressed under her jaw, a tender neck he kissed each morning. But he slowly nodded. There was a failsafe if Sigma was ever under attack by a hostile force.

But first he needed to get his people out of harm's way. This war was between Painter and Mapplethorpe. He picked up the phone. 'Brant.'

'Sir!' His aide's voice was curt and ready.

'Sound Protocol Alpha.'

'Yes, sir.'

A new klaxon rang out, ordering all personnel to evacuate to the nearest emergency exit. Mapplethorpe just wanted a clear path to the child. To protect his people, Painter intended to provide that.

Sean headed to the door. 'I'm going up. I'll attempt to negotiate, but if I fail . . .'

'Understood.' Painter turned, pulled a drawer, and removed a Sig Sauer P220 pistol. 'Take this.'

Sean shook his head. 'Firepower isn't going to get us out of this.'

His friend left. Painter gripped the pistol and studied the screen. He had one last duty to Sigma. He shifted to his computer and typed in the fail-safe code, then pressed his thumb to the fingerprint reader.

A red square appeared, layered over a blue schematic of the facility's air-ventilation system. The default countdown was set at fifteen minutes. Painter doubled the time and synchronized it with his watch to go active at 0100. He stared between the door and the wall screen. He had a lot to accomplish in such a short time. Still . . .

Typing rapidly, Painter entered the final code to activate. The numbers started counting down.

With pistol in hand, he ran for the door.

7:05 A.M.
Southern Ural Mountains

As the sun first peeked over the surrounding mountains, Monk shoved with his pole and drove the raft deep into the reeds. The prow ground into a muddy bank. At long last, they'd made landfall, as soggy as that might be.

'Stay here,' he ordered the kids.

Using the pole, he tested for solid footing. Satisfied, he climbed off the raft, then turned and helped Pyotr and Kiska onto a hillock of grass nearby. Konstantin leaped on his own, as spry as ever, but the boy landed roughly. His exhaustion showed in the dark lines under his eyes and the tremble as he stood. Marta fared little better, lunging with both legs and landing in a knuckled crouch.

Monk waved them onward. The way remained muddy and sodden for another quarter mile, but slowly the ground rose out of the swamp and firmed underfoot.

The forest shed the watery willows and stood taller with birches and spruces. Meadows opened, green with wild gentian and edelweiss.

They reached the top of a rise, and a clear view spread ahead of them.

A mile away, a small town, split by a silver-flowing creek, dotted the lower slope of the neighboring mountain. Monk studied the place. It appeared long deserted and abandoned. The derelict mix of stone and wooden buildings climbed the slopes around a switchbacking gravel road. An old mill neighbored the rocky creek. Its waterwheel lay fallen and broken across the stream like a bridge. Several other structures had collapsed in on themselves, and the place had a wild overgrown look to it, buried in high grasses and lush with juniper bushes and fir trees.

'It's an old mining town,' Konstantin explained. The boy unfolded the map, to check their bearings. 'No one lives there. Not safe.'

'How much farther until we reach the mine shaft?' Monk asked.

The boy measured with his thumb on the map, then pointed to the ramshackle collection of buildings. 'Another half mile past the town. Not far.'

Konstantin glanced off to the right of the town. His expression soured. He didn't have to say anything. Half hidden behind the shoulder of the mountain, a large greenish black body of water stretched off to the horizon.

Lake Karachay.

Monk checked his badge. It still registered a reddish hue. But to reach the town, they would have to head directly toward the lake, deeper into its radioactive shadow.

'How hot is that place?' Monk asked, nodding to the town.

Konstantin refolded the map and stood. 'We should not stop for a picnic.'

Monk stared back at the boy, appreciating his attempt at levity. But neither of them laughed. Still, Monk hooked an arm around the boy as they marched ahead. He gave Konstantin a reassuring squeeze and earned a silly grin in response. A rare sight.

Pyotr and Kiska followed with Marta in tow.

They had made it this far.

There was no turning back.

Half a mile away, Borsakov watched his targets vanish over a ridgeline. With a silent curse directed at the man who led the children, he knelt beside the beached raft used by the others and slipped his rifle from his shoulder. Before he continued, his weapon needed to be cleaned. After the long swim and slog through the swamp, his rifle was caked with mud and full of water. He broke the weapon down and carefully inspected each section: barrel, bolt assembly, magazine. He rinsed and dried all the parts thoroughly. Satisfied, he reassembled the rifle. The familiar routine returned him to a calm, determined status.

Once done, he stood up and shouldered his weapon.

Having lost his radio, Borsakov was on his own, the only survivor from the airboat crash. The pilot's arm had been severed by the fan. Another soldier's head had been caved in, struck by the edge of the flipping boat. The last had been found floating facedown, drowned.

Only Borsakov remained, though he bore a long jagged cut down his calf, sliced to the bone. He had used one of his dead men's shirts to wrap and bind the injury. He would need medical attention to prevent losing his leg to infection from the muddy water.

But first he had a job to do.

Failure was not an option.

Limping on his bad leg, Borsakov set off after his prey.

16

'Wake up!'

Gray heard the words, but his brain took another moment to decipher them. A stinging slap cut through his grogginess. Light filled his head then dissolved into watery images.

Luca leaned over him and shook Gray's shoulders.

Coughing, Gray pushed the man back and rose to an elbow. He stared around the room. He was in a bare cement cell with peeling, blistered paint and a rusted red door. Light came from a single barred window high up on the wall. Beneath the window, Kowalski sat on a moldy thin mattress, his head hanging between his knees, groaning with nausea.

Gray took a deep breath, forced himself to relax, and recalled what had happened. He remembered a hard climb out of the canyon at gunpoint, a short helicopter ride, then a cargo plane on a rain-swept airstrip. He fingered a bruise on his neck. Once aboard the plane, they'd been drugged.

Gray had no idea where they'd been taken.

'Elizabeth . . . Rosauro . . . ?' he asked hoarsely.

Luca shook his head. He slumped against the wall

333

and sank to his bottom. 'I don't know where they are. Maybe another cell.'

'Any idea where *we* are?'

Luca shrugged. Kowalski groaned.

Gray gained his feet, waited for the world to stop spinning, then stepped toward the window. It was too high to reach on his own.

Kowalski lifted his head, noted where Gray was staring. 'Pierce, you've got to be kidding.'

'Get up,' he ordered. 'Help me.'

Kowalski held his stomach but rose to his feet. He clenched his fingers together into a stirrup. 'What do you think I am? Your personal ladder?'

'Ladders complain a lot less.'

Gray mounted the man's grip, reached to the lower lip of the window, and with Kowalski's help, he chinned up to the bars. He gazed across a strange landscape. A town, half consumed by forest, spread outward. The place looked dilapidated and shell-shocked. Roofs were covered in moss or collapsed, windows shattered into broken fangs, fire escapes dripped with icicles of rust, and weeds and bushes sprouted out of cracked asphalt. Across the street, a faded billboard advertised some sort of fair, depicting a Ferris wheel and carnival rides. In the foreground, a stylized version of a strappingly robust family headed toward the amusements.

Across the city, Gray spotted the same Ferris wheel from the billboard outlined against the barren sky. A lonely relic of former glory. Gray's limbs grew leaden at the sight. He knew where he was. The abandoned amusement ride had become emblematic for the city.

'Chernobyl,' he mumbled and dropped back down to the floor.

But why had they been brought here?

Gray recalled the pathologist's report on Dr. Polk's body. The radiation signature suggested the professor had been poisoned here. Though further testing by Malcolm Jennings had clouded this assessment.

What was going on?

Over the next ten minutes, Gray searched the entire cell and tested the door. Though rusted, it remained secure. Gray heard sounds of someone out there: a shuffle of foot, a soft cough. Most likely a guard. He must have heard them talking and radioed his superiors because shortly thereafter a tromping of boots approached the door.

Too many to ambush.

Gray stepped back as the door pulled open. With pistols pointed, soldiers in black-and-gray uniforms stormed into the room. They opened the way for a tall man to step forward, framed in the doorway. His features were not unlike those of the father from the faded billboard outside. His face was all angles and hard corners; a trimmed beard defined a strong chin. He wore a navy blue suit with a red silk tie, tailored handsomely to his physique. Even down to his—

'Nice shoes,' Kowalski commented.

The man glanced to his polished black oxfords and frowned at the unexpected assessment of his wardrobe.

'Well, they are,' Kowalski said with a note of defensiveness.

The newcomer's eyes shifted to Gray. '*Dobraye utro*, Commander Pierce. If you'll come with me, we have some business to discuss and not much time.'

Gray remained where he was. 'Not until you tell me where the two women—'

A hand waved dismissively. 'Elizabeth Polk and Dr. Shay Rosauro. Both fine, I assure you. In fact, their accommodations are a bit more refined. But we had very little time to prepare. If you'll come this way, please.'

The six soldiers with pistols diminished the politeness of the invitation. Led out into a hallway, Gray studied his surroundings. Cells lined both sides, plainly an abandoned jail. Through some of the open doors, he spotted standing water, rusted overturned beds, and refuse piled high into corners. It made their cell's accommodations seem generous in comparison.

The hallway ended at a guard station. It had a view across an overgrown, weedy jail yard. In the distance, off by the horizon, Gray noted the tall ventilation tower that marked the Chernobyl reactor.

Closer at hand, a chair squeaked with an almost nervous sound.

Gray turned. A table stood in the middle of the room. Masterson sat behind it, straightening in his seat, again dressed all in white, looking well rested and smug. Gray had to refrain himself from leaping over and snapping the bastard's neck. But he needed some answers, and cooperation seemed the best way of obtaining it.

Forced to a chair on the opposite side of the table, Gray sat down. A gun remained pointed at the back of his head.

Another stranger waited in the room. She stood behind the table. Her black hair framed a smoky face, stoic and unmoving. She was also dressed in a black suit, a close match in style to that of the man who had led Gray here. The stranger crossed to the table and sat down, barely acknowledging Masterson.

The man folded his hands atop the table. 'My name is Senator Nicolas Solokov. Perhaps you've heard of me.'

Gray said nothing, which caused the man's mouth to quirk with disappointment.

'No? Well, that will be changing,' he responded. He waved to the slim woman. She crossed to Gray, moving with a stiff grace. She sank to a knee beside his chair, tilted her head, and reached toward his hand. Before she touched him, she cocked an eyebrow, inquiring permission.

Gray shrugged. She gently lifted his hand and rested

her palm beneath his. Her fingertips tickled the underside of his wrist. Her eyes stared deeply into his.

'We've already had a conversation with Elizabeth Polk,' Nicolas said. 'Dr. Polk's daughter informed us of your discovery in India. Truly amazing. That information alone was worth transporting you all here. It's fascinating to contemplate that our heritage extends all the way to ancient Greece, to the famous Oracle of Delphi.'

Gray cleared his throat. '*Your* heritage?'

He waved to the woman. 'And Elena's. We're all from the same genetic bloodline.'

Gray remembered Luca's story. 'From the lost Gypsies.'

'Yes. Dr. Masterson has informed me that you were told about the unfortunate, but necessary acquisition of those children. In fact, my father was one of those Gypsy children. And I believe you've met another of our extended family. Little Sasha. A girl with a special talent.'

Gray knew to whom he must be referring, but he kept his features bland, feigning ignorance.

Elena turned to Nicolas and spoke softly in Russian.

The senator nodded. 'So you have met Sasha. Please do not trouble yourself to lie.' He motioned to the woman at his feet. 'Elena is quite – well, perceptive, shall we say. Her touch is very sensitive, measuring the heat of your skin, your pulse. She is also keyed into your pupils and breath. Nothing escapes her. She is my personal lie detector.'

Nicolas pointed to his ear. Elena turned, and with her other hand, she parted her hair behind her ear. Gray spotted a familiar curve of surgical steel. The same implant as the girl's. The woman was the adult equivalent of Sasha, only with a different savant talent.

'She is quite remarkable,' Nicolas growled, his words warmly proud, but with a hint of something darker beneath.

Gray studied the man, noticing something missing. 'So then where is your implant?'

Nicolas's eyes narrowed back upon him. Gray enjoyed the flicker of irritation on his face, plainly a sore point. The man's fingers combed over his right ear in a self-conscious gesture. 'Such a course was not my path, I'm afraid.'

Gray's mind tracked the implication. If Nicolas wasn't augmented, then he must have been born without any savant talent. Yet someone had placed him in a position of power in Russia. Why? What was the endgame here?

Nicolas continued, 'Back to Sasha. From all the turmoil going on in Washington, we've been having trouble gaining clear intelligence on her whereabouts. That was the main reason you were brought here from India.'

Versus being shot on the spot like Abhi Bhanjee.

'We are concerned about Sasha's welfare and want her returned. So first of all, we'd like to know where she is and who has her.'

Gray stared straight at Nicolas. 'I don't know.'

At his side, Elena shook her head.

'Would you like to try again? I'm attempting to keep this civil. But we do have four of your friends here.'

'I can't say for sure,' Gray answered. 'The last I saw her, she was in the care of our organization.'

Nicolas glanced to Elena, who nodded. It was the truth.

'And I assume you do not work for John Mapplethorpe, since the traitor attempted to assassinate you and Dr. Masterson at the hotel in Agra.'

'No, in fact, we're fighting to keep the child away from him.'

'Wise. That man is far from trustworthy. So then perhaps we truly can negotiate. Especially since we now have something worth trading.'

'First, what do you want with the girl?' Gray asked.

'She belongs here. With the rest of her family. We can care for her much better than anyone in your country.'

'Perhaps so. But *why* do you want her? To what end?'

Nicolas stared at Gray, studying him with shrewd eyes. Gray sensed a depth of cunning, along with a hard conceit, someone seeking recognition, compensating perhaps for a lack of talent elsewhere.

Gray pressed that weakness. 'Do you have a plan that goes beyond the exploitation of children like Sasha?'

His eyes sparked. 'Do not underestimate the scope of our initiative. Nor paint us with such malicious intent. We have nothing but the most humanitarian goals in mind, to better the world for all. The sacrifice required of a few children is infinitesimally small when compared to the atrocities that go ignored every day in the world.'

Gray read the need for validation behind the growing heat in his words. 'What goals?'

'Nothing short of changing the course of human history.'

Here the man's vanity shone brightly. He even sat up straighter and leaned toward Gray.

'Every few centuries, a great figure rises who abruptly changes history – someone who alters the fundamental path of mankind. I'm talking along the lines of the great prophets. Buddha, Muhammad, Jesus Christ. Someone who thinks so differently, who sees the world through such unique eyes, that his very viewpoint bends humanity in a new direction. From where do such figures arise? Where does this uniqueness of mind come from?'

Masterson stirred, stretching a kink in his back.

Gray recalled the professor's discussion about autism and its role in human history. And the quote he had used. *If by some magic, autism had been eradicated from the face of the earth, then men would still be socializing in front of a wood fire at the entrance to a cave.*

'Why wait for the right toss of the genetic dice?' Nicolas asked. 'If such uniqueness could be recognized, singled out, and harnessed for the good of all, imagine the new age of enlightenment that could be fostered. Especially if such uniqueness could be heightened to astounding levels.'

Nicolas's eyes settled on Elena.

Gray began to understand the scope of the project's vision. It was no mere spy program. Nicolas's organization planned to take control of the reins to human history by using the augmented individuals like draft horses. And Gray began to suspect *why* Nicolas had been put in such a place of power. Someone was grooming him as a figurehead, propped and supported behind the scenes by the augmented children. Gray tried to imagine all that talent at the bid of one individual.

Gray could not hide his horror and shock. 'How do you plan to—?'

'That's enough!' Nicolas barked. 'Now that you better understand our intent, you can understand why we want Sasha returned. She is important to the program . . . and especially significant to me.'

Gray read something in his eyes. 'Why you?'

'Why?' He stared hard at Gray. 'Because she's more than a test subject, she's my daughter.'

Elena's fingernails scraped the underside of Gray's wrist. The woman turned sharply toward Nicolas. Apparently this was as equally surprising to her. No wonder Gray and the others had been dragged all the way to Chernobyl.

'Before this day is over, you will know what I am capable of.' Nicolas leaned toward Gray, his eyes fiery with determination. 'And I will get my daughter back.'

8:20 A.M.
Southern Ural Mountains

General-Major Savina Martov stood in the heart of Operation Saturn. Behind her, the mine train waited on the tracks, snapping and crackling, smelling of smoke and oil. It rested a hundred yards from where the tracks ended at Mine Complex 337, an abandoned uranium mine that honeycombed the neighboring Ural Mountains. M.C. 337 was where the prisoners housed at Chelyabinsk 88 had spent eighteen hours a day laboring in the dark, slowly being poisoned.

Now it served as a dumping ground for broken mining equipment and piles of rock from Operation Saturn. Over the course of five years, a small team of miners and demolition experts had filled several old shafts to the brim with the debris dug out of this site.

Operation Saturn occupied a small man-made cavern off the train tracks. The blasted room – the size of a hotel lobby – was framed by oil-soaked scaffolding and crowded with mining equipment: conveyor belts, hydraulic winches, rock dusters, water pumps, hoses, all surrounding a compact drill rig with a drummed tungsten-carbide bit. Most of it would be left where it stood or hauled out with the next train.

Savina watched a backhoe dump a load of rock and rubble into one of the ore cars behind her. The train would make one last shipment to M.C. 337.

All was on schedule.

Still, she stood with her fists on her hips, legs apart, surveying the operation site. Her conversation with Nicolas still had her agitated. She had known he was bullheaded and prone to rash and dramatic decisions. She regretted informing him about Sasha. She had not thought he would react so foolishly. Where was his dispassion in such matters? They still had *ten* Omega subjects, more than enough to seed the new site in Moscow. The ten alone were powerful enough to hand him the world, to guide humanity to its new Renaissance, led by a resurrected Russian Empire. And the future czar would not have *one* Rasputin to counsel him, but *ten*. Ten prodigious savants, who together and augmented, could bend time and distance to serve him.

Did he not see that?

What was one child against such a vision?

Two if you counted Nicolas's son, Pyotr. But the boy's talent, while strong, was of little value. What use was empathy when it came to forging a new world? If anything, it was a hindrance. All that would be lost with the boy was his genetic potential. A significant loss, but not insurmountable. And there was still hope of recovering the boy. The last she'd heard from Lieutenant Borsakov was that he was about to head into the Asanov swamps. It would be hard to find anything in the dark, but with the sun now up, she expected results at any moment. Or so she had assured Nicolas.

And ultimately it did not matter. Nicolas would grow to see this.

A technician in a white smock, hard hat, and respirator mask approached her. He was an engineer from the St. Petersburg State Mining Institute. 'Ready to test the board and iris.'

She nodded. After this final shakedown, the operation site would be evacuated. She'd had to push her crew these last two days in order to meet the shortened timetable. Nicolas's operation had been scheduled to proceed today, followed by Savina's in two weeks. But with the recent betrayal by Mapplethorpe, the decision had been made to initiate both operations on the same day. Once she heard of Nicolas's success, she would proceed.

'Are there any problems?' she asked the engineer.

His voice was muffled in the respirator as they walked. 'We've run all the diagnostics, rechecked the ammonium nitrate fuel oil concentrations, performed one final GPR scan of the overburden, and troubleshot all electrical systems. We're ready on your order to clear the site and open the iris. We're going to test-fire it now.'

'Very good.'

Savina followed the man under the arch of scaffolding. The vehicle-mounted drill rig was already being driven out of the way. Men worked around the tight space: in the rigging, on the floor, and amid the equipment. She looked to the upper wall of the cavern. A two-meter-wide shaft sloped upward at a steep angle, lined by an idle conveyor belt, dripping with water from the hoses. Lights glowed at the far end of the shaft, almost half a kilometer away. Tiny shadows moved within the glow, motes in the brightness. The demolition team was doing one final inspection.

Savina appreciated their thoroughness.

Over fifty bore holes – as thick around as her thumb and a meter deep – had been drilled into the end of the shaft and packed with ANFO supercharges. The bores needled through a fault that lay beneath Lake Karachay. Wired to detonate in sequence, the charges would crack a gaping hole in the bottom of the poisonous lake, dumping its slurry of radioactive strontium and cesium straight down the shaft.

'Over here, General-Major.' The technician waved her away from the center of the cavern.

Set into the floor was a three-meter-wide circular hatch. She had obtained it from the Sevmorput Naval Shipyard in Murmansk. It was the latest missile silo door, composed of six flakes of half-meter-thick steel in the shape of an iris.

She stepped off of it and over to where a diagnostic laptop rested on a worktable. The technician had the engineering schematics open on the screen. Other men had stopped to watch.

He spoke into a radio, listened, then nodded to Savina. 'We're set in the control room. Ten seconds until firing.'

Savina crossed her arms. The control room was back in Chelyabinsk 88, in one of the old abandoned Soviet-era apartment buildings. Technicians manned the small room of monitors and computers. Once the site was evacuated, thirty different cameras would provide coverage of the area.

The engineer counted down the seconds. 'Three . . . two . . . one . . . *zero.*'

A snap of an electrical circuit sounded from the silo door, and its steel petals opened like the iris on a camera. As they peeled wider, a low roar of water echoed up to her. She stepped to the iris and stared over the edge. A vertical shaft dropped two hundred meters through the rock.

The engineer joined her and pointed a heavy flashlight down the throat of the mine shaft. Far below, she spotted a silvery rush, reflecting the light. An underground river. There were several such waterways draining the Urals, massive aquifers flowing down from the highlands. On the far side of the mountains, the waters flooded into the Caspian Sea, but here the aquifers drained through a series of rivers, specifically the Techa and Ob, all the way to the Arctic Ocean.

Savina turned and looked up the sloped shaft that led to the fault line under Lake Karachay. It contained over one hundred times more strontium and cesium than was released in Chernobyl. And Chernobyl's toxic plume had circled the globe. She stared back down the vertical shaft to the flowing aquifer.

It had been an ongoing threat. Geologists were well aware of the faults that underlay Lake Karachay. It was only a matter of time until an earthquake burst one of those fissures and dumped all that radioactivity into the drainage basin of the Ural Mountains. Studies done by geophysicists from Norway estimated that such a catastrophe would sterilize a good portion of the Arctic Ocean, one of the planet's last great wildernesses. From there, its poisonous pall would sweep halfway around the planet, concentrating its worst effects across northern

344

Europe. Conservative estimates put the death toll from primary radiation and secondary cancers at one hundred million. And that could easily double or triple from the resulting economic and environmental damage.

She stared from the sloped shaft above to the river below. Such a disaster had always been a constant but barely acknowledged threat. All nature needed was a little shove.

Then the world would burn.

Her breathing grew harder at the enormity of what was about to unfold. Out of that radiological fire, a new Russian Empire would rise, like a phoenix out of the ashes of their own nuclear legacy.

She would let nothing stop her.

She had spent her life and soul here in the Warren, all to serve the Motherland. And after so many sacrifices, so much bloodshed, what was left of Russia? Over the past decades, Savina had watched the Motherland devolve into this corrupt, pitiful shadow of itself. Here at the end of her life, she would offer it hope again. That would be her legacy, brought about by her own son.

She would burn away the corruption and create a new world.

'General-Major? Is there anything more?'

She shook her head and controlled her words. 'I've seen enough.'

The engineer nodded and crossed to a steel lever beside his workstation. It looked like a giant handbrake on a car. He pinched the release on the lever, cranked the bar up, and shouldered it in the opposite direction. The iris swept closed at her toes and sealed the shaft. There was still work to be done. Miners, who had stopped to see the silo doors open, went back to work, crossing over the top of the iris, as they had for the past two years since dropping that first shaft.

Operation Saturn was ready to commence.

Savina turned away and headed toward the waiting

train. She also had final preparations back at Chelyabinsk 88 to complete. She checked her watch. Nicolas should be heading to the ceremony at Chernobyl in another hour. Despite his rash actions of late, he did have everything under control. With or without him, systems were in place and would run their course. All was in order. Nothing could stop it from happening.

As she stepped into the train car and the doors sealed, she glanced back to the heart of Operation Saturn. She tried to picture the millions that would die, but they were an abstraction, a number too large to contemplate beyond cold statistics. She faced forward as the train lurched into motion and headed back toward the Warren at Chelyabinsk 88. The teachers and researchers should be readying for their own evacuation. Computers were being wiped, records incinerated. The children were also being prepared – but not for evacuation. They would be taking one last train ride themselves.

All of them, except the ten who would be with her.

Savina pictured the faces of the other children. Sixty-four, including the infants. It was a number too small to view as only an abstraction. She knew a majority of the children by name. As the train trundled toward the Warren in the dark, Savina leaned a hand against the wall. Her knees trembled, and a wave of emotion swept through her. She did not fight it. It welled up out of her chest and choked her throat. A few hot tears streamed down her cheeks. In this private moment, she let her emotions run their course. She recognized her humanity and allowed herself a moment to grieve.

But only this moment.

By the time the train began slowing, she wiped her face and patted her cheeks. She took several deep breaths. There was no turning back.

Necessity was a cruel master.

And she would have to be just as cruel.

Nicolas climbed into the limousine with Elena. A caravan of vehicles flowed out from the staging area in front of the Polissia Hotel. Politicians and officials were being shuttled or had private escorts. Since midnight, news crews from around the world had been setting up cameras and prepping vans that sported towering satellite antennas. Since first light, celebrities and dignitaries had been drifting over there, for interviews, for tours, for a moment in the limelight.

In the next hours, the eyes of the world would be upon the sealing of Chernobyl, a final act to end the old nuclear era and launch a major new summit to address the issue far into the future.

But Nicolas had his own issue at the moment.

As soon as the limousine door clicked shut, Nicolas had his first moment of privacy with Elena. He turned to her. 'I'm sorry. I should have told you about Sasha and Pyotr.'

Elena shook her head very slightly, furious. She had not spoken a word to him since his interrogation of the Americans. Even now, she shifted to stare out the window of the limousine. Sasha and Pyotr had always held a special place in her heart. It was more than the usual affection. She had a personal connection, too. It had been Elena's older sister, Natasha, who had given birth to them, dying in labor.

'You know the policy at the Warren,' Nicolas pressed as the limousine set off down the road. 'Birth records are sealed.'

It had been a guideline from the start at the Warren. Familial lines for the most part were kept secret. Children knew their immediate brothers and sisters, to discourage inappropriate fraternization, but that was all. Breeding was dictated and controlled by the geneticists.

But Nicolas had been no ordinary offspring. As the son of the founder, an entire history had been fabricated for him, starting in Yekaterinburg, where his mother had given birth to him at a local hospital, using the false surname Solokov. His mother would have used the name Romanov, but that might have been too obvious. From the very start, he had been groomed for a special destiny. As such, he was granted certain privileges.

'I checked the fertilization clinic's records one day,' he said. 'I was curious if I had any children. It was then that I discovered that Sasha and Pyotr were my own. But I was forbidden from saying anything.'

He reached a hand to her knee, but his palm hovered, fearful of touching her. 'In fact, it was because of the production of such talented children that my mother encouraged *our* union. In an attempt to repeat such a fortunate genetic cross.'

Elena would not turn his way. A part of him enjoyed her coldness, this control. He wanted to touch her, but she had not yet given him permission.

'Please, *milaya moya,* forgive me.'

She ignored him.

Sighing, he stared ahead.

Through the privacy glass, Nicolas spotted the rise of Chernobyl. A tall ventilation tower, ringed by maintenance scaffolding, climbed high into the sky. It rose from a jumble of cement buildings. Crammed against one side stood a massive blocky crypt of black steel and concrete. It looked damp, as if sweating. It was not a mystery why the structure was called the Sarcophagus. It looked like a black tomb, and at its heart lay the ruins of reactor number four.

Nicolas had seen pictures of the inside, a blasted landscape of scorched cement and twisted steel. In one room, there was a clock, charred and half melted, that forever marked the time of the explosion. Within the

Sarcophagus, over two hundred tons of uranium and plutonium remained buried within the ruins, most of it in the form of solidified lava, formed from the radioactive fusion of molten fuel, concrete, and two thousand tons of combustibles. Pieces of the exploded core could be found everywhere, some embedded in the outer walls. In the lowest levels of the facility, seeping rainwater and fuel dust collected into a radioactive soup.

Was it any wonder that a new solution was necessary?

Off to the left was that answer.

It went by many names: the Shelter, the Arc of Life, the New Sarcophagus. The hangar-shaped arch rose thirty-seven stories into the air. Weighing over twenty thousand tons, it stretched over a quarter kilometer wide and half again as long. It was so cavernous inside that engineers feared it might form clouds and actually rain within the structure. On the underside of the arch, robotic trolley cranes waited to dismantle the old Sarcophagus piece by piece, operated by technicians safely outside the Shelter.

But things were already on the *move*.

The entire arch rested on greased steel tracks and was even now being slowly hauled along the rails, pulled by a pair of massive hydraulic jacks. It was the largest movable structure ever built by man. And by eleven o'clock this morning, the Shelter would be pulled over the old Sarcophagus and sealed up against the neighboring concrete building, totally covering the old crypt, and thus closing forever an ugly bit of Russian history and heralding a new start.

It was fitting that such an event would mark the beginning of the summit to come. A summit that would unfortunately never take place.

The limousine headed toward the stands that lined the south side of the old Sarcophagus. The seats were already filling with the invited VIPs. Speeches had begun on the stage that fronted the stadium seating, leading up to the official joint U.S.-Russian statements, picked to coincide with the final seal of Chernobyl. The entire series of events was timed to the clockwork pull of the giant arch.

As was Nicolas's plan.

A moment of fear flickered through him. Not unlike when he stood on the news podium as an assassin lined up for a fatal shot. Only the risk this morning was a thousandfold worse.

Fingers closed around his hand as it rested on the seat. He turned and found Elena's hand upon his. She stared out the window, still angry, letting him know this was not over. Her fingernails curled and pressed hard into his palm, a promise that he would be punished later.

He leaned back as she dug deeper.

The pain helped focus him.

Ahead, the arch closed slowly upon Chernobyl.

He knew what was to come.

And he certainly deserved to be punished.

10:04 A.M.

Gray paced the cell when he heard something thud heavily against the door. Kowalski scrambled up, and Luca straightened from where he was leaning against the wall.

'What the hell now?' Kowalski muttered.

The scrape of a metal bar sounded, and the door pulled open.

A figure stepped over the booted legs of a guard on the floor.

'Hurry,' the man said and waved his ivory-handled cane. 'We have to get out of here.'

Gray stared in disbelief.

It was Dr. Hayden Masterson.

Confused, Gray remained frozen in place, caught between wanting to slug the man and shake his hand.

Masterson read his shocked expression. 'Commander, I work for MI6.'

'British intelligence?'

He nodded with an exasperated sigh. 'Explanations will have to wait. We have to go. Now.'

Masterson headed down the hall, dragging them in tow. Gray stopped long enough to collect the guard's sidearm, a Russian pistol called a Grach or Rook. The man had been knocked out, his nose broken. It seemed Masterson's cane was more than show.

Gray caught up to Masterson. Suspicion rang in his voice. 'You? You're an operative with MI6?'

Kowalski mumbled behind him, 'Not exactly James Bond, is he?'

Masterson continued to hobble along, but he glanced over to Gray. 'Retired MI6 actually.' He shrugged. 'If you call this retirement.'

Gray remained guarded, but he could think of no upside for this man freeing them from the cell.

Masterson continued in a wheezing rush. 'I was recruited after I graduated from Oxford and stationed in India during the Soviet occupation of Afghanistan. I retired ten years ago, then stumbled into this mess when someone offered me good money to spy on Archibald. It didn't take long to learn the Russians were behind it. So I contacted MI6 and let them know. It was designated low priority. No one considered Archibald's work a threat to global security. To tell the truth, I didn't either. Not until he was kidnapped and ended up dead in D.C. I tried to light a fire under MI6, but who listens to an old man these days? I couldn't wait. Call it old instinct. I knew something bloody large was afoot. So I'm afraid, after losing Archibald, I had to use all of you to force an introduction.'

'Use us,' Kowalski said. 'They killed Abe.'

Masterson winced. 'I tried to stop them, but our friend was too quick with that whip-sword of his.' He shook his head sadly. 'Maybe this is a younger man's game after all.'

'But wait!' Kowalski stumbled with a sudden realization. 'You were going to shoot *me*!'

Gray dismissed his concern. 'Masterson was putting on an act.'

A nod. 'I had to be convincing.'

'You damn well convinced me!'

'And it was lucky I was so successful.' Masterson turned to Gray. 'The bloody bastard is planning on taking out half the world's leaders today.'

'What?'

Masterson drew them to a stairwell next to the old guard station and lowered his voice. 'More men downstairs. They've had me holed up here. As much a prisoner as any of you. I'm off to free Elizabeth and Dr. Rosauro.' He waved down the hall past the guard station. 'If I could borrow that shapely companion of yours, we'll try to reach a phone and start an evacuation.'

'Take Luca, too,' Gray said. He wanted the civilians as much out of harm's way as possible. Plus the Gypsy leader's presence would go a long way to convincing Rosauro that Masterson was aboveboard.

Luca nodded his agreement.

'Fine. I can use his help,' Masterson said. He pulled a Russian Army walkie-talkie from his jacket and passed it to Gray, so they could communicate. 'But in the meantime—'

Gray cut him off. '—I have to stop Senator Solokov.'

Masterson nodded. 'You've got less than an hour. I don't know what he's planning, something to do with the ceremony over at Chernobyl.'

'What ceremony?'

Masterson pulled out a piece of paper from his jacket pocket, unfolded it, and passed it to Gray. 'They're enclosing the old Sarcophagus at Chernobyl,' he said and nodded to the sheet. 'Under a large steel hangar.'

план выполнения убежища

Саркофаг   Новое Убежище

Саркофаг   Новое Убежище

As Gray studied the sheet, Masterson listed the dignitaries and leaders who would be in attendance at the event and quickly summarized the morning's ceremonies. 'As to Nicolas's specific plans, all I could get was the name. Operation Uranus.'

'Operation Your Anus?' Kowalski said. 'That sounds painful.'

Gray ignored him and headed for the stairs. 'Where's Solokov now?'

'Headed to Chernobyl.'

As Gray descended with Kowalski, he pictured the towering ventilation shaft. Whatever the bastard was planning, it must involve the reactor. But the name for the offensive – Operation Uranus – why pick that name? While training for the Army Rangers, Gray had learned of its historical context from his strategic studies classes. Operation Uranus was a Russian offense during World

War II that ended the bloodiest battle in human history, the Battle of Stalingrad.

So why that name?

Something troubled Gray, something nagging, but the tension locked it away. Ahead, two guards manned the exit to the jailhouse. They had their backs to Gray.

He lifted his stolen Rook pistol.

Worries would have to wait.

17

As the sun shone on a crisp morning, Monk crunched along the gravel road that wound through the ghost town. Weeds and bushes grew waist high, making it feel as if they were wading through green water. Konstantin kept abreast of him, while Pyotr and Kiska trailed. Marta followed, too, but she was drowned away in the green sea, parting the grasses as she maneuvered through them.

'There's little coal in the mountains here,' Konstantin lectured around a bone-cracking yawn. 'All the mining in the region is for metal or metallic ores.'

Monk knew the kid was wired between exhaustion and terror. The tall boy spoke quietly to keep himself awake and to combat anxiety.

'Cobalt, nickel, tungsten, vanadium, bauxite, platinum . . .'

Monk let him prattle as he kept a watch on the town to either side. The buildings looked hastily constructed, made of clapboard with elevated plank sidewalks that bordered the road. They passed a one-room schoolhouse with intact windows and still lined with wooden desks inside. A couple of old trucks, Soviet-era green, sat rusted into the roadbed. The only brick building had

Cyrillic lettering along the facade. Monk could not read it, but it appeared from the shelves inside to be a general store and post office. Next to it stood a saloon with dusty bottles still on the shelves.

It was as if one day the townspeople had simply stepped out of their respective doors and left without ever looking back.

Monk did not have to guess why. From this higher vantage point, Lake Karachay spread wide, rimmed by muddy banks and reflecting the sunlight in a sparkling lie that hid its toxic heart. Monk glanced to the badge hanging from his pack. The red hue had grown to a darker crimson. He checked it every few minutes.

Konstantin noted his attention. 'We must stay no longer than another hour. It is very dangerous here. We must get underground soon.'

Monk nodded and stared up. The entrance to the mine lay another mile above them. He could make out the steel outbuildings and skeletal derricks that framed a larger structure hugging against the mountain. Two large metal wheels flanked the central building, *tailing* wheels, used to dredge up debris from the diggings below. The gravel underfoot probably came from that mine.

Monk set a faster pace.

Ahead, the only other substantial structure appeared as the road swung a hard switchback to climb another level up the mountainside. The mill rose three stories high, the tallest building here. It was built of logs with a tin roof. Its wooden waterwheel, green with moss and lichen, had broken off its moorings and lay toppled across the creek. An old flood must have torn it free.

As they headed toward it, Kiska cried out.

Monk swung around and saw Pyotr standing stock still, as upright as a pole, his eyes huge, bright with terror.

Monk's chest clenched.

No . . . not here.

Marta loped a circle around the boy, also sensing his distress. Like Monk, she didn't know where the danger lay or from where it might strike – but they both knew what the boy sensed.

Monk flashed back to the tiger charging at him, one ear gnarled.

Zakhar.

The beast shouldn't have been able to track them, not across all that open water. But tigers were strong swimmers. The hunter must have forded the swamp and waited to ambush its prey here. Monk did not doubt such cunning from Zakhar.

Monk searched the tall grasses, the jumble of buildings. The creature could be hiding anywhere. The hairs along Monk's arms prickled, almost sensing the feral eyes upon him. They were out in the open, exposed. And without a single weapon. They'd lost their only dagger when Marta had attacked Arkady.

'Back,' Monk said, pointing to the brick building. 'Move slowly. Toward the store.'

Despite all the windows, it would make the stoutest stronghold. They might find something they could use for defense among its shelves. Monk pulled Pyotr to his side. The boy quaked under him. As a tight group, they retreated along the path they'd forged through the grass.

Monk kept an eye behind him, mostly because Pyotr did the same. He trusted the boy's intuition. Where the road curved toward the mining station, the mill house towered across the creek. Monk knew tigers often sought the highest ground: a tall boulder, a lofty tree branch, a mountain ledge, someplace where they could leap upon their prey.

As if sensing it had been discovered, a shadowy striped shape slid like a flow of oil from one of the upper-story windows near the back of the mill. If Monk hadn't been concentrating, he would've missed it. The tiger vanished into the tall grasses.

'Run,' he urged Konstantin and Kiska.

Monk pulled Pyotr up into his arms with one tug.

The two children ahead of him shot forward, stung by terror and fueled by adrenaline. Monk followed, with Marta racing beside him.

Behind Monk, a heavy crack of board sounded as something heavy bounded off the waterwheel and across the creek. The general store's door was open, only thirty yards away. It would be close. He prayed for a walk-in freezer, somewhere they could barricade.

The *crack* of a rifle split through his terror.

Gravel exploded with a bright spark at his toes.

Monk dove to the side, rolling through the high grass, cradling and cushioning Pyotr with his own body. He kept rolling until he ended up behind one of the rusted hulks of an old truck.

The sniper had shot from the lower half of the street.

It had to be one of the Russian soldiers.

Turning, Monk spotted Konstantin and Kiska leaping like frightened deer across the planked sidewalk and through the open door of the store. Marta followed them with one bound. One of the windows shattered as a rifle shot echoed. But the trio had made it inside safely.

Monk sheltered behind the truck and hunkered down. He could not reach the store without crossing open ground.

He glanced up the street.

There was no sign of the tiger. Not a blade of grass moved. No rasp of gravel under heavy paw. The sudden shot must have dropped Zakhar low, startling the cat as much as them. It lay hidden out there.

Monk crouched, trapped between the tiger and a sniper. But that was not the only danger. Another hazard smothered over them all. Beyond the town's edge, Lake

Karachay shone brightly, radiating outward with its toxic pall. Even standing still here was death.

12:30 A.M.
Washington, D.C.

As an alarm klaxon continued to sound, Yuri stood alongside Sasha's bed, shielding her with his body from McBride. The child had snugged into her sheets, hands over her ears, hypersensitive to the bells and shouts. Across the bed, Kat Bryant went to Sasha, consoling her with a palm atop her head. Behind the woman stood the pathologist Malcolm Jennings and a guard.

Yuri faced McBride. The man crouched a few steps away, his back to the corner of the room, his hand twisted in the blond braid of his hostage, Dr. Lisa Cummings. He held his cell phone pistol against her neck.

They were at an impasse.

And Mapplethorpe was already pounding his way down here with commandos. Yuri's blood burned with the thought of the bastard getting his oily hands on Sasha. He could not let that happen.

Yuri shifted to the stainless-steel instrument table and picked up a syringe from among the vials of drugs used to treat Sasha.

'Yuri!' McBride snapped at him with warning.

He answered in Russian, knowing McBride understood. 'I will not let you have Sasha,' he said and stabbed the needle into her intravenous line.

As he pushed the plunger, he saw McBride shift his gun away from his hostage and toward him. The syringe just contained saline, a ruse. Yuri whipped around and flew straight at the man. At the same time, Lisa stamped her heel on the man's instep and smashed her head back into his face.

The pistol fired, explosive in the small space.

Struck in the shoulder, Yuri spun half a step. He barely noted the pain. He crashed into McBride, knocking Lisa out of his grip. Yuri slashed at McBride's throat and jammed the *second* syringe he had palmed off the instrument table, popping into the jugular. The syringe contained a non-diluted concentration of Sasha's medications. At full strength, it was a toxic pharmacology of chemotherapeutics, epinephrine, and steroids.

Tangled together, McBride emptied his clip into Yuri's stomach. Muffled by his body, it sounded like loud claps and felt as if someone were punching him in the gut. Still, Yuri slammed the plunger home, sending the poisonous slurry straight for the heart.

McBride screamed.

Yuri fell with the man to the floor. He knew what McBride was feeling: flames shooting through his veins, pressure detonating in his head, heart squeezing with agony. Hands pulled Yuri off McBride and rolled him to the floor. He spotted Kat draped over Sasha, protecting her from the gunfire, keeping the child's head turned away.

At his side, McBride writhed up into a convulsive seizure, spittle flying, turning bloody as he bit through his tongue. The body would live, but not his mind. The drugs would burn through his brain, leaving him a hollowed husk.

Lisa leaned over Yuri. 'Help me!'

More hands appeared, applying pressure to his belly. Blood spread across the floor. Kat joined him, cradling his head. He coughed. More blood. He reached a hand, knowing she would help.

'Sasha . . . ,' he gasped out.

'We'll protect her,' Kat said.

He shook his head. He knew this already, did not doubt her heart. 'More . . . more *rebyonka*.'

He had trouble focusing – mind and vision. The world darkened, and the pain sank into coldness.

He tried to speak, to tell her where. 'Chela . . . insk . . .' His hand scrabbled to the floor, drew two numbers in his own blood: 88.

Her hand closed over his. 'Hold on, Yuri.'

He wished he could, for Sasha, for all of them.

Darkness clouded over; voices drifted away down a long tunnel. He offered the only thing he could with his last breath.

Hope.

He clenched Kat's hand and forced out one final message.

'He's alive . . .'

Stunned, Kat sat with Yuri's head in her lap. Had she heard him correctly? She stared down into his open eyes, now lifeless and glassy. He had been frantic at the end, as if seeking some last penance, even slipping into Russian. Fluent in the language from her former days with Naval Intelligence, Kat had understood some of it.

More *rebyonka*.

More children.

Like Sasha.

She stared at the girl in the bed, now guarded by Malcolm.

Yuri had babbled after that, tried to write something, but it was garbled nonsense. But what about what he'd said at the very end?

Kat turned to Lisa.

Her friend knelt in a pool of the man's blood. 'He saved my life,' she mumbled and placed a hand on Yuri's chest. Busy with her ministrations, Lisa had not heard his last words.

Beyond Lisa, McBride's body had stopped convulsing.

His eyes were open, staring, just as lifeless and glassy, but his chest rose and fell.

Kat sat, unable to stand, her gaze focusing back to Sasha, to the pile of drawings.

Yuri's words filled her world.

He's alive.

His fingers had clamped onto her hand.

A message for her alone.

She knew whom he meant, but that was impossible.

Still, his last words loosened something inside her, stoked what had never fully gone cold. Her breathing grew heavier. With each breath, the fire grew stronger inside her, burning away doubt, blazing light into the dark places in her heart. A part of her dreaded to let go of that darkness; there was security in the shadows. But she refused to staunch these new flames.

Instead, the fire propelled her to her feet.

She grabbed the guard's abandoned gun from the floor. Straightening, she spoke in a rush to the entire room. 'It's not secure here. We'll strike for an exit . . . if not, we'll find someplace we can fortify.'

As Lisa unhooked the girl's I.V. line, Kat spotted the coloring book, still open on the bedside table, scribbled in green crayon, a man on a raft.

Impossible, but Kat knew it to be true.

Monk . . .

He's alive.

10:20 A.M.
Southern Ural Mountains

The American should be dead.

Borsakov cursed his missed shot. He lay flat in the shadow of a mining shack. The rifle stretched out in front of him, his cheek resting against the stock of his weapon.

362

He had not expected the sudden bolt of his targets – straight back toward him. It had required repositioning and firing before being fully set. Plus he suspected his sights were incrementally out of alignment after the abuse in the swamp. He had not been able to test-fire the weapon and calibrate its sights. The shots would have warned the targets of his approach.

Still, he had them all pinned down.

Two children and the chimpanzee hid in the brick building. The American and the boy behind the truck. Borsakov slid backward, keeping to the grasses. All he had to do was cross the street, and he'd have the American within his sight line again.

This time he would not miss.

He moved stealthily and low across the road, keeping to shadows for as long as possible. He reached the far side and crouched behind an overturned barrel. He leaned out, ready with his rifle.

Down the street, he had a clear view behind the truck now.

Borsakov's fingers clenched on his rifle in fury and confusion.

No one was there.

The American and the boy had vanished.

Pyotr huddled inside the truck, curled in the footwell. Monk had lifted him and shoved him through the half-open window, then disappeared between the two buildings behind the truck. Before he left, he had motioned Pyotr to remain low and duck far into the space in front of the seat. Leaves and beetles shared his hiding place. He clutched his arms around his knees.

Somewhere in the dark places in his mind, where he feared to look, he remembered hiding like this: cramped, breathless, hunted. Another life. Not his. Stone had encased him then, rather than rusty steel.

Hovering between then and now, he felt the pinpricks of lights out in the darkness. Stars in the night sky. If he stared long enough, they would grow brighter, falling toward him. But the night sky had always scared him. So he shied away, back to the moment.

As he did so, a hunger filled him. But like the memory before, this appetite did not belong to him. Close by, a large heart thundered, swallowing Pyotr's feeble beat. Strange odors swelled through his senses: wet grass, the whispers of hot blood in the air, the feel of gravel underfoot. A breath drew heavily, much larger than his own small chest. The scent of the hunt fired through him.

Then another musk came with it.

A new scent.

Another hunter in their midst.

But this scent carried more than pungent odor.

Memory of searing agony came with it.

Spine prickling, fury burned away hunger.

As Pyotr huddled tighter, that large heart stalked forward, padding toward him.

Monk fled along the rear of the roadside buildings and headed toward the lower half of the street. His back and chest burned, scratched and impaled by splinters from the narrow squeeze between the two clapboard shops. He had secured Pyotr in the truck, safe from the tiger for the moment – but not from the sniper. His first priority was to lure the soldier away from the children, to get him chasing after Monk into the mix of buildings below.

Survival and outwitting the soldier would have to follow that.

Monk ran low. He stuck close to the buildings and avoided piles of dry leaves and foundation gravel. He moved silently until he reached where the lower switchback cut downward. Rounding the last building, he edged back to the main street. Had he gone far enough?

Holding his breath, he peeked around the corner and scanned up the street. He spotted the brickwork of the general store, the rusted truck, and the roadway of weeds and high grass. Nothing moved. A breeze flowed down the mountain and feathered the tips of the grass blades.

But there was no sign of the sniper.

He had to be out there, possibly sneaking up on the children. Monk could not risk a hostage situation if the sniper grabbed one of the kids. Monk bunched his legs under him. He had to dash across the street and down to the lower level of the ramshackle town. The crunch of gravel would make plenty of noise.

But he had to be convincing to draw off the soldier.

Taking a deep breath, Monk burst out of hiding and pounded across the gravel. 'Run!' he yelled and waved an arm to imaginary children. 'Just keep running!'

Let the sniper think that all the children were with—

—*crack*—

Fire impaled Monk's thigh. His left leg went out from under him.

He landed hard, his arms out to protect him. Gravel tore skin from his palm and stumped wrist. He let momentum roll him farther down the street. A second rifle blast ripped through the grass over his head with a sharp whistle.

Monk dropped flat, but he spied through the grass and saw the soldier rise. He had been hiding farther up the street, about halfway toward the brick store. Rifle on his shoulder, he sidled straight at Monk.

The soldier had anticipated his adversary circling to the rear. He had hidden in wait, ready to ambush.

But the soldier wasn't the only one hunting.

Fifty yards up the street, a parted V of grass swept straight toward the soldier, like a torpedo through water.

Borsakov kept his face stoic, but a dark satisfaction rang through him. He had the man down, immobile, defenseless. He would end this here, make the American pay for the deaths of his comrades on the boat, make him suffer: a bullet through the kneecap, perhaps another through his shoulder.

As Borsakov took another step, a shift of gravel sounded behind him, a whisper of grass blades, rushing like the wind.

Not the wind.

He knew.

Borsakov twisted around. He started firing before he'd even secured his stance. He squeezed hard, rifle chugging with automatic fire in a wide swath. A feral scream of rage ripped through the blasts as Zakhar burst out of the grass and leaped straight at him: legs wide, black claws bared, muzzle curled back from curved yellow fangs.

Borsakov fired and fired. Blood burst in sprays from the striped fur – but he knew there was no stopping the monster.

It was fury and pain, revenge and hunger, lust and determination.

In the face of such horror, a scream burst from Borsakov's throat, guttural and raw, a primal cry of terror.

Then the tiger landed and pounded him to the ground.

Monk shifted higher, watching the tiger savage the soldier's body. It reminded him of the bear ripping into the massive wolves yesterday. Monk heard the moist crack of bone, and the man's scream cut off. The soldier's body was shaken like a rag doll, gripped by the neck, blood fountaining.

Monk had seen enough and bounded straight at the tiger, his left leg on fire, dripping with blood.

The soldier's weapon had been flung from his body as he was smashed under the eight hundred pounds of feral muscle and claw. The rifle landed halfway between the tiger and Monk. They would not survive this monster without it.

A growl spat toward him.

Zakhar's eyes fixed on Monk. In that black regard, Monk knew the cat recognized him, the murderer of his brother. The tiger crouched atop the broken Russian's body, muscles rippling, hackles high, fur sticking straight out in all directions. Blood flowed across the tiger's chest and flanks, blurring stripes. The cat survived on pure fury.

Reaching the weapon, Monk slid on his knees and scooped up the rifle. One-handed, Monk struggled with the weapon, tangling with its strap and fumbling to bring it up and find the trigger.

He would never make it in time.

Zakhar's rear legs bunched for the kill—

—when a second feline scream echoed down the street. It was not as loud, but it rang out in a perfect yowl of fury and grief. Monk recognized it, having heard it just hours ago.

The death cry of Arkady, brother of Zakhar.

Recognizing it, too, Zakhar leaped up, twisted in midair, and landed in a crouch, tail high. A hiss flowed from the giant cat, less fury, more wary confusion.

Monk lifted the rifle and aimed for the metal cap screwed over the back of the skull. He drew a fix just below it.

Steps away, Zakhar's feral hiss escalated into a whine of pain, of grief, looking for his lost brother.

Firming his stance, Monk squeezed the trigger.

The rifle kicked with a sharp retort.

The tiger jerked, then dropped flat into the grass.

Monk sank to his side, leaning on his stump. He

shouldered the rifle. He knew his aim had been true, a merciful kill shot through the base of the skull. He checked his own wound. The soldier's bullet had ripped a gash in his thigh, but it had passed clean through.

He'd live.

Monk took several breaths, then forced himself to rise.

From down the street, Konstantin and Kiska appeared. Monk knew he owed his life to little Kiska and her perfect pitch and mimicry. Heard once, she had emulated Arkady's cry, amplified by the rolled sheet of tin Konstantin now tossed aside into the grass.

Marta bounded out of the store and straight for the truck.

They would collect Pyotr and move on. Limping, Monk studied the mine complex above the town. They still had a hard climb, but Monk had something to do here first. He hobbled over to Zakhar and placed a hand on the tiger's bloody shoulder, wishing the beast the peace it had never known during its life here.

'Go on now, big fella . . . go join your brother.'

12:43 A.M.
Washington, D.C.

Painter raced down the empty hallway toward the stairs. Alarms rang, accompanied by the Protocol Alpha siren. Evacuation of the facility was almost complete. The emergency exits emptied into a neighboring underground parking garage. Painter did not doubt that Mapplethorpe had men guarding those exits, making sure the child didn't escape. But at least the base personnel should be out of the underground cement bunker.

All except those caught during the initial attack.

After setting the fail-safe, Painter had stopped first at the communication nest of central command and had tapped into the video feed. He'd found that outside communication had been cut off, indicating someone had the schematics to the command structure, but they'd left internal lines open. From the top floor's cameras, he watched Mapplethorpe's commandos gather a dozen hostages, their wrists secured behind their backs with plastic ties.

It could've been worse. At this late hour, Sigma had been lightly staffed. Satisfied, Painter had prepared what he'd needed, and once done, he turned his attention to the danger closest to his heart. He shoved open the door to the stairwell and almost knocked Kat Bryant on her rear end.

She carried Sasha in her arms.

He struggled to comprehend.

Beyond Kat, he spotted Malcolm Jennings and a security guard.

'What? How?' he stammered out.

Lisa shoved past Malcolm and hurried up to him. She was covered in blood. His heart hammered, but she seemed uninjured. She wrapped her arms around him and gave him a fast hug. He felt the shudder of her relief, matched by his own – then they parted, professional again.

'What happened?' he asked.

Kat related in terse, dispassionate thumbnails, finishing with, 'We're attempting to evacuate.'

'You'll never make it out with Sasha,' he said. 'All the exits are surely covered.'

'Then what do we do?' Lisa asked.

Painter checked his watch. 'Well, by escaping on your own, you've already made my life easier.' He pointed back down. 'Take Sasha to the gym locker room. Secure her in there. All of you.'

'What about you?' Kat asked.

He kissed Lisa on the cheek, turned toward the door, and headed out. 'I've got one last thing to do – then I'll join you.'

'Be careful,' Lisa said.

Kat called back to him. 'Director! Monk's still alive!'

Painter halted, glanced behind him, but the stairwell door slammed shut. *What?* He had no time to inquire what she had meant. It would have to wait. He sprinted back down the hall and returned to where he had started, back to the communication nest. Slowing, he tested the air. A sweetness permeated the space, as it should all of central command.

It was the first stage of the fail-safe program: feeding a gaseous accelerant into the air. It took a minimum of fifteen minutes to reach critical levels. And while it was safe to breathe for at least a couple of hours, they didn't have that long. In another ten minutes, the fail-safe would ignite sparks throughout the base and trigger a firestorm across all levels of central command. The flash fire would last only a few seconds, fed by the accelerant in the air, searing every surface within the concrete bunker. Then sprinklers would kick in, dousing the flames immediately.

Inside the communication nest, Painter checked the row of monitors, receiving video feed from cameras on every level.

He stalked along them until he found the one he was looking for. It showed Mapplethorpe standing beside Sean McKnight. He held a pistol to Sean's back. Behind them, commandos began disappearing down an open stairwell door.

Painter tapped on the audio from the camera.

'—madness,' Sean said. 'You can't circumvent channels like this. Do you think you can perform an unsanctioned assault upon another agency, then try to clean it up afterward?'

'I've done it before,' Mapplethorpe growled. 'It's all a matter of producing the results to match the offense.'

'In other words, the ends justify the means,' Sean

scoffed. 'You'll never get away with it. Two people are dead.'

'Is that all? Like I said, I've done this many times before. Abroad and here.'

Painter cut into the conversation. He spoke into a microphone that broadcast through speakers on that floor. 'Mapplethorpe!'

The man jolted, but he kept his pistol steady. He searched around, then found the camera on the wall. He regained his composure, his lips settling into a sneer of derision. 'Ah, Director, so you haven't evacuated with the rest of your people. Very good. Then let us end this quickly. Bring up the girl, and no one else needs to get hurt.'

Painter spoke into the microphone. 'We've already taken out your man, Mapplethorpe, and hidden the girl where you won't find her.'

'Is that so?' Mapplethorpe sniffed a bit at the air. 'I see you've activated Sigma's fail-safe program.'

Painter felt a chill. The man had obtained more than just their base schematics; he'd tapped deep into their protocols. Sean had warned him about Mapplethorpe. The bastard had his fingers everywhere, a black spider dancing in the intelligence web. His oily and bland demeanor hid a much more dangerous core.

'And I believe you've set the timer for zero one hundred,' Mapplethorpe said, confirming the depths of his intel. 'We've been unable to decrypt the code to stop it, but something tells me we won't have to. Not with my holding twenty hostages above. Twenty of your men and women. With families and lives beyond these walls. I don't think you've got the brass balls to let them die, to be slain by your own hand. Whereas I—'

Mapplethorpe lifted his gun to the back of Sean's head.

'—have no such qualms.'

The man fired. The pistol blast overloaded the

speakers, turning into a digital pop and squawk. Sean fell to his knees, then to the floor.

Painter's chest tightened, unable to take a breath. Disbelief rang through him. A part of him expected Sean to stand back up, to shake off the attack. But just as quickly, a flame as hot as the coming firestorm burned through Painter. Stunned at the man's brutality and callousness, Painter could form no words.

Unlike his adversary.

Mapplethorpe's voice returned. 'We're coming for that girl, Director. And no one is going to stop us.'

18

Gray secured the black belt over the Russian field jacket, camouflaged in forest green. He stamped his feet more securely into the boots. Kowalski tossed him a furred cap. The stolen uniform fit decently, but his partner's outfit looked ready to burst at the seams. The two Russian soldiers, stripped to their underclothes, had been posted at the front of the jailhouse. Caught by surprise, it had not been hard to knock them out and secure the uniforms.

'Let's go,' Gray said and headed to a motorcycle.

'Shotgun,' Kowalski called out.

Gray glanced over, realizing the man was not talking about a weapon. They both had AN-94 Russian assault rifles.

Kowalski eyed the sidecar to the IMZ-Ural motorcycle. 'Always wanted to ride in one of these,' he said and climbed into the open car.

Gray shifted the rifle over a shoulder and hiked a leg over the seat.

Moments later, engine growling, they shot through the old prison gates and out into the weed-strewn streets of Pripyat. Gray checked his wristwatch.

Twenty minutes.

Leaning lower, he throttled up, goosed the gas, and sped through the faded, rusted city. The asphalt was broken, and shattered glass threatened the tires. Around every corner, they met unexpected obstacles: abandoned rusted skeletons of automobiles, moss-covered old furniture, and even a strangely surreal stack of band instruments.

Despite the hazards, Gray raced at breakneck speeds, taking corners hard enough to lift the sidecar off its tire. Kowalski whooped a bit at these turns. They passed the occasional soldier patrolling the streets, who lifted a rifle or arm in greeting as they raced past; at other times, Gray spotted a flash of a haunted face peering through a broken window, one of the stray scavengers of the city.

Reaching the outskirts of Pripyat, Gray sped toward the horizon as a trio of deer sprang away from the roar of the cycle. He aimed for the towering ventilation stack of the reactor. Even over the roar of the cycle, he heard snatches of amplified voices rolling out from the grandstands. According to Masterson, Senator Nicolas Solokov was planning some attack on those gathered here to observe the sealing of the Chernobyl reactor.

But what was the man's plan?

What was Operation Uranus?

As Gray raced down a freshly paved asphalt road, he studied the growing hulk of the Chernobyl complex ahead. His eyes were drawn to what looked like a gargantuan Quonset hut off to one side. The arched steel hangar reflected the morning sunlight like a mirror.

And it was moving.

Like oil on water, the sunlight flowed over its curved exterior. It closed slowly upon the Chernobyl reactor. Most of the complex was gray concrete and whitewashed surfaces, but along one side, a hulking structure stuck out along one edge, blackened like a dead tooth. It marked the grave of reactor number four, a massive black Sarcophagus. The rolling hangar, open at one end, sought to swallow the structure under its high arch.

As they drew closer, Gray's mind shuffled through possibilities. Archibald Polk had been exposed to a deadly level of radiation, possibly from here. Whatever Nicolas was planning had to involve the old reactor. Nothing else made sense.

Masterson had warned that security would be high near the grandstands, especially with the number of dignitaries in attendance. The stands stood a quarter mile from the reactor. Gray weighed which path to take: to head for the grandstands or the reactor. What if he was wrong about the reactor? Could there be a bomb somewhere among the stands?

As the bike shot across the open plain between Pripyat and Chernobyl, a broadcasted voice reached him, echoing and hollow, extolling the virtues of nuclear cooperation in the new world. There was no mistaking that voice. Gray had attended several events at the White House.

It was the president of the United States.

Gray factored this into his account. The Secret Service would surely have canvassed the site, swept it multiple times, set up a strict protocol. Additionally, the Secret Service would have agents on all sides of the reactor, again searching for any threat.

Gray studied the number of parked vehicles, the sea of satellite antennas. The entire grandstand area was cordoned off with fences, gates, and patrolling guards – on foot and in open jeeps. While his disguise worked at a distance, Gray doubted the ruse would get him through to the stands. He had no identification, no passes for the event.

As he weighed his options, speeding toward the immense site, he was awed by the sheer size of the project. The giant steel hangar slowly trundled along a pair of tracks, pulled by whale-size hydraulic jacks. It had already reached the dead reactor and had begun to close over it, arching high into the sky, its steel now nearly blinding with sunlight, so tall that the Statue of Liberty could stand on her own shoulders and still not reach the roof of the arched hangar.

Even Kowalski whistled his appreciation at the dimensions of the rolling structure. He finally leaned over and called out, 'What's the plan when we—?'

Gray lifted an arm, silencing him. A new voice had cut into the president's speech. Like the president, this speaker was also familiar. He spoke Russian, then repeated his words in English, playing for the international audience.

Senator Nicolas Solokov's voice boomed toward Gray. 'I protest this travesty!' he bellowed. 'Here we all are, congratulating ourselves for erasing a shameful piece of Russian history – for *hiding* it, as though it never happened, sweeping it under a steel rug. But what about those killed during the explosion, what about the hundreds of thousands doomed to die of cancers and leukemia, what of the thousands of babies born into deformity, pain, and mental debilitation? Who will speak for them?'

Gray was now close enough to see the stage that rose before the amphitheater seating. Figures were too small to make out, but giant video screens flanked the stage. One displayed the Russian president, the other the United States's leader. Each president stood behind a podium. In the center of the stage, another figure stood amid chaos. Nicolas Solokov. Guards tried to haul the senator from the stage, while others protected him so he could speak. From all the milling confusion, Nicolas must have barged onto the stage to initiate this dramatic, televised protest.

Off to the side, men in black surrounded and shielded the president.

Whatever Nicolas had planned, it had begun. Gray

leaned lower and gunned the engine. The motorcycle rocketed down the blacktop toward the stands.

The speaker squawked with electronic feedback, then Nicolas continued, shouting, 'You all believe a handsome coffin like this marks an end to a blasted legacy, but it is all sham! The monster has already escaped its cage! No matter how large a lock or how strong the steel, you cannot put that monster back behind bars. The only real end to this legacy is to fundamentally change our attitudes, to set true and lasting policy. This ceremony is nothing more than a pale charade! All posture, no substance! We should be ashamed!'

Finally, the guards overwhelmed the senator's supporters. Nicolas's microphone was ripped from his hands. He was dragged bodily off the stage.

The Russian president began speaking in his native tongue, sounding both angry and apologetic. The U.S. president motioned the agents to disperse, not wanting to appear spooked by a showboating politician. Speeches slowly resumed.

Behind them, the arch continued to swallow the reactor.

Gray slowed his bike. He still had a choice to make: to head to the grandstands or the reactor. He considered Nicolas's protest, his dramatic exit. It had all been artfully staged. The senator had plainly orchestrated a reason *not* to be at the event, to be taken away. But where? He would not leave that to chance. He would not risk being trapped in harm's way. Whoever had dragged Nicolas from the stage must be in his employ, removing him to safety.

Beyond the gaggle of TV vans, Gray spotted a green army jeep hightailing it away from the media area. It was on a dirt road that paralleled the eight-foot-tall tracks of the massive archway. The rutted path headed away from the reactor and curved around the end of the tracks toward the rear side of the complex.

Gray spotted a suited figure in the backseat.

Nicolas.

Gray stared upward. The blinding steel structure now consumed half of the blackened hulk of the Sarcophagus. In another fifteen minutes, it would close completely over the crypt. The grandstands rested a quarter mile away from the reactor.

Gray had to make a choice.

He pictured Nicolas Solokov seated behind the desk in the guard shack during the interrogation. From the cut of his clothes to the patterns of his speech, the man was arrogant and self-assured, an ego matched only by a need to control. It radiated out of him.

Nicolas would want to *watch* what was to come.

So why was he heading *behind* the reactor?

Unless . . .

Gray swung the cycle off the blacktop and cut across the open fields. He headed straight for the end of the tracks, intending to intercept the vehicle as it rounded the bend in the road.

'Pierce!' Kowalski yelled. 'Where are we going?'

'To save the president.'

'But the grandstand's over that way!' Kowalski pointed an arm in the opposite direction.

Ignoring him, Gray bounced the cycle like a dirt bike across the rolling plain. Kowalski clutched tightly to the handrails. Gray gunned the engine and sped faster over the wild terrain. Mud and grass spattered behind him.

Ahead, the jeep raced alongside the four hundred yards of tracks. The vehicle was almost to the end. It would be close. Gray was still a football field away from the road.

And they'd been spotted.

An arm pointed toward their racing motorcycle. From the distance, Gray and Kowalski would appear to be Russian soldiers out for a joy ride. Confusion should reign for a moment in the jeep. That's all they would have.

'Kowalski!'

'What?'

'Can you take out one of their rear tires as they make that curve?'

'Are you nuts?' he asked, his voice rattling with the bike.

'Hang on.'

Gray angled the bike into a dry sandy wash. Floods had swept the stretch fairly flat and smooth.

'Take your shot!' he yelled to Kowalski.

The large man already had his assault rifle up. Kowalski braced himself in the sidecar and brought the rifle to his shoulder. Gray heard him almost purr to his weapon. 'C'mon, baby, make Daddy proud.'

Directly ahead, the jeep had reached the end of the tracks. It slowed to make the sharp turn but still took the corner hard. The driver fought to hold his vehicle to the road.

Gray heard a *pop-pop* from the sidecar. The Russian AN-94 fired double shots with every squeeze. At the same time, the jeep suddenly fishtailed as the driver lost control, his left rear tire smoking and tossing tread. It skidded sideways and slammed into a concrete pylon between the ends of the track.

Kowalski hooted his satisfaction and rubbed the side of his weapon. 'Thank you, baby!'

Further self-congratulation was cut off as their cycle left the sandy wash and sailed back into coarser terrain. Spitting rocks, the cycle tore forward and reached the roadway in seconds.

The Russian jeep rested where it had crashed, one side crumpled, killing one of the soldiers in the front passenger seat. The other three occupants had piled out and retreated into a jumble of concrete barriers and low metal shacks that filled the space between the two track rails.

As Gray rounded into view, a roar of clapping erupted from the grandstands, along with cheering. The ceremony was reaching its climax. Covered by the noise, Gray barely heard the shots fired at them. The bike's front tire blew, but Gray had anticipated an attack and aimed the cycle to the far side of the crumpled jeep. He slammed to a skidding stop behind it and rolled off the bike.

Kowalski tumbled out alongside him, and together they sheltered behind the crashed vehicle.

More rounds pinged off the front of the jeep.

Gray risked a fast peek around the rear bumper. He spotted a suited figure fleeing straight down the center of the tracks, which rose eight feet tall to either side, built of concrete and steel.

Nicolas Solokov was making a three-hundred-yard dash for the goal – in this case, the back end of the rolling archway. Gray tried to get a shot at him, but a bullet struck the bumper and whistled past his ear. He caught a glimpse of a smoking pistol, borne aloft by a raven-haired woman.

Elena.

Cursing, he dropped back.

Kowalski yelped, nicked in the shoulder.

The woman and a soldier held them pinned down.

Gray checked his watch.

Ten minutes.

Nicolas heard gunfire behind him and tried to race faster down the concourse between the raised tracks, but he'd twisted his left ankle after the crash. He had to trust Elena to keep him safe.

Two workers walked behind the backside of the steel Shelter. The massive structure rolled slowly along the rails, creeping a foot a minute on Teflon bearings, drawn by the massive hydraulic pulling jacks to either side.

A garage-door-size service hatch lay open ahead and offered access to the inside of the looming Shelter. It was the main reason Nicolas had fled from the others. He could not be sitting in front of that open door when Operation Uranus came to fruition.

He hobbled as fast as he could down the packed gravel roadway between the tracks. He had to get through that door, across the interior of the Shelter, and out the rear side before it closed.

Even he couldn't stop Operation Uranus.

All he could do was get out of its way.

The plan had been formulated back in 1999, when the Shelter Implementation Plan had first started. The SIP's goal was to stabilize and cover the old Sarcophagus. Engineers had been warning for years that the old crypt could collapse at any moment, exposing two hundred tons of radioactive uranium to the atmosphere. By that time, sections of the old Sarcophagus had already begun to crumble. Tiny holes and fissures had formed. So the first phase of the SIP sought to stabilize the Sarcophagus. That meant patching holes, shoring up structural wall pillars, and securing the rickety ventilation stack. This was all done while the Shelter's massive arch was being constructed a safe four hundred yards away.

That initial structural work was completed in 1999 – but it held some secrets. After the fall of the Soviet Union, corruption ran rampant. It had cost little to have four concussion charges secretly planted into the new wall pillars. They had remained dormant and inactive until yesterday. Last night, one of Nicolas's men had sent a signal to the buried charges, setting the timers to match the closure of the Shelter over the Sarcophagus. Once set, there was no turning back.

At exactly two minutes before the Shelter sealed, the

charges would blow. No one would even hear them. All that would be noted was a crash of concrete, followed by the collapse of an entire section of the Sarcophagus's wall – the side that faced the grandstands. For an entire two minutes, the stands would be bathed in massive amounts of radiation before the Shelter finally sealed against the concrete wall behind the Sarcophagus. The exposure would not be enough to cause immediate fatalities. In fact, no one would feel anything. But during those two minutes, everyone in attendance would absorb a lethal dose of radiation.

They would all be dead within a matter of weeks.

In attendance were the Russian prime minister and president, alongside the leaders from across the Americas and the European Union. If successful, Nicolas's mission would throw the major world governments into disarray, so that when the radiological bloom spread globally from his mother's operation at Chelyabinsk 88, the world would need a strong voice, someone who had spent his career warning of just such a catastrophe.

They would turn to the only survivor of Operation Uranus.

And over the coming months – guided by the secret cabal of savants – Nicolas would demonstrate a remarkable prescience, intuitive knowledge, and brilliant foresight.

Out of the fire to come, Nicolas would quickly rise to power in Russia, and from there, stretch his influence globally. The Russian Empire would rise from these radioactive ashes to guide the world in a new direction.

It was such a thought that fueled him now.

He limped up to the two men following the back end of the Shelter. He pulled the pistol from his pocket. Two head shots. Almost point-blank. They dropped like leaden sacks to the gravel. There could be no witnesses.

Nicolas hurried through the open service hatch that pierced the back wall of the hangar. It took a dozen steps to cross through the hatch. The Shelter's steel walls were twelve meters thick.

Once through, Nicolas entered the heart of the Shelter.

Despite his desperation, he gaped at the sheer wonder of the massive space. The arch of steel climbed a hundred meters overhead and was two and a half times as wide. Cavernous did not describe the place. Like stars in the night sky, hundreds of lamps lit the vast interior, positioned along steel scaffolding that lined the inside of the Shelter. Overhead, a maze of yellow tracks crisscrossed the roof. Giant robotic cranes waited stationary, ready to tear apart the old Sarcophagus. Giant hooks the size of ships' anchors and skeletal pronged grips hung from the trolley cranes.

Just inside the Shelter, Nicolas stopped long enough to hit the giant red button that closed the service hatch. It trundled slowly closed behind him, creeping down on giant gears.

According to their original plan, Nicolas and Elena were to hole up outside in a control booth on the far side of the Shelter. The booth, which controlled the winch engines, was heavily lead-lined to protect the operator from any radiation. It was also positioned on the opposite side from the concussive charges, so exposure should be minimal.

Nicolas needed to reach that booth, but if Elena remained pinned down between the tracks back there, he wanted to protect her from the burst of radiation that would come. Though not in a direct line of the exposure like the grandstands, her position could still be exposed to scatter radiation through the open rear hatch – maybe not enough to kill her, but it could destroy her chances of having healthy children.

So to protect his own future genetic heritage, Nicolas sought to shield her. But more than that, he could not totally discount that he did care for the woman. His mother would interpret such tender feelings as weakness, but Nicolas could not deny his heart.

As the door slowly lowered, Nicolas headed off.

'Elena!' Gray called out from behind the jeep. 'You must help us!'

There was no answer.

At least not from Elena.

'Pierce, I don't think you're going to talk your way out of this,' Kowalski said. His partner crouched a few steps away. His shoulder wept blood through his jacket, but it was only a graze. 'She's one crazy bitch. Why is it always the crazy ones who are such good shots?'

'I don't think she's crazy,' Gray mumbled.

At least he hoped not.

He had seen how she had reacted to the revelation that Sasha was Nicolas's biological daughter. A mix of shocked dismay and protectiveness. There was some connection between Elena and the girl, something more than just an augmented sisterhood.

He had to trust he was correct.

'Sasha came to me!' Gray called out. 'Sought me out. She guided us here for a reason.'

Silence stretched. Then a soft voice finally spoke. 'How? How did Sasha guide you here?'

Elena was testing him.

Gray took a deep breath. He lifted his rifle in the air and tossed it aside.

'Pierce . . . ,' Kowalski growled. 'If you think I'm throwing my gun away, you're as nutty as she is.'

Gray stood up.

Across the gap, the Russian soldier's rifle shifted toward him. Elena also rose and barked at the soldier, keeping him from shooting outright. Elena wanted to know more about Sasha. Across the way, the Russian pair shared a fortress of concrete pylons. Elena kept her pistol pointed at him.

Gray answered her question. 'How did Sasha guide us? She drew pictures. First she guided the Gypsies to my door. Then she drew a picture of the Taj Mahal, which guided us to India, where we discovered your true heritage and history. You have to ask yourself *why*. Sasha is special, is she not?'

Elena just stared at him with her hard, dark eyes.

Gray took that as agreement and continued, letting her see and hear the truth in his words. 'Why were we sent to India? Why even engage us at all? Why now? There has to be a reason. I think Sasha – consciously or unconsciously – is trying to stop what you're planning on doing.'

Elena showed no flicker of acknowledgment, but Gray was still alive.

'She sent us on a path to discover your roots: from the Oracle of Delphi, through the Gypsies, to now. I think there was some reason your lineage was begun. Perhaps the fulfillment of a great prophecy that is yet to come.'

'What prophecy?' Elena asked.

Gray noted a flicker of both recognition and fear. Was there some nightmare etched into their psyches? Gray pictured the mosaics found at the Greek stronghold in India, including the last mosaic on the wall, a fiery shape rising out of smoke from the omphalos. Gray took a chance and quickly described what they had found, finishing with, 'The figure looked like a boy with eyes of fire.'

The pistol in Elena's arm began to tremble – though it still didn't waver from its aim at his chest. Gray heard Elena mumble a name that sounded like Peter.

'Who is Peter?' Gray asked.

'Pyotr,' Elena corrected. 'Sasha's brother. He has

nightmares sometimes. Wakes screaming, saying his eyes are on fire. But . . . but . . .'

'What?' Gray pressed, intrigued despite the time pressure.

'When he wakes, we all do. For just a moment, we see Pyotr burning.' She shook her head. 'But his talent is empathy. He's very strong. We attributed the nightmares to some quake of his talent that radiated outward. An empathic echo.'

'It's not just an echo from Pyotr,' Gray realized aloud. 'It's an echo going back to the beginning.'

But where does it end?

Gray stared over to Elena. 'You cannot truly want what is to come. Sasha plainly did not. She brought me here. If she wanted Nicolas's plan to work, all she had to do was remain silent. But she didn't. She brought me to *you,* Elena. To you. To this moment. You have the chance to either help Sasha or destroy what she started. It's your choice.'

Her decision was instantaneous, perhaps born out of the fire in her brain. She pivoted on a toe and fired. The Russian soldier dropped, killed instantly.

Gray hurried over to her. 'How do we stop Operation Uranus?'

'You cannot,' she answered, her voice slightly dazed, perhaps dizzy from the sudden reversal of roles, or perhaps merely waking from a long dream.

Elena handed Gray her pistol, as if knowing where he must go. He was already sidling past her and heading off between the rails. If she didn't know how to stop Operation Uranus, perhaps Nicolas did.

'You must hurry,' she said. 'But I . . . I may know a way to help.'

She turned and glanced toward the back side of the complex, where Nicolas had been headed originally.

Gray pointed to the motorcycle. Though the front tire

was flat, it would still be faster than on foot. 'Kowalski, help her.'

'But she shot me.'

Gray didn't have time to argue. He turned and sprinted through the forest of concrete pylons. The way opened ahead, lined by the tracks to either side. At the other end of the concourse, he spotted Nicolas limping through a wide door in the massive steel wall and vanishing into the darkness.

Gray pounded down the way.

Down to six minutes.

As he flew, he saw the black gap in the steel wall begin to narrow. The door was closing.

They'd escaped the jail, but now what?

Elizabeth ran behind Rosauro, while Luca trailed and guarded their backs with a pistol. Using his cane, Masterson limped as best he could next to Elizabeth. She helped the old man by holding on to his elbow.

Their first priority was to find a phone and to raise an alarm. But the entire city appeared haunted and desolate. Birches grew out of broken streets, weeds grew everywhere, buildings were scribed with lichen and moss. How were they going to find a working phone here?

'The next intersection!' Masterson gasped and waved his cane while taking a hop on his good leg. 'To the left. The Polissia Hotel should be at the end of that next block.'

Masterson had suggested the destination. Apparently the hotel had been renovated for a gala the prior night and was being used this morning as a shuttle station for guests invited to the ceremony.

But what about uninvited guests?

Elizabeth had caught a glimpse of Gray and Kowalski flying away on a motorcycle as they'd made their own escape. She hoped they were okay and could do something to stop that bastard. As she fled with the others, her head ached and her eyes strained. Tension and fear wore her down.

'I'm sorry, Elizabeth,' Masterson wheezed.

She glanced at him. She knew he was apologizing for more than just involving her and the others in this escapade.

'I truly didn't think your father was in any bloody danger,' he explained. 'I thought the Russians' interest in Archibald's work was just a matter of industrial espionage, stealing data. I never thought it would result in his death.'

Even though she understood the professor's position in the past and recognized the international threat now, she could not find her way to forgiving him. Not for her father, and not for involving them in all this without their consent. She was tired of secrets – both her father's and this man's.

As they neared the intersection, two Russian soldiers stepped from a doorway. One dropped a cigarette and ground it underfoot. The other lifted his rifle and barked at them in Russian.

'Kak tebya zavut?'

'Let me handle this,' Masterson said and waved for Rosauro and Luca to lower their weapons.

The professor straightened his white hat and leaned more heavily on his cane. He doddered to the front and called out in Russian, *'Dobraye utro!'*

Masterson spoke fluently. All Elizabeth understood were the words *London Times*. Masterson must be attempting to pass them off as visiting press.

The soldier lowered his weapon. 'You are Englishers.'

Masterson nodded with a broad, embarrassed smile. 'You speak English. Brilliant. We've gotten ourselves lost and could not find our way back to the Polissia Hotel. If you'd be so kind, perhaps you could escort us back there.'

From the crinkling of the soldiers' brows, they must not have understood him that well. Masterson was using their own lack of fluency to unbalance them, to deflect them from questioning the cover story. But the soldier with the rifle did understand their goal.

'*Polissia Gostineetsa?*' he asked.

'*Da!* Now there's a good chap. Could you take us there?'

The pair spoke in rapid snatches of Russian. Finally one shrugged and the other turned with a nod.

Behind them, a scream of a motorcycle erupted, shattering the quiet town. Far down the street, in the direction of the jail, a motorcycle with a flashing blue light and sidecar swung into the road, bearing two soldiers with furred caps. They were spotted. Shouts called out in Russian toward them.

Suddenly the pair of soldiers in front of them stiffened.

'Trouble,' Masterson said and pushed Elizabeth down the street. 'Run!'

Rosauro spun on a heel and snap-kicked the closest soldier in the face. Bone cracked, and he fell stiffly backward. The other guard lifted his weapon, but Luca was quicker on the draw with his pistol. Blood exploded from the soldier's shoulder, twisting him around as if mule-kicked, but his weapon chattered with automatic fire, sweeping toward them.

Masterson rolled and shielded Elizabeth, while both Luca and Rosauro dropped flat to the street. The professor fell against her and knocked her to her knees. Luca's pistol cracked again, and the gunfire ended.

Masterson slid off her and slumped to the road. Elizabeth had felt the shuddering impacts into his body. He rolled to his back while blood pooled under him.

'Hayden!'

He waved her off, still holding his cane. 'Go!'

The motorcycle screamed down the road toward them all.

Rosauro yanked her up.

Luca fired at the motorcycle, but it swerved behind cars and debris for cover. Return fire from the soldier in the sidecar sparked the pavement around them.

'I'm sorry, Elizabeth,' Masterson said again, blood bubbling at his lips.

'Hayden . . .' She covered her mouth, unable to find the words to thank him, to forgive him.

Still, he saw it in her eyes and gave a tiny nod of acknowledgment with a shadow of a smile, content. 'Go . . . ,' he said hoarsely, eyelids closing.

Rosauro pushed her down the street toward the next intersection. Luca kept firing one-handed behind him as he ran – then the slide on his pistol popped open, out of ammunition. Strafing fire chased them.

Rosauro guided them alongside the edge of the road, putting a rusted truck between them and the cycle. 'Around the corner!'

But they'd never make it.

No longer under fire, the cycle roared straight for them.

Elizabeth looked over her shoulder. As the motorcycle swerved through the bodies in the street, Masterson suddenly rolled with the last of his strength and jammed his cane into the front wheel of the bike. The stout rod snapped and sent the cycle flipping up on its front tire and over. It crashed upside down and slid across the rough pavement, casting sparks and leaving a bloody smear.

Rosauro urged them all onward. 'Hurry!'

Hopefully the cycle's roar had covered most of the gunplay, but they had to be away from here as quickly as possible. Reaching the intersection, they headed along the next street. A quarter mile down the road stood a bright hotel, freshly painted, lights glowing. A few polished black limousines waited at the curb.

They hurried toward it. Luca tossed aside his empty pistol, and they did their best to straighten and dust off their clothes into some semblance of normalcy. They slowed when they reached the hotel and strode toward it, as if they belonged. No one accosted them. The hotel was mostly deserted, just a pair of drivers lounging in the lobby. A few staff members also worked behind a desk. Everyone else appeared to be at the ceremony.

Rosauro crossed to the front counter. 'Is there a phone we could use? We . . . we're with the *New York Times*.'

'Press room . . . over there,' a tired-eyed young man said in halting English. He pointed toward a door off the lobby.

'*Spazeebo*,' Rosauro thanked him.

She led them through the door. The room was square with a low counter that ran along the full perimeter of the space. A central table held mounds of office supplies: reams of paper, stacks of pads, pens, staplers. But what drew Elizabeth's attention were the two-dozen black telephones that rested along the wall counter.

Rosauro headed to one side, picked up the receiver, and listened for a dial tone. She nodded her satisfaction. As she dialed, she said, 'I'll alert central command. They'll spread the word and get an evacuation started.'

Elizabeth sank into a neighboring chair. In the momentary calm, she began to tremble all over. She could not stop. Masterson's death . . . it broke something inside her. Tears started flowing – grieving for the professor, but also for her father.

Rosauro finished dialing and waited. A frown slowly formed, and her eyebrows pinched together.

'What's wrong?' Luca asked.

She shook her head, worried. 'There's no answer.'

12:50 A.M.
Washington, D.C.

Painter knocked lightly on the locker room door and

pushed it cautiously open. He was met by a pistol pointed at his face. Kat lowered the weapon, her eyes relieved.

'How's everyone?' he asked and followed her inside.

'So far, so good.'

A Sigma corpsman took up her position at the door. Kat led Painter into the main room, lined by banks of metal lockers and benches. At the back was an archway that led to the showers and sauna.

Kat led him to a neighboring aisle. He found Malcolm on a bench, and Lisa seated on the floor, her arm around Sasha. The girl stared up at him with large blue eyes and rocked slightly. Her gaze found Kat's, and her entire body relaxed.

Lisa stood. She had changed into a fresh pair of scrubs, no longer covered in blood. Kat bent down, picked up Sasha, and sat on the bench with her. She whispered in the girl's ear, which drew a small smile from the child.

Lisa slipped into Painter's arms, then stared up at him for a breath. 'What's wrong?' she whispered, concerned.

Painter thought he'd been hiding it well, but how did one completely mask the fury and grief that filled him now?

'It's Sean,' he said.

Kat and Malcolm glanced over to him.

Painter took a deep breath. 'The bastard killed him.' He could still hear the gunshot, the snap of feedback, and see his friend's body fall.

'Oh, God . . . ,' Lisa mumbled and pulled tighter to him.

'Mapplethorpe's heading down here, searching for the girl.' Painter checked his watch.

Kat noted his attention. 'The fail-safe?'

'Set for four minutes.' Painter prayed he had everything prepared correctly. The air was now heavy with the sweet-smelling accelerant.

'If we have to defend the room,' Kat asked, 'do we have to worry about the gunfire igniting the air?'

He shook his head. 'The compound functions like aerosolized C4. It takes a strong *electrical* spark to set it off, not a flash of fire.'

Lisa kept to his side. 'Then what do we do from here?'

Painter waved them to their feet. He wanted to protect them as best he could. He would lose no others. But he didn't have much to offer.

'We'd better hide.'

Mapplethorpe followed his commando team down the hall.

He had employed this same group of men many times in the past, a mercenary team that included former British S.A.S. and South Africa's Recces. They were his muscle across the world political map. They shied at nothing that was asked of them: assassinations, kidnappings, torture, rape. Whatever clandestine operation he needed run, these men would get it done. Best of all, afterward they would simply disappear, leaving no trace, just shadows and ghosts.

It was hard men such as these who kept the country secure. Where others feared to tread, these soldiers did not balk.

The point man reached a door at the end of the hall. Its sign read LOCKER ROOM. The soldier held up a fist. In his other hand, he clutched an electronic tracker.

Earlier, Trent McBride had reported that the child's microchip transmitter was still functioning. There was no place she could hide. They'd picked up her signal on this level.

The commando waited upon his order to proceed.

Mapplethorpe waved him through the door. He

checked his watch. The fail-safe was set for another three minutes. In case Painter Crowe decided not to abort the firestorm, he wanted the girl nabbed and evacuated. If they were quick enough, it should not be a problem. An emergency exit lay at the other end of the hallway and led off to an underground garage.

Ahead, the soldiers burst through the door and ran low and fast into the next room. Mapplethorpe followed in their wake, closing the door behind him. He heard quiet orders flow among the group as they spread through the rows of lockers.

Mapplethorpe followed the commando with the tracker, flanked by two more soldiers. The lead man ran along the lockers, his arm held high. He finally reached the source of the signal, dropped his arm, and pointed.

In the silence, Mapplethorpe heard a faint whimper coming from inside the locker.

At last.

A padlock secured the door, but another soldier whipped out a small set of bolt cutters and snapped the lock off.

Mapplethorpe waved. They were running out of time. 'Hurry!'

The head commando tugged the locker's handle and yanked the door open. Mapplethorpe caught a glimpse of a digital tape recorder, a radio transmitter – and a Taser pistol wired to the door.

A trap.

Mapplethorpe turned and ran.

Behind him, the pistol fired with a pop and a crackle of electricity.

Mapplethorpe screamed as he heard a loud *whuff* of ignition, sounding like the firing of a gas grill. A flash of heat, and a fireball blew outward. It picked him off his feet and carried him down the row. His clothes roasted to his back. He breathed flames, his scalp burned to bone. He struck the wall, no longer human, just a flaming torch of agony.

He rolled and burned for a stretch of eternity – until darkness snuffed him away.

A floor below in the gym locker room, Painter heard the screams echoing down from the medical locker room directly overhead. He had set the trap above, knowing Mapplethorpe would come searching for the girl's signal. He had planted one of the Cobra radio transceivers used to draw off the helicopters back at the safe house. Like before, he set the device to mimic the girl's signal.

As a boy, Painter had often gone hunting with his father on the Mashantucket Reservation, his people's tribal homelands. He had grown skilled at the art of baiting a trap and luring prey. Today was no different.

His false trail had drawn the others like moths to a flame.

And like those moths, they met a fiery end.

Painter felt no remorse for his trap. He still pictured Sean McKnight falling to the floor. Two other staff members had also been killed. Painter checked his watch. The second hand swept past the twelve, crossing the fail-safe deadline set for one o'clock.

He held his breath, but nothing happened.

Earlier, after setting the fail-safe, he had fled to the mechanical room and manually disabled the electronic sparking system. He had needed the levels flooded with the accelerant gas, but Mapplethorpe had been right. Painter could not let the men and women captured by the commando team die, not even to protect the girl. So he had set the trap instead, localizing the firestorm to the one room and luring Mapplethorpe and his team to it.

With a majority of the soldiers dispatched and its

leader killed, the others would likely disperse and vanish into the night.

Lisa leaned against him. 'Will the fires spread?'

The answer came from above. Sprinklers engaged and rained both water and foam over them.

'Is it over?' she asked.

Painter nodded. 'Right here it is.'

Still, Painter knew things elsewhere were far from settled.

10:53 A.M.
Pripyat, Ukraine

Gray sprinted toward the closing steel door at the back end of the massive hangar. He pounded down the roadway between the tall rails. He passed the bodies of two dead workers, shot in the head.

His heart thundered in his ears, but he still heard cheers echoing from the distant grandstands, as if this were a track meet and he was sprinting for the finish line in the four-hundred-meter dash. Only in this race, the spectators' lives depended on him crossing the finish line in time.

With a final burst of speed, he reached the hatchway and dove on his belly under the descending door. It was like entering a crawl space beneath a house. The door was yards thick, composed of plates of steel. He scrabbled forward as the edge continued to drop, pressing down on him. Panic fired his heart. He kicked and paddled, worming his way forward as he was flattened farther under the thick door.

Finally, he reached the end and rolled out into a cavernous space. He took in the sight in a heartbeat: a vast interior, lined by scaffolding, enclosing a ten-story blocky structure of concrete and blackened steel. It was the infamous Sarcophagus, the gravestone over reactor four. By now, the hangar had been hauled almost completely over the crypt. Beyond the Sarcophagus rose a wall of concrete. The hangar would end its crawl and butt up against that wall, sealing the Sarcophagus completely.

But for now, an arch of sunlight spanned the Sarcophagus like a fiery rainbow. It was all that was left open to the world. As Gray stared, the sunlit rainbow grew incrementally narrower.

Off to the left, Gray heard someone speaking in Russian outside the hangar, proud and bold, broadcasted loudly from the grandstands. He also heard the continual steady drone of the hydraulic jacks as they pulled the hangar the last few feet.

Then to the right, a pistol fired.

Gray pictured the bodies outside.

Nicolas was leaving an easy trail of bread crumbs to follow.

As Gray sprinted in that direction, he kept low as he dodged around several stacks of plate steel, a pile of broken concrete, and a forklift. The air smelled of oil and tasted rusty. As he reached the corner of the Sarcophagus, he freed the pistol from his belt.

Peering around the corner, he spotted a figure limping toward the narrowing arch of sunlight. He was about twenty yards from escaping. Gray leveled his pistol.

'Nicolas!' Gray barked at him.

Startled, the man tripped around.

'Don't move!' Gray shouted.

Nicolas searched for a second, then turned and fled. Gray could not risk killing the man. Not until he found out what was planned. So he took careful aim and shot. Nicolas's good leg went out from under him. He sprawled onto the floor.

Gray rushed toward him, but a man such as Nicolas did not rise to his height of power by folding under stress. The senator rolled behind a stack of steel I-beams. Shots fired back at Gray, forcing him to duck to the side. He took shelter behind a pallet of lumber.

'*Chyort! Rodilsya cherez jopu!*' Nicolas cursed at him in Russian, his voice edging toward hysteria. He yelled at Gray. 'We can't stay here, you *svoloch*! We have less than three minutes.'

Beyond the man's hiding place, Gray watched the sliver of sunlight between the massive concrete wall and the trundling hangar pinch ever closer together. There was only four feet of space left. No wonder Nicolas was in a hurry.

'Then tell me how to stop Operation Uranus!' Gray called back.

'There is no way to stop it! It's all been set in motion. All we can do is get out of the way . . . *now*!'

'Tell me what you've done.'

'Fine! Concussion charges! Planted inside the pillars on the other side of the Sarcophagus. They'll rip a wall down and expose everyone on that side to a lethal dose of radiation. There's no way to defuse them. We *MUST* go now!'

Gray attempted to digest what he'd heard, trying to seek a solution. Even if he ran outside and screamed for an evacuation, it would be too late.

'There's no reason for us to die with them,' Nicolas continued. 'The world needs a new direction. Needs strong men. Like myself. Like you. Our group's goal is to better the state of mankind, to forge a new Renaissance.'

Gray remembered the senator's earlier discussion about propping up a new prophet onto the world stage. So this is how he planned to do it, creating world chaos, then offering a solution, one promoted by a figurehead who was guided by the prescience and knowledge of augmented children.

'Even if we die here,' Nicolas pressed, 'it won't be the

end. Plans are already in motion that cannot be stopped. Our deaths would serve no purpose. Join us. We can use such men as yourself.'

In truth, Gray could think of no way to stop what was to come.

Beyond Nicolas, the walls continued to close.

'Two minutes!' he called to Gray. 'There's a lead-lined control booth just outside. We can still make it if we leave right now!'

Nicolas shifted behind his hiding place, plainly considering making a run for it. But with a twisted ankle on one side and a wounded leg on the other, he must know that path was certain death.

Then again, so was staying here.

Nicolas finally tossed out his pistol and stepped into the open. He faced Gray, arms out to either side, tottering on his legs. 'If this is the only way to live, so be it!'

Gray cursed under his breath. Unable to stop the deaths to come, his only recourse was to apprehend the mass murderer who had orchestrated the deadly operation. Gray stepped out into the open with his pistol leveled.

At that moment, the drone of the hydraulic pumps climbed into a screaming roar. With a groan of twenty thousand tons, the massive arch began to shudder.

What was happening?

Kowalski stepped over the dead soldier to join Elena at the control panel. While Gray had fled on foot, Elena had driven the motorcycle like a NASCAR driver on crack. Kowalski had clung so hard to the sidecar's handles that his fingers still trembled. They had rocketed to the rear side of the steel archway and sailed up to a concrete bunker that trailed big cables.

It was the control shack for the hydraulic jacks.

A fierce but brief firefight followed.

Kowalski had tried to help, but Elena spun like a ballerina with a machine gun. She danced and pirouetted through a hail of bullets as if anticipating each shot. She took out four soldiers. Kowalski managed to kill only one.

Nicolas's men, Elena had said once the gunfight ended.

Once inside, Elena had set to work. Bent over the control board, she pushed the hydraulics toward the redline, seeking to close the hangar faster.

Just outside the shack's window, one of the towering motors smoked, looking ready to blow. On one of the screens, flashing red warning signs blinked.

That couldn't be good.

Kowalski stepped out of Elena's way and stared at a row of monitors. They displayed video feed from inside the hangar. On the middle screen, Kowalski spotted two tiny figures on the floor.

Gray and the Russian guy.

From the angle of the camera, Kowalski could see what Gray could not.

Oh, crap!

'Elena!' he called out. 'A little help here!'

He turned in time to see her suddenly slump toward the floor. He reached out and caught her around the waist. His hand found the shirt under her dark jacket soaking and hot. He parted the coat and saw her entire left side drenched in blood. It seemed her dancing had not been as flawless as he'd thought.

'Why didn't you say something?' he said with an ache in his voice.

She waved to the monitors. 'Show me.'

Gray struggled to comprehend the sudden acceleration of the hangar's closure. The momentum of twenty thousand tons was not easy to get moving quickly, but it was definitely closing faster, accompanied by the scream of hydraulic motors.

'No!' Nicolas cried out.

Gray realized the anguish in his voice was twofold: *fear* that he now had even less time to escape, and *dismay* that his plans would be ruined if the hangar sealed too soon.

'Let's go!' Gray said, pointing his pistol at the man.

Nicolas lowered his outstretched arms – and revealed what was hidden behind the pile of I-beams. The man's hand had been out of view until now.

A second pistol.

It pointed at Gray's belly and fired.

Gray managed to twist sideways, but the bullet still burned a line of fire across his stomach. He pointed his own weapon and fired. The shot, thrown off by the sudden attack, ricocheted harmlessly off the floor. Even worse, the pistol's slide popped open.

Out of bullets.

The same could not be said for Nicolas.

The Russian drew a dead bead upon Gray.

As a consequence of his concentration, Nicolas missed the movement along the roof of the arched hangar. A massive yellow trolley crane swept above them and dropped a giant hook.

The whistling as it plummeted finally drew Nicolas's eye. He glanced up as the massive steel hook, large enough to anchor ships, slammed into the pile of beams next to him. He tried to leap aside, but the impact knocked half the pile over, pinning his legs.

His pistol skittered across the concrete floor.

'Help me!' the man groaned, desperate, panicked.

No time.

Beyond the pile, the narrowing gap between the steel arch and concrete wall was little more than a foot wide. Gray vaulted over the collapsed pile of beams and sprinted for the exit.

As he reached the slit of sunlight, Nicolas screamed at him. 'You've not won, you *svoloch*! Millions will still die!'

Gray had no time to question him. He shoved into the crack and wormed between the squeezing walls, concrete on one side, steel on the other. The vault was a dozen yards thick. He scooted as fast as he could. Still the pressure began to squeeze his chest, trying to hold him for the final crush.

He took one last breath and exhaled all his air, collapsing his chest. He shoved the last few feet and fell out of the crack with a great gasp of air, landing on his hands and knees.

Like being born a second time.

Behind him, he missed a figure standing off to the side of the hangar. She slipped into the crack as he vacated it.

Gray turned. 'Elena! No! You'll never make it!'

He rolled to his feet and lunged for her. But she had already slid deep into the crack, deeper than he could follow with his larger form. She moved swiftly, her lithe figure fading farther and farther away.

Gray prayed she'd make it safely to the other side, but it was still certain death. Only then did he note the long smear of blood trailing into the narrowing crack.

A growled voice spoke behind him.

'Where's Elena?' Kowalski asked.

Gray watched her vanish out of the crack. He shook his head.

Kowalski stared up and down the side of the hangar. 'She left me up there. After she dropped that anchor on that bastard. Said she was coming down here to help.'

Gray turned away. 'I think that's where she's headed.'

Nicolas lay on his back, his legs weighted under a half ton of steel beams. Through a haze of agony, he heard footsteps stumbling toward him. He turned his head. Elena came up to him.

His eyes winced with a pain deeper than any broken bones. 'Oh, *milaya moya,* what are you doing here?'

She sank next to him.

Blood soaked through her shirt.

'*Lubov moya . . . ,*' he said with a mix of pain and protectiveness. He lifted an arm, and she fell into his embrace. He held her and rocked her gently as the last of the sunlight squeezed away.

A commanding grind of steel on concrete sounded with a note of finality as the Shelter sealed. A few moments later, a crumbling crash echoed as the far side of the Sarcophagus collapsed. The concussion charges had worked as planned, but the Shelter was already closed tight around it, sparing those outside.

He wasn't so lucky.

Nicolas stared up at the lighted archway. The inner steel surfaces were all lined by a thick coat of polycarbonate, all the better to reflect radiation and hold it inside.

Not that it mattered, but Nicolas lifted the flap of the dosimeter badge secured to his jacket pocket. The surface had been white when he'd put it on this morning. It was now solid black.

He let it go and reached another arm to cradle Elena better.

'Why?' he asked.

There were many questions buried in that one word. *Why* had Elena betrayed him? Nicolas knew she must have. Nothing else made sense. But also *why* did she come back?

Elena did not answer. He shifted and saw the glaze to her eyes.

Dead.

And so was he.

The *living* dead.

He knew what end awaited him. He had lived his professional life exploring such deaths. It would be as agonizing as it was humiliating.

As he cradled Elena closer to him, something slipped from her hand and landed on his leg. He reached out and grabbed this last gift from her.

His pistol.

She must have collected it from the floor.

This is why she had come.

To say good-bye and to offer him a way to escape with her.

He nestled into her and kissed her cold lips one last time. *'Ty moyo solnyshko . . .'*

She was indeed his sun.

Holding her, he raised the gun to his lips.

And took his escape.

19

With a rifle over his shoulder, Monk climbed the last switchback of the road. Ahead, the mining complex clustered in front of a granite cliff face. The metal outbuildings and old powerhouse had all oxidized. Roofs and gutters dripped icicles of rust, windows were broken or shuttered, and corroded equipment lay where they'd been dropped decades ago: shovels, picks, wheelbarrows.

Off by the cliffs rose tall mounds of old mine tailings and waste rock dumps. Amid the stone piles rose the tower of a tipple, with its loading booms, hoists, and various chutes used to tip ore ears and unload them into trucks.

As Monk limped on his hastily bandaged leg, he wondered how he knew so much about a mining operation. Had his family been involved—

His head suddenly jangled through a series of flashbulb-popping images: *an older man in coveralls, coated in coal dust . . . the same man in a coffin . . . a woman crying . . .*

An electrical stab of pain ended the flickering bits of memory.

Wincing, he led the children and Marta through a

405

maze of conveyor belts, ore car tracks, and dump chutes toward their goal. A pair of rails led to a gaping opening in a cliff face. It was the main entrance to the mine.

As they crossed, Monk looked over his shoulder.

Lake Karachay spread below. Monk estimated it was two miles across the width here, and three times as long. He searched the forested mountains on the far side, looking for any evidence of where they'd started this journey.

'We must hurry,' Konstantin reminded him.

Monk nodded. The older boy walked between the two younger children. Marta trailed. He led them toward the opening.

As he neared, he discovered a problem. A large wooden barrier, constructed of stacked and mortared wooden logs, blocked the mine shaft from floor to roof.

From the condition of the complex outside, it looked as if no one had been here in ages. But Monk spotted a pile of cigarette butts and empty vodka bottles at the foot of the barrier. Fresh boot prints covered the sandy floor. The mine below was not as abandoned as it appeared. Someone had been taking a break here recently.

Monk glanced behind him. There were no parked trucks or recent tire tracks crossing the complex, so whoever had been lounging here had left by another means. Konstantin had already described that means.

An underground train crossed under the lake from Mine Complex 337 below to Chelyabinsk 88. Whoever labored in the mines must ordinarily exit out the other side.

Monk prayed they would not be expecting visitors at their back door.

He crossed to the rectangle of riveted steel set into the barrier.

'What do we do?' Monk asked. 'Knock?'

Konstantin frowned and crossed to the door. He lifted the latch and pushed. The door swung open, unlocked.

Monk fumbled his rifle around and pointed it through the door. 'Warn a guy before you do that!' he whispered.

'No one comes here,' Konstantin said. 'Too dangerous. So no need for keys. Only sealed to keep bears and wolves away.'

'And the stray tiger,' Monk mumbled.

Konstantin dropped his pack, opened it, and fished out their flashlight. He passed it to Monk, who shouldered his rifle.

Ducking through the door in the main tunnel, Monk pointed his flashlight. Massive wooden beams shored up the passageway as it slanted into the mountain. A set of steel tracks headed into the darkness, extending beyond the reach of the flashlight's glow. Closer at hand, a pair of ore cars rested on the tracks near the barrier.

Down the way, Monk noted shadowy branching tunnels. He suspected the mountain was honeycombed with shafts and tunnels. No wonder the current miners occasionally wandered up out of the Stygian darkness for a little light, even if it was in the shadow of a poisonous lake.

Monk asked for directions as they headed out. 'So where to?'

Konstantin kept silent.

Monk turned to him.

The boy shrugged. 'I do not know. All I know is *down*.'

Monk sighed. Well, that was a *direction*.

Flashlight in hand, he descended into the darkness.

Savina noted all the smiling faces. Excited chatter spread among the older children, while the younger ones scurried around, trying to dispense nervous energy. They were in direct contrast to the very youngest among them, those under five and too immature for their implants.

Those few remained quiet and detached, demonstrating varying levels of untreated autism: sitting silently, staring vacantly, plagued by repetitive gestures.

Four teachers sought to organize their sixty or so charges.

'Stay in your groups!'

The train waited beyond the open blast doors at the back of Chelyabinsk 88. It would be transporting the children for a short pleasure ride. The young ones were occasionally allowed such a luxury, but today the train was on a one-way trip. It would not be returning, coming to a dead stop at the heart of Operation Saturn.

Behind Savina's shoulders, the old Soviet-era industrial apartments stared down at the children with hollow eyes. The teachers also had the same haunted look despite their bright words.

'Did all of you take your medicine?' a matronly woman called out.

The medicine was a sedative combined with a radiosensitive compound. While excited now, in another hour the children would be drifting into a disassociated slumber. It would ease any anxiety when the charges blew at the far end of the tunnel and initiated Operation Saturn. The first dump of lake water through the heart of the tunnel and its subsequent blast of radiation would transform the radiosensitive compound in the children's bloodstream into a deadly nerve toxin, killing them instantly.

The group had considered simply euthanizing the children via lethal injection, but such an intimate act of killing strained even the most professional detachment. Plus afterward, all the small limp bodies would have had to been hauled, loaded, and transported to the heart of Operation Saturn. The plan was for the radiation, blasting for weeks as the lake drained, to burn the bodies and denature the DNA beyond examination – that is, if anyone ever dared approach the bodies. The radiation levels in the tunnel would defy penetration for decades.

So in the end, the current plan was deemed efficient, minimally cruel, and offered the children one last bit of joy and frivolity.

Still, Savina stood with her arms behind her back. Her hands were clenched together in a white-knuckled grip, necessary to keep from grabbing children and pulling them from the train.

But she had saved ten.

She had to console herself with this reality.

The ten best.

They remained in the apartment building behind her, where the control station for Operation Saturn was located. Once done here, the ten Omega subjects would be transported to the new facility in Moscow. It was time for the project to climb out of the darkness and into the sun.

It would be her legacy.

But such a rise had a cost.

Bright laughter and merry calls trailed behind the last of the children. They argued over who would get to ride in the open ore cars and who would be in the front or rear cabs. Only a few older voices wondered why they were going without any of the adults, but even these sounded more excited than concerned.

With the last of the children loaded, the train hissed, hydraulic brakes sighed, and with a snap of electricity, it rolled off down the tunnel. Laughter and shouts trailed back to them. A moment later the blast doors slowly sealed over the end of the tunnel, cutting off their happy voices.

The four teachers headed away. No one spoke to anyone. They barely made contact. Except for a thick-waisted matron in an ankle-length apron. As she passed, she lifted a consoling hand toward Savina, then thought better of it and lowered it again.

'You didn't have to come,' the woman mumbled.

Savina turned away without a word, not trusting her voice.

Yes . . . Yes, I did.

11:16 A.M.
Pripyat, Ukraine

Gray sat in the back of the limousine. Up front, Rosauro drove, with Luca in the passenger seat. They rocketed past the first checkpoint on their flight out of the city. The Chernobyl Exclusion Zone stretched in a thirty-kilometer radius out from the reactor complex. It had two checkpoints, one at the ten-kilometer mark and one at the thirty.

Gray wanted to be outside that second gate before anyone realized something was amiss at the reactor. It would not take long for the dead bodies to be discovered and for the place to be locked down.

Earlier, as Gray and Kowalski had fled overland back to Pripyat from the site of the ceremony, he had called Rosauro on the walkie-talkie that Masterson had supplied him. She had reported an inability to reach Sigma command. He had instructed her to keep trying. By the time Gray arrived at the hotel, lines of communication with Washington had reopened. Rosauro had commandeered one of the limousines. She had also stolen the driver's mobile phone.

Gray clutched the phone now, awaiting a call from Director Crowe. Painter had his hands full over in Washington, but at least Mapplethorpe was out of commission and Sasha was safe.

Gray shared the back of the limousine with Elizabeth and Kowalski. His partner sat bare-chested as Elizabeth treated the gunshot wound to his shoulder.

'Quit wiggling!'

410

'Well, it goddamn hurts.'

'It's just iodine.'

'Sooo, it still stings like a son of a—'

The woman's scowl silenced any further expletive.

Gray had to give the man credit. Kowalski had saved his life at the hangar by dropping that half-ton steel hook. Though Elena might have done the deed, it had been Kowalski's sharp eyes that had noted the threat and saved him.

Still, they weren't out of danger yet.

Gray turned and stared out at the roll of passing hills, dotted with copses of birches. His heart continued to pound. His mind spun through a hundred different scenarios. As they raced away from Chernobyl, he knew they should be heading *somewhere*.

Nicolas's last words plagued him: *You've not won . . . millions will still die.*

What did he mean? Gray knew it had not been an idle threat. Something else was scheduled to happen. Even the name of Nicolas's plan – Operation Uranus – had bothered Gray before. The name was taken from an old Soviet victory during World War II against the Germans. But the victory was not won by the single operation alone. It was accomplished via a perfectly executed tandem of strategies. *Two* operations: *Uranus* followed by *Saturn*.

As Gray fled the hangar, Nicolas had hinted as much. Another operation was set to commence, but where and in what form?

The phone finally rang.

Gray flipped it open and pressed it to his ear. 'Director Crowe?'

'How are you doing out there?' Painter asked.

'As well as can be expected.'

'I've got transportation arranged for you. There's a private airstrip a few miles outside the Exclusion Zone, used to accommodate the ceremony's VIP guests. British

411

intelligence has offered the use of one of their jets. They're apparently trying to save face for not listening close enough to Professor Masterson, one of their own former agents. By the way, I've gone ahead and sounded the alarm. Word is spreading like wildfire through intelligence channels about the aborted attack at Chernobyl. For safety's sake, evacuations are already under way, but so far you're ahead of that chaos.'

'Very good.' Gray could not discount that the director's firm voice had helped take the edge off his anxiety. He wasn't alone in this.

'You've certainly had a busy day, Commander.'

'As have you . . . but I don't think it's over.'

'How do you mean?'

Gray related what the Russian senator had said and about his own misgivings.

'Hold on,' Painter said. 'I've got Kat Bryant and Malcolm Jennings here. I'm putting you on speaker.'

Gray continued, explaining his fears of a second operation, something aimed at a larger number of casualties.

Kowalski also listened as Elizabeth packed a bandage over his wound. 'Tell them about the jelly beans,' he called over.

Gray frowned at him. Back at the hangar, Elena had attempted to warn Kowalski about something before she'd departed to Nicolas's side, but the man had clearly misunderstood, losing something in the translation.

'You know,' Kowalski pressed. 'The eighty-eight jelly beans.'

Kat's voice whispered faintly from the phone. 'What did he say?'

'I don't think he understood what—'

'Did he say *chella-bins*?'

'No, *jelly beans*!'

Kowalski nodded, satisfied. Gray mentally shook his head. He could not believe he was having this conversation.

A confusing bit of chatter followed as Painter, Kat, and Malcolm discussed some matter. Gray didn't follow all of it. He heard Kat say something about the number eighty-eight drawn in blood.

Malcolm's voice spoke louder, excited, directed at both Gray and Kat. 'Could what you both have heard been the word *Chelyabinsk*?'

'Chelyabinsk?' Gray asked aloud.

Kowalski perked up.

Gray rolled his eyes. 'That might be it.'

Kat agreed.

Malcolm spoke quickly, a sure sign the pathologist was excited. 'I've come across that name. During all the tumult here, I hadn't had a chance to contemplate its significance.'

'What?' Painter pressed.

'Dr. Polk's body. The radiation signature from samples in his lungs matched the specific isotope content of the uranium and plutonium used at Chernobyl. But as you know, subsequent tests clouded this assessment. It wasn't as clear as I'd initially thought. It was more like his body had been polluted by a *mix* of radioactive sources, though the strongest still appeared to be the fuel source at Chernobyl.'

'Where are you going with all this?' Kat asked.

'I based my findings on the International Atomic Energy Agency's database of hot zones. But one region of the world is so polluted by radioactivity that it's impossible to define one signature to it. That region is Chelyabinsk, in central Russia. The Soviet Union hid the heart of its uranium mining and plutonium production in the Ural Mountains there. For five decades, the region was off-limits to everyone. Only in the last couple of years has the restriction been lifted.' He paused for emphasis. 'It was in Chelyabinsk that the fuel for Chernobyl was mined and stored.'

Gray sat straighter. 'And you think it was *there* that Dr. Polk was poisoned – not at the reactor, but where its fuel was produced. In Chelyabinsk.'

'I believe so. Even the number eighty-eight. The Soviets built underground mining cities in the Ural Mountains and named them after the local postal codes. Chelyabinsk forty, Chelyabinsk seventy-five.'

And Chelyabinsk 88.

Gray's heart pounded harder again. He now knew where they had to go. Even had the postal code.

Painter understood, too. 'I'll alert British intelligence. Let them know you'll be going on a little detour. They should be able to get you to the Ural Mountains in a little over an hour.'

Gray prayed they still had enough time.

Millions will die.

As the limousine reached the second checkpoint and was waved through by a bored-looking guard, Painter continued. 'But, Commander, in such a short time, I can't get you any ground support out there.'

Gray spoke as the limousine sailed out of the Exclusion Zone and into the open country. 'I think we've got that covered.'

To either side of the road, older-model trucks had parked in low ditches or pulled into turnouts. A good dozen of them. Men sat in the open beds and crowded the cabs.

In the front seat, Luca leaned over to Rosauro and spoke in a rush. She slowed the limousine, and Luca straightened and waved an arm out the passenger window.

The signal was plain to read.

Follow us.

As the limousine continued, the trucks pulled out and trailed after them. Like Director Crowe, Luca Hearn had sounded his own alarm, using the phones back at the hotel after they'd initially failed to raise central command.

Gray recalled the man's words in describing the Romani: *We are everywhere*. Luca was proven right as his clarion call was answered.

Behind the limousine, a Gypsy army gathered.

11:38 A.M.
Southern Ural Mountains

The farther Monk descended into the mine, the more he became convinced the place was deserted. He heard no echo of voices or thrum of distant machinery. And while this eased his mind that they'd not be discovered, it was also disconcerting. With the silence, it was as if the place were holding its breath.

Monk headed down a steeply slanted access tunnel, his wounded leg burning and painful. Without a map, Monk had to follow the trail of whoever left the cigarette butts and bottles at the front gate to the mine. It wasn't a hard track to discern. The sandy bed of the floor showed clear boot prints. The miner took a direct route back, crossing down some steep access chutes.

And though the place seemed deserted now, Monk had found plenty of evidence of past activity: fresh tailings dumped into shafts, shiny new gear leaning on walls, even an abandoned ice chest half filled with water and floating cans of beer.

Konstantin trailed with his sister, while Pyotr remained glued to Monk's hip. The child's eyes were huge upon the dark passages. Monk felt the fever of his terror as Pyotr clutched to him. It wasn't the cramped spaces that scared him, but the darkness. Monk had occasionally clicked the lamp off to search for any telltale evidence of light.

At those moments, Pyotr would wrap tight to him.

Marta also closed upon the boy, protective, but even

the chimpanzee trembled in those moments of pitch darkness, as if she shared Pyotr's terror.

Monk reached the bottom of the chute. It dumped into another long passageway with a railway track and an idle conveyor belt. As he searched for boot prints, he noted a slight graying to the darkness at the end of the tunnel. He crouched, pulled Pyotr to his side in the crook of his stumped arm, and clicked off his flashlight.

Darkness dropped over them like a shroud. But at the far end of the passage, a faint glow was evident.

Konstantin moved next to Monk.

'No more light,' Monk whispered and passed the boy the darkened flashlight. If he was wrong about the place being deserted, he didn't want to announce their approach with a blaze of light.

Monk swung up the rifle he had confiscated from the dead Russian sniper. 'Quietly now,' he warned.

Monk edged down the tunnel. He walked on the ends of the railroad ties, avoiding the crunch of the gravel bed. The children followed in his footsteps. Marta balanced along one of the rails. As they continued, Monk strained for any voices, any sign of habitation. All he heard was an echoing drip of water. It was a noise that had grown louder the deeper they descended. Monk was all too conscious of the neighboring presence of Lake Karachay.

He also became aware of a growing odor, a mix of oil, grease, and diesel smoke. But as they reached the bend, Monk's keen nose detected another scent under the industrial smells. It was fetid, organic, foul.

Cautiously rounding the turn, Monk discovered the passage ended in a central cavern, blasted out of the rock. It was only a hundredth the size of Chelyabinsk 88, but it still rose three stories high and stretched half the size of a football field.

Most of the floor was covered in parked equipment

and piles of construction material: coiled conduit, stacks of wooden beams, a half-dismantled column of scaffolding, piles of rock. Off to one side rose a tall drill rig, mounted on the back of a truck. The place looked as if it had been hurriedly evacuated. There was no order to it, like someone packing a moving van in a hurry, just dumping things haphazardly.

At least they'd left the lights on.

Several sodium lamps glowed at the opposite side of the room.

'Careful,' Monk said. He motioned the children to hang back, to be ready to bolt and hide among the debris if necessary.

Monk crept forward, staying low, rifle ready at his shoulder. He zigzagged across the space, holding his breath, cautious of his footing. Reaching the far side, he discovered a tall set of steel blast doors, sealed and reflecting the lamplight. They looked newer than the mine works. To the right stood a small shack, about the size of a tollbooth. Through its open door, Monk spotted a few dark monitors, a keyboard, and rows of switches.

Nobody was here.

Monk noted the tremble in his rifle. He was wired and edgy. He took a deep settling breath. The fetid reek was much stronger. Off to the left, Monk noted black oil pooled beyond a stack of equipment. He crept out and peeked around the corner.

Not oil. Blood.

He found the source of the smell. A tumble of bodies draped the back wall, tangled in a heap, outfitted in mining gear or white laboratory coats. Blood and gore spattered the walls behind them.

Death by firing squad.

Someone had been cleaning house.

Behind him, Konstantin appeared, creeping out into the open. Monk returned, shook his head, and pointed to the computer shack. He didn't want the children to see the slaughter. He motioned to Pyotr and Kiska to remain where they were.

Konstantin joined Monk as he strode toward the blast doors. 'I've been here before,' the boy said. 'We're allowed to ride the train sometimes. These are the substation controls.'

'Show me,' Monk said.

Konstantin had already highlighted what General-Major Savina Martov was planning, nicknamed Operation Saturn. It lay beyond these doors.

The two crammed into the shack, and Konstantin studied the substation's controls, his eyes flickering over the Cyrillic lettering. Monk could almost hear his mind flying at speeds beyond normal mentation. After a moment of study, his hands flew over the board, flipping switches with deft assuredness, as if he'd done this a thousand times before.

As he worked, Monk asked, 'How did you learn about Operation Saturn?'

Konstantin glanced to him with a wincing look of embarrassment. 'My skill is rapid calculation and derivative analysis. I work often in the Warren's computer laboratory.' He shrugged.

Monk understood. You could turn a boy into a savant but he was still a boy: curious, mischievous, pushing boundaries.

'You hacked into her files.'

He shrugged again. 'A week ago, Sasha – Pyotr's sister – she drew me a picture. Gave it to me in the middle of the night. When we were all woken by one of Pyotr's nightmares.'

'What picture?'

'The train here, with many children on board, all dead and burning. It also showed the mining site just past the blast doors here. So . . . so the next day, I broke into the files about the operation. I learned what was planned and when it was scheduled to happen. I didn't know what to do. Whom to trust. Sasha left with Dr. Raev for America, so I talked to Pyotr.' Konstantin shook his head. 'I don't know how Pyotr knew . . . maybe he doesn't even know . . . it's sometimes like that.'

Konstantin stared up at Monk for understanding.

Though he didn't completely, Monk still nodded. 'What did Pyotr know?' he pressed.

'He is a strong empath. He sensed you would help us. He even knew your name. Said his sister whispered it to him in a dream. They are very strange, those two, very powerful.'

Monk heard a trace of fear in the boy's voice.

Konstantin even glanced warily back toward Pyotr, then set back to work. 'So we came for you.'

With a final flick of a switch, a row of monitors glowed to life across the top of the control board. They showed black-and-white images, views from different angles of a small cavern, rigged with scaffolding. On the floor was bolted a large steel iris.

The heart of Operation Saturn.

Motion drew Monk's eye to the centermost screen. It showed a train rested outside the mining site. Open ore cars were loaded with children. Some had climbed out and stood around in confusion. Others appeared to be laughing and playing.

Konstantin clutched Monk's sleeve. 'They . . . they're already here.'

Savina sat in the brightly lit control station, flanked by two technicians. They were running final diagnostics on two computers. The station was in a converted subbasement bunker beneath one of the abandoned apartment buildings. There were no windows. Their eyes on the world came from seven LCD screens wired into the walls. They displayed video feed from the cameras in the tunnel and at the operation site.

She stared at the parked train for another breath, then stood up, unable to remain seated. She felt a familiar crick in her back. She had failed to take her steroid injection, too busy with all the final preparations. She turned away from the view of the train. Not because it hurt to look – which it did – but because anxiety ran through her.

She checked her wristwatch. It was more than half past eleven o'clock, and she had still not heard from Nicolas. She exited the control room, so the others did not see her wring her hands. It was a weak matronly gesture, and she forced herself to stop. She headed to the stairs and climbed toward the level above. Not with any destination in mind, only to keep moving.

From her contacts in the intelligence community, she had already heard the rumblings of an 'accident' at Chernobyl. A radiation leak. Dead bodies. The place was being evacuated. And if Nicolas had been successful, such a mass departure was too late. Perhaps her son had been caught up in the resultant chaos and had been unable to report to her yet. Her operation was set to commence in another forty-five minutes, once she heard confirmation from Nicolas.

As she climbed the stairs, she imagined him gloating in his success, possibly even enjoying a secret tryst with little Elena. It would not be unlike Nicolas to celebrate first and attend to business afterward. Anger tempered her anxiety.

She finally reached the floor above the control station. It had been converted into a domicile for the technicians: bedrooms, exercise space, and a central communal area full of sofas and dining tables. The only occupants at the moment were ten children. She knew each by name.

They turned to stare at her, their heads swiveling all at once, like a flock of birds turning in midflight. Savina felt a flicker of apprehension, a recognition of the foreignness of their minds. The Omega subjects were savants so talented that their skills crossed the threshold of the physical to a realm where Savina could not travel.

Boris, a thirteen-year-old with eyes so blue they appeared frosted, seemed almost to be studying her. His talent was an eidetic memory coupled with a retention that frightened. He even remembered his own birth.

'Why were we not allowed to go with the others?' he asked.

More heads nodded.

Savina swallowed before answering. 'There is another path for all of you. Do you have your bags packed?'

They just stared. No answer was necessary. Of course their bags were packed. The question displayed the level of her own nervousness. Before her lay the power that would fuel the Motherland into a new era. And deep down, Savina knew such a power remained beyond her full comprehension.

'We will be leaving in an hour,' Savina said.

Those ten pairs of blue eyes stared back at her.

Footsteps sounded behind her. She turned as one of the technicians joined her.

'General-Major,' he said, 'we're having some glitch with the blast doors on the other side of the tunnel. If you could advise us how to proceed.'

She nodded, glad to focus her mind upon a problem.

She followed the technician back to the staircase. Still, she felt those ten pairs of eyes tracking her, cold and dispassionate, icy in their regard. To escape their judgment, she hurried down the stairs.

*

'Open the doors!' Monk called to Konstantin.

From inside the control station, the boy nodded. Electric motors sounded, and large steel gears began rolling the blast doors out of the way, splitting down the middle.

Konstantin came running over to him, out of breath. 'Five minutes,' the boy warned.

Monk understood. Konstantin had sent the tunnel's digital camera system into a diagnostic shutdown and reboot. The clever kid had engineered a five-minute blackout. They had that long to evacuate the children from the train before the cameras were back online.

There was little else he could do. The master control station lay at the other end of the tunnel. Once the subterfuge was detected, the other station would kill the power to Konstantin's shack.

They had only this one shot.

As the doors parted, Monk squeezed through, followed by Konstantin. Marta also loped after them. The old chimpanzee wheezed with exhaustion, but she didn't slow, even passing Monk.

The old girl knew they had to hurry.

A hundred yards away, the train rested on the tracks.

Monk ran toward it, hopping a bit on his wounded leg. Konstantin called out in Russian, yelling at them to get off the train and out the blast door. The boy waved both his arms.

'Just clear the train,' Monk said. 'I must get moving as quickly as possible.'

Monk jangled alongside the train as he ran. He carried two assault rifles over his shoulders, each with sixty-round magazines. Konstantin had already given him a lesson on the manual drive mechanism for the train. It wasn't much.

Get in the front cab, shove the lever up.

Reaching the train, Monk trotted along one side,

Konstantin along the other. 'Everyone off the train!' Monk shouted. 'Out the doors!'

Konstantin echoed his orders in Russian.

Still, chaos ruled for a full half minute. Children yelled or cried. Hands grabbed at him, milling and jostling. But the kids were also well trained to follow orders. Slowly the tide shifted, and the children began to drift down the tunnel toward the doors.

No longer crowded underfoot, Monk reached the last car, a covered cab. He leaped through the open door and went to the front end. A small driver's seat was flanked by a green and red stick. Green for go. Red for the brakes. A small dashboard displayed gauges and voltage readings.

Monk did not have time for finesse. He leaned out the window. 'Konstantin!'

The boy's voice echoed to him. 'Clear! Go!'

Good enough.

Monk shoved the green lever forward. Electricity popped, casting a few sparks into the darkness ahead. The train lurched forward, then began to roll off down the tunnel.

Four minutes.

He had to get this train to the other end of the tunnel before the camera system rebooted. It was up to Konstantin to herd the children out of the tunnel and close the blast doors. Monk had instructed the boy how to jam the gears so that the doors would remain closed.

Konstantin also had one other task.

Monk had confiscated a pair of the miners' radios. Once Monk reached the far doors, he would signal Konstantin to open them. If all went according to plan, Monk would have the advantage of surprise – and two fully loaded assault rifles. While likely a suicide mission, what choice did he have? The children were safe for the moment, but if Operation Saturn succeeded, how many millions more would die? Monk had no choice but to storm the master control station, guns blazing.

Initially, he had considered sabotaging the mine site, but Konstantin had paled at that suggestion. The charges – fifty of them – were primed with radio detonators. Even if he could scale the half kilometer of shaft in four minutes to reach them, any mishandling of the explosives risked setting them off.

So the matter was settled.

With a rattle of wheels, the train sailed down the dark tunnel, lit by occasional bare bulbs. The front cab also had a single headlamp, which cast a glow ahead of him. As the train trundled faster and faster, Monk noted kilometer markers on the wall. According to Konstantin, the tunnel ran four kilometers long.

Monk found himself holding his breath, counting off a full minute in his head. Along the right side, he saw the number 2 stenciled into the wall.

Halfway there.

At best, he would have less than thirty seconds to spare.

Not great, but not bad.

Then the lights went out, as if the hand of God had clapped.

Under Monk, the train sighed, as if echoing his despair. Without electricity, the train rolled to a stop in the pitch darkness.

Behind him, from the back of the train, a child screamed in raw terror. Monk's body clenched. He knew that voice.

Pyotr.

Savina stared at the bank of darkened monitors in the control station. She shook her head. Minutes before, one of the technicians had summoned her down here, worried about a glitch in the system, something to do

424

with the blast doors at the far end of the tunnel. By the time she'd got down here, the cameras were off-line, running a diagnostic subroutine.

No one had ordered it.

Suspicions hardened her veins. Something was wrong. Rather than sit idle, she took a preemptive move and cut all power to the tunnel.

'M.C. three thirty-seven,' Savina said. 'There's a substation over at the mining complex.'

One of the technicians, an electrical engineer, nodded to her.

'And as I recall, there's a camera built into the control shack over there. To allow you to communicate with technicians on the other side.'

The man nodded again – then his eyes widened. 'It's on a system independent from the tunnel.'

It was a precaution engineered in case of breakdowns like now, leaving the two stations still able to communicate.

'Bring up that camera.' She tapped one of the monitors.

The engineer typed rapidly at his computer. A few moments later, the screen snapped to life in grainy black-and-white. The camera was small and utilitarian, angled above the control board of the shack to give a good view of the operator on that side.

Savina leaned closer. Out the shack's open door, the camera caught a milling of children in the cavern beyond. Many children. The ones who had boarded the train.

Savina struggled to comprehend, when a taller boy stepped into view of the camera. He was tall, dark-haired, with a long, angular face. Her fingers tightened. She knew that boy.

Konstantin.

What was going on?

With all that had happened this morning, she'd had no time to follow up on Lieutenant Borsakov's hunt for the American and the three children. She watched

Konstantin wave an arm and call silently to the crowd of children. Borsakov had obviously failed.

But what were they doing over there?

She searched the crowd, looking for the American and the other two children. She sought one child in particular, the one she wanted back.

Pyotr screamed as the blackness smothered him. His eyelids stretched wide searching for any light, Marta held him in her strong arms. The two had used the confusion at the other end of the tunnel to sneak aboard the last car and hide.

Pyotr knew he had to stay with the man.

But the darkness . . .

Pyotr gasped, drowning in the black sea. He rocked and rocked while Marta tried to hold him. It was his nightmare come true. He'd had the same dream often: where his shadow rose up and consumed him, smothered him until there was only darkness. The only way to defend against it was to set himself on fire, to burn like a torch against that darkness – then he would wake screaming.

Other children said they saw him on fire in their own dreams. At first he thought they were making fun of him, but after the first few times, they all started looking strangely at him, seldom talked to him, rarely played with him. Teachers grew angry, too. They scolded, didn't let him have sweetcakes with honey, said he upset the other children to the point that no one did well on their tests for days afterward. They blamed him for scaring everyone.

And it scared him, too, down to the bones – and that was only a dream. *This* darkness now was no dream.

Panicked, he strained to escape it, but it was everywhere. He sought light where there was none. Even that path terrified him, but it was better than the smothering inkiness.

Out of the darkness, pinpricks of light appeared like fiery needles punched through black cloth, willed into being by his terror. Just a few, then more and more. He stared upward as the starry landscape spread and pushed back the darkness.

But he knew the truth. These were no stars.

As Pyotr strained, his heart fluttered like a trapped bird. He stared upward as the stars grew brighter, swelling larger as they fell closer. He knew he should turn away. But his eyes opened wider . . . as did the darkness inside him. It also sought the light, howling out of the dark pit, needing to be fed.

Stars began to fall faster and faster, a few at first, then others followed. From all directions, they swept down upon him, crashing toward him.

He heard the cries and felt the hammering hearts. They filled him with their light. He fell backward as the night sky collapsed upon him and lit his core on fire.

Distantly, he heard a simian howl of warning.

Because Marta knew his secret.

In those waking moments after his nightmares, when he woke screaming, it wasn't just fear – it was also exhilaration.

Something was dreadfully wrong with the children.

After cutting the power, Savina had continued to study the camera feed from M.C. 337. Though she had no audio, it was plain the children remained agitated, milling in confusion, some crying, most walking or standing shell-shocked. The only one who appeared in control was Konstantin. He moved among them, appearing into view, then disappearing again.

Savina kept a watch to see if Pyotr was among them.

Though she had ten Omega subjects, if the boy was there —

Then one of the children in view dropped to the floor. A neighboring child turned to the slumped child, then she also fell, as if clubbed. More and more children collapsed. Panicked, one boy ran past – then he, too, succumbed.

The technical engineer also noted the same. 'Is it the neurotoxin?'

Savina stared, unsure. The radiosensitive compound was inert unless exposed to high doses of radiation. The readings at M.C. 337 had never been that high. A moment later, Konstantin reappeared. He carried a limp girl in his arms. It was his sister Kiska. He turned straight at the camera. His eyes full of terror.

Then Savina saw it – like a light snapped off in his eyes. The fear vanished to a dullness and down he went.

It wasn't the neurotoxin.

Konstantin and Kiska hadn't consumed the medication.

A thump sounded from overhead. Then another and another.

Savina stared up.

Oh, no . . .

Turning, she ran for the stairs. She flew up them two at a time. Her back cramped, and her heart pounded with a lance of pain. She burst into the room where the ten children had been waiting for her.

They had all collapsed, in chairs, on the floor, heads lolling, limbs slack. She rushed to Boris, knelt beside him, and checked the pulse at his throat. She felt a weak beat under her fingertips.

Still alive.

She rolled him over and lifted his eyelids, which hung at half-mast. The boy's pupils were dilated wide and nonresponsive to light.

She climbed back to her feet and stared around the room.

What was happening?

20

Painter hurried down the hall. He didn't need any more trouble, but he got it.

The entire command bunker was in lockdown mode after the attack. As he had suspected, after the fiery death of Mapplethorpe, the few remaining combatants ghosted away into the night. Painter was determined to find each and every one of them, along with every root and branch that supplied Mapplethorpe with the resources and intelligence to pull off this attack.

In the meantime, Painter had to regain order here.

He had a skeleton team pulled back inside. The injured had been transported to local hospitals. The dead remained where they were. He didn't want anything disturbed until he could bring in his own forensic team. It was a grim tour of duty here this evening. Though Painter had employed the air scrubbers and ventilation to clear the accelerant, it did nothing to erase the odor of charred flesh.

And on top of resecuring the facility here, he was fielding nonstop calls from every branch of the intelligence agency: both about what had happened here and about the aborted terrorist act at Chernobyl. Painter stonewalled about most of it. He didn't have time for debriefings or to play the political game of who had the bigger dick. The only brief call he took was from a grateful president. Painter used that gratitude to buy him the latitude to put off everyone else.

Another attack threatened.

That was the top priority.

And as the latest problem was tied to that matter, he gave it his full and immediate attention. Reaching the medical level, he crossed to one of the private rooms. He entered and found Kat and Lisa flanking a bed.

Sasha lay atop it as Lisa repositioned an EEG lead to the child's temple.

'She's sick again?' Painter asked.

'Something new,' Lisa answered. 'She's not febrile like before.'

Kat stood with her arms crossed. Lines of worry etched her forehead. 'I was reading to her, trying to get her to sleep after everything that had happened. She was listening. Then suddenly she sat up, turned to an empty corner of the room, called out the name Pyotr, then went limp and collapsed.'

'Pyotr? Are you sure?'

She nodded. 'Yuri mentioned Sasha had a twin brother named Pyotr. It must have been a hallucination.'

While they talked, Lisa had retreated to a bank of equipment and began powering them up. Sasha was wired to both an EKG and EEG, monitoring cardiac and neurological activity.

'Is her device active?' Painter asked, nodding to Sasha's TMS unit.

'No,' Lisa answered. 'Malcolm checked. He's already come and gone. Off to make some calls. But something's sure active. Her EEG readings are showing massive spiking over the lateral convexity of the temporal lobe. Specifically on the right side, where her implant is located. It's almost as if she's having a temporal lobe seizure. Contrarily her heart rate is low and her blood pressure dropped to her extremities. It's as if all her body's resources are servicing the one organ.'

'Her brain,' Painter said.

'Exactly. Everything else is in shutdown mode.'

'But to what end?'

Lisa shook her head. 'I have no idea. I'm going to run some more tests, but if she doesn't respond, I can think of only one possible solution.'

'What's that?' Kat asked.

'Though the TMS implant is not active, the spiking EEGs are centered around it. I can't help but believe those neuro-electrodes are contributing to what's happening to her. Her electrical activity is frighteningly high in that region – as if those wires in her brain are acting like lightning rods. If I can't calm her neural activity, she may burn herself out.'

Kat paled at her assessment. 'You mentioned a solution.'

Lisa sighed, not looking happy. 'We may need to remove her implant. That's where Malcolm went, to make some calls to a neurosurgeon at George Washington.'

Painter crossed and put an arm around Kat's shoulders. He knew how attached she had become to the child. They had lost many lives protecting her. To lose her now . . .

'We'll do everything we can,' Painter promised her.

Kat nodded.

Painter's beeper buzzed on his belt. He slipped his arm free and checked the number. The Russian embassy. That was one call he had to take. Gray should be landing at Chelyabinsk in another few minutes.

As he glanced back up, Lisa waved him away with a small tired smile. 'I'll call you if there's any change.'

He headed for the door – then a sudden thought

intruded, something he had set aside and not yet addressed. He frowned questioningly over to Kat.

'Earlier,' he said, 'I don't know if I heard you correctly.'

Kat looked at him.

'What did you mean when you said Monk was still alive?'

12:20 P.M.
Southern Ural Mountains

Monk sidled along the train in the pitch dark. He ran his stumped forearm along the cabs as he moved down the tracks. He stretched and waved his other hand in front of him. Stumbling over railroad ties and larger stones in the gravel, he worked his way from the front of the train toward the back.

A moment before, as Monk had stepped out of the train, Pyotr had stopped screaming. It had cut off abruptly. The silence was even worse, creating a stillness as complete as the darkness. Monk's heart pounded.

Reaching the next ore car, he hiked up over the edge and waved his arm into the open space. 'Pyotr?'

His voice sounded exceptionally loud, echoing down the tunnel. But he didn't know where the boy was or even if he was still on the train. The only option was to work methodically backward.

Monk hopped back down and moved toward the next car. He stretched his right arm out again, sweeping ahead of him—

—then something grabbed his hand.

Monk yelped in surprise. Warm leathery fingers wrapped around his. He reflexively yanked his arm back, but the fingers held firm. A soft hoot accompanied the grip.

434

'Marta!' Monk dropped and gave her a fumbling hug in the dark.

She returned it, nudging her cheek against his, and gave a soft chuff of relief. Her entire body trembled. He felt the pounding of her heart against his chest. She broke the embrace but kept hold of his hand. She urged him to follow with a gentle tug.

Monk gained his feet and allowed her to guide him. He knew where she was taking him. To Pyotr. Moving more swiftly, Monk reached the last cab. Unlike the open ore cars in the middle, the last cab was enclosed.

Marta hopped through an open door.

Monk climbed in after her. The old chimpanzee shuffled and herded him to a back corner. He found Pyotr on the floor, flat out on his back.

Monk's hand patted over him, defining his shape out of the darkness. 'Pyotr?'

There was no response.

He felt the boy's chest rise and fall. Fingers checked his small face. Was he injured? Had he taken a fall? His skin was feverish to the touch. Then a tiny hand wandered like a lost bird and discovered Monk's fingers – and gripped hard.

'Pyotr, thank God.' Monk scooped him up and sat with the boy in his lap. 'I've got you. You're safe.'

Small arms wrapped around his neck. Monk felt the burn of the boy's skin, even through his clothes.

Pyotr spoke, at his ear. '*Go . . .*'

Monk felt a chill pass through him. The tone sounded deeper than Pyotr's normal tentative falsetto. Maybe it was the dark, maybe it was the boy's raw fear. But Monk felt no tremble in his thin limbs. The single word had more command than plea.

Still, it was not a bad idea.

He stood and lifted the boy up. Pyotr seemed heavier, though Monk was past the edge of exhaustion into a bone-deep fatigue, near collapse. Marta helped guide him to the door. He jumped out and landed hard. With the boy in his arms, he hurried back toward the front of the train. He had brought one rifle with him, but he'd left the other in the front cab.

Reaching the car, Monk asked, 'Can you—?'

Even before he finished the question, Pyotr clambered out of his arms and gained his own feet.

'Stay here.' Monk quickly climbed inside, grabbed the second rifle, and slung it over his shoulder.

He returned to Pyotr. The boy took his hand.

Monk expelled one hard breath. Which direction? The train had stopped halfway along the tunnel. They could either return to Konstantin and the other children or continue ahead. But if they had any hope of stopping this madwoman, Monk saw no advantage in going back.

Perhaps Pyotr thought the same thing. The boy set off in that direction. Toward Chelyabinsk 88.

With two rifles strapped to his back and a boy and chimpanzee in tow, Monk marched down the pitch-black tunnel. They had come full circle and headed back home. But what sort of welcome would they face?

The doctor shook his head. 'I'm sorry, General-Major. I don't know what's wrong with the children. They've never demonstrated this type of catatonia before.'

Savina stared across the room. A pair of nurses and two soldiers had helped spread the ten children on the floor, lined up like felled trees. They'd brought in pillows and blankets from the neighboring bedrooms. Two medical doctors had been summoned: Dr. Petrov specialized in neurology, and Dr. Rostropovich in bioengineering.

In a sheepskin-trimmed jacket, Petrov stood with his fists on his hips. The medical team had been in the process of evacuating when called over here. A large caravan of trucks and vehicles was already lined up for departure.

'I'll need a full diagnostic suite to better understand what's happening,' he said. 'And we've already dismantled—'

'Yes. I know. We'll have to wait until we reach the facility in Moscow. Can the children be transported safely?'

'I believe so.'

Savina stared hard at the doctor. She did not like his equivocation.

He nodded his head with more certainty. 'They're stable. We can move them.'

'Then make arrangements.'

'Yes, General-Major.'

Savina left further details to the medical staff and headed back down to the control bunker below. While dealing with the matter here, Savina had also been in contact with her resources in the Russian intelligence and military communities. The information gridlock at Chernobyl seemed to finally be loosening. Contradictory reports and rumors swirled around events at the ceremony: everything from a full nuclear meltdown to a foiled terrorist attack by Chechen rebels. The firming consensus was that there had definitely been a radiological leak, though the extent remained unclear.

And why had Nicolas remained silent?

The worry gnawed a ragged edge to her temper and patience.

And now the strangeness with the children.

Savina needed to clamp down on the chaos and focus on the matter at hand. No matter what the circumstances were at Chernobyl, Operation Saturn would proceed. Even if Nicolas had somehow failed, she would not. Her operation alone would unsettle the world economies, kill millions, and spread a radioactive swath halfway across the globe. It would be harder, but with the savant children still under their control, they would persevere.

With such a focus in mind, she cast aside the confusion and sought the cold dispassion of the resolute. She knew what she must do.

Reaching the bunker, she found the wall screens still dark, except for the grainy view of M.C. 337. She studied the spread of small bodies on the rocky floor. There was still no sign of movement over there.

She turned to the two technicians. 'Why aren't the other cameras back online?'

The chief engineer stood up. 'The diagnostic reboot finished a few minutes ago. We were waiting on your orders to power systems back online.'

Savina sighed and pressed her fingertips to her forehead. Did everyone have to be dragged by the nose? She motioned to the board. 'Do it.'

Despite her desire to snap at the man, she kept her voice even. While she had ordered the shutdown, she had indeed left no standing order regarding the power situation.

To avoid any further misunderstanding, Savina pointed to the view of M.C. 337. 'Keep the power cut off to the other substation. All except its camera.' She didn't want any more surprises from that side.

As the two technicians set to work, lights flickered across the board, and the dark screens filled with images of the tunnel and the heart of her operation. Everything appeared fine – except for one glaring exception.

The train was no longer parked beside the mining site.

Savina pointed to the screens. 'Bring up the cameras, sequentially down the tunnel. Find the train.'

Fingers punched keys at the master control, and snapshots of the tunnel flipped across the screen, dizzying her head. Then halfway down the passage, the train appeared. It sat idle on the tracks. Savina stepped closer to that monitor and studied the ore cars and cabs. She saw no movement. Someone could be hiding, but Savina didn't think so.

'Continue down the tunnel,' she ordered.

More digital images flowed. She spotted movement on one.

'Stop!'

A single wall lamp lit this section of the dark tunnel. It lay about a quarter klick from the blast doors. As Savina watched, figures appeared out of the darkness, walking into the light from the deeper tunnel.

Savina's fingers tightened on the edge of the control board.

It was the American . . . leading a child by the hand.

As they drew farther into the glow, Savina recognized the boy.

Pyotr.

Straightening, Savina glanced to the grainy image from M.C. 337. All the children remained collapsed. So why was this one boy still up and moving?

'General-Major?' the engineer asked.

Savina's mind spun but failed to settle on any explanation. She shook her head. As if sensing the eyes upon them, the pair stopped in the light. The American looked behind him. His eyes narrowed with confusion.

As the power returned and pools of lights flickered into existence, Monk knew the cameras must also be online. Without much reason or ability to hide, Monk continued several steps, heading toward the nearest lamp. It was only then that he realized something was amiss.

Or rather *missing*.

He searched behind him. Marta was gone. He had thought she had been following him in the dark. She moved so silently. He stared back down the throat of the tunnel. He saw no sign of her. Had she remained back at the train? Monk even searched ahead, thinking maybe she had gone scouting in advance of them. But the tunnel ended in two hundred feet at a set of tall blast doors.

Marta was nowhere to be seen.

Speakers off by the doors spat with static, then a crisp voice spoke in English. 'Keep moving forward! Bring the boy to the door if you wish to live.'

Monk remained frozen, unsure where to go from here.

12:35 P.M.
Kyshtym, Russia

Seated in an old farm truck, Gray led the caravan through the gates of the airstrip and out onto a two-lane road that headed off into the mountains. Walls of towering fir and spruce trees flanked the road, creating a handsome green corridor.

In the rearview mirror, Gray watched the small mountain town of Kyshtym recede and vanish into the dense forest. The town lay on the eastern slopes of the Ural Mountains, only nine miles from their destination, Chelyabinsk 88. Like the entire area, the town was not without its own legacy of nuclear disaster and contamination. It lay downwind of another nuclear complex, designated Chelyabinsk 40, also known as *Mayak*, the Russian word meaning 'beacon.' But Mayak was not a shining beacon to Russian nuclear safety. In 1957, a waste tank exploded due to improper cooling and cast eighty tons of radioactive material over the region, requiring the evacuation of hundreds of thousands. The Soviets had kept the accident a secret until 1980. As the road turned a bend, the town vanished, like so much of the Soviet Union's nuclear history.

Continuing onward, Gray settled into his seat. The road crossed a bridge with guardrails painted fire-engine red. A warning. The bridge spanned a deep river that marked the former boundary of restricted territory. The road wound higher into the mountains.

Behind Gray trailed a dozen trucks of different makes and models, but all well worn and muddy. Gray shared the front seat with Luca and the driver, who were conversing in Romani. Luca pointed ahead and the driver nodded.

'Not far,' Luca said, turning to him. 'They already sent up spotters to watch the entry road. They report lots of activity. Many cars and trucks heading down the mountain.'

Gray frowned at the news. It sounded like an evacuation. Were they already too late?

In the bed of the truck, four men lounged, half covered in blankets. Gray had been impressed with their arsenal hidden under the blankets: boxes of assault rifles, scores of handguns, even rocket-propelled grenades.

Luca had explained the lax control of such weaponry on the Russian black market. The small army, gathered from local Russian Gypsy clans, had met them in Kyshtym. They swelled the ranks of the men Luca had brought with them from the Ukraine. Gray had to hand it to Luca Hearn: if you needed to gather a fast militia, he was the Gypsy to call.

In the trucks behind them, Kowalski and Rosauro followed. They had left Elizabeth back at the jet, safely out of harm's way, guarded by a trio of British S.A.S soldiers.

Everyone had to move swiftly. Speed was essential. The plan was to strike the underground facility, lock it down, and stop whatever was planned. The nature of Operation Saturn remained a mystery. However, considering it was in the heart of the former Soviet Union's plutonium production facilities and uranium mines, it had to be radiological in nature.

Senator Nicolas Solokov's words still haunted him.

Millions will still die.

Gray had learned the man was born about ninety miles from here, in the city of Yekaterinburg. This was the region the man represented in the Russian Federal Assembly, which meant he knew the area and its secrets. If someone wanted to plot a nuclear event, here would be a great place to do it.

But what was planned?

Back in Kyshtym, Elizabeth paced the length of the jet. Her arms were folded over her chest, her chin low in concentration. She was worried for the others, fearful after hearing what Gray and the others sought to stop.

Millions will die.

Such madness.

Anxiety kept her on her feet, for the team, for the fate of millions. She had a laptop open on a table. She had tried to work, to keep busy. She had begun downloading her digital pictures from her camera. Professor Masterson had kept her camera safe after she was kidnapped by the Russians. He had returned it to her following their escape from the jail in Pripyat.

On the screen, the photos scrolled as they downloaded into the laptop.

Pacing past, she caught a glimpse of the omphalos, resting at the center of the chakra wheel. Despite her worry, her heart still thrilled at the thought that the stone was the original Delphic artifact. For two decades, historians knew the smaller stone at the museum was a copy, the fate of the original a mystery. Some scholars hypothesized that perhaps some oracular cult had survived the temple's destruction and that they'd stolen the stone for their secret temple.

Elizabeth drew back to the laptop. She stared at the omphalos. Here was that proof. She sank into the chair as a sudden realization struck her. She remembered what was carved inside the museum's copy: a curving line of Sanskrit.

It was an ancient prayer to Sarasvati, the Hindu goddess of wisdom and secret knowledge. No one knew who inscribed it there or why. But it was not unusual to see religious graffiti from one religion marking another.

Still, Elizabeth began to suspect the truth. Perhaps the copy of the omphalos had been left behind like a road marker. She scrolled through the images and came upon the photo of the wall mosaic, depicting a child and young woman hiding from a Roman soldier underneath the dome of the omphalos, where the Sanskrit poem was written. It read, *'She who had no beginning, ending, or limit, may the Goddess Sarasvati protect her.'* It could definitely be referring to the last Oracle, a prayer to protect her lineage. Lastly, the goddess Sarasvati herself made her home in a sacred river. Many religious scholars believed that this mythical river was the Indus River, where the exiled Greeks made their new home.

Elizabeth suspected that someone had left that secret message for others to follow. As she and her father had.

She brought up the image of the original omphalos again. She had taken several pictures, including the triple line carved upon the stone that warned of the trap – written in Harappan, Sanskrit, and Greek. She brought up that image.

There had been another example of this triple writing on the chamber walls. Beneath the figure of the fiery-eyed boy. She brought that up, too. Beneath the mosaic, the line of Harappan was intact, but half of the Sanskrit and Greek had been worn away. Only a letter or two remained legible.

She read what she could. ' "*The world will burn . . .*"'

The line nagged, reminding her of what Gray and the others sought to prevent. She stared at the image of a boy rising in smoke and fire from the omphalos and felt a chill of concern. But what was the rest of the message? The only intact line was the one written in indecipherable Harappan. It was a challenging word puzzle.

Unless . . .

Elizabeth jolted upright and leaned closer, her earlier worries forgotten. She glanced between the two images on the screen. She began to understand what she was looking at. She had lines of Harappan translated into Greek and Sanskrit. *Translated*. She breathed harder. On the computer, she had the beginnings of a digital Rosetta stone for this lost language.

She returned back to the broken line of passage beneath the smoky boy. She studied it, compared, and pulled up pictures of the writing on the stairwell wall, too. She began to spot commonalities.

Could she translate it?

Sensing something important, she set to work.

12:45 P.M.

General-Major Savina Martov studied her adversary. She stared at the American on the screen. He remained stopped within the pool of light by the tunnel lamp. She lifted the microphone to her lips.

'Move to the doors now!' she barked sharply.

From the way he jumped at her words, the man had heard her. There was no problem with the speakers near the blast doors.

444

'General-Major,' the engineer said. 'I have a priority call for you from the Arkhangelsk Missile Base.'

Savina tilted back and picked up the handset. One of her contacts was established at the base there. 'Martov here.'

'General-Major, some disturbing intelligence is coming out of the Ukraine. It seems that Senator Nicolas Solokov is dead.'

Savina inhaled sharply. She kept any stronger reaction in check. Still, her throat tightened. Her contact did not know Nicolas was her son, only that he was intimate and supportive of her operations here.

The contact continued speaking. 'Rumors are still swirling as to the details surrounding the events. Some say he was killed by terrorists, while others say he may have had a hand in the actions there. All that is certain is that he is dead. Cameras from inside the sealed Shelter show his body, along with his assistant. He was shot in the head. Radiation levels are still too high to safely remove his body, but measures are under way. I can't say . . .'

The man's words droned on, but Savina had stopped listening. Tears welled up in her eyes. She tilted her head back to keep them from spilling. As the man finished, Savina thanked him for the call and hung up.

She turned her back slightly from the technician and engineer.

Nicolas was dead.

Her only son.

Maybe a part of her had known this already. For the past hour, she had been unable to shake a pall of despair. Her breathing had grown heavier. *Nicolas* . . .

'General-Major?' the engineer asked softly.

His gentleness only angered her. She turned her attention to the screen. The American still hadn't moved. As if her grief were oil, her frustration set flame to it. A fury built inside her. The American had been thwarting her all day, and now defied her.

No longer.

Tears dried in the heat of her vehemence.

Her son might be dead, but she had given birth to another child, to the dream that would rise out of the ashes here. Family blood was not the only way to leave behind a legacy. She would finish what had killed her son. She would find another figurehead to take his place. It might take longer, but it would be done. The world had stolen her son. But she had the power to strike back.

A fierceness entered her voice that made the engineer take a step back. 'Enough!' She pointed to the two screens on the left. They depicted the heart of Operation Saturn. One displayed a view up the shaft toward the planted charges; the other centered on the iris set in the floor. 'Initiate Saturn! On my mark!'

The engineer and technician swung to their stations. They tapped furiously.

Savina stared at the man on the screen. If he wouldn't bring Pyotr to her, she would light a fire under the man. There would be no retreating, no escape.

'Green across the board,' the engineer said tersely. 'Awaiting your mark.'

'Go!'

She took a deep breath and watched the two screens. One monitor flashed with light. She heard a distant muffled explosion. Rocks tumbled past the camera, followed by a surge of mud, smothering the view. On the other screen, the iris rolled open as a sluice of rock and mud washed down atop it with a heavy wallop. Moments later, black water flowed from above, gushing in a solid column. The engineers' calculations proved perfect. The arc of the water sluiced straight down the open maw of the iris.

It had begun.

The world had killed her son. But her brainchild would live. Though she had initiated the operation with a fury that was equal parts hope and retribution, she could not deny a dark vein in her steel. As the water flowed, she knew she would have her revenge on the world for what it had stolen from her today.

She turned her attention to the American.

Once whetted, her vengeance sought a new target.

She was not done.

Monk picked himself off the ground. The explosion still rang in his head. Trapped in the enclosed space, the concussive force had slammed against his ears like the clap of giant hands. He had covered Pyotr with his own body.

As his head continued to ring, he helped the boy to his feet. Distantly a heavy roaring echoed from the dark tunnel behind him, sounding like the growl of some great dragon. But Monk knew what he was hearing.

The rush of water.

Tons of water.

He also knew what it all meant – the explosion, the subterranean waterfall – it meant he had failed. Operation Saturn was under way, dumping a toxic slurry into the heart of the world.

The loudspeaker squawked again by the blast doors.

'Drop your weapons!' the woman said with a mix of ice and fire, cold determination laced with anger. 'Bring the boy to the door. And I suggest you move quickly. The radiation levels are rising rapidly. You have less than five minutes before you absorb a lethal dosage.'

Monk had no choice. He shrugged off the rifles and let them clatter to the tracks. Pyotr reached over and grabbed the sleeve of his stumped arm.

Together they hurried the last couple hundred yards, racing as radiation rose in the tunnel. Ahead, the blast doors slowly parted, revealing a line of five soldiers with rifles leveled.

Their welcoming committee.

Pyotr urged him faster, as if the boy knew something Monk did not.

Monk's wounded leg lanced an agonizing spike with every step. His chest tightened. His breathing wheezed. He stared down toward his waist. He still wore his dosimeter badge. It flapped with each step. Monk could see the surface. It showed crimson, but with each passing yard, it grew a shade darker.

Despite his leg, he sped faster.

Monk and Pyotr sprinted for the doors.

As they neared the exit, a massive blast shattered like thunder, coming from out in the cavern of Chelyabinsk 88. Monk's steps stuttered in surprise, but Pyotr tugged him onward.

The guards, equally startled, twisted around. One dropped flat in fear.

Pyotr aimed for the gap. Hitting the line, the boy leaped over the soldier's prone form. His other hand darted and snatched a sidearm from the holster of a neighboring soldier. The boy swung and slapped the weapon into Monk's one hand.

There was no fumbling. It had hit his palm perfectly. Monk swung out his arm. From point-blank range, he fired into the line, using a reflexive skill buried deeper than his erased memory.

He emptied the entire clip, dropping all five men.

Monk tossed the pistol aside. Pyotr dashed forward and grabbed another. He passed it to Monk, snatched his sleeve again, and they were off.

All around the cavern, more explosions rocked. Men screamed and smoke poured from several of the abandoned apartment buildings. As he ran, he spotted the screaming passage of a rocket-propelled mortar or grenade. It slammed into another of the buildings. Concrete and glass exploded outward, showering the soldiers below.

The base was under attack.

But by whom?

Gray raced the truck down the concrete ramp and through the massive doors. On the plane ride here, he had read about these complexes, these cities underground. The Soviets used to bring in orchestras and bands to play for the workers, filling subterranean amphitheaters. Still, Gray was not ready for the sheer size of the place.

Nor the chaos.

Six trucks had led the initial assault.

To soften them up, Luca had said.

Gray couldn't argue. This was Luca's army, not his.

He had one mission.

Gray shot through a wall of smoke. He saw rocket fire slamming into the five-story apartment buildings, collapsing entire sections. Luca was in the bed of the truck, braced with a rocket on his shoulder. Two trucks flanked to either side. Kowalski drove one, Rosauro the other.

After their trucks passed through the mouth of the tunnel, the Gypsies closed off the exit road behind them, blocking the way with a pair of logging trucks, heavy with timber. Two dozen men manned the barricade and kept anyone from leaving.

Gray was impressed by the Gypsies' attack strategy – both now and moments before.

On the way up here from the airport, all the vehicles in the region appeared to be just ordinary rural traffic, wandering the mountainside roads and dirt tracks.

Then, upon a coordinated signal, the entire peaceful-looking countryside rose and turned upon the mountain in a synchronized assault. Rifles bristled out of bunkers built into the centers of hay trucks. Horses broke away from wagons with riders bearing shotguns, covering steeper terrain swiftly. Motorcycles rocketed out of the back of paneled milk trucks and shot up the side roads. The sudden transformation locked the mountainside down in a matter of minutes.

The Russians who had already left the subterranean compound were waylaid on the road, driven into ditches, stripped of weapons, and tied up. By the time Gray reached the mountain entrance, the advance assault team was already barreling into the throat of the tunnel, leaving a trail of smoke and fire for him to follow.

Gray hadn't hesitated. They had no time to spare. Operation Saturn had to be found and stopped.

And Luca's men assisted there, too. Like any good army, the Gypsies had gathered intelligence in advance of an attack. On the way up here, a man in a black ankle-length duster had stood in the middle of the road and waved Luca's truck to stop. Two men in laboratory coats knelt in the roadside ditch, hands behind their backs, rifles held at their heads. The Gypsies hadn't been gentle. Then again, it was the Russians who had slaughtered their mountaintop village and kidnapped their children.

The Russians had started this war; the Gypsies intended to finish it.

The interrogator passed Luca a hand-drawn map, splattered with blood. Luca handed it off to Gray. It was a crude schematic of Chelyabinsk 88, including a circle around the control station for Operation Saturn, located in a subbasement bunker beneath one of the cavern's apartment structures.

With the goal known, Gray careened the truck down

the curving road toward the ongoing siege at the high-rise complex. The initial attack, while dramatic and surprising, had also clogged the road with rubble. One entire building had fallen across the central roadway.

Gypsies in trucks continued to mount a fiery barrage. Others abandoned their vehicles and prepared for a ground offensive.

Gray skidded his truck to where the men gathered and rolled out. Kowalski and Rosauro joined him. Hopping out of the truck bed, Luca called out in Romani. Men responded. After a few exchanges, Luca turned to Gray and hunkered down with him behind one of the trucks.

'The Russians have taken to the buildings, defending more fiercely the deeper you go.'

Gray knew why. 'They've pulled their forces back to defend the control station. If they've not already initiated Saturn, they will soon. We can't wait.'

Luca held up a restraining hand and glanced back toward the gathered ground troops. 'I have a man . . . ah, here he is.'

A small figure ran low over to them. He wore cement-gray clothes and a black cap. The two Romani men spoke quickly.

'This is Rat,' Luca introduced the newcomer.

'Nice name,' Kowalski mumbled.

'He's a scout. Skilled at finding paths no one would think to guard. He may know a way, but it'll have to be a small party. No more than five or six.' Luca looked around at their small group. 'Perhaps just us. *Va*?'

'*Va*,' Kowalski agreed, then glanced to Gray for confirmation.

'The other men will keep the Russians busy,' Luca added, waving to the ground forces and trucks.

'We go then?' Rat asked in stilted English.

'*Va*,' Gray answered, earning a grin from the man and a clap on his knee.

451

They readied their weapons – rifles and sidearms – and followed the small man toward a pile of rubble. Gray could see no way through. Luca motioned to the ground forces as they passed. A sharp warbling whistle spread across the smoky cavern.

Rat waved their small team under a tilted section of wall. Gray ducked and found it led to a basement window of the closest apartment building.

As they slowly continued into the scout's maze, Gray heard a shout rise behind him.

'*Opre Roma!*'

Like a flame set to dry grass, the clarion call spread.

Gunfire and rocket blasts intensified.

Continuing onward, Gray prayed they weren't too late.

Savina moved swiftly down the stairs and into the bunker. She ignored the twinges from her back, the shooting pains down her legs, and her pounding heart. At the first sound of attack, she had the blast doors to the tunnel sealed and locked.

Above, waiting for her, a group of the five strongest soldiers had been summoned by Dr. Petrov. The plan was to abscond with five children, carried on the backs of the soldiers. No more. She could not take all ten. Their best chance to escape was to move quickly and efficiently. The American prisoner had given her the idea. He and the children had fled out a back service tunnel. They would do the same.

But Savina had one last measure to address.

She entered the bunker and found the technician and engineer tearing out keyboards. They had already used magnetic wands to wipe the hard drives. The damage to the controls would guarantee that nothing would interfere with the progress of Operation Saturn.

'Is everything locked down?'

The engineer nodded his head vigorously. 'It would take an electrical genius weeks to repair it.'

'Very good.' She lifted her pistol and shot the engineer through the forehead. The technician tried to run, but Savina swung her arm and dropped him at the foot of the stairs, pierced through the neck. He writhed, choking on his own blood.

She could not risk these two being caught. What they dismantled, they might be forced to fix at gunpoint.

She could not let that happen.

To satisfy herself even further, Savina grabbed a fire ax from the back wall and crossed to the boards. Lifting it high, she smashed both computers and electronics boards. Afterward, she rested the ax on the floor and leaned on its handle. She stared at the row of LCD screens. They still displayed views from various cameras. She considered smashing the monitors, too, but with her back in full spasm, she didn't know if she could lift the ax again.

And in the end, what did it matter?

She shoved the ax to the floor and stared at the centermost screen. Water poured in a toxic black stream.

Let them see what she had wrought.

She smiled, enjoying this one last act of cruelty, then turned and headed for the stairs.

Let them watch the world die.

No one could stop her.

21

Pyotr led the man by his shirtsleeve. They ran through chaos. Soldiers screamed, glass shattered, rifles blasted, flames writhed, and smoke choked. But it wasn't chaos to Pyotr.

He tugged Monk into a sheltering dark doorway as a soldier rounded a corner ahead, searched, then moved on. Pyotr hurried the man down a hall, up some stairs, out a window, and over a pile of rubble to the next building.

'Pyotr, where are we going?'

He didn't answer, couldn't answer.

Reaching another hall, Pyotr stopped. In his head, he stretched outward along a thousand possibilities. Hearts glowed like small pyres, flickering with fear, anger, panic, cowardice, malice. He understood how each would move even before they did. It was his talent, only so much more now.

For he had a secret.

Over the past years, as he woke screaming from his nightmare, waking other children with visions of bodies on fire, there was a reason his other classmates performed so poorly on their tests afterward. The teachers believed it was just because Pyotr had scared them, but they were wrong. Pyotr's talent was to read hearts. They called it empathy. But he had a secret, something he only talked to Marta about.

Something he knew from his dreams.

He could do more than *read* hearts – he could also *steal* them. It wasn't *fear* that made the other children perform poorly; they had something drawn from them. For just a few minutes after waking, Pyotr could do anything. He could multiply big numbers, like Konstantin; he could tell a person was lying by listening to how they talked, like Elena; he could see to hidden places, like his sister; and so much more. It filled him until he burned.

He pictured the stars falling into him, screaming, feeding the emptiness inside him. In his dreams, he had always woken before he consumed them fully. Not today. Pyotr walked through a dream from which he could never wake. He knew he had crossed a line, but he also knew he had no choice. He was always meant to burn.

Pyotr stared out at the chaos with a fiery gaze that was not his alone. Through a hundred eyes, he teased a pattern out of the chaos. Though he could not see the future – or at least no more than a few seconds – his ears took in every noise, his eyes interpreted every flicker of flame or shift of shadow, his heart read deep into what drove a man to choose to step here or there, to take that corner or not, to shoot or run. And with a shadow of his sister's ability, his senses extended a few yards beyond even that.

And out of that chaos, a path took form.

One he could follow.

Pyotr crossed out into the hallway, guiding Monk behind him.

He pointed to the left – and Monk shot the soldier who stepped into view a second later. The man was learning to trust Pyotr's instinct. To move with him, to fire upon command, growing into an extension of Pyotr.

Together, they crossed through the pattern.

Moving through pure instinct.

And that's what Pyotr was now: *instinct* fired by a hundred talents.

He understood fully. Instinct was merely the brain's unconscious interpretation of millions of subtle changes in the environment, both at the moment and leading up to it. The brain took all that chaotic information, saw a pattern, and the body reacted to it. It seemed magical, but it was only biological.

Pyotr did the same now – only a hundredfold more powerfully.

He extended his senses, reading hearts, motivations, trajectories, distances, noises, voices, directions, cadences, smoke, heat . . . and on and on. The million details filled him and sifted through the hundred minds he shared. From out of that chaos, patterns opened, and he knew each step to take.

'Where are we going?' Monk asked again.

Where you need to be, Pyotr answered silently.

Pyotr led him down the stairs again, then pulled the man to the floor as a shot fired overhead. From there, they crawled under a row of steel desks as soldiers searched, then down another set of stairs to a long basement hall with branches into a maze of rooms and other passageways.

Pyotr hurried.

While he saw a pattern, he could not truly see the future. He danced faster along the threads of pure instinct, sensing the pressure of ages upon him. They were running out of time.

The man grew more distressed, perhaps sensing the same.

'Where are you—?'

A new voice intruded, coming from the end of the hall, pitched full of surprise. Pyotr read the pound in the newcomer's heart. A name was called out with a ring of disbelief.

'Monk!'

Gray almost shot him. Rounding into the hall, Gray had found two figures running straight at him, one with a weapon pointed ahead. If not for the presence of the boy, Gray would have shot on instinct.

Instead, he momentarily froze between recognition and shock.

His friend did not. The pistol fired. Gray felt a kick to his shoulder, throwing him back. Pain lanced outward.

Kowalski caught him as he fell and barked as loud as the crack of the pistol shot. 'Monk, you ass! What are you doing?'

Monk halted, tugged to a stop by the boy. His face collapsed into a wary mask of confusion. 'Who . . . who are you people?'

Kowalski still fumed. 'Who are we? We're your goddamn friends!'

Gray gained his feet, his left shoulder blazing with fire. 'Monk, don't you recognize us?'

Monk fingered a red and swollen line of sutures behind his ear. 'No . . . actually I don't.'

Gray stumbled over to him, his mind dizzy with questions, with the impossibility of it all. Was it amnesia or had they done something to him? How could Monk be here? Gray didn't care. He gave his friend a bear hug, earning a fiery complaint from his shoulder. Just a graze, but he would've taken a gut shot to have this man back in his life. He clutched even tighter.

'I knew it . . . I knew it . . . ,' Gray whispered fiercely. Tears welled and rolled. 'God, you're alive.'

Kowalski grumbled, 'He won't be alive much longer if we don't get moving.'

The man was right. Gray let Monk go, but he kept one hand on his friend's elbow, to make sure he didn't disappear again.

Monk looked across the lot of them. 'Listen,' he said and pointed outward. 'I could use your help. There's something I have to stop.'

'Operation Saturn,' Gray said.

Monk did a double take in Gray's direction, then nodded. 'That's right. This boy can—'

Monk suddenly twirled around. 'Where's Pyotr?'

Gray understood his confusion.

The boy had vanished during the chaos.

1:15 P.M.
Kyshtym, Russia

Elizabeth studied the image on the computer screen. It displayed the wall mosaic from the temple in India. Five figures sat on tripod chairs surrounding the central omphalos. From the hole in the stone, smoke swirled upward like a steaming volcano. A fiery boy rose above it, half buried in a column of the smoke.

But it wasn't just the smoke that lifted him.

At her elbow, Elizabeth had papers covered with scribbled lines of Harappan, Sanskrit, and Greek. She had images of the inscriptions on the wall and omphalos. She was not entirely certain of her translation.

The world will burn . . .

She studied the mosaic closer. Five women slouched in their chairs, as if in a trance, but each held one arm raised toward the smoky boy. Her first thought was that it represented a conjuring of the boy or summoning of him. But now she knew better. They weren't *conjuring* him, they were *supporting* him.

She glanced to the line she had freshly translated in full.

The world will burn . . . unless the many become one.

It was a warning. The mosaic foretold what must come to pass or the world would be destroyed in some great fire. Elizabeth remembered Gray's concern that whatever operation was at work in these mountains would kill millions and most likely involved a nuclear or radiological event.

She pictured a mushroom cloud, burning and smoking with hellfire.

It was not unlike the billowing smoke from the mosaic.

. . . unless the many become one.

She scrolled down to the bottom of the image, below the newly translated warning. She touched a finger to what lay there.

A chakra wheel.

Her fingertip traced a petal to the center. The chakra wheel represented the same warning. The numerous petals all led to one center.

The many become one.

She stared again at the five women, lifting a boy high.

Certainty grew in her – not only about the accuracy of her translation, but also about its importance. Elizabeth's body trembled with dread. She had to get word out to someone. She crossed to the satellite phone Gray had left her. He had instructed her to call Director Crowe if there were any problems.

Still, she hesitated. What if she was wrong? What if she caused more of a mess? She considered keeping silent. But she remembered her father, and all his secrets.

Of Masterson and his. She was done with secrets and half-truths, of words not spoken.

No more.

She would not be her father.

Knowing her discovery was important, she raised the handset and tapped in the number Gray had left.

3:18 A.M.
Washington, D.C.

Painter watched as the child was prepped for the operation. He stood with Kat Bryant in a neighboring observation room off Sigma's small surgical suite. Sterile-wrapped equipment waited to be employed for the delicate operation: ultrasonic aspirators, laser scalpels, stereotactic localizers. Trays of steel tools and drills with various burrs lined tables. Inside the room, Lisa, Malcolm, and a neurosurgical team from George Washington University Hospital continued the final preparations.

In the middle, Sasha lay under a thin surgical drape. All that was visible was the side of her head, shaved, coated in orange antiseptic, and trapped in a rigid frame attached to a scanning device. In the center of the surgical field, her steel implant reflected the lights.

Kat, pale and worried, stood with one hand on the window.

Over the course of the past hour, a series of EEG results and CT scans had shown progressive brain damage in the child. Whatever was happening to Sasha, it was slowly burning out her brain. It was decided, while the child was still strong, to remove the implant. It seemed to be the focus around which the storm of neurological hyperactivity centered.

Lisa had used the term 'lightning rod.'

The only way to save her was to remove it. The

461

neurosurgeon had studied all the scans and X-rays. He believed the device could be removed safely. It would be a delicate procedure, but not beyond his abilities.

That had been the first good news all night.

Painter's phone jangled in his pocket. He considered not answering it, but he tugged it out and checked the I.D. From Kyshtym, Russia. He turned his back on the window, flipped open the phone, and answered it.

'Painter Crowe here.'

'Director,' a woman spoke, sounding greatly relieved. It was Elizabeth Polk. 'Gray left this number.'

He heard the anxiety in her rushed voice. 'What's wrong, Elizabeth?'

'I'm not sure. Something I discovered, translated . . . anyway . . .'

Painter listened as she stated her case, her fears, what she believed was the message buried in an ancient mosaic.

'The oracles were all slumped in their chairs, unconscious, drugged, drained. Their sole reason for existing was to support the one who could save the world from destruction. I know this sounds crazy, but I think it's connected to what's going on today.'

As she talked, Painter had swung back to the window overlooking the surgical suite. Her words resonated through him. *Slumped, unconscious, drugged . . .*

Like Sasha's collapse.

He remembered Kat reporting the girl called out her brother's name just before she collapsed.

Their sole reason for existing was to support the one who could save the world from destruction.

Painter saw the surgeon lift his scalpel, ready to begin the operation.

No.

He bolted for the door.

Kat called to him. 'What's wrong?'

Painter had no time. He burst through the sterile

prep area and into the operating room. 'Stop! No one move!'

1:14 P.M.
Southern Ural Mountains

'General-Major, you should head downstairs to the bunker,' the soldier warned. He stood a head taller than her, thick with muscle. 'We shall make a stand here.'

Another soldier dragged Dr. Petrov's screaming form into the room from the hallway. His leg had been blown off at the knee. Blood poured. Other soldiers ran in with the children carried over their shoulders. The group had been chased back to the apartment by the collapse of the Russian forces, retreating before the guerrilla assault.

The large soldier pointed a beefy arm toward the stairwell. 'Please, General-Major. We will hold off as long as we can.'

'The children . . .' Savina said, knowing her plan was crumbling around her. She could not let anyone else steal what she had started. 'Shoot them all.'

The man's eyes grew large, but he was a soldier.

He nodded.

Savina retreated down the stairs. She could not watch. Her legs stumbled under her as she reached the bottom of the stairs. The door to the room was four-inch steel. Barricaded inside, she would wait out the war above. Ahead, she noted the flicker of the screens beyond the doorway. In the center screen, water flooded poison into the earth. As she holed up here, she would take solace as she watched.

Gunfire erupted overhead.

The children . . .

Cringing, she headed for the room.

But a shape stepped into view in the open doorway, blocking her.

A boy.

Pyotr.

Pyotr stood in the doorway and stared up at the woman. She was darkness and shadow in the gloom of the stairwell. He did not truly see her, but he knew her. He focused on the flame of her heart, aglow at the foot of the stairs.

'Pyotr,' she called to him, with a shining note of hope in her voice.

As she stepped toward him, he lifted his arms and reached out – not with flesh but with his fiery spirit. He cupped the flame of her heart between his open palms, holding it like a frightened bird. Then he gently squeezed, smothering her flame.

The woman dropped to her knees with a cry, a fist clutched to her heart. 'Pyotr, what are you—?'

Hope turned to terror as she screamed.

He was not done.

There was another facet to Pyotr's talent of empathy. He could certainly sense others' emotions, but with the force of a hundred behind him, he could do more.

As a hundred eyes stared out of his, he drew from the other children: all the agony of the scalpel, the ache of loneliness, the coldness of neglect, the pain of secret abuse at night. He reached farther back, to a blue-eyed child in a dark church, watching a woman and a man approach. He stole all that fear out of the past and thrust it like a dagger into her heart.

The woman shrieked, arched back, racked and locked in a pain without end.

Yet, likewise, as the dark emotions ran through Pyotr, the same fire grazed him. Hot tears flowed for all the lost innocence, including his own.

He barely registered the pistol as it lifted toward him. The woman sought to blindly kill what tortured her. While he did the same to her.

The pistol blast shattered the silence.

Pyotr fell back when the woman's flame suddenly snuffed out between his palms. As he stumbled back, she fell to the floor, half her face gone. He stared up and saw Monk rushing down the stairs from above, his pistol smoking.

The man leaped over the woman and scooped him in his arms.

'Pyotr!'

Monk lifted the stiff boy. He ran his hand over his small frame. He seemed uninjured, though his skin burned to the touch. He hugged Pyotr to his chest.

The others ran down the stairs behind him.

A brief firefight had eliminated the defenders above. It had looked like the Russians had been about to fire upon a group of unconscious children.

If they'd been a half minute later . . .

The Gypsies remained above to secure the area and watch over the children. They were safe here for the moment.

'Is this the place?' Gray asked.

With the boy in his arms, Monk crossed with the others into the bunker. The control board smoked from deep gashes into the smoldering circuitry. Keyboards lay cracked. Glass crunched underfoot. Everything was shattered, except for a row of wall monitors.

Monk pointed to the center screen, recognizing the room. It was the heart of Operation Saturn. Only now, black water poured like a river out of a hole in the roof and swirled down a shaft in the floor.

'It's already under way,' he said hollowly. 'We're too late.'

On a neighboring screen, Monk spotted the mining chamber where he'd left Konstantin and the others. The kids were sprawled in tangled piles. The view was too grainy to tell if they were still alive. Had the radiation somehow reached them?

A well of despair swept through him.

As Gray fished out a sat-phone, Monk stared at the others: Kowalski and Rosauro. Monk sought any glimmer of recognition. There was none. Who were these people? If they were friends, shouldn't they jar some reaction from him?

As he studied the others, Pyotr reached a hand toward the center screen and placed his palm on it.

'What's he doing?' Gray asked with the phone at his ear.

Monk turned his attention. 'Pyotr?'

The boy stared deeply at the image on the screen.

Kowalski spoke to the left. 'Hey! The train's moving over here!'

Monk glanced over. The train slowly shifted down the tracks, sparking with electricity. The tunnel must still have power, not that they had any control over it.

'Is the kid doing that?' Kowalski asked. 'Moving it with his mind?'

Monk held his breath, then let it out slowly. 'No,' he said and stared at the receding train, suddenly remembering. 'There's someone else out there.'

'Who?' Gray asked.

As Pyotr's hand touched the screen, he cast his senses out into the tunnel, stretching to his limits. Fired by stolen talents, steel and concrete could not stop his reach. As voices faded behind him, he dove into the dark tunnel and swept toward the one flaming star that remained inside, a great heart, one he had loved all his young life.

Pyotr found her cowering in the train, rocking. She had hid out of sight of the cameras because he had asked it of her. She was part of the pattern. But for the moment, nothing mattered. He hurt, deeper than he'd ever been hurt. He simply needed her. Reaching her old heart, he cupped the flame gently and sent her all his love and his need.

She knew he was there and hooted gently, reaching to the empty air. In the dark tunnel, they wrapped around each other, sharing emotions at a level deeper than anyone else.

It was one of their secrets.

He had known the truth the moment they'd first touched hands. Pyotr knew the reason so many children loved Marta, came to her for comfort, to cry in her arms or to simply be held.

She had a talent, unknown to her keepers, a strong gift of empathy, like Pyotr. Two kindred spirits. So he kept her secret, and she kept his.

But it wasn't their only secret.

There was a darker one, wrapped in terror, revealed in a way neither understood but both knew to be true. From the moment they first saw each other, they knew they would die together.

Gray watched the train accelerate down the tunnel toward the site of Operation Saturn. Monk had given him a thumbnail version of the purpose.

'But who's in the train?' he asked. 'Can we communicate with them?'

Monk held the boy as his small fingers were splayed on the screen. 'I think Pyotr is already there. The boy knows how to operate the train.'

'But who's on the train?'

'A friend.'

On the screen displaying the heart of Operation Saturn, the train pulled into view at the edge and braked. A dark shape hopped out of the front car and loped into the chamber.

'Is that a monkey?' Kowalski asked, stepping back.

'Ape,' Rosauro corrected with a sigh, as if she was tired of correcting the man. 'A chimpanzee.'

'It's Marta,' Monk said.

Gray heard the pain in his voice. A storm of radiation had to be surging through there. The figure moved slowly, slipping, knuckling awkwardly, already sick.

'What's she trying to do?' Gray asked.

'Trying to save us all,' Monk answered.

Pyotr stayed with Marta. He pulled her flame close to his, not enough to be consumed, but so he could feed her his strength, let her know what she had to do, that she wasn't alone. Likewise, he caught glimpses through her eyes, through her sharper senses.

He saw the column of roaring water. He felt a heat weakening and burning Marta. The air smelled like rotting fish and frightened both of them, a flow of dark water, from their shared nightmares.

Deadlier than any river.

But they faced it together.

Marta skirted around the gaping hole that swallowed the water so thirstily. It had to be stopped.

There was only one way.

Pyotr knew and told Marta. Konstantin had explained in detail how all the equipment worked: about the explosive charges, about the radio transmitters, about the giant silo doors.

He had also told Pyotr about the lever.

Marta needed no help. She spotted the rod of steel behind a piece of equipment. It could close the silo doors and stop the flow into the heart of the world. Pyotr felt the soft hoots of fear coming from her. He felt them under his own ribs.

You can do it, Marta . . .

She struggled, her skin burned, her fur fell like pine needles, her knuckles blistered in contact with the spray of water on the rock.

Pyotr held her flame and willed her strength.

She reached the lever. It was tilted close to the floor. It needed to be raised straight up. She hunched a shoulder under it, gripped the length with both hands, and heaved with her legs.

The steel would not move.

As death flowed behind her in a burning current, Pyotr felt the strain in her back, in her legs, in her heart.

Her flame flickered in his hands.

Marta . . .

But the lever would not move.

Monk watched Marta struggle with the lever. She was too weak. It would not budge. Pyotr began breathing hard, sharing the old chimpanzee's fear and pain.

'Why won't it move?' Gray asked.

'C'mon, you damn monkey!' Kowalski yelled.

Monk leaned closer, placing his own palm on the screen. He tried to remember the brief glimpse into the room as he had hurried past. As he strained, a sharp jab of electric pain shot through his head. Images from another time and place flashed.

. . . a man covered in coal soot . . . a plunging ride in an ore car . . . a white grin against dusty skin . . . that's a boy! . . . just like, Daddy . . .

Then it was gone.

Monk struggled to retain something, but like a dream upon waking, memory began to dissolve through his fingers. Why did that particular memory dredge up? Buried in it must be something important.

As the memory faded, he caught a glimpse of that coal-dust-covered man slowing the ore car by squeezing the—

'Hand brake!' he gasped out.

He flashed back to the brief peek into the mine site before. He pictured the lever. It'd had a handgrip at its end.

Monk turned to Pyotr. He leaned and whispered in his feverish ear. 'Marta must reach to the end of the lever. She must squeeze the handle. Then it will move for her.'

Pyotr continued to stare, as if deaf to his words, and maybe the boy truly could not hear. Monk had to get him to listen.

Seeming to understand his frustration, the woman Rosauro stepped next to him. 'How are they communicating? Telepathically?'

'No. I think *empathically*. Sharing emotions. I've seen him do it with her before. Just not at such a distance.'

'Then you'll have to reach him the same way.'

Monk glanced at her, as if she were a madwoman.

Gray spoke. 'Rosauro's specialty is neurology. Listen to her.'

The woman spoke slowly. 'Empathy is all about sensation and tactility. You might be able to reach them the same way. Offer something that comforts him. It may open a path.'

Monk pictured Pyotr and Marta. They had been always touching, rubbing, grazing against each other, but Monk remembered what brought the boy the greatest sense of security and comfort.

Shifting, he wrapped his arms around Pyotr as he had seen Marta do so often. He felt the boy's heart race like a hummingbird's. Rocking the boy very gently, Monk huffed in his ear and whispered what must be done.

He willed it with all his heart.
Squeeze the hand brake . . .

Pyotr stayed with Marta as she struggled with the lever – then felt a familiar warmth coming from behind him. He glanced over his shoulder and found a strong heart there, casting a fierce flame. He stared into that fire and sensed what must be done as much as he heard it.

He turned back to Marta and clasped to her, letting her know, too.

But his friend trembled and burned, growing so weak.
Please . . .

She hooted, scared, but one of her large hands slid up the lever and found the grip there. Long fingers wrapped around it and squeezed. Then she heaved again, shouldering the lever and pushing with her legs.

The lever moved, but it was still heavy. With shaking limbs, she fought it straight up and shoved it back. Something snapped loudly.

A great grind of gears sounded.

Exhausted and spent, Marta slumped to the ground.

'She did it!' Gray said.

On the screen, the hole in the floor began closing, snipping off the stream with a steel iris. The river of water, no longer able to drain below, flooded into the mining chamber.

The chimpanzee was flushed out of the room and into the tunnel, but more and more water followed. Though clearly exhausted and burned, she gained her feet and swung atop the train car. As black water rose around her, she loped back and forth across the roof, scribing a path of panic and distress.

Gray's heart went out to the poor creature.

'Get that damned monkey out of there, for Christ's sake!' Kowalski bellowed. He slammed a fist on the broken control board.

But there was nothing they could do. The doors were jammed, and water was swiftly filling the tunnel, which was sealed at both ends. Even if they could open the doors, the radiation level would kill them all. And ultimately, the chimpanzee had already been exposed to many times the lethal dosage.

Rosauro turned her back and stepped away, covering her mouth with concern.

Finally, the old chimpanzee settled to her haunches, hugging her knees. She began to rock. She knew what was coming.

Monk clutched the boy, a single tear running down his cheek.

In his arms, the boy rocked, too, in exact synch with his friend in the tunnel.

Pyotr stayed with Marta as the waters rose. Her heart flashed and swirled in fear. She'd always known the dark water would kill her. He held her now, as she had done with him so many times in the past. He wrapped his warm arms around her and pulled her tight. They rocked together one last time, two hearts sharing one flame.

Marta knew his secret, too.

She hooted softly and leaned her cheek against him.

Pyotr . . .

I love you, Marta . . .

As the waters rose to consume his friend, Pyotr looked into the dark sea that filled him, shining with seventy-seven bright lights, swirling around a brighter fire that was his own heart. One of his teachers had told him how planets circled suns, trapped in their orbits.

He understood.

He knew by consuming those stars he could never let them go. This was no nightmare where he stole only a little of their skill. He had crossed a line of no return. As he stared, he saw those stolen lights grow infinitesimally dimmer. He was burning them up, consuming his friends, his sister.

There was only one way to let them go.

It was the other reason he came to Marta.

He needed her.

Pyotr . . . no . . .

You must . . .

He felt her hands reach tentatively to that bright light inside his dark sea. Her long warm fingers wrapped around his own heart.

Pyotr . . .

But she knew. For the others to live, there was only one path. The others were trapped in his orbit, and if left unchecked, he would burn through them all. The only way to free them was to take away the sun that held them. Then the stars could fly back and return to where they belonged.

So Marta squeezed and squeezed as dark waters rose around her. Focused on him, she was no longer scared. As they rocked, she closed her fingers tenderly, but it still hurt.

Then just before Pyotr's light fully died, he reached to a single star in that dark sea, slightly brighter still than the rest.

Sasha, he whispered and told his sister a secret.

The boy suddenly slumped in his arms. His small hand fell away from the screen. He saw Marta's body get washed from the top of the train and swirl off into the darkness of the tunnel.

Monk lowered the boy to the floor. 'Pyotr?'

The boy stared blindly toward the ceiling, pupils dilated. Monk checked for a pulse. He found one but barely. The boy's chest rose and fell.

Overhead, small cries and screams echoed down. The other children. They were waking, rising to find a room full of dead bodies.

Gray pointed. 'Rosauro, Kowalski, go up and help them!'

Monk glanced to the grainy image from the other end of the tunnel. He watched kids stirring, others already standing. He saw Konstantin help Kiska sit up.

They were okay.

'What about the boy?' Gray asked.

Monk sat on the floor and cradled his thin body. Pyotr breathed, his blood pumped, but Monk stared into his blank eyes and knew the boy was gone.

Pyotr . . . why?

Gray joined him and placed a hand on his shoulder. 'Maybe it's shock. Maybe with time . . .'

Monk appreciated the offer of hope, but he knew the truth. As he had held the boy, he had felt the child let go. Monk's gaze returned to the screen full of stirring children. Monk knew. Pyotr had sacrificed his life for them, for all his brothers and sisters.

Gray settled to his haunches next to him, keeping vigil with him.

The stranger seemed like a good man, and in this quiet moment alone, Monk felt a certain comfort around the guy. Not a memory, just a sensation that he could drop his guard without fear.

So Monk felt no shame as tears rolled heavily and he rocked Pyotr one last time, now just an empty shell of a boy.

22

Painter crossed through the rabble of tents and wagons covering the national Mall. The Gypsy encampment filled the grassy fields and long meadows of the Mall. The tents were a mix of traditional structures made of hazel rods thrust into the ground and covered in sailcloth, and more modern tents, fresh from a sporting goods store. The wagons were just as diverse, from simple structures to massive homes with smoking chimneys resting on tall painted wheels.

The Romani had come from all around the world to this great gathering. Horses were corralled in makeshift pens, children ran throughout, music rang out, great bouts of laughter echoed. And more and more were arriving each day.

The president had an official thank-you ceremony scheduled for the end of the week. Nothing like saving someone's life to get them to extend a grateful hand of hospitality. Not to mention saving the world.

Painter followed a path through the chaos as dogs barked and children scampered out of his way. Tourists also shared the crooked alleyways and narrow bazaars, buying trinkets, having their fortunes told, or merely ogling the merry mayhem. Painter glanced up at the Washington Monument to help align himself and continued onward.

Stepping around a corner, a space opened in front of him, backed by one of the largest and most elaborately decorated wagons. Its wooden doors stood open. Painter spotted a cozy home with a raised double bed, cabinets brightly painted and lacquered in yellows and reds. There was even a small stove with a fancifully carved mantelpiece.

On the steps leading up to the wagon, Painter found Luca sitting with Gray, deep in conversation. The commander's arm was still in a sling. A few steps away, Shay Rosauro was playing a game of daggers with a group of Gypsy men. One of her blades whistled through the air and hit the bull's-eye, knocking off an opponent's knife. From their plaintive calls for mercy, she must be soundly besting them.

Off to the side, Painter was surprised to see Elizabeth and Kowalski. The woman must have just returned from India to attend the ceremony. She was working with both Romani historians and Indian archaeologists to unearth the flooded Greek temple site.

Painter glanced to the right and spotted the banner across the front facade of the Museum of Natural History. It displayed a Greek mountain temple with a prominent capital *epsilon* in the center, announcing the upcoming exhibit about the Oracle of Delphi. With all the publicity of late about the archaeological discovery, tickets were already sold out for months in advance, many bought by the Gypsies here, eager to learn more about the origin of their clans.

Luca spotted Painter's arrival and stood. The Gypsy was dressed in loose pants with a thick belt and matching black boots, along with an open vest over a long-sleeved embroidered shirt. 'Ah, Director Crowe! Welcome!'

476

Painter offered a bow of his head to the clan leader. '*Nais tuke*,' he thanked him in the Romani tongue.

Gray also stood. Like Kowalski, the commander was dressed casually in jeans and a light jacket. Over the past days, they had all found themselves coming here. It had been a long couple of weeks of funerals and grim meetings. Painter wandered here almost every night with Lisa. They would stroll through the camp, in each other's arms, not talking, but listening to the songs and laughter as they passed families gathered around candle-lit suppers. Painter took solace in this fervent and bright reminder of the fullness of life. Painter also found the shared songs and communal camaraderie echoed back to his own childhood, to the tribal festivals on the Mashantucket reservations. It did feel like coming home . . . if just a bit.

But today's gathering was more formal and practical.

They all crossed to a nearby plank table. A pair of massive draft horses were penned nearby.

As they sat, Gray asked, 'So how did the meeting go?'

Luca stared at him with bright eyes.

Painter had just returned from a meeting with representatives from the State Department, the Russian embassy, and several child welfare organizations. The status of seventy-seven children was the point of contention. There were many claims on them.

'The Russians were happy to concede all authority over to us,' Painter began. 'They have enough to clean up as it is. The latest radiological studies from the joint nuclear task force suggest that the partial flooding of Lake Karachay into the groundwater, while locally disastrous and requiring evacuation of lands for miles downstream, will not prove globally catastrophic. The floodgates were closed in time.'

Gray looked relieved. 'And the children?'

Painter had visited the hospital this morning. An

entire wing of George Washington University Hospital had been cordoned off to handle the children flown in from Russia. The neurology team had spent the last weeks slowly and meticulously removing the implants. As the chief neurologist had originally conjectured, the extraction was a delicate but not exceptionally complicated procedure. The last child had her implant removed a couple of days ago. They were all doing well.

'Testing shows some savant talent remains in the children but at a substantially weakened level,' Painter said. 'Whatever communion was shared at the end seemed to have burned out the foundations of the neurological structure that produced their prodigious talent. But contrarily, the change also seemed to lessen their autistic presentation. The children have shown remarkable improvement. Still, whoever takes on the mantle of fostering these children will have to concede to a supervised monitoring of their health status, along with regular psychological evaluations, both in regard to their talents and to their general mental health.'

Painter stared at Luca, who remained stoic, but his eyes shone with hope. Painter finally smiled. 'But the unanimous consensus of the panel is that the children will be released to Gypsy families for that fostering.'

Luca pounded a fist on the table. 'Yes!'

His loud reaction earned a whinnied complaint from one of the draft horses and an equally firm stamp of a large hoof.

Painter spent another half hour going over further details, which helped sober the man but failed to dim the light in the Gypsy's eyes. Finally they all stood and began to disperse.

Elizabeth headed out, with Kowalski at her elbow.

'Now that you're back in town,' Kowalski mumbled to her, running a palm over his shaved scalp. 'Would you want . . . Maybe we could . . . ?'

Gray winced at the man's efforts and nodded for Painter to move to the side. 'This isn't going to be pretty.'

'What is it, Joe?' Elizabeth asked, an eyebrow lifted curiously at the large man.

He stammered, cursed under his breath, then straightened. 'Do you want to go out on a date?'

Smooth, Painter thought, suppressing a grin.

Elizabeth shrugged and led Kowalski out. 'You mean a second date, right?'

Kowalski's brow crinkled like a washboard.

'I think being shot at, kidnapped, irradiated, and saving the world classifies at least as a *first* date.'

Kowalski tripped along next to her, his mind catching up at about the same pace. 'So you'll go?'

Elizabeth nodded. 'As long as you bring the cigars.'

Kowalski grinned. 'I got a whole box of—*aw, crap!*' He stopped and stared down at his shoes. His left foot had landed squarely in a pile of horse manure. 'These are my brand-new Chukkas!'

Elizabeth hooked his arm under hers and headed off. 'It'll wash off.'

'But you don't understand! The leather is hand polished by . . .'

The pair disappeared into the throng.

Gray shook his head. 'Kowalski's got a date. I think hell's just gotten a little bit colder.'

Painter and Gray headed out toward the Smithsonian Castle. Both of them had a ton of work still to do. Sigma command remained in disarray, both politically and structurally. They'd lost some key people during the initial assault, and one entire level remained cordoned off due to the firestorm. Repairs and inspections of the infrastructure were still under way.

But politically things were far dicier. They had managed to capture the neurologist Dr. James Chen, one of the Jasons involved with Mapplethorpe and

McBride. Under interrogation, he was helping them weed out the corrupt Jasons from the legitimate scientists working for the Defense Department. But Mapplethorpe was another matter. He had his fingers throughout Washington's intelligence agencies. It was still unclear if he had been operating solely as a rogue agent or if there were members of the Washington establishment who had supported the man's action. As a result, intelligence camps were circling their wagons, protecting themselves but still pointing fingers.

Even toward Sigma.

So vultures circled, but Painter had the backing of a grateful president. It would take work, but they'd get things running smoothly before long. In fact, Painter was scheduled to meet Sean McKnight's replacement tomorrow, the new interim head of DARPA. The president initially offered Painter the position, but he had declined. Sigma needed some continuity. As the joint brainchild of Archibald Polk and Sean McKnight, Painter could not abandon Sigma.

Painter glanced at Gray. 'I assume you'll be spending all day at the hospital tomorrow.'

He nodded. 'Kat will need company.'

Monk Kokkalis's surgery was scheduled for six in the morning. An MRI revealed what had been done to Monk in the Russian lab, but it remained unknown if the damage could ever be reversed. The Russians had wired a microchip into Monk's basolateral amygdala. The neurologists believed the chip had induced and maintained a *fluid amnesia*. It was a technique already being investigated using chemicals, specifically propranolol as a beta-blocker to erase especially strong memories of trauma. The Russians had been experimenting on Monk, using the biotechnological equivalent.

The surgery had been delayed until Monk finished a series of antiradiation treatments. The neurologists used the extra time to study Monk's case, but they still could not say if he'd ever get his memory back – especially with the other result found during the MRI. In order to install the chip, a small section of Monk's cerebral cortex had been removed.

Painter recalled the horror on Gray's face upon learning that and his dismayed words: *First his hand, now a section of his brain . . . it's like Monk is slowly being whittled away.*

'Has there been any indication that Monk recognizes Kat?' Painter asked.

Gray shook his head. 'The doctors have mostly kept her away. They believe that, while the chip is still in his head, further stress on his memory, like the emotional connection with Kat, might actually cause more damage than good.'

'Still, she visited him.'

He nodded. 'She had to. She went into the room with a group of nurses. Monk conversed with them, but he had no reaction upon seeing Kat. Nothing at all. It practically destroyed her. She has Monk back, but he's still lost to her.'

'Then we'll have to pray for the best.'

September 29, 6:21 P.M.
George Washington University Hospital

The man woke into a room too bright. It stung his eyes and pounded deep into the back of his head. Nausea followed, accompanied by a swirl of details. He swallowed hard a few times and forced his vision to steady.

A slim woman in a blue smock patted his hand. 'There you go, Mr. Kokkalis. Just breathe.' She turned away. 'He's coming around more fully this time.'

The spinning settled. The pounding of the drum inside his head slowed to a dull pressure. He found

481

himself in a hospital room, remembering in bits and pieces. The operation. He lifted an arm and found it strapped to a plastic splint through which intravenous lines dripped both clear saline and a unit of blood. To the side, monitors beeped and whirred.

Monk tried to move his head, but his neck ached, and a tube ran down from a cap atop his head.

A series of doctors came through, shining lights into his eyes, making him do simple motor tests, judging his ability to swallow with ice chips, and performing other cranial nerve function tests. After about ten minutes, they drifted away, chattering about his case, leaving two people standing at the foot of his bed.

Monk recognized the man. 'Gray . . . ,' he said hoarsely, his throat still raw from the endotracheal tube.

The man's eyes brightened.

Monk knew what they all hoped, what he hoped, but he shook his head. He knew the man only from the chaos in Russia. A striking woman in jeans and a loose blouse leaned next to him, her auburn hair down to her shoulders. Her emerald eyes searched Monk for some answer. But he didn't even know the question.

Gray touched her elbow. 'It may be too soon, Kat. You know that. The doctors said it might take months.'

She turned slightly to the side and wiped her eyes. 'I know,' she said, but it sounded like a moan.

With his senses tuned sharp by a trailing edge of nausea, Monk caught a scent in the air, familiar, spiced yet musky. No memory came with it, but his breathing grew heavier. Something . . . something about . . .

'We should let him rest,' Gray said and guided the woman away. 'We'll come back in the morning. It's been a long day. You should be getting her home anyway.'

Gray nodded to a blue stroller behind them. A small child slept, nestled in blankets, head capped like Monk's, eyes closed, a pursed button of a mouth.

Monk's eyes locked on the baby. Staccato flashes burst into existence out of nothingness.

. . . tiny fingers curled around his finger . . . walking down a long, dark hall, tired, rocking the small figure in his arms . . . little kicking feet as he changed a diaper . . .

Just snippets. No coherency. But unlike before, there was no pain, only a soothing brightness that did not fade this time.

Out of that glow, he found a small sliver of himself.

'She's . . . her name . . .' The two turned to her. 'It's Penelope.'

The woman stared at the child, back to him. Her entire form shook as tears spilled in shining streaks of joy. 'Monk . . .'

She rushed to his side, falling over him. She leaned and kissed him gently, her hair draped over them like a tent.

He remembered.

The taste of cinnamon, soft lips . . .

He still did not know her name, but a surge of love swelled through him that drew tears to his own eyes. Maybe he would never know her name, not truly, but Monk knew one thing with all his heart: if she'd let him, he would spend the rest of his life learning who she was all over again.

7:01 P.M.

Gray headed down the hospital corridor, leaving Kat and Monk some privacy. While here, he wanted to check on one last patient. He crossed over to the children's ward. He showed his identification to an armed guard who protected the wing.

Once through, he passed several wards and smaller

rooms. The walls were painted with balloons and cartoon animals. He passed a tall boy in hospital pajamas. He was walking with a smaller girl. Both their heads were shaved on one side. They were chatting enthusiastically in Russian.

All the children seemed to be recovering from their ordeal.

That is, all except *one*.

He crossed down another long corridor to a private room at the very end. The door was open. He heard voices inside.

Gray knocked softly and entered. The room held a single bed and a small play area with a yellow plastic table and a set of children's chairs around it. He found Dr. Lisa Cummings standing inside, filling out a chart. With her medical background, she was assisting the surgeons and doctors, while keeping Painter updated on status reports and abreast of any problems.

Sasha sat at the table, coloring in her book. She wore a pink bonnet that covered her shaved head.

'Mr. Gray!' the girl called to him and popped out of her chair like a jackrabbit and ran over to him. She hugged his leg.

He patted her shoulder.

Sasha came here as often as Gray, visiting her brother.

Pyotr sat in a wheelchair by the window, staring out at the growing twilight. He sat like a mannequin. Upright, stiff, unresponsive.

'Any change?' Gray asked and nodded to the chart in Lisa's hands.

'Some actually. He's now taking food by spoon. Baby food. It's like he's infantilized. The doctors are hoping that over time, he may grow into his body.'

Gray hoped they were right. The boy had saved the world and sacrificed everything to do it.

'Gray, if you can put the boy to bed, we'll let you have some time alone with him.'

Gray nodded.

'C'mon, Sasha, let's go back to your room.'

'Wait!' She let go of Gray's leg and ran to Pyotr.

'Say good night to Pyotr, then we have to go,' Lisa insisted.

Sasha kissed her brother on the cheek, then came running back to Gray and lifted her arms toward him.

Gray knelt down for a good-bye kiss, too, and offered his cheek. She kissed it, then grabbed his earlobe. She leaned in close and whispered, tickling his ear.

'Pyotr's not in there,' she said in conspiratorial tones. 'Someone *else* is in there. But I'll still love him.'

Gray felt a slight chill at her words. Sasha must have overheard the doctors. The prognosis was ultimately grim. Even if Pyotr could recover some manner of life, he wouldn't be the same boy.

Gray rubbed her arm, reassuring her, but he offered her no false hope. It was best she adjust to the reality in her own way.

'Sasha,' Lisa said warningly.

'Wait!' she burst out again and ran to her table. 'I have something for Mr. Gray.' She shuffled through her piles of papers.

Gray waited, still down on one knee.

Lisa smiled. 'She really doesn't want to go to bed.'

The girl came flying back with a page ripped from a coloring book in her hand. She thrust it at Gray. 'Here,' she said proudly.

Gray stared down at a picture of a clown. She had colored it perfectly, even adding some nuance with shading to make the clown seem both sad and slightly creepy. She obviously still retained some artistic talent.

Sasha leaned to his ear again. 'You're going to die.'

Gray was taken aback by her statement, but there was no menace in her voice, only a matter-of-fact tone, as if commenting on the weather. Gray imagined Sasha was struggling to understand the concept of death. She had seen too much of it, and her brother hung somewhere in the balance between the living and the dead.

Gray didn't know what to say. But like before, he wouldn't lie to her. He stood but kept a hand on her shoulder. 'We all die eventually, Sasha. It's the natural order.'

She sighed in the overly dramatic manner of all exasperated children.

'No, silly.' She pointed up to the paper. 'You have to be careful of that! That's why I drew it!'

Lisa pointed to the door. 'That's enough, Sasha. Time for bed.'

'Wait!'

'No.'

Crestfallen, she allowed Lisa to drag her away. She waved back at Gray, using her entire arm.

Once they were gone, Gray crossed over to Pyotr. He liked to sit with the boy, to let him know he was not forgotten, that his sacrifice would be remembered. He also came here because of Monk. The boy had meant so much to his friend. Gray felt a certain obligation to keep Pyotr company.

But in truth, the visits were also a balm on his heart. He felt a strange calmness with the boy that was inexplicable, as if some empathic aura still surrounded the child.

As Gray sat now, he considered all that had happened. He remembered the boy dragging Monk into view down the hall. Gray now understood what Pyotr had been doing. His sister had saved Monk's life by plucking him out of the sea and out of their lives, and Pyotr had been returning him, like putting a borrowed wrench back into a neighbor's toolbox.

All that had happened . . . Gray knew it hadn't been luck, nor even coincidence. He stared at Pyotr and pictured Sasha, too.

It had all been orchestrated.

And as Gray stared, he also recalled Nicolas Solokov's goal: to manipulate the savants in order to produce the world's next great prophet. The next Buddha or Muhammad or Christ. Gray had also discussed such speculations with Monk while the two had visited Pyotr here.

Afterward, his friend had nodded to the boy.

Maybe the Russians were more successful than they had imagined.

Either way, like so many great people, Pyotr had paid the ultimate sacrifice. Now they would never know the truth. And maybe it was better that way.

Gray sighed and pushed away such melancholy thoughts. In his hands, he folded Sasha's coloring page and glanced down to it. Apparently, besides everything else, Gray now had to worry about creepy clowns. As he creased the paper, he saw that the child had drawn something freehand on the blank page on the back.

Unfolding it, he stared down at a shape, finely drawn in black crayon.

It was a small Chinese dragon, beautifully executed.

An icy jolt of recognition shot through Gray. His hand rose to his throat. Tucked under his shirt was a pendant bearing the same dragon in silver, a gift from an assassin, both a promise from her and a curse.

Gray glanced to the doorway. Had Sasha seen the charm sometime? He stared down at the crayon drawing, knowing in his heart she hadn't.

It was a warning – but not about clowns. As he stared, Gray realized Sasha had been pointing *up* to the page in his hands. From her low vantage, she hadn't been indicating the clown. She had been pointing to the page's *underside*.

To the dragon symbol.

In the quiet of the room, Gray sensed a looming danger. He whispered the name tied to that threat.

'Seichan.'

EPILOGUE

The boy sits by the window and stares out at the twilight world beyond. He is not ready to go out there yet. He still has much to adjust to in this new home. It fits him poorly and makes it difficult for him to think.

He can see his reflection in the glass: dark hair, small features, a familiar face. But it does not yet feel like his own. That, too, would come in time. As he stares, he watches the leaves falling past the window, drifting on the wind.

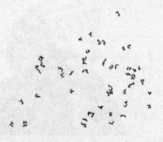

There is no fear now, even as more leaves fall. That which lies deep inside him fills in the spaces with shadow and shape. Formed out of memory. What comes is still more familiar than his own reflection in the glass. He knows it was the face he once wore.

He still remembers the darkness, a black sea swimming with lights. He remembers the dying sun in the middle, strangled away so that others might fly and shine. But in that last moment, the boy who had once worn this body had kept a secret from them all. As he left that dark sea to places beyond, he pulled another light out of harm's way and dropped it into that empty dark sea.

So it might live anew.

Outside now, more leaves tumble, and shadows of memory fill in gaps, forming the true face of the one who wore this body now.

This old face would be forgotten eventually, but not the boy who gave up his life so something new could be born. Often in his dreams, he sees that boy running over fields, topping a hill, waving back – then gone.

So happy now.
The new boy who sits in the chair stares out the window.
Sometime he will run again, too.

AUTHOR'S NOTE TO READERS: TRUTH OR FICTION

Like Dr. Archibald Polk, I started this novel with a fascination in human *intuition*. Does it exist? Where does it come from? So as usual, I thought I'd end this adventure by noting where many of the ideas and facts originated, dividing them by subject matter.

The Greek Oracle of Delphi. I spent some time in the prologue on the myths and realities surrounding the Oracle. Whether these women could truly see the future or not might be up for debate, but what we do know for certain is that the Delphic Oracle's prophecies were indeed fundamental in changing the course of Western civilization. As to the details – such as the mystery of the capital *epsilon* and the strange hallucinogenic gases – they are all factual. A great book for anyone interested in exploring this subject in greater detail is *The Oracle: The Lost Secrets and Hidden Message of Ancient Delphi* by William J. Broad.

The Jasons. This organization of scientists who work alongside the Defense Department is a real organization

493

and is still operating. For a truly absorbing read into their history and accomplishments, pick up a copy of *The Jasons: The Secret History of Science's Postwar Elite* by Ann Finkbeiner.

Project Stargate. This was a real program run out of the Stanford Research Institute and funded by the CIA. Their strange successes into remote viewing are factual.

Brain manipulation. There was much speculation in the book about brain plasticity, about augmentation with transcranial magnetic stimulation, and about how humans are 'natural-born cyborgs.' How much of that is true? *All of it.* For an enlightening and entertaining exploration into the mystery of the human brain, I suggest you read *The Brain That Changes Itself: Stories of Personal Triumph from the Frontiers of Brain Science* by Norman Doidge, M.D. As to Monk's induced amnesia, there are chemical techniques employed today that can erase selected memories, specifically through the use of propranolol.

Can we see the future? Nobel Prize-winning scientists say yes. The experiments on gamblers and soldiers described in this book are real and have been repeated at universities around the world. According to those distinguished researchers, we do seem capable of seeing for about three seconds into the future. How is that possible? That remains unanswered. As to the stories about the amazing savants in India – like the Indian boy who was taken to Oxford and the woman who met Einstein – they are based on fact. You can read more about these histories in *Intuition: Knowing Beyond Logic* by Osho.

India and Gypsies. The history of the Romani and their roots in the Punjab region in India is factual. This origin is also the reason the chakra wheel is prominently centered on the Romani flag. As to India's caste system, the plight and status of the 'untouchable' classes is a true concern. In fact, some historians believe it was just such a friction among castes that drove the Gypsy forefathers out of India. For more details about this struggle, there is a disturbing article in *National Geographic* in the June 2003 issue, titled 'India's Untouchables.' Oh, and if you're ever visiting the Taj Mahal, there truly is a revolving restaurant atop the Deedar-e-Taj Hotel. I recommend the *pani pani* or *golguppa*.

Russia's radioactive legacy. The descriptions of Pripyat and the planned closure of the old Sarcophagus under a giant arch of twelve-meter-thick steel is factual. Details about the old Soviet Union's plutonium factories in the Ural Mountains, as disturbing as they may sound, are also true. There are indeed underground cities where prisoners were housed to work the uranium mines. Most miners died before ever earning their freedom. And today, the Chelyabinsk region of the Ural Mountains remains one of the most polluted places on the planet. In fact, Lake Karachay does exist, and according to the Natural Resources Defense Council in Washington, D.C., the radiation level on the shore is sufficient to deliver a lethal dose to someone in less than an hour. So as Konstantin warned, it's not a good place for a picnic. Worse yet, the lake is leaking radiation into the neighboring Asanov swamp. Fault lines do cross under the lake. An earthquake potentially threatens to do just what Savina Martov sought to accelerate. Such a disaster would kill the Arctic Ocean and sweep over northern Europe.

Strange weapons. In this book, I employed sonic flares, radiosensitive poisons, whip-swords, shotguns that shoot Taser rounds, even a cell phone that converts into a gun. As you might guess, they're all real.

Autism and Autistic Savant Syndrome. While the exact cause for autism remains unknown, the latest research initiated by the Autism Genome Project in collaboration with the National Institute of Health has found that certain genes, along with environmental factors, contribute to the presentation of the disorder. For a better understanding of such unique minds, I highly recommend Dr. Temple Grandin's book, *Thinking in Pictures: My Life with Autism*. Another book that I found insightful about autism and savant syndrome was the memoir by Daniel Tammet, *Born on a Blue Monday: Inside the Extraordinary Mind of an Autistic Savant.*

In fact, the seed for this novel came from a quote by Dr. Temple Grandin. She was kind enough to permit me to use it: *'If by some magic, autism had been eradicated from the face of the earth, then men would still be socializing in front of a wood fire at the entrance to a cave.'* To my mind, it echoes the quote at the beginning of this novel from Socrates about the Oracle of Delphi: *'The greatest blessings granted to mankind come by way of madness, which is a divine gift.'* It makes one wonder if such unique minds truly guided the path of mankind's history.

To answer that, I'll end with a partial list of famous historical figures who are believed to have displayed some level of autistic tendencies.

Hans Christian Andersen	*Jane Austen*
Ludwig van Beethoven	*Emily Dickinson*
Thomas Edison	*Albert Einstein*
Henry Ford	*Thomas Jefferson*
Franz Kafka	*Michelangelo*

Wolfgang Amadeus Mozart   *Isaac Newton*
Friedrich Nietzsche   *Mark Twain*
Nikola Tesla   *Henry David Thoreau*
Alan Turing   *Nostradamus*

You be the judge.